BOOST
AND SUE

A novel

By Katrina Cain

For my partner: Without you the sun does not rise and the stars do not shine. You are my everything, my one true love.

"The thief must no longer steal,
but rather labor, doing honest
work with his own hands, so
that he may have something to
share with one in need. Take
no part in the fruitless works
of darkness; rather expose
them, for it is shameful even to
mention the things done by
[the disobedient] in secret; but
everything exposed by the light
becomes visible, for everything
that becomes visible is light."

*Ephesian*s 4:28, 5:11-14

INTRODUCTION

Many of the situations that arise in this novel would be judged by many to be patently unfair. This is very true, however, only because the concept of "fairness" does not really exist. There is actually only "justice" and "equity," but no fairness. Allow me to explain this with a simple example.

Say a 200-pound man and a 100-pound woman are going to share a bed—how should the bed fairly be divided? What is fair? Well, there are two ways to divide the bed. The first is to say, each one is a person, each person is equal, they should each receive an equal share of the bed to be fair, so this amounts to a 50-50 split. This fairness is called "equity." However, there is a second way to divide the bed. Because the man is substantially more massive than the woman, he should receive a share of the bed commensurate with his size. Thus, he would receive two-thirds of the bed while the woman receives one third, based on her smaller mass. This 67-33 split is also fair, and this fairness is called "justice."

Now any reasonable person can immediately see the conundrum—we can rightly divide the bed 50-50 or 67-33 and both results are actually logically fair, but there are two quantitatively different expressions of fairness. How can this be? Because there is no such thing as fairness, only justice and equity. Let's look at a real public policy example.

In the State of Connecticut (a small and reliably "blue" state) actuaries working for insurance companies have done the computations to show that male drivers on average cause more automobile accidents than their female counterparts. Therefore, because of their higher risk driving, males pay a higher rate for car insurance than females, who pay a lower rate. This is justice. In neighboring Massachusetts (another small and reliably "blue" state) it is illegal by statute to treat males and females differently under the law, and therefore male and female drivers are charged the same rate for auto insurance. This is equity.

Clearly, in these two very small, very similar New England states, policymakers have concocted two different calculations of fairness for automobile drivers, and yet both are patently fair. All I ask when you read this book is that you remember that life is inherently not fair, because "fairness" does not actually exist.

One more thing—if you fancy yourself a legal eagle then read the italics, and if you're more like the rest of us then skip them. Enjoy!

FIRST BOOST AND SUE: THE TOWN OF SIMSBURY

All of this started because my employee took a picture of the box that displayed the serial number. She had no reason not to—it was one of the six sides that she could have electronically captured—but had she photographed one of the five other sides, I would not be in this situation. Let me be crystal clear: I am, and always have been, an eBay seller, ever since the site first started and Paypal was handing out ten dollars to each new user in the late 1990's. That's so long ago that Elon Musk was perfecting e-currency and hadn't even started Spacex, Tesla, and the Boring Company.

I am an eBayer, putting myself through Trinity College to achieve an undergraduate degree in Women, Gender, and Sexuality that I am fully aware will be worthless without further schooling when I finish. What a long and winding academic path to choose! But the issue at hand was business related.

I was selling a newfangled robotic pool vacuum with a list price of $399.00, which I had purchased from a nearby pawn shop. So, I spend my days in school learning about heteronormativity, intersectionality, and the coercive patriarchal autocratic hegemony, and when I am not in school, I am driving from pawn shop to pawn shop buying excess inventory. Nowadays, all the pawn shops have their own dedicated eBay seller on staff, but in the mid-2000's this was not the case.

This young woman Amanda was working for me in my two-bedroom, third-floor apartment in the West End of Bristol. I had met Amanda at a young people's twelve-step meeting in nearby Canton on a Tuesday night—she's a dyke who lives at home with her parents and was trying to save and move out and get a place with her girlfriend. I think that's sweet and romantic. It's what I'm all about, and I'm more than happy to help her out.

Essentially, when you get down to it, Amanda runs my business. She photographs items, uploads photos, writes a small description based on a similar item, prices the item, calculates the shipping method and cost, and lists it for sale. Furthermore, she reprices items that are slow to sell, she watches our competitors, and she does the fulfillment of all the media items, including CDs, DVDs, and books. She knows how to find the proper mailers, the right configuration of odd stamps, the printing of labels for international airmail packages and for items over twenty dollars that require tracking, and I handle only the larger items.

Enter this pool vacuum. It required a larger box (probably an eighteen-inch cube that we ship the electric welders in) and so she probably figured I would take care of it. I'm absolutely sure she simply snapped a photo of whichever side was easiest, but I didn't want to tell her. I didn't want to admit to her that as a business, we cheat. I didn't want to tell her that we cheat to make a living and that's how I was able to pay her. Allow me to explain how this works for anyone unfamiliar with the pawn shop.

Someone brings a piece of jewelry to the pawn shop. The guys there don't care where the item came from. Rather, their job is to strip the emotional value off of an item and transform an item into some inert object. That customer's wedding ring with an inscription from husband to wife becomes a lump of scrap metal set to be melted into a bar on 47th Street in Manhattan after a bunch of middlemen weigh it and ceremoniously test its purity. There is no more love associated with that piece of jewelry: it is scrap, set to be discarded and destroyed. That is the role of the pawn shop, except they don't just buy jewelry but deal in any item of value. The going rate used to be between twenty-five percent and a third of retail, and since the advent of eBay, half of the eBay price.

The pool vacuum arrived. It is new in its original box and is high-end, specifically designed for some wealthy individual's inground pool, and it retails for $399.00. Doubtless the pawn shop paid $125.00 for it, and then they sold it to me for $175.00 in cash. I'm selling it for $300.00 online, and after $25.00 in shipping and $35.00 in fees, I have saved the customer a hundred dollars and I have earned $65.00 for slapping a label on a box and tendering it for UPS transport. This is how I make my living, and since I started school full-time I hired Amanda for eleven dollars an hour and take slightly less money. Regardless of how much I cheat in other areas, I pay Amanda right—I take out payroll taxes and pay her FUTA and FICA and send her a W-2 at the end of the year. I've kept her legit. So why don't we take pictures of serial numbers in our listings? Ask Detective Mansour who is standing in my apartment, waiting for me to come home.

Amanda had let in the officer. He came in with a second officer from the Town of Simsbury, Connecticut police department and asked her if this were her apartment. She said no and immediately called me, and since I was just out running an errand I was back home almost instantly. I marched up to the third floor of the apartment at the corner of Park Street and Tulip Street in Bristol. I had moved into the third floor because it was cheaper, but after carrying my share of eighty-pound welders and big screen televisions upstairs I was seriously reconsidering my decision.

The officers were not very happy to see me. "Name?" one of them said.

"Susan Sturbridge," I said.

"Have you ever been known by any other names?" the detective asked.

"I've never been married," I replied.

"That's not what I meant," said the officer.

"What exactly do you mean, *officer*?" I asked.

"It's detective. And it looks like...well it looks like perhaps you looked a little different before..." The officer stumbled.

"Are you asking me if I'm transgender?"

"Yes. What was your name when you were a man?"

"You realize that is a *very* insulting question to ask a transwoman," I responded.

"Well, what *was* your name before?" the officer continued.

I handed him my license. "Susan Sturbridge. That's my legal name. Now can you please tell me what this is all about?"

"What's the name on your birth certificate?" asked the other officer who was now examining my identification.

I started fuming. I wanted to cry. I was in the process of transitioning from male to female, and while I had changed my name and had been taking feminizing hormones to change my license, I hadn't changed my birth certificate yet. At this time, in the State of Connecticut, one needed to have surgery before a birth certificate would be changed. I was years away from that, and the officers sensed that.

"If you tell me why you guys are here, I will tell you the name on my birth certificate," I said.

"We're not here to play 'Let's Make a Deal,'" said the officer, clearly annoyed. "What is your birth name?"

"Seth," I said. "Seth Sturbridge was my name when I was born. Now I am Susan. Are you happy now? Why are you here?" I was angry.

"We're investigating larceny," Detective Mansour said. With that he conferred with the other officer quietly, and then he spoke again. "We want to know how you got *that*," he said, extending his arm to point into the spare bedroom which I used to store my inventory.

"The pool vacuum? Super Pawn. Right down on King Street, Route 229."

"You mean Middle Street?"

"Whatever. King Street. Middle Street. It's all Route 229."

"Do you happen to have a receipt?" Mansour asked.

I responded promptly. "Actually, I do." I dug through my receipt box and found the slip that was dated about a week ago. It was handwritten, on Super Pawn letterhead, and along with some other merchandise, it clearly read "1 robotic pool vacuum $175 tax inc."

"Mr. Sturbridge..." began the other officer.

I forcefully interrupted him. "It's *Miss* Sturbridge..." Amanda laughed softly.

"I'm sorry, Miss Sturbridge, that item is stolen property and we are going to be confiscating it."

"You absolutely are not," I countered. "Not unless you are going to pay me for it." The officers both had a hearty laugh.

"It's evidence in an open investigation. It's going to be seized."

"So, I'm just out $175?" I asked, growing more upset.

"Well, you're more than welcome to go back to Super Pawn and see if they'll reimburse you," said Mansour. "But we're not leaving your apartment without that pool vacuum." He paused. "And those golf clubs."

"Golf clubs?" I asked incredulously. "Amanda, did you let them into the inventory room?" I was absolutely livid. Amanda's lip started to quiver.

"They're cops, Susan," Amanda answered softly. Unfortunately, I raised my voice.

"Amanda! You didn't have to let them in! You could have just made them wait outside until I came home!" Amanda started crying really softly, and instantly I felt like a horrible person. I forgot the police were even there. "I'm sorry. I'm sorry honey. I shouldn't have raised my voice. When this is over, I want you to take the rest of the day off and I'll pay you." She smiled through tears. I turned back to the officers.

"So, you're saying someone walked into a store and walked out with *that*? It must weigh forty-five pounds! How on Earth did they hide it?" I was absolutely incredulous.

"Actually, Miss Sturbridge," Mansour said, "Someone wrote a bad check for it."

"Well that makes a little more sense. But isn't that check fraud? Or passing a bad check? Isn't that a financial crime? It's not larceny…"

"It *is* larceny," the officer countered. "And until you showed us the receipt from Super Pawn we believed you were in receipt of stolen goods. That's just another form of larceny, but it's the same penalty under the law. This is sixth degree larceny. It's a class C misdemeanor. You're looking at maybe three months in jail. And believe me. A lady like you is not going to York with the females. You're going to men's jail." The officers laughed with one another.

"Well, I don't know what my gender has to do with anything, and I'm not about to be incarcerated. I'm not a criminal. I bought a legal item through a legal transaction at a legitimate brick-and-mortar store and I have the receipt. That's a one hundred percent legal transaction, is it not?"

"Oh, Miss Sturbridge, we're not saying you didn't legally purchase the product. But we're still seizing it."

"You're not," I said flatly.

"We are. I can absolutely guarantee you that we're not leaving this apartment without the pool vacuum and the golf clubs. Or we can take you in on a breach of peace charge and your little employee here can bond you out."

"No, no," I responded. "I don't want to be arrested. I just don't understand why you need to seize the vacuum. If the person wrote the bad check, why do you need the item as evidence? The crime speaks for itself. You have the bad check. *That* is the evidence."

"We're restoring it to its rightful owner," Mansour countered.

"Oh, you mean the pawn shop?" I asked sarcastically.

"No. The pool supply store in Simsbury. It belongs to them."

"Technically," I replied, "It belongs to me. What I really want to know is how you are so sure that this precise unit is the one that matches the check that you are investigating."

"The serial number," Mansour said. "The serial number is in your eBay listing."

"No way," I answered. I looked directly at Amanda. "Amanda, I told you we only put model numbers in our listings and not serial numbers, right? You know that!"

"Of course I know that," she said. "I never, ever, put serial numbers in the listings."

"Let me see the listing," I said to her. Amanda brought the laptop over. Sure enough, barely legible in the photo, but it was there in the picture. She saw it as soon as I did."

"I'm sorry, Susan," she began. "It was just heavy. I just took a picture without even moving the box. I'm really sorry." She lowered her head. "This is all my fault."

I placed my hand gently on her arm and she looked up at me. "It's not your fault, Amanda. You didn't mean it. It's just an oversight. I'm not mad at you." I looked over at the officers. "I'm mad at them. Guys. Tell me something. If I put that photo up on the Internet, isn't it possible that the owner saw mine for sale, copied my serial number down, and then just said that was the one? Maybe he hadn't even recorded the serial number. What do you have to say to that?"

"Miss Sturbridge. The owner of the pool supply store made a police report about the theft…"

I interrupted him. "Stop calling it theft. It's check fraud."

"Please don't interrupt me," Mansour said. "It's all larceny. Look up the law if you need to. The owner of the store had a copy of a receipt with that serial number on it along with the number on the bad check. This is open and shut."

"Bullshit," I retorted. "He runs the store. He's the owner. You didn't get that receipt from a customer. It came from the owner. All he had to do was see my listing, make a new receipt, and call you. Done."

"Are you calling the store's owner a liar?" Both officers stood erect.

"Maybe I am, maybe I'm not. All I'm saying is that there's reasonable doubt. Isn't that your standard?"

"It's actually not, Miss Sturbridge. We get a statement that a pool vacuum was sold with a bad check to a booster who sells it to the pawn shop and you buy it, it sucks to be you. Someone has to eat it. And that person is you." Mansour smiled at me.

"What if I make a complaint to your Captain for discriminating against me for being a transwoman?" I offered.

"You could," Mansour said, "But remember that your employee here let us in, and we saw the stolen merchandise before we saw you. We're taking it. Like it or not."

I had to concede. "I understand," I said. "I'm going to let you take it. I'll just sue you later for the money." Mansour was entirely unfazed.

"It's a free country, Miss Sturbridge. Sue who you want. But there's no tort here."

"That's for a judge to decide, not a cop," I replied disgustedly. "Just take the damn thing and go." Mansour picked up the vacuum while the other officer went farther into my inventory room and picked up the set of golf clubs I had for sale. "Wait a minute!" I said. "Those golf clubs don't have serial numbers! They're not even listed on eBay yet!"

Mansour looked at me and smiled wryly. "First, they match the description of a set of clubs that was also purchased illegally using a bad check. And second, they came from the same store, right?"

My ears turned red and I tasted bile. "Now I'm really going to sue you," I said. They picked up the vacuum and the clubs and handed me a receipt for seized property. I looked at it and fumed. "You don't understand," I continued. "I really am going to sue you and I'm going to win! How dare you come into my house like this! Get out of here!"

"You have a good day, Miss Sturbridge," said Mansour as he banged the box in the doorframe. I slammed my door on them and could hear them laughing going down the back stairs.

"Screw them," said Amanda.

"I agree," I said in a daze. "Screw them. Go home Amanda. I'm really sorry that I made you cry. I'll pay you out for the rest of the day. Go see your girlfriend."

"Thanks, Susan. I'll see you tomorrow morning."

"See you sweetie," I said and hugged her. I fumed for a while, just staring at that little slip of pink paper, alone in my apartment. I do not like police. I hadn't had any police contact since I'd gotten clean from drugs. It's just so disconcerting when they interact with you, and then they just had to rub it in about my gender. I just hate men. I put on my tallest shoes, did my makeup, and drove down to Super Pawn.

It's a short drive from Park and Tulip to Route 229. The pawn shop was in a strip mall that housed a sports bar, a cheap Chinese food restaurant, a tanning place, and an unmarked door in back that housed the illegal poker club run by Big Daddy. Definitely class C real estate on a busy thoroughfare in Bristol, a small city home to about 60,000 people and ESPN.

When I walked in, I was greeted warmly. "Susan!" they all said. "How are you, Hon?" One owner, Brian, was at the pawn counter standing with one hand on the counter while he took a long drag off a Marlboro red with his other hand, and his gun planted firmly at his hip. The other owner, Dino, the old man, was behind the jewelry counter. There were two young women in their twenties watching television behind the counter as well. Brian's cousin Al was standing at the gun counter on a dating site on the computer, surrounded by rifles and shotguns overlooking a counter of handguns. Brian's no-good cousin Anthony was playing X-Box behind the pawn counter. Several other men were playing setback in the back room where the inventory was stored. I was the only customer in the store.

"Susan, we got more merch," Brian said.

"Sorry Brian. I have a problem."

"What happened?"

"The cops were just at my house."

"No way."

"Yeah. They seized the pool vacuum and the golf clubs."

"Shit, Susan, I'm really sorry," said Brian.

"They said bad checks were written for them and that they were stolen property. The only reason they didn't arrest me was because I had your receipts."

"Shit, Susan." Brian lit another cigarette. "Dino!" yelled Brian. Al left his post at the gun counter and sauntered slowly over, as did the old man. "Dino. Christian's on the junk again. He's making mistakes." The men all looked at me.

"Can we speak candidly?" I asked. Brian motioned for me to come into the back room. "Explain this to me. How does he get this stuff?"

Brian looked at me quizzically. "You know, Susan, before you we didn't have any, you know, shemales in our crew."

"The correct word is 'he-she,'" chimed in Al.

"It's actually not either, guys. I'm, just a woman."

Dino laughed. He spoke very kindly. "We know that Susan but we've known you since you were little, coming in with your dad to buy hand tools and silver coins. Your first bike came from here! It's just hard for us when we've known someone so long being one way and all of a sudden you just change. We accept you for being a woman. It's just hard for us."

"We never call you Seth," laughed Al. Brian punched him hard in the arm.

"Shut up, Al. We said we wouldn't call Susan that any more. She's a woman, and she's turning out to be a beautiful young lady."

"You're just saying that because I spend five grand a week here," I retorted.

"No, I care," said Brian's cousin Anthony. "When are you getting your tits done? That's what I'm waiting for…"

"You are sick, sick, sick, Anthony," said Dino. I ignored his crassness and attempted to educate.

"Actually, Ant, my tissue is still growing and so the surgeon won't operate until they finish growing on their own. So I just have to wait."

"How long?" asked Anthony.

"I really don't know. It could be a year. It could be three years. I don't know. Anyways… Brian. How does this stuff come in?"

All the men looked at Brian. He paused, then said, "If you tell anyone what I'm about to tell you, I will deny it, and then I will shoot you."

"Geez, Brian. That's pretty harsh. I'm part of the team," I answered. He continued.

"There's a place in Hartford that make fake IDs, down the street from the C-Town and by the Copart. All these guys do is fake IDs. They have a tight crew. You give them forty dollars and a name and address and they take your picture and give you an ID. Any state you want. They look legit. So our boy Christian is part of a crew. He goes in with his crew and they buy maybe four or five IDs."

"Four or five?" I had never heard of such a thing.

"Yeah. Because they use them up. Then Christian prints up these fake business checks on a Dyesub printer and he lists a fake company with himself as the proprietor. They pose as property managers, HVAC companies, welders, mechanics, you name it. The checks look perfect. He even learned to make the MICR right and everything. Then they pose as contractors and drive to all these specialty stores that don't use Telecheck and scam the employees."

"That seems like too much work," I said. "There must be something easier to do with checks," I reasoned.

"Should I tell her?" Al asked Brian.

"Go ahead," said Brian.

"Christian used to print fake payroll checks," said Al. "He would find addicts that he would sell a little dope to that had regular jobs and told them he would cash their checks for them. Well, he would just write down the bank account and routing number, and then print fake payroll checks made out to himself."

"Does that work?" I asked.

"Easy money," replied Al. "He would use different aliases with different fake IDs, print fake payroll checks for a g-note apiece, then just drive from Bank of America to Bank of America just cashing fake checks. And he got paid cash."

"He bought a Harley from us with a paper bag full of c-notes," said Brian. "Then he got caught and did eighteen months in prison. When he got out he started doing this instead. Safer. We've known him for years."

"So he just drives around passing bad checks?" I asked.

"Yup," said Brian. "They go to Jersey and New York and PA for a few days, and this is how they support their dope habit."

"I liked their first scam better," I said. "If you're going to do all this work driving around, why not just get a real job? It just seems like a ton of work."

"It's the life they like," said Brian. "They shoot dope all day. They probably make 150K a year and it all goes into their arms. They have nothing to show for it at the end of the year."

"Then every once in awhile," said Dino, "They get pinched and they go to can and they're on vacation for awhile. But three hots and a cot. TV. Other guys in their same line of work to socialize with. They don't mind. Then they just get out and do it all over again."

"That's crazy," I said, very happy at that moment to be free from drugs and alcohol and firmly rooted in twelve-step recovery. Brian lit another cigarette.

"What do I owe you for the clubs and the vacuum?" he asked while pulling out a wad of hundreds from his back pocket.

"The vacuum was $175. The clubs were $600." Brian peeled away eight hundreds from his stack. He had always taught me to carry two wads of cash—your real bankroll and a fake. That way, if you get rolled, you hand the dude the fake one and leave. And, you always put a dollar bill on the top of your c-notes to hide your wad's value. Brian still did just that.

"Keep the change for your trouble," Brian said as he handed me $800. I looked at the cash in my hand and felt very, very grateful. The men hadn't asked me how the cops found me. Or if my employee had made a mistake. To them, it was just the cost of doing business.

"You said you had more merch, Brian?" I asked.

"Yeah. Four Dewalt combo kits."

"What's that going to cost me?"

"Eight hundred," said Dino and they all laughed aloud.

"I just can't get ahead with you guys!"

"And you never will," said Al. I handed back the eight hundred to Brian.

"So we're square now?" I asked.

"Ralph will carry the four kits out for you. You got the truck today?" Brian loved my truck, a blue '78 Ford F-150 from Maine.

"No, I got the car," I said. "They'll fit." I gave Ralph my keys and he loaded the merch. Ralph did odd jobs at the pawn shop, like fixing the small engines that came in and sweeping up, and had a little boosting habit of his own.

Those kits were valuable. I could make $75 apiece on them if I kept the whole thing together, or $100 apiece if I broke them down and sold the tools individually. A hammerdrill. A drill/driver. A work light. A reciprocating saw. A charger. Two batteries. And a case. I mean, just the batteries were $100. All 18V XRP. This was a very nice score for me today.

I thanked the men and left for my home, cooked a nice strip steak black and blue and dipped it in some Worcestershire sauce and had half a bag of salad. I was still angry about everything that had happened, but the food definitely calmed my nerves. I got to thinking about how to sue the officers.

I was really not a litigious individual. This was the absolute first time I was ever suing anyone. I'd always heard people say, "I'm going to sue!" and "I'll see you in court!" but I didn't really know where to start. Based on some quick Google research it appeared that I should send a demand letter first. So I authored one to the captain of the police department and cc'ed the mayor of the town. Here's what it said:

June   15,   2005

Dear   Captain   Stevens,

I am writing to you because last week Detective Mansour of the Simsbury Police Department made a bad seizure of property from my home that he stated was stolen in reference to Simsbury Case #05-10342. He seized a set of Callaway golf clubs with no serial numbers, no engravings, no personalization, and no customization and claimed that they "matched" property taken from a   store   in   Simsbury.

When he showed me the police report with the information on the clubs, he showed me that the criminals involved in the case (of whom I have no knowledge of their identities or whereabouts) were charged under 53a-128 of the Connecticut General Statutes for issuing a bad check. Even if the check amount were over $1000 and the crime were thus a class D felony, the holder of that check (in this case, the Simsbury business owner) is not entitled to seize any property from me or any   other   individual.

Pursuant to the penal code, the convicted criminal becomes a debtor to the holder of the check, and the holder must pursue collection of that debt in accordance with Section 52-565a of the Connecticut General Statutes, which does not include seizure by police of property that is legally mine. When I explained this (in slightly less detail) to Detective Mansour in my home, he told me that   I   was   mistaken,   and   he   did   have   the   right   to   take   this   item.

I am sending a copy of this letter to the First Selectman of Simsbury to let him know of this transgression.   Simply,   I   want   the   golf   clubs   returned   to   me.

I understand that the police who came to my home were doing their job—they believed that because of my online business that I might have somehow been involved in the illegal activities of others. However, once I provided a receipt for the purchase of those clubs, the detectives should have left my home. I am attaching a copy of my State of Connecticut Form OR-138 showing that I have been registered with the State as a small business since 2003. I am also attaching a copy of my Form OS-114 from the previous quarter showing the sales taxes paid and gross sales of my business, which were well over $80,000 in those three months. I have a federal employer identification number, and run a legitimate business just like the store in Simsbury that unfortunately had property seized that is similar to my inventory, but since mine was legally obtained, mine cannot be taken from me.

At Trinity College I studied legal theory and am well-aware of my rights and my ability to file suit against the town to seek punitive damages for the massive headache this illegal seizure has become. As I stated above, since seizure of property (in this case from its rightful owner!) is not a legal route to debt collection pursuant to 53a-128.

Please call me to set up a time when I can pick up the clubs. I have also enclosed a copy of the "receipt" Detective Mansour gave me, in case you need to alter this document or create another one if it will no longer be applicable for purposes of my IRS Form 4684 filing next year.

I appreciate your timely response,

Susan   Sturbridge

cc: First   Selectman   Dennis
enclosures

After receiving no response, I decided to sue the town. I now had to fill out a piece of paperwork called a summons for the small claims action. (I had decided to file in small claims because it only cost $90 and I didn't know the first thing about regular civil court with all sorts of motions and such. This was a simple issue with, hopefully, a simple resolution.) I completed the summons and wrote the following complaint:

I am filing suit against Detective Mansour, as representative of the Simsbury Police Department, as well as First Selectman Dennis, as representative of the Town of Simsbury. I have included a copy of the unanswered letter I sent to the First Selectman's Office one month ago which explains in more detail this issue.

Simsbury Police Detectives seized property from my home on June 9, 2005. They seized a TurboBot robotic pool vacuum cleaner and a set of Callaway Big Bertha Fusion Graphite

Golfing Irons. The TurboBot pool vacuum had been purchased with a bad check by someone I do not know. I legally purchased the item from a local Bristol merchant, and provided the receipt to the police, who cleared me of any wrongdoing. They claimed that the item was "stolen property." I explained that I had not stolen it, and that since their suspect had written a bad check for the item, it became a civil matter of debt collection. They responded that CT statutes state that "stolen property" is defined as "property obtained through theft or other illegal means," which includes check fraud. I countered that since I purchased the product legally and provided a receipt, it was not stolen property, since I legally obtained it. I told them that they should use the fines collected from the prosecution of the bad check criminal activity to reimburse the original owner. They refused, and bullied me into surrendering the item.

They also seized a set of Callaway Big Bertha Fusion Graphite Golfing Irons. They claimed that this property (found while snooping around my inventory room) was wanted by Simsbury Police for an investigation. They could not give me any more information, but suggested that unless I wanted a train of other police departments tramping through my home, that I would be best advised to surrender the item to them. They told me the item would be returned if it did not match the item missing from Simsbury. After not hearing from their office for some time, I did some detective work of my own and visited Captain Peter Stevens of the Simsbury Police Department. He released a copy of the first page of the Lost/Stolen Property Report naming the missing property that the detectives supposedly seized. The clubs are not the same. The clubs they seized were graphite shafted. The "missing" clubs were steel shafted. There is a difference of $240 in the price of these items. Simsbury claimed that the serial numbers (which were not noted on any official reports and could have easily been adjusted or added) matched on the clubs. Even if the serial numbers matched (an impossibility) they cannot seize property legally obtained (I had a sales slip for these as well) since they were not stolen. But since they do not match, I believe the Simsbury police department should have returned those clubs immediately.

The Simsbury Police Department explained that the items would not be returned to me.

I am seeking to recover the full retail value of the items that were part of this wrongful seizure: $2686.00

Respectfully   submitted,

Susan   Sturbridge

I mailed everything out Priority Mail as instructed and patiently expected a response. It didn't take long to get one. The Scarsella Law Firm represented the Town of Simsbury in all legal matters, and as large as a Hartford player they were, that is how small my case was to them. What they did first was transfer my case to the regular docket and out of small claims. (I would find out much later that firms often do this because small claims decisions are not appealable while regular docket cases are.)

So I waited again, then got a notice saying I had to attend a "status conference" at the Hartford JD Civil Court at 2pm in about a month. I had no idea what that would entail, but on that day I put on my best White House Black Market dress and my tallest heels and showed up when I was told.

The Hartford court building is a court that looks like courts on TV—large Ionic columns and stone stairs outside and very ornate wooden adornments in the interior. I asked where civil caseflow was and sat down, since they had lunch from 1pm to 2pm and I was a couple minutes early.

Lots of individuals who looked like attorneys were milling about the open lobby—all of the men and women wore suits and were all carrying file folders and briefcases. Caseflow finally opened and they sent me to Courtroom B. It was definitely luxurious, lavishly appointed with beautiful woodwork and carvings on the benches. Then a frazzled-looking man with glasses and a sharp grey suit walked in. "Miss Sturbridge. Hello. I'm Attorney Easton for the Town of Simsbury. How are you?" I was struck by his candor, his kindness, and his professionalism. And he respected my gender identity. A class act.

"I'm well Attorney Easton. How are you?"

"Fine." he replied.

"What do we do next?" I asked.

"We talk to the judge," he replied. An Asian clerk came out and verified who we both were, even though we were the only ones in the courtroom. In a moment the judge came out from his chambers, and older man in a long robe. Easton stood so I stood. "Hello, Your Honor," he said. I parroted him.

"I was just looking at this complaint," the Judge began, "And I believe we can settle this today. Are you in agreement, Attorney Easton?"

"Yes, Your Honor."

"Miss Sturbridge, would you mind telling me what happened?" He had kind eyes, and was patient. I told him the entire story from the beginning. When he spoke again, he was candid and frank.

"Mr. Easton. Can you explain to me why your officers seized a set of titanium golf clubs from Miss Sturbridge's residence when the official police report states clearly that the golf clubs were steel? I don't play golf but I know that a set of titanium clubs is more expensive than a set of steel ones. She has provided evidentiary documents as part of the complaint."

"Yes, Your Honor. It appears that there was a simple misunderstanding, a scrivener's error or a clerical error made by the officers. I can assure you that there was no malfeasance. I believe this is a simple oversight and you have my client's apologies."

"All right. Miss Sturbridge," the Judge continued, "I read your complaint and heard your account and I believe that the preponderance of the evidence suggests that the pool vacuum is indeed stolen property, but that the golf clubs were not. Will you accept being paid for the clubs but not for the vacuum?"

"I will Your Honor." I had neglected to mention until now that Brian had given me a blank receipt and I had filled in the value of the golf clubs as $800 rather than $600 to avoid this contingency. They were worth much more than that retail, but neither the Judge nor the Attorney knew what I actually paid. I just fudged the number a bit.

"Can I have the clubs back in lieu of payment?" I asked Attorney Easton. (If I got those clubs I could sell them for fifteen hundred dollars.)

"Unfortunately, they have already been returned to the golfing store. We are willing to make a fiduciary restitution."

The Judge continued, "I understand Miss Sturbridge, that the value of the clubs in question is $800."

"That's correct."

"So, Miss Sturbridge," the Judge said, "You will receive $800 plus ninety dollars for cost of suit and $5.60 for postage for a total of $895.60?"

"That's perfect, Your Honor," I smiled and shook Attorney Easton's hand.

"I will send you a release and a withdrawal to sign," he said, "and then when I get them back I'll issue you a check."

"Can I just come to your office to do this," I asked.

"Just give me a couple of days to get the check from the town, and then we can finish."

We parted ways. It was my first experience with the civil justice system, and it was a very good one. When I looked back at the whole thing globally, everyone did exactly as I thought they would. The boosters kept boosting. The pawnshop returned my $775 I outlaid for the merch (actually, they gave me $800) and then I turned that $800 into $1100 the next week. And I just earned $895.60 from the Town of Simsbury. It was an excellent day! I called my girlfriend.

"I'm taking you out to Max à Mia in Avon tonight," I said.

"My favorite restaurant?" she asked. "Why?"

"I had a legal victory today. I made just shy of $900 and I didn't have to sell anything."

"Oh, honey, you should save that money," she said. "You're in school!"

"No, Honey, I insist. It's literally free money. What would be the point of this whole thing if I didn't share it with you? I've never made that much in one day before. Let's go out and celebrate! Get that nice salad you like with the polenta croutons and we'll get some sea bass or halibut. Let's go!"

"Okay!!" she said excitedly.

With that, the boosting and suing began in my life. I had always boosted, but I had never sued too—this opened a whole new realm of possibility. It would happen many more times as detailed in this book. But before I skip ahead to talk about the other times I was successful, I need to give you a little context. I'll go back to the beginning.

DENYING GENDER

_____I have always been a female. That is to say, though I was born with an external genital morphology that is customarily associated with boys and men, I have always felt like a female. When I was in kindergarten I knew something was wrong—girls had one bathroom and boys had another, and I knew that boys had penises and girls did not, but I was just too young to put everything together. When I was about eight, I remember my parents telling me to say my prayers at night. Each night I would pray, "Dear God, please let this life just be a bad dream and I will wake up tomorrow and be a girl." I prayed that way every night and it never happened, but I was still too childlike to know why.

Wanting to alter my reality began when I was around ten. It was at that point that I knew I was transgender for certain. Up until then, I thought that maybe we were all both men and women and we just didn't talk about it. Remember, if you can imagine it, it could be true. That was my mantra as someone who was ten dealing with some pretty serious issues of ontology. At age ten I started wearing my sister's clothes in private, always at night because I didn't want to get caught by my parents. I had secured a grocery bag full of old clothes (a donation bag, maybe?) and would wear them at night. Somehow I had a bra that fit me—I'm pretty certain I boosted it from TJ Maxx or Marshalls when I was with my mother buying clothes. But the central piece was always the breasts. So that brought with it another problem. What could I use that could feel like a real breast?

First I tried water balloons. This seemed like a good idea. However, when a water balloon is filled up on the small side (picture breasts on a ten-year-old male's body) they were way too firm. They felt like water balloons, not breasts. Somewhere I had read that during air burst testing (to check their integrity) that condoms got to be the size of watermelons. So I trusted they wouldn't break. The only reason I knew where to get them is because at the car wash they sold them in a little machine that took quarters. So I stole eight quarters from my parents' change jar and left the house in the middle of the night to get two condoms from the machine. I filled them with water and they were perfect—soft and supple like real breasts. I had found my solution!

So it would be night time. I would have on the bra and the water balloon condoms and the women's clothing. Until one day I got caught. I was going in and out of my room to the bathroom so I could see myself in the mirror with the breasts. It woke up my parents and so they asked me if everything were alright. I scurried out of the bathroom and into my bed and my father chased me in. He knew I was hiding something. I turned away from him and covered my "breasts" with my arm. I wouldn't turn around and was crying. Finally my dad saw the bra strap.

"You're wearing a bra?!"

I cried and he hit me, one of the only times I can remember. I have since forgiven him and hold no grudge against my father. It took a lot of work but it was worth it. I kept wearing the bra and breasts for the next few years until I was about thirteen. When I was a preteen I used to steal money any way I could, with the express intention of buying myself a woman's wardrobe. I skimmed money out of my parents' wallets and stole a couple of women's purses who just happened to be walking their dogs or playing at a playground with their kids. I had amassed about $200, which is a lot for a thirteen-year-old with no allowance.

After telling my parents that I was a girl and them flatly rejecting that for me, I fell into a deeper and deeper depression, and just had a terrible psychological state. I was never suicidal—I remember thinking that that electrical impulses travel at the speed of light in the brain, but a bullet travels at hundreds of miles and hour. If I ever shot myself, from the time the bullet left the chamber until it killed me, that time could literally be an eternity of hell. So I lived in a constant state of ennui, and I dug into my studies. But there was this small piece in my mind that I could not compartmentalize, something no thought emanating from the rational frontal cortex could remove. It was definitely something deeper—amygdala or brain stem—and something more formative. Daily, I was in the process of denying my identity.

By this time I had some of my sister's clothes that fit me and some random clothes that appeared to be hand-me-downs my parents were saving for when my sister was older. These weren't really feminine clothes—they were pink or magenta or purple—but they weren't good looking pieces so I hatched a plan. There was a very special (and now defunct) store called Rena's Unique Boutique. By some estimations it would be a "stripper store" or a "transvestite store," but I knew from seeing their ad that they sold everything that I needed.

I was thirteen years old and had never been on the Internet (it was only 1993). I owned a rusty red 20" bike with no gears and only foot brakes, but I was used to it. I had no map, one pair of clothes, and a backpack. I took my $200 and left the house in the dead of night early one Sunday morning. I rode my bike with no gears and no lights in the predawn hours from Terryville to Seymour, which is about twenty-five miles.

The only way I knew how to get to this place was Route 8, the highway, and clearly I could not ride my bike on the highway. So I followed a southerly route the best that I could, travelling through Thomaston, Watertown, Waterbury, Naugatuck, and Beacon Falls to get to Seymour. I arrived in the morning before the store opened, so I stopped at Stop and Shop for some breakfast and sat with my bike down by the river in a meditative state.

Finally the store opened and it was glorious—a store chock full of sexualized women's clothing. I didn't dare buy shoes. I couldn't afford them and my feet were still growing—but I wanted everything else. I introduced myself to the woman proprietor and told her I felt like a girl even though I was a boy, and that I wanted to look and feel pretty.

"You're so young!" she said.

"I know," I responded. "Just make me look pretty."

With that she found me a lacy black bra and properly fitted me for it. She got me breast forms that filled the bra and looked as real as possible. She got me a shiny silver dress, a miniskirt, and a couple sexy tops. It all cost me about $150. I thanked the woman profusely, told her I would be back when I had more money, and rode my bike back to Terryville.

I was still very much of a criminal mindset, sociopathic even, and especially now that my bankroll was depleted, I wanted more money so I could expand my wardrobe. Also, I really wanted to dress as a woman in public rather than only in my room. Looking back on this as an adult transwoman, I'm sure I looked hideous, but I stashed my bike at an abandoned house and changed. I put on one of my new blouses and new skirt and thought, "I'll just walk into church and sit in back, and when the women go up for communion I'll just snag one of their purses and walk out. Then I'll hustle back to the abandoned house, change, and go home."

I got so far as getting dressed and walking up the road to the church, but I couldn't go in. All of my past crimes had been crimes of opportunity while this was intentional larceny. What if I got caught? What a mess that would be! If they detained me, they would notice I was not a female, and then everyone in our small town would be gossipping about that crazy Seth Sturbridge. I couldn't do that to my parents, no matter how much I despised them. So I didn't steal, but walked right back to the abandoned house. But there was something about it—it was thrilling walking around in public as a female. I felt so *normal*, so *right*, so *comfortable*.

In my case I rode the final part of my journey back home, and when I was within a mile of my home, a police officer stopped me. "Your mother is worried sick about you, Seth," he said. "I'm taking you home."

I'd never seen my mother so distraught. Her face was blotchy and red from hours of crying and she was bawling uncontrollably. "My baby, my baby," she kept saying, hugging me and sobbing.

I was stoic, not crying, didn't even feel bad—they must have believed I had borderline personality disorder or was just a sociopath. These were the people that I hated. My father hit me and called me a faggot when he caught me wearing women's clothes. My mother told me that if I became a woman I would be a freak, I would be unhappy, no one would be friends with me, I would never get a job, and I would waste my life. How did I come from these people?

The officer left and my father opened my backpack, discovering fake tits and women's garments. "This is why you left in the middle of the night?" he asked. I said nothing and he looked at me with disgust. My mother had stopped crying and she asked me where I'd gone.

"Seymour," I said flatly.

"What's in Seymour? You rode your bike to Seymour in the middle of the night? Do you know how dangerous that is? You could have been hit by a car and killed!" My mother had always lived in a fear-based world. After many years and a large amount of introspection, I came to see that fear and faith could not dwell in the same house and I sought to rid myself of fear, anger, and all of its precursors and effects.

"Mom," I said, "I just want to be a girl. And I needed some nice girl's clothes." My mother began rummaging through my backpack.

"You mean you want to be a slutty girl!" she exclaimed. "Look at this stuff! I am so embarrassed that you are my child. Is this what you think a woman is? A pair of breasts and some slutty, skimpy skirts and dresses? If you really were a girl, you would know that all this here is *not* what makes a girl a girl."

"Then what does?" I asked with my lip quivering.

"A vagina," said my father as he left the room.

"Honey, we know you struggle with this," she said. "God gives all of us different struggles and this is something you have to deal with. We're going to make an appointment with the psychologist right away. This behavior is just not normal."

"It would be normal if I were a girl."

"No it wouldn't be!" she huffed. "Girls don't ride bikes twenty miles in the middle of the night to buy clothes."

"Well what did you want me to do?" I asked. I was desperate. "If I had asked you to take me to the store and buy me women's clothes, what would you have said?"

"I'd say absolutely not. That's a waste of money."

"It's not a waste! I want them. I *need* them."

"And where are you going to wear them?" she asked.

"Out."

"Out? Honey everyone will make fun of you and call you names. Just be happy you're a boy. You're a bright, beautiful, and handsome boy." She paused a moment. "Is it that you are attracted to boys? Is that what this whole thing is about?"

"No, Mom," I replied. "That's gross. I like girls. I want to kiss them. But I also want to look like them and do my hair nice and dress like them and have a girl's name. When I close my eyes and look in a mirror I see a girl, but when I open them I see a boy. It just doesn't make any sense."

"Well it just doesn't make sense to me either. Let's just not talk about this again. You can keep the clothes, but just wear them in your room by yourself. You know how this affects your father!"

And that was the end of that. I kept the clothes—I eventually got to wear them at Halloween in high school so I did get to wear them out in public after all. Among everything else, I remember I just longed for the winter months to come when we wore pants instead of shorts. Then I could shave my legs and they would be covered so that the boys wouldn't see them and make fun of them. But it made me feel right, somehow.

Everything changed once I got to high school. I went to private high school because my grades and test scores were high and I got a scholarship. I had always grown up as a precocious child, but I really dove into my studies as an escape from reality. When I had just turned fourteen I found an even better and quicker escape from reality—alcohol and drugs. Once one of the kids brought in some alcohol and I tried it, I was hooked. Pot was even worse. And so it began, 1994.

Once I tried booze I just had to have more. However, I had a hard time procuring it at fourteen since I had no older siblings and had not yet made friends with the juniors and the seniors. So, shocker, I stole it. There was a neighborhood IGA store in town that sold beer. So I hatched a plan. I'd carry down a paper grocery bag with bottles and cans in it for redemption. I recycled the cans in the machine that was right next to the "in" door, then folded up the paper bag and put it in the shopping cart.

Next to get the alcohol. I would put a 30-pack in the cart, be it Coors cans or Bud Lite or Budweiser or whatever cheap beer they sold there. I would go back to the bottle machine (where there was no camera), open the grocery bag, slide the 30-pack in, and place it right next to the redemption area, just next to the "in" door. Then I would go back to the cashier and cash out for the bottles and cans I had brought inside. When I exited the store, I would quickly trip the "in" door, grab the 30-pack that was an arms length away, and just walk out. I thought I was pretty slick at fourteen!

What I hated the most was that I could never bring the beer in the house because my parents didn't drink and they would find it. So I would always have to hide the 30-pack outside. So while I always had alcohol (I repeated that stunt again and again) it was always warm. I don't think that I realized at the time that I was an alcoholic. I just figured that I was in high school, and so I drank now, just like everyone else. Except for the fact that I was drinking by myself and stealing booze, and neither of those was a good indication of what was to come.

I fell in love the first time I smoked marijuana. I had bought a nickel or dime bag from another freshman that also sold valium, but I found out at an early age I have a naturally high tolerance for benzodiazepines and never really abused those drugs. I had no pipe or rolling papers, but I knew the idea. My parents had gone out to a church meeting and I was home alone, and this is when I opted to try the stuff. I wanted to be alone in case I had a bad reaction or something else happened, so I didn't want to be around other people.

So I simply took a toilet paper tube and put tape over one end, cut a circular hole in the tube, and then pushed a little piece of tinfoil into the hole to make a bowl. Then I poked holes in the foil with a pin and taped the foil down so it would be airtight. I will never forget that first time I got high. It was 6:15pm. I went out on the back porch for what seemed like an eternity, came back inside, and it was 6:16pm. Time, something I had thought of as so fixed, completely changed and literally I began to question my entire reality with all sorts of chemicals. I had found the secret to fixing all of my problems: drugs.

At fourteen, my body was changing in so many ways and I hated all of them, but now I found a way to hate myself but still be able to function as a young man in a society that I desperately wanted to view me as a female. When a boy becomes a man, in many different cultures including ours, as he grows and matures, people notice. So when I started growing facial hair, and my vocal chords thickened permanently and my voice changed, and as I put on more and more muscle mass, my family noticed and told me that I was becoming a young man, With every agonizing day that passed, and with every irreversible change that was occurring, I knew in my heart of hearts that it would be harder and harder to ever look like a natal female, something we now call "cisgender". This reality fueled my drug use.

Soon I was using acid and mushrooms and ketamine and I was tripping at school. I was a complete disaster. But I maintained my grades and my activities and was at the top of my class. The biggest problem I had with the drugs was that they cost money, so if this were to be my habit, I was going to have to boost.

I continued to steal from my parents, but then I realized I could steal calculators. Everyone in school had these Texas Instruments graphing calculators that cost around a hundred dollars apiece, and people were constantly losing them or getting them stolen. So, I began skulking through the halls and classrooms in the evenings or on free periods. I'll never forget, there was this student in my class Andy Carbone who would pay you twenty-five dollars for a calculator. His older brother brought them to the pawn shop and got paid thirty-five dollars, so he learned to arbitrage and made ten dollars apiece for just being the fence. He was the first fence I ever met, and I loved his work—making money selling stolen goods rather than stealing oneself. It seemed like such a better idea!

Now we had Internet at school—this was before Google, but we had Yahoo! And Infoseek and Netscape Navigator, as were the times. So I basically looked up other ways to get high. I knew all about cocaine and crack and opiates and heroin, but they all seemed so dangerous and I didn't really want to kill myself. Crystal meth was not a phenomenon yet in our part of the country. But I did discover a multitude of information about a drug called dextromethorphan hydrobromide, the main ingredient in many over-the-counter cough medicine preparations.

Robitussin getting you high? I would never have believed it. But I read all about the dosing and the brands—you needed Coricidin Cough and Cold, the purple box, what the kids call "triple c's"—and I decided to try it. So at age fifteen I went to visit the local drug store and stole a box of Coricidin and took the sixteen pills that were in the box. Turns out, it was amazing. My body felt like it were being pumped up with helium and my brain felt clear, without any excess noise. Peaceful. My body buzzed and hummed, my tactile sensation was heightened, my sense of time and space were significantly altered. It lasted about three or four hours, and after one use, I was hooked. A large portion of that was also that I needed to steal a calculator to purchase a bag of weed, but this drug I could steal directly from any CVS, Walgreens, Rite Aid, Stop and Shop, Walmart, or Target.

When I was sixteen I was boosting regularly but also discovered another high that I could steal—inhalants. It turns out that the compressed air duster used for cleaning computers and in photography got one pretty high when inhaled directly out of the bottle. Difluoroethane gas. The school actually bought it in bulk for the photography students, so once I found out where it was stored I had another addiction: Dust Off. On a free period I would sneak off campus and then suck down a can under the bridge by the river. Very, very, vivid hallucinations. Lots of physical effects. Utterly distorted time and space and reality. Inhalants were great, but I ended up stopping when I was around nineteen or twenty because I thought I'd inhaled so much gas that I was giving myself brain damage.

When I was sixteen I also ended up with gold in my hands: a set of locker codes. As it turned out, any locker sold by the school store was imprinted with a code on the back. This way, if an administrator needed to open a locker for any reason they could check the code on the back with the master list, get the combination, and open the locker.

It was just after football practice (and yes, I played football). I thought that if I were just hyper-masculine, maybe I could just destroy this feminine part of me that was the cause of such intense agita. I found out later that this had been a pattern of many other transwomen, who often took very masculine jobs like firefighter and police officer and military personnel. These individuals, and me as well, all believed that if we acted masculine enough we could convince the world (and probably ourselves) that we were men and we were okay. However, concurrent with this I was nonetheless destroying my body with drugs, and engaging in risky behavior.

But the locker codes. The man who ran the men's locker room, Arthur Brand, had left the code sheet right near the window where the students brought their laundry for some reason. So I knew what to do immediately. He went in back, I ran up and grabbed the list and bolted. He never saw me.

Now I had the power to break into anyone's locker at any time. There were about 300 people in the school. I thought of everything of value that I could steal and it made me giddy. But I needed to be stealth about it. So I was a bit of a math nerd and used my calculator for everything, and as part of this, I learned to program it. So I wrote a simple program. It prompted you for the locker number, say 256. You type in 256, press enter, and voilà—it would spit out 34-1-23 or whatever the combination was. I could now discreetly walk up to any locker with my calculator and open it. It was like having a master key.

I was saving it for the end of the year. I already knew I was going to work at the local health food store over the summer, loading and unloading produce. My first job, $5.25/hour. But I needed to make much more than that if I wanted to keep my drug habit going.

It was April. I had cleaned out the two pharmacies in town and the three places in Bristol that stocked Coricidin. I couldn't steal the Dust Off from Staples because there were cameras everywhere (though I highly doubt it was the compressed air duster that the people behind the cameras were looking at for people to steal from an electronics store). I didn't feel like drinking the cough syrup because it made me feel very nauseous and I usually threw up, which was gross. The other available brand, Mucinex, had giant horse pills and contained guaifenesin, which also made me sick. So I was down and out. What did I do? I went to the fence. Andy Carbone. I told him I had a proposition for him: I would sell him my program for $100, and could steal anything he wanted to, as long as he left some stuff for me.

Big mistake. Oh, I got the $100, which I immediately spent on weed and acid. But Carbone got caught the first day. I don't know how to this day—someone must have see him and reported it. And that prick, to save his ass, turned me in.

This was a big deal. They almost expelled me. The only thing that saved me was that it was my first offense and I was an honor student at the top of my class. I can still remember the disciplinary hearing. Mr. Reardon asked me if I'd ever used this program. I told him no. He asked me, then why do you have it? I told him because I just wanted to have the power to be able to use it. He argued for my expulsion: he thought I was definitely a sociopath. That I wanted the power to do something rather than actually doing it: he thought that was more criminal than actually stealing.

But the majority won out and my ass was saved. I mean, I played football and lacrosse and did track and field. I was the lead in our musical theater productions. My writing was published in the literary magazine. I had a position in student government (which got stripped from me). I was the vice president of the debate team. The point was, besides this lone act of indiscretion I was the model pupil. And they appreciated that. No one had yet made the connection to drugs and alcohol because I always engaged in that behavior off-campus.

My senior year I skated by. I had gotten into college and was happy. I was really embracing being a male, and was drinking and drugging more than ever. I had my own car to use after working all summer and making $200 a week, and I graduated with my class, somehow. The next job I got was an absolute godsend.

There was an amusement park in Bristol and Southington called Lake Compounce that hired seasonal workers, mostly high school and college students home on break. I went to prep school and had a great academic record so they took me with no problem. My job was working on the midway in the games department. What a summer! I spent my days guessing people's weights and ages (I got pretty good at it! Another useless skill.) Or I was at the ring toss. And I spent my nights smoking weed and riding the roller coasters. I could not have asked for a better setup. I met more drug dealers than I ever had before at that park, but the best part was the money.

Not the salary. That was peanuts. It was near minimum wage. But the money. Each game had its own blue apron. So when you were moved from game to game after a break, you switched aprons. Those aprons had slots for cash like spots in a cash register. And there was zero accountability. So you would walk into a new game after a break. No one's around, check the apron, pocket maybe five or ten bucks out of there. More people come, take all of that money. And like I said, zero accountability. By the end of the summer I'd saved up $3,600 in addition to my pay. All cash, all untraceable.

I had to keep going to the bank to get big bills. They must have thought that I was a male stripper. I was big and muscular, with a big goatee. I looked like an animal, and I acted like one. At one point the amusement park noticed that money was missing from the games department. They called in a few of us who they suspected of stealing one at a time into a management office. This big black guy showed me a tiny camera and said we had been being recorded, and if we had anything to say about the missing money we could just be fired and not arrested.

I didn't believe him for a second. I knew if I were on camera stealing the police would already be there and I'd be leaving in handcuffs. So I adhered to the bro code—deny 'til you die. They rolled a few of the weaker ones, or ones that already had a record, but I went right back to work, right back to boosting.

That was my last time at my parents' house for a really long time. I hated the both of them for treating me the way they did and not letting me transition, and getting in the way of my self-destructive drug use. Normal teenage stuff. But I was on my way up to a Potted Ivy, Amherst College, for what I hoped to be a bacchanalian and drug-fueled experience. I didn't think I'd have to boost anymore since I had that $3,600, and nothing was going to be easier than working at Lake Compounce to make illegal bank. So I went off to school, as masculine and burly as they come, still hiding my gender identity, addicted to drugs and alcohol, and boosting to beat the bandwagon. I just fell in deeper.

GROWING PHALARIS

Phalaris arundinacea is a plant otherwise known as reed canary grass. This species of phalaris is also used as a source for the psychedelic drugs DMT, 5-MeO-DMT and 5-OH-DMT (bufotenin), as well as hordenine and 5-MeO-NMT. Although the concentrations of these compounds is lower than in other potential sources, such as Psychotria viridis and Mimosa tenuiflora, large enough quantities of the grass can be refined to make an ad hoc ayahuasca brew, and this is exactly what I did in college.

By my junior year, I was growing it in my room. It looks like any perennial grass, and when it is small looks just like common lawn grass. No one would ever think that it had anything to do with drugs, but they still might wonder why you were growing flats of grass in a house, apartment, or dorm. I had a whole setup I borrowed from my magic mushroom growing phase, and I modified it to work for the Phalaris.

The key to the Phalaris grass is this very special molecule called dimethyltryptamine, or DMT. I know that those who use fentanyl or carfentanil will argue that the drugs are stronger, I cannot imagine a drug being stronger than DMT. What makes it special is its rapid onset: five to seven seconds. The reason this occurs is because dimethyltryptamine is also an endogenous neurotransmitter. To understand this, consider the analogy of carbon-14 in carbon. So among the norepinephrine we see a few DMT molecules in the brain. They are naturally-occurring and we all have them.

Then consider this—this molecule that is found in your brain is also found in a number of plants. That it is found naturally in one's own brain differentiates it from other drugs. (Since it's Schedule I and yet we are all born with a tiny amount in our bodies, I could just imagine a future when the police would simply arrest you for the tiny amount inherent in your own mind!) So whereas other hallucinogens (mushrooms, dextromethorphan, LSD, etc.) take awhile to metabolize, when one smokes DMT, one knows exactly what it is. As quickly as a hit of crack, almost immediately one's entire visual and physically perceptible world disappears. One is instantly brought to a new space, where one encounters intelligence, spirit, and unimaginable power. And then a couple minutes later you are back to reality. And it all happens so fast, and it's all because you are making a quick tweak to an endogenous neurotransmitter. In the same way that a solid piece of steel is really a lot of protons, neutrons, and electrons and a lot of empty space, nothing more than a probability wave that every piece of matter making up that steel doesn't just spontaneously turn into energy and cease to exist, our reality was just based on a chance likelihood of a certain quantity of DMT in our brains. It fascinated me.

DMT doesn't just come from Phalaris—I just grew that because it's the easiest to cultivate and gives a good yield. Banisteriopsis caapi is a popular one. It's an Amazonian vine that contains tryptamine hallucinogens that has been prepared for millennia in a ceremonial brew called yaje or ayahuasca, where a potent MAOI is added to make the chemicals orally active. This brew has been drunk by psychonauts from many countries for many millennia who are looking for a spiritual vision quest. Overseen by the shaman, the user experiences deep and long-lasting hallucinations and experiences a sense of profound learning from this plant-teacher.

It always appealed to me because I am transgender. Back in ancient times, in cultures without autocratic and coercive patriarchal hegemonies, the transgender person was considered revered. These transpeople became healers, shamans, medicine people, who guided those between life and death as they stood between male and female. Transgender individuals (and intersex individuals) were considered holy and special, and they were charged with overseeing the special plant-teachers which are the roots of the chemicals I speak about today.

So after the Phalaris grass stopped growing taller, I harvested it, and did a polar/nonpolar and acid/base reaction to the plant matter. I ground it in a blender with some distilled water and made what looked like a green milkshake. Then using denatured alcohol, naphtha, hydrochloric acid, and lye, I created the finished product: a small amount of brown powder with the look and texture of dark brown sugar but the smell of burnt plastic. This is mostly DMT.

I divided it up into doses, put each dose into a folded piece of tinfoil, and saved them for my trip out West following the band Widespread Panic on tour. Touring was really fun. I was dating this woman named Sarah who had a 1971 yellow Volkswagen microbus and her plan after graduation was to take her "boyfriend" (me) and live in the van and drive all over the country. Before we left we were going to need supplies.

So I went in the dead of night—three or four in the morning—and went to all the common rooms of all the dorms and picked up all the leftover liquor, wine, and beer from the previous night's festivities. I boosted any food I could find, and when we were ready to go, we had two trunks in the bus—one filled with food and one filled with liquor. It was perfect.

To make money on tour I went to eBay. Always eBay. I bought 1000 lighters from China that arrived in a big cardboard box with Asian characters all over it for $110. That's only eleven cents per lighter. Then I got my get-up. I had sunglasses, red devil horns, no shirt, a rope for a belt, and a pair of shorts. I would walk from car to car and camp to camp yelling "Lighters! One dollar!" And trust me, when you're touring with a band and smoking a lot of cigarettes and weed, you use up lighters. Not to mention all the ones that get lost. Lots of people would say, "Lighter guy! C'mere!" And then I began my real sales pitch: DMT, $25 a hit.

No one was selling DMT on tour. You could get mushrooms, acid, dust, E, pot, but no one had DMT. Most people had only heard of it. The people who had done it before smelled it and knew exactly what it was. The 5-Meo-DMT smells the same but other than that it's the only powder with that special burnt plastic smell. Word that the Lighter Guy had DMT spread around the campers and I ended up sold out. But I couldn't grow in the van. It would have to wait until I got back home, but there were other ways to make money. While I drove, Sarah was sewing those backless tops that hippy girls wore, and she sold those. We were very industrious. Drugs all day, drugs all night, concerts when the jam band came around, and lots and lots of sex. Very fun time. But things didn't end well. The summer was ending, the tour was over, and Sarah wanted to settle down in Albuquerque, NM. I had no aversion to this city, and I had no aversion to Sarah. She used to dress me up in one of her white dresses to have sex with me (she was a swimmer and was 5'11" so I fit in some of her clothes) and she was always working on top and we were always coming together. Very good time.

However I had an illness I wasn't taking care of (besides the addiction). I had bipolar disorder, a serious mental illness which might have even been called schizoaffective disorder because my manic episodes tended to leave me in a psych ward for awhile after breaking with reality. Well, I broke.

Sarah and I were spending our last night together in the microbus before I was to take a Greyhound bus back to her house in Tennessee where my 1987 Volvo 740 GLE station wagon was waiting for me. (I rearranged the letters in Amherst to spell "Hamster" on the back of it for ha-has.) So it was our final night together and we took a lot of acid. I still remember being parked next to this lone tree in the desert and the sun went down and it looked like a giant flea on the back of a dog ready to pounce up. I stared at that flea for hours thinking it would jump off the Earth, and luckily, it did not.

But I was tripping so hard I was still tripping at the bus depot as I boarded the Greyhound. I had a bottle of whiskey with me, but it's still a long ride from Albuquerque, NM to Bristol, TN. I made it, and was in a mania when I got back to my car.

I said hello to Sarah's mom and sisters (she had three) and told them how she was doing. I left out all of the drug parts but I figured her mom knew—her mother and I had smoked weed together before. It was the first time I'd smoked with someone's parent. Anyway, they sent me off with a kiss and a hug.

And I was driving up I-81. What a ride. Over three hundred miles through the length of Virginia. But I didn't make it too far. I was heading north on I-81, and I was literally having a psychotic break. I felt like there were helicopters following me and filming my vehicle, and I was driving eighty-one miles and hour because I was on Route 81. What a mess! So I pulled over because my driver's side back wheel felt funny. Like the tire was low. It was slightly swaying back and forth on the road.

So I pulled over and looked at the tire. Not flat. Not low. Didn't know what was going on. So I got back in the car and kept driving until, "Wham!" The driver's side back wheel *came off* and lodged in the wheel well. The whole car went slamming down onto the brake rotor at over 75 mph and I dug a giant slice into the highway as I desperately steered the car into the median.

What a disaster! One or two of the lug nuts were loose and the wheel had been wobbling on the studs until finally one of the studs snapped and the whole wheel went flying off. I'd never seen an accident like that. Luckily I was not near an eighteen-wheeler at the time or I might not be writing this book. But anyway, I had AAA and got a tow truck and the driver couldn't believe what the rotor looked like. "Look at that," the driver said, "You took off a couple inches of that rotor, burned right off!" the rotor looked like it had been cut with a torch in a straight line across the circular brake part. The tire was still good, but I needed a wheel, studs, and a new rotor. Most of the garages in the area only fixed American cars, and it took me a good two days to get back on the road. I drank a lot of whiskey and just waited, then drove back to Connecticut.

My plan was to go home, get the rest of my clothes and things, pack the Volvo, then drive back to Albuquerque to live with Sarah. That did not happen. My parents took one look at me and brought me to the psych ward. I was barely functioning at this point. I had run almost out of money, my bipolar was acting up, my addiction was raging. I spent a lot of time thinking in the psych ward—how did I get here? It turns out it was more than just the DMT and the acid and the mushrooms and the weed and the booze. I have to back up a couple years.

When I showed up on campus I had just turned eighteen. They called me "Birthday Seth" because I had arrived on my birthday. At the time, Amherst was a great place to be, but I sought out the lowest common denominator.

My first priority was marijuana. As it turned out, I met this senior Stephanie in one of my theater classes and it turned out that her boyfriend had graduated the year before and rented an apartment in town. His name was John Mizzy and he was from Texas, making his living selling dime bags to MoHos (girls from Mount Holyoke College, an all-women's school in the five-college system to the south) and was more than happy to sell me enough weed to put a pretty big dent in a bread bag.

He bought cheap Mexican schwag by the pound and then brought it on the bus in a big army surplus bag from Texas to Massachusetts, which he claimed was the best way to move a large quantity of weed quickly and safely. So he sold me maybe a quarter pound and I was very happy.

Of course you don't want to smoke schwag out of a nice glass piece, so I opted for the biggest thing I could find—a six-foot bamboo bong. It was so massive that you couldn't light it yourself—this was a two-man operation. The bong came via USPS to my school post office box, and I just carried this massive package back to my dorm room. I planted some of the seeds, more of an experiment than anything else, as I wanted to see if I could grow weed.

Well, they started growing, and my roommate was not happy. His name was Chris and he was "hardcore," meaning he didn't drink or use. He was such a loser. But he complained to the R.A. and the next thing I knew I was kicked out of freshman housing and given a very large single in the basement of a senior dorm named Milliken, right next to the A.C.'s office for a close eye on me. When students found out some of them were really pissed. A freshman girl wrote into the paper and said, "Is this how we punish people? Move them out of crowded doubles into a spacious single in a senior dorm?" You have no idea how much this idea would continue to resonate further into my life as a transwoman.

So I had my freshman room in the basement of a senior dorm, which meant I was networking with the older students. Not to mention that Milliken, besides the Zoo, where they didn't flush when they peed (if it's yellow let it mellow, if it's brown flush it down) and drank everything out of mason jars (they were all hippies), was definitely the druggy dorm. I was in the right place for once in my life.

I used my newfound freedom to my advantage. I threw a party for my friends who were freshmen while I was in Milliken. In the freshman dorms you were not allowed kegs, but the other dorms had students of all mixed ages so kegs were allowed. I got a keg and a tap and had a rager with all my freshman friends in my room in the basement of the senior dorm. Life was good. Then the drugs got me.

Not the pot. We burned through all that schwag and I moved up to indoor, grown and cultivated by Mike and Victor on the first floor of the Zoo, the hippy dorm. It was my first time seeing living pot plants. Mike used to sit around shirtless and trim the little plants like it were very meditative to him. He was definitely a weed dealer and those plants were more his personal supply.

I'm sure the college knew what was going on. Before Massachusetts legalized pot in 2016, the Pioneer Valley and north up to Belchertown and Orange and Athol had decriminalized marijuana. Our own college dean told students he'd rather see students smoking pot instead of drinking, because no one ever went to the hospital for smoking weed. So, even with all the pot I wanted, it still wasn't enough.

I started buying a lot more stuff from a now-defunct company called JLF Poisonous Non-Consumables. There was a list of all drugs that were legal and got you high on Erowid or one of those sites that encouraged reporting drug use anonymously into a set of blogs and threads. This company JLF basically sold everything on the list. From the rare tryptamines (5-Meo-DMT, 5-Meo-DIPT, AMT, et al.) to Amanita muscaria (toadstool mushrooms) to San Pedro cactus (a legal plant precursor for mescaline) to chemicals like L-Dopa and harmine, morning glory seeds, nutmeg, psilocybin mushroom spores, spore syringes, grow kits, to even DXM, this company sold everything related to legally getting high.

I opted for a product called alpha chloralose based on the trip reports. It was cheap, relatively safe, and was used as a tranquilizer for large birds. So I bought the powder (white and bitter) then went to the health food store and bought the empty gelcaps to put it in, packed about 750mg into a pill and tried it. It was excellent, like ketamine but without the K-hole experience. Excellent time.

Now there was this senior in Milliken who we all knew was just a garbage head. His name was Neil Connelly. He was in my dorm and I ran into him one day. I told him I had these pills and they were a tranquilizer. Did he want to try one? Five dollars. He said sure. Then, a typical addict, he says, "give me three," as he hands me fifteen dollars. I said, "As long as you don't take them all at once. You could overdose. Just take one, and save the rest. That's all you need. I just did it."

He assured me that everything was fine. Didn't see him for a couple days. Next thing I know, there are two Amherst town police at my dorm door. Not fake campus police. Actual police. With guns. They were investigating an incident where a student, Neil Connelly, was at Cooley-Dickenson Hospital on a respirator because he had overdosed on something and his respiration had slowed to a near-lethal point. He said I had sold him the pills. "What were they?" the cops asked.

I was scared to death. I had never been interrogated by police before. This was a first. I told them the truth. It's a chemical called alpha chloralose, which is a bird tranquilizer, and I bought it from this company called JLF Poisonous Non-Consumables. They were incredulous, but I had the proof. "His initial blood screening showed up as PCP. That's phencyclidine. Dust. You don't know anything about PCP?"

I quivered. I had never done dust, and I had no intention of doing it. I had heard only bad things about it. It turned out that there was a UMASS-Amherst student who was recently on dust and fell out of his high-rise window and died, and they hadn't found the dealer that sold it to him. So when they were interrogating me they thought they had found their man. I gave them the rest of the alpha chloralose and told them to forensically test it, that this was all he had taken, and I had no PCP. They took down all the info off my license and told me that they were watching me. Great.

Neil got better and came back to school, but that run-in with the cops was not my only problem with this. Once the school found out, the deans were very unhappy. They had a disciplinary hearing. Neil was there. They sentenced me to drug rehab and told me I had lost my privilege to live on campus for the rest of the semester. But it didn't stop there. Because of my lousy academic record (I ended the semester with a C, a D, an F, and a W for withdrawal) I was going to have to spend a semester off from school, then spend another semester at another college getting nothing below a B, and then I could return.

Sounded like a plan. Rehab didn't resonate with me. I was this preppy kid in Worcester with prostitutes and junkies. I just looked around and said, "I am not at all like any of these people." I didn't understand that I was, indeed, just like them. Younger maybe, hadn't lost as much, but just like them. My life was just a series of yets. Many of those yets had happened to these other people, but for me, they were in the cards for later.

When I got back to campus I had no room. Luckily I only had about a month left of school. The first couple of nights I slept in "the Tunnels." There was a system of steam tunnels and an underground walkway all below the campus that carried all the pipes and wires and these big steam pipes that brought heat from the physical plant to the buildings. There was no way I was sleeping in my car in Massachusetts in November. I'd rather be ninety degrees in the tunnels then forty degrees in the car.

But after a couple days I couldn't stand it. I needed help. This girl Christina Belafonte had gone to high school with me and was presently at Smith College in Northampton. I called her and told her my situation and she told me I could come stay with her until the end of the semester. Well that was a treat. I was the only "man" staying over at the women's college. I showered next to them, shaved next to them, brushed my teeth next to them. It was really really nice being one of the girls, even if I were still presenting as a boy.

I never got into trouble there, but I couldn't stay for the whole semester. Christina's roommate, this really nice girl named Jenn, finally said she didn't want me sleeping on their couch because she had gotten a boyfriend from UMASS-Amherst and he needed to be able to visit and not find another "dude" in the room. I acquiesced. But it was a nice three weeks. I'll always remember Jenn because she's the one that told me that the creators of Scooby Doo had gone to the UMASS system, and the characters of the show (five of them) were based on the five colleges in our system. So, Fred, with his ascot, came from Amherst, and you can guess the rest. It was all kind of perfect in a perverse, animated sort of way.

So with one week left in the semester I pleaded with my friends back in James 411 (I had lived in James 410) that I needed to stay on their couch for a week. They had a triple and it was already crowded, and one of them didn't want me there, but majority rules and with a two-to-one vote I was allowed to stay. I brought lots of good weed as tribute and it was nice to not have to ride the PVTA bus just to get to campus.

In a way I missed the walk of shame at Smith. Every morning when I left there were several men slinking across campus back to their cars or to the bus stop who had spent the night with some poor female, and I liked being in that category, like it was a mark of pride.

So that was that. I came to college with $3,600 cash, blew that, was in rehab for a month from early October to early November, and I left on concurrent academic and disciplinary probation. Not that great of a start at school.

The next year was uneventful. I took a job at Fleet CCO in Farmington (former Shawmut Bank, now Bank of America) where I did contingency underwriting for home equity loans. It was a good job, and in hindsight, if I never went to college and just stayed there I'd probably be a VP at Bank of America right now. My job was analyzing all of the things besides income and credit score that went into a loan, so I looked into titles and appraisals and flood insurance, etc.

That was the type of work I was capable of if I stayed off the marijuana. I was still doing the Coricidin (they didn't drug test for that) and don't worry, I had consequences. I crashed two cars in the two months high on that crap. Luckily when the cops came both times, they thought my eyes and speech were so screwed up because I had a concussion (I never wore a seatbelt) rather than because I was high.

Trinity College flew by. I went there for a semester before going back up to Amherst. I didn't live there to save money, but I took four classes and got all A's as I was supposed to. I didn't have a marijuana connection anymore so I just took Coricidin and drank. But Trinity was fun. I liked it. The kids were preppier somehow. Amherst kids were more hippy or different looking. At Camp Trin-Trin everyone looked like they had just walked out of an Abercrombie and Fitch catalog.

I had also gotten a girlfriend once I left Amherst, this young woman named Karen Tremblay. After I started at Fleet, I reached out to others from my high school to socialize with. My friend Alicia went to Connecticut College in New London and she invited me to visit. She specifically wanted me to meet her friend Karen. "You sound the same," she'd said.

So I met Karen, and sure enough, she was studying ethnobotany. She knew all about Ott and Shulgin and McKenna. We talked for hours and hours and immediately fell for each other. We kept that relationship for many years, from when I was eighteen until I was twenty-one. We were actually engaged. She lived with me at one point. So she was slightly older than me and graduating, and I didn't see her for a few months because she went to live at Heifer Project's main farm in Arkansas.

She was definitely a farm girl, though she was originally from Boston. So she got room and board and lived and ate for free and worked on this farm. Heifer Project is an international charity that instead of donating money to people in need, they donate animals. So for your contribution to them they will give a family in need a female goat, with the stipulation that once the goat has kids, those kids should be given away to another needy family. They give away hives of bees, sheep, cows, oxen, chickens, you name it. It's a great charity and I give to it even today.

So she went to Arkansas to live for a little while then came back to live in Massachusetts at the satellite farm in Rutland. But I was not faithful when we were apart, and I don't know if she were either. I started dating this girl Svetlana from Bulgaria, and she was just immensely beautiful. She was so beautiful that when I brought her home for Thanksgiving my father literally said to me, "What does she want with you?"

She looked amazing. She was 5'10", DD natural breasts, jet black hair, and little ethnic features. She was a stunner. The best part was, she knew I was trans. See, with Karen, we bonded over ethnobotany and entheogens and she was looking for a man and I was going to be that man. With Svetlana it was different—we bonded more naturally, being in the same class, then becoming friends, and then lovers. I'll never forget that first class I met her in, called the Language of Movement, a theater arts class. The professor had us choose a partner and Svetlana chose me. Then we were to just stand slightly apart and just stare at each other without speaking for ten minutes. Trust me, if you have never done this exercise, it is a gift. I think I fell in love with her right then.

Anyway, Svetlana accepted me for being transgender. So when I told her I felt like a girl, she said, "Then I will treat you like one," and she started giving me her clothes to wear, which I fit in. Now I never left the room, but it was so sweet and so kind and exactly what I needed. Despite my anatomy, when we made love she tried to be as soft and sweet with me as she could (I'm a submissive bisexual femme) and it was just lovely.

I should say besides these women in my life, I did try sleeping with men. So when I got up to school I thought, maybe I'm not transgender, maybe I'm just gay. Maybe this is what it feels like to be gay. Gay men, for the most part, seem kind of effeminate. So I slept with a gay guy, and it was gross. Then I thought, maybe society has taught me that this is gross and it's really not and I just need to relinquish my religious hang-ups. So I did it again. And it was gross. So then I knew, sadly, I wasn't gay which meant I must be trans. I didn't end up sleeping with another man from 1997 til 2009, after I had transitioned and got my breasts done.

What amazed me about this little situation was that what I learned in Women's Studies several years later was that sex, gender, and sexuality are three separate and distinct things. Now this thought process is in opposition to the heteronormative patriarchal "mainstream" thinking that says sex and gender are the same thing (which means transsexuals are anomalous and are mentally ill) and sexuality is based on sex, such that men have sex with women and not men. (This is enforced and coercive heteronormativity, which excludes gays and lesbians from mainstream culture and causes them to be oppressed.) Well what I discovered after taking hormones for years was that in fact, my sexual proclivities had indeed changed. Whereas when I was a male I was strictly straight and was attracted only to females. Feminists would argue that once I transition to being a female I would still only be attracted to females.

Not so, feminists. Once being on feminizing hormones and having breast implants, I became attractive to straight men. And they were attracted to me and I to them. All of a sudden, I was bisexual. And I certainly was not attracted to gay men, but straight men? If they were cute? Of course. So I learned a valuable lesson about why feminists are wrong. Not to mention that feminists on the whole detest transwomen. We tend to uphold the traditional femininity that they reject in opposition to the patriarchy. So while they are busy burning bras and not wearing makeup, I am piling on the eyeliner and eyeshadow and the foundation and blush and lipstick and getting breast implants, wearing suggestive clothing and high heels. My sexual appeal as a woman empowers me. And I am the opposite of a feminist. It took me getting a later degree in Women, Gender, and Sexuality to figure that out.

But back to Svetlana. It was 2000. I was trying to have sex with both Svetlana and Karen. Karen seemed to be the girl I would marry if I were from Terryville, my home, kind of a cow town. She was a farmer, an earthy girl, a truck-driving girl, a strong girl, a country girl. Svetlana was educated and erudite. A princess. She would be the kind of girl I'd marry if I were up at Amherst, the only place I'd ever meet a Bulgarian anyways.

And I loved Svetlana. She made me not want to get high. I taught her how to drive. (At the time, I believe it was very hard for people to get cars in Bulgaria. There was a waiting list. And her parents were professors who lived at the University in Sofia, so they didn't drive.) In hindsight I felt bad. All I had to teach her on was an old Volvo wagon that was standard shift (four-speed with a push-button overdrive) so she had to learn to drive and how to manage a stick. But personally I used to think we all needed to learn to drive standard so that we could drive trucks and stuff. It's just that by 2018 we have eight-speed automatics and automatics can get better mileage than standards now anyway.

So that was interesting, teaching a foreigner how to drive. She definitely ran over a whole bunch of flowers in a median and also crashed into a hedge. But I was proud to teach her. She still remembers it to this day and we joke about it.

Svetlana came from a different culture. I'll never forget. Her English wasn't perfect because she learned in school rather than through immersion so I needed to constantly explain metaphors and idioms to her. And then she wouldn't know a word so she would say something like, "Look! A night butterfly!" and I would say, "Yes, that's a moth." I remember she said, "I like night butterfly much better." And who's going to argue with someone that looks like that? The other thing I remember was how she ate an apple. I guess people in Bulgaria tend to be poorer so they don't waste. So she would just eat the apple straight through the core, not around it. Though I remember Tom Sawyer or Huck Finn asking someone if they wanted the core of their apple, I couldn't imagine someone in this era eating right through the core. Especially someone as educated, erudite, well-travelled, and beautiful. She was a trip.

Enter Karen. I'm hanging out with Svetlana and she calls me: "I need a place to stay," she said. "My volunteering is done at the farm. Can I stay at your dorm 'til the end of the semester and then we'll stay the summer?" What could I say? This was my girlfriend. "Of course." Well that meant the end of my relationship with Svetlana. But that was about to end anyway.

All the while I was juggling these two women, I had a new scam to make money—selling drugs. But the market was crowded where I was. But not the online market. This was before Silkroad of course. So remember I mentioned JLF Poisonous Non-Consumables? They sold another product I loved, dextromethorphan. Pure dextromethorphan hydrobromide. No more cough syrup. No more eating forty-eight pills. I could order the pure chemical, pack it into a gelcap, take the single pill and be high for eight hours. And it cost about a dollar a pill. A dollar!

There are about 454 grams in a pound. Being American, Mark Niemoller (the man who ran JLF until the feds raided his business and seized over two hundred fifty thousand dollars of his cash and threw him in jail for selling rare tryptamines) sold things in pounds rather than kilograms. Today, everything comes from China—it's international. So just like they are pumping out fentanyl by the kilogram and creating a public health crisis in America, they pump out DXM by the kilo as well.

But back in the day, good ol' Niemoller sold DXM by the pound. It was $650 a pound. So, 454 grams for $650, or $1.43 per gram. So I hatched this plan. I had an eBay account. Why not buy the DXM from JLF, then jack up the price and sell smaller bags of twenty or twenty-five grams (fifteen to thirty doses) on eBay for a profit? It's simple arbitrage—move from one market where a product is undervalued and with lower demand to a new market where it is overvalued and had a high demand? So I did it. I made a listing, titled "25 grams pure dextromethorphan hydrobromide DXM pure powder $75." I was almost tripling my money. It was sick. And the orders rolled in.

Back in the day, eBay was so new. It was like the Wild West and there were very few rules. In my listing I said it was a research chemical and not for human consumption, that it would be packaged discreetly, and that it would be delivered quickly. The response was overwhelming. I had to order more powder from JLF. Many people just emailed me and asked me if I could just sell it to them off eBay and just use Paypal so there was no record. I was on a suicide course anyway so I didn't care. I sold to everyone, repeatedly tripling my money.

Then it happened. It was bound to. Four seventeen-year-old seniors at the Peddie School (a very elite prep school in New Jersey) used their parents' credit card and bought a bag. I had no idea anything was amiss. It came in as a regular order to a NJ post office box. I would never sell drugs to kids. (I would never sell drugs period now, but at the time I'm just saying that for the record I did have some sense of morality or scruples.) But I did. And they all took the drug, they all took too much, and they all overdosed and ended up in the hospital.

It made the newspaper in the Star-Ledger: "Teens sick after buying drug on eBay." It turned out that for years afterwards if you Googled "DXM eBay" the first thing that came up was this story about me. (In the future, the same thing would be true if you Googled "chipleader with tits," but that's a story for later.) The four students were expelled weeks before graduation. It was a big deal for these families and they wanted someone's head.

So the next thing that I knew, I got a call from my mother saying, "The FBI is at our house." My poor mother. She didn't deserve that trauma. I got questioned. They thought I was manufacturing it. They thought I ran a drug factory. When I showed them the receipts they knew I was just a middleman. JLF was already under investigation. So they let me go. No punishment. What I had done was not a crime. Dextromethorphan is an unscheduled chemical. It was not, at the time, illegal to sell.

New Jersey changed that. Because of my incident, the state of New Jersey made it illegal to sell DXM to their residents. That made two states, NJ and GA. I can personally take responsibility for having a law changed in New Jersey. I got back at Jersey later for banning my customers by raping their malls, but I'll get to that later as well.

Nowadays the law has caught up to all of this. You would go to federal prison for many years doing what I did. The CFR and USC caught up with these outliers and now it would be illegal to sell DXM powder unless it were clearly marked as a pharmaceutical with a particular dosage to take (the normal dose is around thirty milligrams). So if you sold someone twenty-five grams of this stuff and the standard dose is in milligrams any reasonable person would infer that you are encouraging abuse (with a dosage range of .5 to 1.5 grams) rather than use. I am quite sure a jury of my peers would send me to federal prison if I ever did this again. Not only that, imagine if someone died? I'd probably get a six to ten year bid at York CI.

So I learned my lesson. Sort of. (That sums up this book in a nutshell.) I then sent out a mailer to all my customers I had in my database. I told them that eBay had shut me down but I could still sell. I set up a website called DXMSTORE.COM. I accepted checks and money orders to my school address. Then I solicited. When people sent me money, I sent them nothing. I made even more money than selling drugs. I was selling nothing! Fabulous! And what were people going to do, go to the cops and say they were trying to buy drugs and got burned? No way. They ate it. And I ate with their money. Lots of Vietnamese, Thai food, and Japanese food, my favorite. So I shut the site down, and kept the money.

Now this was all too much for Svetlana. When I broke down and told her that the FBI was at my parents' house and I had been caught selling drugs, she broke up with me. It turned out that she had an older brother that was an addict and she saw the life he led and wanted no part of it. I was devastated and heartbroken—she was the best thing that ever happened to me—but I still had Karen. I moved on.

I finished the semester, and got housing for the summer in Seligman with all the other students staying the summer. All this time, juggling two girls and an online-dealing job, I had also managed to partake in a work-study job on campus. I worked for the physical plant. Maintenance. My job was to make the signs for anything that required the sign-making machine, to cut all the blinds to replace that were torn or broken in the dorm rooms, and the best part, I let kids into storage to get their belongings.

This is where my boosting really shined while I was at school. I had a master key that opened all of the storages in the basements of the dorms. Most things in storage were for people who were abroad for the semester. So, let's say someone needs something out of storage. They call the physical plant, and get my boss Mikey. Mikey calls me on the radio and dispatches me in a white bread truck that said Amherst College in purple letters on the side, and I let the student in to get his or her stuff. Well, while I was waiting for them I was casing the place—what could I take?

Well, televisions and fridges were easiest. I got $25 apiece for those at the pawn shop in Connecticut. So after the student would leave, I would go in and grab the refrigerators and TVs and put them in the bread truck. It's a victimless crime, I thought. People are going to come home from being abroad and their TVs and fridges would be missing. First of all, they couldn't pin it on me. Lots of people had access to that storage area. Second, when the kids would come back, their rich parents would just buy them more stuff.

That was something that really stuck in my craw as a high-schooler and then college student. Going to prep school and private college, both on need-based and merit-based financial aid, I was always "the poor kid." So in high school, while sixteen and seventeen-year-olds were pulling up in Mercedes and BMWs, my mom was driving me to school in a 1986 Dodge Colt Vista wagon. At Catholic grammar school we were all sort of on the same playing field, but as time went on I saw huge amounts of financial disparity. Trust me, being the "poor kid" isn't great at prep school or college. It's like a curse.

So I would load up the station wagon with televisions and refrigerators, then drive them out of state. The out-of-state piece I knew was important because on the off chance that someone had saved a warranty card or written down the serial number of his or her unit, the pawn shop by law had to report the serial numbers to law enforcement for the purpose of stopping criminal activity. So I didn't want my name associated with stolen goods and then be on the radar of police. So I moved them out-of-state since everything was so state specific. And this is how I really got to know the guys at Super Pawn.

They knew I was boosting the stuff (otherwise, how could I have a steady stream of college mini fridges and televisions?) but they didn't care. A lot of time I would take the two or three hundred dollars and go down to the casino to see if I could double up quickly at the blackjack table (I hadn't learned poker yet) and I did well enough to keep going. Plus it was a rush, gambling with money from boosting.

Another thing I would do was steal schoolbooks. I'd be wide awake at 4am from the DXM so I would take my big black shoulder bag (I called it my "stealin' bag") and go from dorm to dorm and common room to common room when everyone was asleep. And if anyone had left out any type of schoolbook—into the bag it went. Then there was this book dealer in the town of Amherst that was shady and would pay me cash for them without an ID. I boosted everything that wasn't tied down.

I even took my show on the road to UMASS-Amherst. I was taking an astronomy class to learn about cosmology, and our school didn't offer the program. So I took the bus up the street to

UMASS to take the class in the science building, which was a giant high-rise. (Fun fact: another tall building at UMASS-Amherst, the library, has books only on every other floor. Turns out when the architects designed the building, they neglected to account for the weight of the books. It was structurally unsafe with books on every floor, so there are only books on every other floor. 100% true.)

So after my class, I would take the elevator up to the top floor and work my way down, walking down the extremely long halls with no cameras looking for anything of value I could steal. I used to find a lot of books and throw them in the stealin' bag, but after doing it a bunch of times there were no more. So one night I went to each floor. There was a standpipe and a firehose in a little cabinet on every level. Each one of these hoses had a brass nozzle on the end that came off. I took all of them and filled the black bag with yellow brass. I believe at the time the scrapyard was paying about $1.50 a pound for yellow brass, so I made enough money that night to buy a bag of weed.

Back to my love life. Svetlana had dumped me, the first woman who actually accepted me for being transgender, and I was living with Karen in Seligman for the summer. Then I got the call from Dean Monroe. "Seth," he said, "we understand from the local police that the FBI was investigating you for selling drugs to some teenagers that left four students in the E.R. As this is incredibly similar to what you did before, it would be a second offense. You will likely be expelled or face a more serious suspension, though that is looking unlikely. We are not going to convene the disciplinary committee until the end of the summer, but as of right now your right to live on this campus is gone and you have a day to pack up and leave."

Damn. And I had just gotten a summer job in Shelburne Falls, a half-hour up the road. My job was taking a set of hand-written sermons written by this woman's father who was a pastor and immortalizing them into a book. The transcription was made more difficult by the fact that the sermons were in cursive and the writing was very sloppy. But it paid well and Karen had gotten a job at a farm in Hatfield up the road selling organic produce at a farmers market in Boston on the weekend and she worked the fields during the week. Where were we supposed to live?

Karen suggested we could camp, but that would mean no showers and sleeping on the ground. I had camped before in my life and it didn't seem like a viable option, considering we were going to be working in two different places and I needed to be dressed business casual in the mornings. I got in the car and explored, trying to find somewhere we could go.

I happened upon the Peace Pagoda in North Leverett, MA. There was a Cambodian Buddhist temple up there in the wilderness of Western MA. Some wealthy Cambodian had bought the land and was in the process of building enormous structures in the woods in this small cow town. I drove up a long gravel road where there was a parking lot, parked the car, and walked about a quarter mile into the woods.

There, in front of my eyes, was an enormous Buddhist temple. It was beautifully adorned and just looked out of place in the wilderness. There was no one around. I walked up to the main entrance. I was Catholic. I'd never been to a temple like this before. When I walked in there were rice mats to put your shoes on so I dutifully removed mine, walking up to the altar.

There were Christmas lights and flashing lights and spinning lights and candles and a big gold Buddha. There were several people sitting on orange pillows dressed in orange. I found out later that these were the monks that lived there. They were all chanting in Cambodian and I did not understand them. I walked up to the altar and bowed, and then closed my eyes and sat cross-legged on the floor. It was a very meditative place—this temple out in the woods with these bald old men chanting rhythmically and this trippy altar. It was surreal.

I got up after a while and put my shoes on and walked outside. There were chickens walking around, a bunch of abandoned-looking vehicles, a dirt driveway with mobile trailers parked alongside it and numerous short old women dressed in white that I found out later were nuns that lived there as well. As I walked around taking it all in, a young Cambodian boy ran down the hill and spoke to me in English.

"Hi, my name is Vy. What's your name?"

"Seth," I said in reply. "What is this place?"

"It's a monastery. There's a temple, another temple we're building up the hill, and the Pagoda at the top of the hill. That's where they buried a special monk."

I found out later that when a monk dies, they cremate the body, then dig through the ashes for what they call "relics." If the monk were especially holy, they would find small things that looked like red, green, and blue "stones" or "jewels" within the ashes. These were supposed to be the physical manifestation of the monk's enlightenment. When these were found, it was a joyous occasion, and they would enshrine these relics in a pagoda like the one at the top of the hill.

"Can I see the Pagoda?" I asked Vy.

"Sure, come with me."

He led me through the woods up a narrow dirt path. We walked and walked and suddenly I had this major déjà vu. I had been here before, either in a dream or a trip. It gives me the chills writing about it right now. I had seen this before, a large white dome surrounded by trees and to see it in reality was spectacular.

It was over a hundred feet wide and probably fifty feet tall. A giant white dome with a gold piece on top that looked like a weathervane. There was a walkway around the whole thing and gold statues of human figures several times larger than people at various intervals around the dome. The writing on the dome was Asian.

"The monk is in there," said Vy as he bowed to the dome. I bowed to it too. It was surreal. "Let me show you the coy pond," he said. We walked away from the pagoda to a coy pond, with rock walkways all around it and brightly colored fish swimming in the water. "That's the old temple." He pointed to a rock garden.

It turns out that in the 1970s there was a white supremacist faction in North Leverett, a town that was almost all white, which was concerned with this influx of Cambodian refugees. These monks and nuns were granted asylum because they were persecuted in Cambodia, and they had the threat of death hanging over them for practicing their religion. So they sought asylum in the United States. A wealthy Cambodian family built the first temple for them, and a group of whites in the town burnt it down. It was an arson, a serious matter, and the men were brought to justice and punished.

It was a really sweet tribute, however. The monks and nuns left the foundation of the temple (all that remained) and turned the rest into a rock garden for peaceful meditation. How holy, I thought. These people are peaceful. They want to remember the past but make it a meditation, as the rest of their life is. Vy and I walked around silently. Then he yawned, and motioned me to follow him down a different path. We walked past another building.

"That's another nun's house," he said.

That was Sister Ruth's house. She was a white woman with a shaved head who wore all white and spent her days in prayer. There was a man, her servant, that lived with her. It turns out that years ago, the man came to her home, forced himself on her, and raped her. He was caught, arrested, processed, and went to court. Before his sentencing, Sister Ruth spoke to the prosecutor and begged him not to send this man to jail because he wouldn't learn anything there. She asked them instead of the seven-year sentence to sentence him to live with her under house arrest for seven years and she would teach him to pray. The prosecutor was dumbfounded, but she said he was safe and ready to repent. That was fifteen years ago and he was still there.

We kept walking down the hill.

"Vy," I said. "I'm looking for a place to stay. Is there any way my fiancée and I can work here in exchange for a place to stay?"

"I don't know," he said. "Let's ask the monk."

He made sure to tell me that when you first meet a monk it is necessary to bow to him three times. So he brought me to the monk, I bowed three times, and he spoke slowly to the boy in Cambodian.

"Come downstairs. The monk wants to show you something."

We went down the back stairs. The monk kept talking and gesturing with his hand around the room at various places.

"That needs to be painted," Vy said while motioning to the trim, "And we need to hang two doors. If you can do that, you can stay here."

I was deliriously overjoyed. I was very rapidly solving our housing crisis, and had met some very interesting individuals.

"Tell the monk that my fiancée will bring the people here extra vegetables from the farm where she works too," I said.

He told the monk and the old man's face lit up. He smiled and bowed to me. I was in awe.

"The monk says come with him."

We walked back upstairs, where there was an office with a computer with a Cambodian keyboard and some papers. The monk handed me a piece of paper and a card.

"This is our tax-exempt card," said Vy, translating for the monk. "And this is one of our credit cards. Go to Home Depot and buy all the supplies you need and bring the receipt."

"Done," I said. "I'll do it tomorrow. Let me reconvene with Karen."

And with that I left. That was definitely my God working in my life. I was driving around looking for a safe place to camp for free, and instead I found an old Cambodian man who never met me and gave me a credit card. Who does that? Not in my world, that's for sure. What kind of faith this man had! It brought tears to my eyes. And all I could think about was the Old Testament, with the Israelites wandering in the desert and God gave them manna to eat, so that even though they were in the wilderness, they lived another day. One door closes, another opens.

I got back to Karen and told her the good news. She couldn't believe it! (She didn't really care about the FBI and the drug stuff. We had used DXM together and she liked it, and I explained to her that it was probably the cheapest, longest-lasting, most potent non-lethal high that you could find. And it was legal, sort of.) She packed up her Geo and I packed up the Volvo and we said goodbye to Amherst College. I didn't know what the future held, but I was sure I could get through it okay.

When we got back to the monastery it was almost dinnertime. Vy ran out to greet us.

"Hi Seth," he said. "This must be Karen."

"It is," she said.

"Let me show you your house," he said.

This boded well, I thought. We followed a different dirt path through the woods and came to a line of three prefab 12x18' sheds, each one having an orange outdoor extension cord running out of it. There was a huge reclining Buddha statue at the end of the path. Karen and I opened the door and went inside. There were a couple orange pillows like in the temple, and two rice mats for sleeping, and a rice mat to put our shoes. Humble, but ours.

"Before you bring the things up here," said Vy, "It's time to eat. We're having a dinner in your honor tonight!"

"Seriously?" I asked.

"Yes!" said Vy. "Come with me."

We went to the first trailer along the dirt path. This was apparently their kitchen and dining room, and it smelled distinctly of fish. The monks came in, nodded to us, got their food and ate.

Vy said softly, "The monks eat first, then the nuns eat. You will be eating with the nuns."

The monks ate the special meal: it was fish head soup over rice. It wasn't until later that I realized they ate this almost every day. It was finally our turn to eat. I was a "man" so I got served first. The wrinkled old nun gave me an old plastic bowl, put rice in it, then searched the broth to find the largest remaining fish head. She piled it on my rice and poured some stock on it. There was also some sort of green herb they served with it. She handed it to me, smiling, pointing at the fish head and saying something in Cambodian.

Vy said, "She is telling you to eat the eye. That is the delicacy."

I looked at the fish head, then looked at her. She smiled back so longingly and happily. I picked the eye out of the socket with my fork, and I just couldn't do it. I thought I would retch. Vy saw my expression and looked at the others.

"Give it to her," he said and pointed to another old lady. She looked thrilled. I flipped the fish head over and took both eyes out and put them in her bowl. Karen was a vegetarian. She looked mortified. She told Vy she didn't want any fish, so the nuns gave her a bowl of rice with some herbs. She gave a little bow to them and began to eat, and I started to eat my rice as well. The stock tasted great, but I wasn't sure how to eat the fish. I waited for the rest of the nuns to get served and start to eat and watch them. They picked the meat off the face and gill area. It felt a lot like getting the meat out of a lobster's leg—lots of work for not a lot of protein. But I did it. I ate fish face meat and rice and they were glad. It was our ceremonial dinner. I'll never forget it.

It was amazing to me as a transwoman the gender differences at the monastery. The monks lived in this very modern building with nice amenities and the nuns lived in trailers. And the eating habits were odd, too. When we were done eating we excused ourselves, and I apologized to Karen. She laughed at me.

"You're the one who had to eat the fish head! Gross! But I love you." She kissed me.

Life went very well at the monastery. I worked Monday through Friday in Shelburne Falls about a half an hour west of North Leverett and Karen worked in Hatfield about twenty minutes south of there. She would get up each day at 4:30am, and she would be out by five, home by 3:30pm. On the weekends I did the odd handyman jobs around the monastery that I was directed to do. Weekends Karen went to Boston with all the week's produce, and Sunday we would bring the monks and nuns bushels of leftover peppers and cucumbers and corn. The nuns were ecstatic. They loved all the fresh vegetables and cooked many soups.

One day Vy's uncle came to the monastery. He was a Cambodian man named Chhum. He spoke broken English, clearly an immigrant, but he could communicate. Vy told him I went to Amherst College and was here for the summer.

"Oh. Amherst. Very smart. You tutor my son?"

I told him sure. Of course I did it gratis since I was getting room and fish face meat board. He gave me his address at an apartment complex in town, south of the college. We made a time.

"See you!" he said.

Turns out I met their whole family. Chhum and his wife Vithy and their boy Edward. He needed help in math, and I was a math and physics major, so it was a good fit. He was only in algebra one so the work was easy. And he gave me a bunch of lychee candy when I was finished. We made a time to meet again. When I went back and rang the bell, Chhum told me he needed my help with something. I said sure.

"Start with Edward. Then I come back. You come out."

I did just that, and in about twenty minutes Chhum returned. He had a box truck that had the name of an Asian food wholesaler. Apparently it was his company. I hopped in the passenger seat of the cab and we drove across the complex to his personal dumpster. He opened the dumpster and then the back of the truck. It stunk. He had about 1500 pounds of rotten mangoes. He and I threw the boxes in, one at a time, into the dumpster. It was nasty work.

When we were done I asked, "Chhum, is that illegal?" He shrugged.

"I not pay to throw away."

And with that we made the whole complex smell like rotten fruit. I went back in and continued tutoring Edward.

I got back home and Karen was crying. She was standing in our house, and she had opened a black garbage bag I had brought in from the car that had all of my bras and intimates and dresses and blouses and skirts.

"I'm sorry, honey."

She burst right out at me.

"Are you a faggot? Am I marrying a faggot?" She started to cry and whimper. I had flashbacks to being a kid and having my dad hit me.

"I can explain," I started.

"Explain what?" she said. "You're a fucking faggot."

I pleaded with her. "But I love you! I..."

She grabbed my arm. "I'm taking my tent and I'm going camping until I figure this out." And with that she grabbed her things and slammed the door. I sank into despair.

I called out sick the next few days from work and just got high and drunk in my little shed. It was really pathetic. I wanted Karen to come back. I had given her a diamond. I don't know what I was thinking. The drugs had so warped my thinking that this all seemed okay. I'll just dress like a woman when my wife is out, and she'll never know. I didn't know she'd react like this. Then things got worse. The next day I got a phone call from the dean. My disciplinary hearing would be next week. Shit.

I called Chhum. I told him they were having a disciplinary hearing and I needed all the help I could get. Could he possibly testify as a character witness that while I had to leave school, I was still trying to help others and volunteer. He told me he would do better. I was extremely nervous.

Karen came back a couple days later. She handed me back her diamond and said she was leaving to move back in with her parents in Boston. It felt like a kick in the gut. First I lost Svetlana over drugs, but she was okay with me being trans. Then I lost Karen for being trans, but she was okay with the drugs. It just didn't make sense. I went to hug her and she said coldly, "Don't touch me. Don't call me." And with that, Karen Tremblay exited my life.

My job in Shelburne Falls had ended. I had done everything at the monastery that they asked of me. Now just the disciplinary hearing. I was so nervous the day of it, and put on a jacket and tie and went to the room. I had told Chhum when and where to meet me.

The hearing started. Two deans were there, three professors, three model students, and then there was me. They were going over the details of what happened. I couldn't deny any of it, and could only plead for mercy. As the case went on, I saw Chhum come to the window and knock during the session. I apologized to the council. "That's my witness. Can I just get him in here?"

One of the deans took care of it, meeting Chhum at the door and exchanged a few words with him. Then he came back in.

"Mr. Chhum is parking his van and will be right in." I never guessed what could have happened next.

Chhum opened the door and had two monks dressed in orange robes and six nuns dressed head to toe in white, all bald, Cambodian women. Chhum motioned them where to sit. The nuns waved at me. I bowed to the monks. The deans mouths were agape. Chhum proceeded to tell them that I tutored his son and helped him with his business. Then he introduced the monks and the nuns each by name and translated as each of them spoke in Cambodian.

The nuns said how pretty and tall my fiancée was, and how she brought them fresh vegetables each week. They said how I ate with them and cleaned with them and I was always kind and gracious. Then the monks spoke. The first one described how trustworthy I was, that he gave me a credit card when he had just met me and I worked as a handyman at their monastery. The other monk shared about how I lived there and ate with them and meditated with them and I was wise and of great faith. Then, when they were done, Chhum marched them out of the hearing and back into the van and back up to North Leverett.

The council went behind closed doors and conferred. They came out a short time later. The dean said, "Mr. Sturbridge, when we had our initial review of your case, I was quite positive that we were going to expel you for your conduct. But I have to say, in over twenty years of doing this work, no one has ever brought monks and nuns to testify to character. We are all impressed. You are suspended for a total of two years, and provided you complete a semester at another school earning all A's and B's you are welcome to return and graduate as a Lord Jeff."

And they left. Two years? I hadn't even told my parents yet. Both women had left me. I was still an active addict. I had no job. Nothing tying me to Amherst or especially North Leverett. I needed a change. I packed up my stuff from the monastery, bid them a beautiful goodbye with great thanks, and I got drunk and drove back to Connecticut. It was going to be a new chapter in my life. Everything that was fixed had changed. Uncertainty was my certainty. It was time to regroup. It was 2000. And I needed guidance.

ONE HUNDRED LETTERS TO ONE HUNDRED INDIAN CHIEFS

Did I mention I like to drive? Well I do. It's symptomatic of the bipolar, I imagine. Driving long distances calms my brain and I find it very meditative. With both women out of my life, no job, nothing connecting me anywhere, I decided to travel a bit, especially out West. Where to? I'd let the universe decide.

So I wrote one hundred letters to one hundred Native American chiefs off of a database I found online. Most were in the West. It was a simple letter. I asked for room and board in exchange for teaching their kids mathematics. Responses did not come flowing in. But I got three. One was from a tribe in Michigan offering me a job at their casino. One was out in California but they wanted me to be a certified teacher. And the last one was from the Warm Springs Indian reservation in Oregon, who took me up on my offer. I only needed one.

I spoke with the woman at the school, Edna Matters, and we talked quite awhile. She explained that many of the students had special needs and had FAS or FAE (fetal alcohol syndrome or fetal alcohol effect, respectively) and that it would be slow going. I didn't want to tell her that the entire reason I chose the reservations to work on was because I knew of the rampant alcoholism. I had some idea I was an addict, and I wanted to help those who were suffering on account of the disease of addiction.

It took me a few days to get out there. When I got there I found a simply horrible situation for these people: they had basically the worst land in all of Oregon. It was a lifeless desert—I didn't even know there was a desert in Oregon! Driving on the road into the reservation, there was a car that had flipped and was on the side of the road, and it was riddled with bullet holes. I wondered how poor these people were who couldn't get a truck to tow away a wrecked car for recycling.

The only attraction they had was a casino at Kah-nee-tah and some natural hot springs that some people thought would heal them. Other than that it was a desolate, lifeless place. I got to Edna's home where I would be staying. It was a double wide. She was white and her husband was Native American. The whole time I was there he did nothing but drink beer and watch television. She was the principal of the school and I would work for her. I started in two days. I told her I would go explore the reservation.

I took off in my Volvo. Most of the reservation looked like run-down single and double wides with the occasional small fixed foundation home. There was a lot of graffiti. A lot of signs that were shot with shotguns. A lot of rusted out cars in lawns. A lot of rural poverty. I went down a dirt road into the forest and sure enough, I was on a big hill and I picked up something in my tire. I pulled over. I dared not change the tire on that incline with a scissor jack. I needed a hydraulic jack. I needed help.

So I parked the car and headed down the road toward the reservation. No sooner then I went a quarter mile than a black bear lumbered in front of me. Though I am "bear aware" now, at the time black bears were very rare in Connecticut and I had never seen one. Of course now the population has exploded and there are hundreds if not thousands of sightings in Connecticut. But back in 2000 there were none. I had never seen a bear. He walked in front of me, lifted his head up to smell, and then kept walking.

I was absolutely petrified. I had no weapon. No bear spray even. (In my later trips to the Northwest I always carried bear spray. You can take a gun and unload a clip into a bear's head and their skulls are so thick that they just get angry. But the National Park Rangers don't carry guns—they carry bear spray, which is just a concentrated giant can of mace. It sprays about fifteen feet, blinds the bear, and allows you to escape.) After this my car never did not have bear spray in it.

I walked a little further. Adrenaline pumping. A car full of kids came up the road and saw me, and they pulled over.

"You okay, man?" they asked.

I told them I'd just seen a bear. I must've looked like I was ready to piss my pants but they just laughed at me.

"Black or brown?" the young man asked.

"Black."

They all laughed even more. "They don't hurt you!"

I told them I had a flat and I needed a hydraulic jack. They turned around and went back (they were probably all taking a ride to get high) and soon enough a Native American in a pickup truck rode up to me.

"You're the one staying with Edna," he said.

"Yes. I got a flat. I can change the tire but I just don't have a good jack."

He went to the bed of the pickup and pulled one out. "Sue told me you're going to help the kids. We really appreciate that. She told me you were from one of the top schools in the country. That's pretty cool. Thanks for helping. When do you start?"

"Two days."

"Nice. Well, get acclimated and make sure you drive into Madras. That's the closest city. They have a grocery store and everything you'll need."

"I'll check that out today, thanks!" We fixed the tire and I was on my way.

The tire was fixed but I was broken. I had driven much of the way out without stopping. If you ask me now, I say there's nothing to see til you get to Colorado. Pennsylvania is long rolling hills and farms. Ohio is flatter, more farms, a little more urban, and some factories. Indiana is farms. Illinois is farms until you get to Chicago, and then it's traffic and an urban jungle. Iowa is rolling hills of corn and hay bales. Nebraska is all flat and all corn and soybeans. Then it gets interesting in eastern Colorado. Rolling golden hills. Then as you get closer to Denver you can see the Rockies.

Once I had made the trip many times (with and without my father) I used to always do the same thing. I would make sure to get to Iowa the first night, not Des Moines but maybe Iowa City, somewhere in eastern Iowa to spend the night. Then spend the next day getting through Iowa and Nebraska and spending the second night in Colorado. But coming home was different.

I didn't want to waste the ten or twelve hours in a room—I just wanted to get home. So I would take drugs to stay awake, then drive straight through from Grand Junction, Colorado (on the west side, named because it's where the transcontinental railway meets the north-south railway in the west—it has rail yards larger than I've ever seen. I've never seen so many tracks in one place). And I would leave Grand Junction and drive home to Connecticut in one shot. It's about thirty-two to thirty-six hours of driving, depending on the traffic and the weather.

But this first trip to Oregon I didn't know any of this. I also didn't know that typically people who were bipolar (manic-depressive, to use the parlance of the times) manifested their first symptoms around my age, and the disease was exacerbated by drug use and a lack of sleep. The point is, I drove all the way across the country and slept eight or nine hours the whole time. I was in a complete manic state.

Another manifestation of my disease is psychosis (it is also called "schizoaffective disorder") which comes on in periods of immense stress or after being in a prolonged mania from not sleeping. I had never had a bipolar episode, but that was about to change. I lost touch with reality the same way as one does using DXM or mushrooms or acid or ayahuasca, except I hadn't taken a drug. I was psychotic.

I laid down at Edna's house to sleep on an air mattress and was up all night, mind racing. When I left the next morning to check out Madras, I was simply not in reality. I thought I was being guided by the radio and by reading license plates and street signs. I was sure I was in a movie and all the people I saw were just extras (think, *The Truman Show*) and I saw signs from God. I heard voices. I needed hospitalization. Well, I got that.

Driving into Madras I became obsessed with the grid of the town. I'd had a pickup truck in front of me heading into town whose license plate began with "6C," so I became obsessed with finding the intersection of 6th Street and C Street since I thought that would be the end of the "maze" that I found myself trapped in. I didn't know what I was going to find there, but I was dead set on getting there.

While driving through Madras, I realized at one point that I was headed the wrong direction and needed to make a U-turn. But as I made the turn I clipped a trailer someone was towing behind a pickup and dented it. The guy pulled over and got out and started yelling at me. I started yelling at him, and things escalated. I got back in my car and drove away. He called it in and shortly I was being pulled over by three cops.

They arrested me for reckless driving and leaving the scene of an accident. My first arrest. When they put the cuffs on me I told them they burned and I started screaming. They put zip ties on me instead, put me in the car and got me to the station, then brought me to a holding cell. That's when I tried to "escape" by flushing my clothes down the toilet. The toilet was full of clothes and I kept flushing and flushing and all the water ran out over the cell and out the door. The cops brought me to a psych ward where I was given a shot of Haldol and I was chained to a bed. I finally slept and when I woke up after about sixteen hours, I was groggy, but in reality.

They kept me there for two or three weeks. I saw an endless slew of psych nurses and APRNs and PAs and psychiatrists. They put me on a mood stabilizer called lithium and an antipsychotic called Zyprexa. I got out of the fog and felt normal. The sum total was this: I had a psychotic break caused by what's called a manic episode. That mania resulted from a disease known as bipolar disorder that I have, and was now officially diagnosed with. I would need to take medication for the rest of my life to be normal.

The prosecutor decided to drop the charges and they nolled the case. Because I had no prior record and the psychiatrist told them it was a medical issue and out of my control, they agreed to let me go. My father flew out to Oregon to help me drive my car back, and I took the long, slow ride to Connecticut.

The whole ride I was thinking of a new way to boost and make money. I hatched yet another plan. Whereas now, the Canadian currency is stronger than the American dollar, back in the early 2000s it was the opposite. I had been a bit of a numismatic as a child and had a fairly large collection of coins. These new machines called Coinstar had just appeared, and I wanted to fool the machine with Canadian currency. So I tried. I took all of my Canadian money to Stop and Shop. It ate all the quarters—it wouldn't even return them. It ate the dimes. It ate the nickels. But it didn't eat the pennies. They registered as American money, even the multi-sided polygonal ones. So, I had my plan. To put it in practice.

Montreal was a little far (I had been there with my parents as a child) but there were a couple of cities and towns closer to the Vermont border. I looked up banks in the city of Sherbrooke, and there were three. I called each one. I told them I was a coin collector and I wanted a large number of pennies. The first bank said no. The second said only if I were a customer. But the third, the Bank of Quebec, said no problem. How many did I want? I said $1,500 worth—that's 150,000 coins.

The woman paused. "We can do that," she said. "But it will take two days."

I told her no problem. I gave her all of my information and told her I'd be there by one o'clock on Thursday. I drove up through Massachusetts and Vermont smoking some weed to pass the time, and got to customs. I told them I was looking at McGill for grad school and they waved me through.

I brought $1,000 American. I went and spoke with the woman at the bank I'd talked to on the phone and she welcomed me. I changed the currency and got $1,500 Canadian. I brought my car out front and they wheeled out the cartons of pennies on a hand truck. Each box was $50. They brought thirty bricks in three trips. I loaded up the wagon, moving them as close to the center as I could. My wagon was so loaded down it looked like I was towing a boat. I thanked the polite Canadians and started driving back.

I had a bottle of rum that I dared not open until I got through customs a second time. I told the agent I had taken a day trip to the casino in Montreal, and he waved me back in. I started drinking. I had mapped out all the Coinstar locations that were between northern Vermont and Connecticut on the computer. (Remember, this is before GPS on the phone.) I had a white five-gallon bucket in the passenger seat, the rum in the center console, and I set the cruise at 65mph and drove with my knee, unwrapping rolls of pennies as I drove, taking the occasional sip of rum. I kept filling my white bucket and made my first stop at White River Junction.

There was a pile of wrappers on the floor of the front seat. I picked up the white bucket, dumped it into the Coinstar machine, and it took every penny. Then I got in the car again and did the same thing for hours—drive a little, fill the bucket, drink a little rum, stop at the next store, turn in my receipt. I got all of them processed, and got home around 9pm. I calculated my day. I took $1,000, turned it into $1,500. The fees on Coinstar were 9% or $135. The gas (which was closer to $1 a gallon than $2, $3, or $4) and the rum and a quick bite to eat in Canada cost me $65, and I ended up with $1,300 at the end of the day.

I was psyched. I made $300 in one day, and all I did was smoke pot, drive around buzzed on booze, and made a mess of my car. I put that crime in the memory bank. The best part about it was that it was victimless. The coins would all get mixed together. Coinstar would notice, and they wouldn't want to take the loss. They would process the coins and roll them up and send them to banks. The banks were not going to take the loss. They were most likely just going to sit there or get sent back to the federal government. Victimless crime. I used to feel bad about diluting the money supply, but it turns out that after fifteen years, those coins went from being worthless, to parity, to being even more valuable than ours. If someone just held those coins for that time, they would have the same return as any number of index funds, without the crash of '08. Victimless crime.

Back to Connecticut. I stayed for the winter months, taking a customer service job at a fly fishing supply outfit in Torrington. But as soon as spring started, I got the itch to travel again. Also, though I was no longer in school and had started dating this girl Sarah up at Amherst, visiting when I could. Then came May, and I just stayed in her room until she graduated. (This is before we started following Widespread Panic that summer.)

So, when she graduated, as a present I took her on a trip to the Adirondacks in upstate New York. We were camping in Saranac Lake in the Volkswagen bus, when I got arrested a second time. It was Friday afternoon, and while Sarah was at camp sewing clothes for our pending trip, I went into town to get some supplies. Of course I stopped at the local bar. I was already very drunk.

All I know is I got in an argument with the bartender, and when I walked out I grabbed a bottle of tequila from behind the bar and just took it. I got back in the bus and drove back to camp but I never made it there. The cops pulled me over on the main road, searched the bus, found the tequila, and thankfully didn't charge me with DUI. I left the yellow bus at the side of the road and got booked.

I asked about court. The lieutenant said, "Listen, it's Friday and court is closed. We can't arraign you until Monday. You'll have to stay in the holding cell all weekend, and then you might not get out on bond because you're out-of-state. If you plead guilty to petit larceny right now, you can pay a $600 fine, and be on your way. What do you say?"

I didn't want Sarah to worry, and I didn't want to stay in holding all weekend, so I took the deal. In hindsight, of all my arrests, this would stick with me the most. In New York, there's no contest plea or nolle after a certain amount of time or after programs. There is guilt and not guilty. Even to this day, if one does an FBI background check on my fingerprints, one will find this seventeen-year-old arrest.

But I paid the fine and left, walked back to the bus, and drove back to camp.

"You've been gone awhile," Sarah said.

"You don't want to know," I said.

"Did you get stopped? She asked.

"Yes," I told her. But none of the details. She didn't care anyway. We had great lovemaking that night.

Then we drove back to Amherst. I had been drinking (of course) and it was night when we got back. One of the taillights in the bus was out, but I hadn't rigged it yet so we got stopped by the cops.

"Have you been drinking?" the officer asked me.

"No," I said.

"I can smell it. Out of the car."

He gave me a breathalyzer. I was at .20. He immediately arrested me and booked me in Amherst jail. Then I was in the cell and he told me I needed to blow again, and brought in a larger machine.

"No way," I said.

"You have to."

I said, "I don't have to. I'm already in jail. What are you going to do, send me to worse jail?"

He didn't like my attitude. "If you don't blow, your license will be suspended for six months."

"What do I care? I don't live here."

"Suit yourself."

Sarah bonded me out. Turns out as I found out in Northampton court a short time later with the help of a public defender who was a pre-law professor at Smith College of all places, that the portable roadside device gives the police officer probable cause, but it doesn't count as admissible evidence at trial. Only the permanent unit at the police station is used for that. So good thing I didn't blow. The judge dismissed my case, and I lost my license in Massachusetts for six months. Oh well, I was going to leave for Tennessee anyway to begin my trip with my new lover. Too bad for those suckers. I skated out of trouble once again.

Not getting in trouble took me longer to get better. I didn't realize how low my addiction had taken me. I had been arrested in different states and had no consequences. I was like a wild animal. I had that long time on the road with Sarah I'd already mentioned, and I ended up in the psych ward. When I got out I went back to my parents' but the using just increased. I was getting high every day. Anything to not experience reality. Something had to give.

ORGANIZED CRIME

I surrendered to the disease of addiction on 1/28/02. That was not my first clean date, which wasn't until 9/9/02, after which point I stayed clean for over ten years. January 28th was my mother's birthday, and it was the date I agreed to go into drug rehab on my own.

From the time I got out of the psych ward after driving back from Tennessee to that January my life was in a downward spiral. I hated the lithium—it made this background humming noise in my brain that would not go away, and it made me feel stupid and unmotivated. The Zyprexa caused me to gain twenty-five or thirty pounds. I felt sluggish and sleepy. And I was still getting high every day. I went to holidays high, weekends high, weekdays high. I was just high.

I had used so much DXM that my body temperature was off. I felt warm all the time. I would go out in December in a tee-shirt and jeans and be fine. I had also lost my sense of taste almost completely—I didn't taste my food anymore. I couldn't sleep properly, and I looked pale, shrunken, and sick. I looked chronic. By drinking so much instead of eating I was nutritionally unbalanced. I was coming apart at the seams. With my family's beckoning I sought help from others.

I went to Silver Hill in New Canaan. Fancy rehab. Nice food. Places to smoke. Nowadays I think you can go to detox for $10,000 and it costs about $50,000 for a stay and they don't take insurance. But at the time I had good insurance and they took it.

It was a twenty-eight day program. You started in detox and then got moved to what looked like dorms or sober houses. The longer you stayed, the less you were supervised, and the fewer groups you went to. I'll never forget what happened. The first day I had a three-hour block of time to myself I was at about twenty days in. And the first thing I did after twenty days clean, was walk out the front gate and go into the town of New Canaan, found a CVS, and stole two boxes of Coricidin. I waited in agony for the evening when I could take them and not get caught.

And that was the crazy thing—I didn't get caught. I got high in rehab, stayed up all night, and finally got to bed around 6am. And the whole time I was coming down (and craving more) I'm saying to myself, why did I relapse? This is crazy. I went here to get better. And when I woke up the next day it hit me like a ton of bricks.

The three principles of abstinence-based recovery are honesty, open-mindedness, and willingness. So what was wrong? I hadn't been being honest with myself. The honest truth was, *I was not a man*. I was a woman! No wonder I couldn't recover. I was living a lie. I was living and pretending to be a man when I was really a woman. No wonder I couldn't stay clean.

The very next day I went to my counselor and explained the situation. I told him I was transgender and wanted to transition. I wanted to start ASAP. Could I please wear a skirt on the unit? (I was housed on the men's side.)

He said, "Absolutely not. It will disturb the other patients."

"Disturb the other patients?" I said, "This is a mental hospital. Everyone here is disturbed!"

He would not accede. But at least I had a bit of an awakening in there that I needed to have. I could not stay clean and be a man. I needed to practice rigorous honesty in all my affairs. I was a woman. And if I didn't make this fundamental change, I would not be able to stay clean.

I stayed the twenty-eight days, though instead of having twenty-eight days clean I had eight days clean. But I kept that a secret. I had learned what I needed to, and that gave me the insight I craved. I would need to transition and become a woman. Easier said than done.

I moved back in with my parents who were 100% against me transitioning. They made this patently clear. I took a job at a catalog company in New Hartford doing customer service and order entry. Every day I commuted to New Hartford for my little eleven-dollar-an-hour job, and every day I drove home and went to a twelve-step meeting. However, it was an ugly time. I would stay clean for a week or two, then use. A month. Use. I couldn't stay clean, and I knew it was because I wasn't living as a woman. I was in a bad cycle.

Everything changed on 9/9/02. I had a spiritual awakening. A moment of clarity. It was Saturday night and I'd driven to High Watch Farm in Kent for a Saturday meeting. It was a three-speaker AA meeting. They still have it there today. Same format, and a prime rib dinner before it if you liked to make a donation. So I went to this very large meeting, and at break I went out to smoke and I saw this man Mike.

Mike was my counselor at Silver Hill. He was gritty. He was real. He was an addict. He had nine years clean and was now a drug and alcohol counselor. I learned so much from him. Not just slogans and snippets, but real-life stuff.

"Mike!" I said as I gave him a hug. "I'm so glad to see you! What are you doing up here?"

"I'm a guest here," he replied. I was blown away.

"What do you mean?"

"I relapsed," he said. I was heartbroken.

"What happened?"

"Well, after almost ten years I thought maybe I could just drink a little. So I had a drink and everything was okay. 'Til I drank again and again. And then a month later I picked up heroin. And a month after that I lost my job, my car, my house, my wife, and I'm in rehab." He smiled pathetically.

And I saw it as if it were illuminated by God's hand: the reality. I was twenty-three and had not stopped. If I didn't stop, I was going to be twenty-three, thirty-three, forty-three, fifty-three, with no job, no girlfriend, no money, and living at my parents' house. Forever. Ad infinitum. And right then and there, seeing Mike, God spoke directly to me and I really surrendered, and stopped using.

Part of stopping using, I had said, was that I had to live life as a woman. Easier said than done. I was six feet tall, about two hundred thirty pounds, with broad masculine shoulders, thick muscular body parts, large hands and feet, and no way of learning to be more feminine. My parents balked at me. I told them I was going to move out. They told me on what salary? Your eleven-dollar-an-hour job would be ending in February or March. I challenged them. Yes. I will find a roommate in the program. And I did. Tiffany.

December first we moved in together into a little apartment on Jennings Road in Bristol on Birge Pond. I had a 1994 Volvo 850 turbo black sedan, about a grand in my wallet, a computer, some clothes, no furniture, no nothing. I applied for a Discover card and went to Salvation Army and bought furniture. I was too proud for food stamps (not later) but I ate mac and cheese and ramen and chicken legs and baked beans.

Tiffany worked at a group home in West Hartford for mentally-retarded adults, and I worked in New Hartford. My job ended about two months later, at which point I had to boost. It was all I could do. I stole three-packs of pregnancy tests, nicotine gum, pricey antacid. Anything small I could hide down my pants and sell on eBay for a profit. Razor blades. Rogaine boxes. Target. Walmart. CVS. Rite Aid. Stop and Shop. Endless petty thievery. It helped pay the rent.

Until I started something better. And legit. I had really thought through the transgender thing. I had to accept that I might not have a child. I might never find a partner. I might never have a job, because someone might not hire me because I am trans. So I started a business organically from the bottom up.

I started at the library. They had $.25 books. Some of them had price stickers on them. $15. $20. So I started picking through the library books and finding profitable and positive arbitrage. I would buy them for twenty-five cents and sell them for five dollars. Then I remembered the pawn shops, and how they all sold CDs and DVDs for between three and four dollars. I asked, how much could I have them for if I bought fifty? Two dollars. (They paid one.) So I went through all their inventory. I'd buy a massive number of CDs and DVDs. I learned through trial and error which movies I could profit off of and which ones were losers. Same with the CDs.

Pretty soon, I had a little inventory on a bookshelf, in alphabetical order and an Amazon store and an eBay store named Rugbykingpin. I was an online media seller. Between that and the boosting I was surviving.

Then one day I went to Super Pawn. Brian greeted me.

"Seth," he said, "You wanna buy anything besides CDs and DVDs? That's small peanuts you're dealing with. If you want to make more money, you're going to have to expand."

"What do you mean?"

"Let me show you. Ralph, Come here." Ralph hustled over. "Bring me that tote that Stevie brought in today." Ralph disappeared and came back with a grey tote filled with men's electric razors. "You can have that whole tote for two hundred dollars," said Brian.

I looked in there and flipped through the merchandise. They were all blister packs. Norelco razors. All of the packages were slit open near the UPCs and some of the UPCs were damaged.

"Twenty-five apiece," said Brian.

"I don't know, Brian. Am I gonna earn?"

"Guaranteed. Each one of those goes for around $50. You're paying $25. Just try it and see what happens."

Reluctantly I handed him two c-notes.

"Come back tomorrow and I'll have more," he said.

I brought them home and made the listings. I stopped off at the post office and picked up some Priority Mail boxes, and I made a fixed price listing. I explained that there was a little slit in the package and that the UPC may be damaged, but the razor was new and unopened. I priced them at $49.99, lowest price online. I went to bed, and when I woke up, I had eight different sales to eight different men across the country. Six dollars in fees, six dollars to ship, I netted a profit of thirteen dollars on each one times eight was $104. I just made a c-note while I was sleeping. I boxed everything up and brought them to the post office. Then I went back to Brian. I walked in and he was all smiles.

"What happened?" he asked.

"I sold all of them," I responded, beaming.

"In one night? Holy cow, Seth!"

"I know, right?"

"That means you priced them too low. How much did you charge?"

"Fifty."

"You should have made it fifty-five, made another forty bucks."

"I didn't know, Brian. This was a test, you know?"

"I get it. I got more merch. You wanna try some other things?"

He brought me in the back. He had these big expensive Braun razors in big squarish boxes. I had seen them on TV. They self-cleaned and worked wet or dry. They were top of the line.

"I'll give you those for seventy apiece."

"Seventy dollars? Isn't that steep?"

"Seth, these retail for $150. Sell them for $125. You'll earn, I promise you. You just stick with me and I promise you'll earn." He sold me six razors for $420. "Give me $400," he said. "We're square."

I went home and did what he said—I listed them for $125. They were a new product and they were gone in two days. I ended up opening a UPS account where I dropped the items off at Staples. I turned $400 into $600 in two days. And I worked about two hours. It was excellent.

Things soon progressed. I was selling digital cameras, camcorders, graphing calculators in new packages, women's and men's Rogaine, packs of razors just like I used to get. They got electric toothbrushes—Sonicares, Oral B's, Waterpiks, and that was just the beginning. First I was seeing the stuff I knew how they got. They cut the sensor off with a razor blade, stick them down their pants, walk out the store. Lather, rinse, repeat, at every Walmart in a fifty-mile radius. We got laser rangefinders for hunting, scopes for rifles, golf games from Brookstone, boxes and boxes of video game cartridges, wireless weather stations, Galileo thermometers, anything relatively small and easy to conceal, I bought it. I was getting in deeper.

Then a new crew started hitting Home Depot. They were pros. Three of them. I met them coming in one day. They all looked like heroin addicts or crackheads or meth addicts. Their faces were sunken and they had acne and sores, their teeth were bad, and their clothes were too big. I never asked Brian for any of their names. I never introduced myself to them. If they were in the store when I was there, I just waited for them to be done. Then Brian literally took the items from them, tacked on a little for himself, and sold them to me. He stopped giving me receipts. He just handed me a pile of blank ones and said to write what I wanted to.

The Home Depot stuff was the best. Milwaukee, Makita, Dewalt, Paslode. Brand names, all new in the package. No cuts, tears, brand new and sealed. They brought in mountains of the stuff. I was constantly filling the trunk of my Volvo. I had to start ordering large cardboard boxes from Uline for shipping. We got drills, drivers, hammer drills, impact wrenches, nail guns (cordless and corded), reciprocating saws. Diamond-tipped carbide blades to cut concrete. Those were $100 apiece. They would bring in ten at a time. Dremels, bits, impact hammers, batteries by the totefull.

I asked Brian how they got the stuff. He laid it out for me. They could easily get the blades. Get a flat orange cart. Lay down eight or ten blades. Get 80-pound bags of concrete or 94-pound bags of Portland cement and stack the stuff ten high on top of the blades. Check out in the garden department in case there's an alarm. No cashier in their right mind is going to move ten 80-pound bags of concrete to see if there's a thousand dollars worth of saw blades under them. Next Home Depot, bring back the cement and say you got the wrong kind, and do it all over again. They cleaned out Home Depot.

Then the not-so-flat big items were a little different. They needed three people. Usually, the first one was doing the saw blade trick while the other two shopped. They had a shopping list with the exact same items on it. One Dewalt 18V XRP hammer drill. Two Milwaukee batteries. One Paslode cordless nail gun, etc. Then each man would put the identical items in each cart.

While one made a key or somehow wasted time near the front of the store (maybe he went to the Pro Desk and bullshit about a sheetrock project while he had a free cup of coffee) the other one would check out and pay. When he exits the store, he hands the receipt to the third guy in the lot. The third guy walks the receipt in and immediately slips it to guy making the key or at the Pro Desk. He goes out to garden and grabs a plant. Shows the receipt to the garden cashier and says, "I already bought this stuff. I just wanted a butterfly bush." Or azalea. Or rhododendron. Or whatever. It was getting returned anyway. Even the best cashier couldn't catch these guys at work. This guy had a real receipt for the store with the correct date and a timestamp of a few minutes earlier for that exact stuff in his cart. They would charge him for the plant, and wave him through.

Then they mix and match receipts and return the merch they bought at different stores, saying their boss didn't need the stuff. They had the receipt. Easy return. They would walk out with a g-note of blades and a g-note of merch from every store. And they filled trucks and vans with the stuff and brought it to Brian. They had all different fake IDs, paid cash, all untraceable.

Brian was getting so much merch he didn't know what to do with it. Rugbykingpin blew up. The first year I did $20,000 in sales. The second I did 100k. The third I did 500k. It was too much merch for me to handle all by myself. And since I was still doing the CDs and DVDs for myself to keep a sense of uprightness, I needed help. I hired Amanda.

I was dutifully going to twelve-step meetings and I started school again, this time at Trinity College in Hartford. I was able to transfer a lot of my credit from Amherst, and the rule was that the GPA of the transfer credits didn't transfer. So all those Cs and C-minuses I got disappeared and just became Mechanics and Hyperbolic Geometry.

I wanted to become a women's studies major. The program at Trinity was called Women, Gender, and Sexuality. I gave up on a career in math or physics and opted for a humanities degree. It didn't matter at this point—I was running my own small business that was outgrowing my apartment. I had honesty, open-mindedness, and willingness when it came to the program, and when it came to being transgender, but not with respect to money making. As it turned out, I found out later that all this worked because Brian was cheating the taxman. He would pay the boosters on the books. Then I gave him cash off the books. Then I just wrote whatever I wanted on the blank receipts there was no copy of, cheated on my own taxes, saying the cost of goods sold was whatever I felt like on my Schedule C. There was no accountability and the government was getting robbed.

Once Amanda started working for me, I began transitioning by taking feminizing hormones. I found an amazing endocrinologist in New Haven that dealt with transwomen.

At our first meeting he asked, "Do you want children?"

"Maybe?" I said.

He said, "I can't treat you yet. Go to Yale and freeze your sperm. When you're done, I'll give you a Lupron shot, and some estradiol and prometrium, and you can go from being hormonally male to hormonally female in a month." Cool beans. I did just that. I also started wearing breast forms every day and was changing my wardrobe and shoes to being exclusively female.

The hormonal change was literally incredible. The first manifestation of it was when I was driving on I-84 East around Slater Road and I just started bawling uncontrollably, for no reason at all. The next thing was the feelings. When I was a man I experienced emotions, but I never felt feelings, like in the body, except on the rarest of occasions. (Perhaps seeing that bear—I felt fear in the form of a chemical release of adrenaline.) But as a woman I had feelings. Feelings in my chest and stomach and lower back and I could "feel" everything. It's like I didn't know my body was turned off before and now it was turned on for the first time. It was like being blind and then seeing. Unreal.

At that same time I transitioned, I met a girlfriend. I followed the advice of the people in the program and had no new relationship in the first year. After the 365 calendar days were up, I still didn't have a relationship. I was very happy being single. I was clean, my business (though cheating the IRS and based on boosting and fencing and not in recovery at all) was thriving, and I had started college again. When I was at college I met this busty blonde woman named Jackie.

She was in two of my classes and was a women's studies major as well, and was an adult like me. (She was 39, I was 25.)

I immediately thought she was attractive (she objectively was) but not as a partner. She needed a man. She had just broken up with her husband and had moved from a big house in Farmington to a little condo with her son. She immediately asked me for help selling things online. I obliged. The first time I went to her new condo in Farmington I walked up the steps and was bringing a housewarming gift. Simultaneously, this other woman was about to walk up to her door to give her a housewarming gift.

Her name was Ava, and when I saw her my heart stopped. She was 5'1", probably 110 pounds and very petite, not the kind of girl I'd ever been attracted to before. (Karen, Svetlana, and Sarah were all at least 5'9" to 5'11") but her face and her eyes. She was so dark and ethnic. I didn't know if she were Arabic or Armenian or Persian but she was something exotic. Green eyes, poker straight hair, the smallest little hands and feet, and impeccably dressed.

Jackie opened the door to both of us standing at her stoop. She introduced us and Ava left—she was literally dropping off the gift and then had to change to go to the gym.

"She works out. Nice." I thought,

She looked around thirty-five and drove a new Lexus. She lived in another unit in the condo. She left and I helped Jackie go through all these ridiculous collectibles called Liddle Kiddles, which were tiny dolls. I didn't think they'd be worth anything but she said they were. I ended up selling them for quite a bit. Later that day, with Jackie, she told me that I needed to pick up her son from school, and did I want to take a ride? Sure.

I got in her lime green Beetle and we talked and talked. Her son got in the backseat. I just said it. "Jackie—I think I want to sleep with Ava."

Jackie's son let out a big laugh. "What do you mean?" asked Jackie.

"I think she's hot. I've never been with an older woman. I'd just like to sleep with her."

"Susan," she said, (Jackie was always perfect with my pronouns and my name) "Ava is not just someone you sleep with. You have to date her."

"Good. Then I want to date her. Could you tell her that?"

"Sure. Why don't you write her a note and I'll put it on her door when we get back."

So I did just that. I wrote her a note saying, "My name is Susan, we met at Jackie's house. It was really nice to see you today. I'd love to take you out for some hot food."

And I left my phone number. She called me the next day and accepted. Turns out, she called Jackie before I left the note and said, "Who was that today? He was so cute!" And Jackie explained, he's not a 'he' he's a 'she,' and her name is Susan. She's a transwoman. She's transitioning. But after hearing that Ava still took a shot with me, Thirteen years later we still joke that "hot food" means "sex".

It turns out that Ava wasn't 35, but I didn't know this for some time. She finally told me her age. 48. WTF?! I was 25. She was 48. This was crazy! It turns out she was Lebanese, which is why she was so beautiful. Both parents from Lebanon. And oddly enough, her two sisters had both married Polish men. On our first date I picked her up on Trumbull Street in downtown Hartford.

"Is this a Toyota?" she asked me.

I was so insulted. "This is a Volvo. You drive a Toyota. What do you think a Lexus is? It's just a Toyota with an 'L' on it." But she had bought me a single rose as a gift, and I gave her a little magnet with a picture of the Lord on it that said "Jesus is coming, look busy." I thought it was ironic. It's still on our refrigerator today. And that was the beginning of my next relationship. I started dating Lebanese Ava. It was a beautiful time. Things only got better.

POKER CHAMP

I had to move into my third apartment. I started with the apartment on Jennings road I shared with Tiffany. After our six month lease was up, she told me I was too messy and she didn't like the inventory all over the house. I moved out, but we stayed good friends for many years until she finally relapsed and got married to another woman (not in the program). I went to her wedding with Ava—it was my second lesbian wedding. It was cool. They were both femmes so they both wore dresses. I have to say the girl she married parents didn't look thrilled but Tiffany's family and friends were all having a good time.

So then I moved into my second apartment at the corner of Park and Tulip in Bristol and I had a roommate Caroline. She was half black and half Native American and she had adopted parents. She had FAE. That's one of the reasons I wanted to live with her—I knew I could help her. She was a high school dropout who worked at a garden center, but her parents were very wealthy and bought her a car and paid the bills. I'm sure she had a trust fund. But she was kind.

We worked well together. She was really into music and I had a CD collection like no other. I was selling thousands of CDs. One of the other things I used to do to augment my business (legally) was to go to these things called postal auctions. They don't do them the same way anymore, but at the time there was this building called the Mail Recovery Center in an industrial park outside Atlanta. From my downstairs neighbor I had bought a 1978 blue Ford F-150. He had wanted to buy this boat in Maine. When he got there he got the truck to pull the boat and the boat for $1000. He asked me if I wanted the truck and I said sure.

So I got my first classic vehicle. I loved that thing. So, first of all it was a shift on the column, and I had never seen that before but it was easy. Down and in for first. Up and out for second. Down and out for third, and up for reverse. It was the coolest truck. It had 250k on it but it still ran. I bought aluminum mags for it and sold the steelies. I started to restore the interior. It was all original inside. Big vinyl seat, no A/C, but power steering and power brakes. Under the hood there was nothing but a 300 straight six and it was two-wheel drive.

I used to drive that truck all the way to Atlanta twice a year for the postal auctions. You had to pay cash, and you had to remove the merch that day. Some people showed up with U-Hauls or box trucks or bread trucks. The first time I went I was interested in just CDs and DVDs. And you could be. So before the auction started, you got a chance to view the merchandise. All the auction lots were divided by type and were behind fencing in what looked like a huge gymnasium. Everything had either been lost in the mail, or had an insurance claim paid on it.

There was an amazing plethora of merch. Musical instruments in a lot. Stamps. Silver coins. CDs and DVDs in giant 36"x36"x36" boxes. Books by the tractor trailer load. Vinyl records. Jewelry. Jewelry boxes. Laptop computers. Phones. You name it, there was a lot of it out there. So in the morning you got a sheet of paper with all the lots on it and you got to inspect everything. Then you were given a bidder number. When the bidding began, they would start everything at $50. You would hold up your placard if you were interested, and as they raised the price to $200 or $400 or $800 if you were still interested you would keep your placard up. Finally they would sell it to the last person raising his or her hand. My first time I bought two things. A lot of jewelry boxes because they were going for $50 and there were about twenty in there and one I really liked that I still use today. I figured I could keep the one I liked and auction off the rest to get my fifty back, and I did. Then I bought a box of CDs for $2500.

I went and paid them (cash only) and went to the loading dock. They used a fork to put the box in my pickup. I couldn't lift it. I also couldn't leave it there. So I drove straight home. Fifteen hours. And I got home around 3am. The next morning Amanda came in and I told her I had a treat for her.

"Uh-oh," she said She said that a lot. We went to the truck. "Holy cow!" she said. "I've never seen that many CDs!"

"Me neither," I replied. We carried them up in totes, brought the big 3' box upstairs as a trophy, and she got to listing. I figured I grossed about $10,000 on those CDs, less whatever was fees, shipping, and what I paid Amanda. It was around $4,000 in profit for driving to Atlanta, staying one night, and driving home. I had the art of arbitrage down.

Meanwhile I'd gotten much closer to Ava. She did her own kind of arbitrage, just take what I do and add a couple of zeros after it. She was the CFO of a private equity firm in Hartford that was relatively small (around 350 million under management) but had a great portfolio. If you don't know about private equity, they invest money by taking private cash and investing by buying small companies, nurturing and growing them, and then selling them after a period of three to five years. By doing this, Ava was able to return around fifteen percent to her investors (mostly it was the Connecticut Teachers Pension Fund) and she was great at her job.

She had started as an analyst at the Aetna in Hartford (always, "the Aetna," not, "Aetna") which was a large insurer. Then after being there for some time, a coworker started a new firm with a new what they call a mezzanine fund or "mezz fund" in Hartford and she brought Ava in at the ground level. Now personally, I believe that private equity firms do exactly what I do, boost and sue, except with bigger numbers. I was in the same line of work as Ava, just with a different manifestation.

They also cheat on their taxes in private equity, but they do so with a little loophole called the "carried interest provision." Basically, what this means is, instead of their company paying the standard 35% tax rate for businesses, they pay only the 15% capital gains rate, since the law says that when they buy and sell those companies, it's the same as an individual buying and selling stocks or houses or condos. It's a loophole, and private equity abuses it.

Then there's what they do. How they operate is just sick. So, for instance they bought a small company that made toothpaste in a niche market. After they bought the company they had to make it more profitable. How do you make people use more toothpaste? They only brush twice a day! Well, they consulted with China where the tubes were made and they made the hole in the tube bigger. That way, the user would squirt out more toothpaste (than he or she needed) every application and hence use more product. If that's not boosting then what is?

Then there was Bumble Bee tuna. How do you screw up tuna? They did it. For those of you who remember, all tuna used to come in six-ounce cans. Then all of a sudden, the cans became five ounces, but they stayed the same price. Who's to blame? Private equity. By changing the size of the can, they saved 17%, not to mention less steel to make the can. And everybody pays. And then Ava takes limos and car services and flies first class around the country doing deals while returning nominal money to my father's teacher's retirement fund on the backs of everybody getting screwed into eating tinier cans of tuna. And forget about suing. Ava's boss just wouldn't pay her bills. She would run up credit lines and then not pay. She would make them come after her, and then she would negotiate a settlement for twenty or twenty-five percent on the dollar. Boosting and suing. That's all the private equity business does. And I learned from the best.

I had mentioned my roommate Caroline. She loved that I had all this music at the house at any time. It got to the point that I had to drive to IKEA and buy more cheap bookcases to store all the inventory. So Caroline would just go through my library and say, "Can I copy this?" And of course I would let her and she built up an amazing collection.

Now me personally, besides classic rock I love jam bands. I loved the Dead and the Allman Brothers and Phish and Widespread Panic and Government Mule and String Cheese Incident. If they jammed out, I loved them. A throwback from my using days. But I also loved pop music, and I started to get a lot of this electronically. Not Napster (remember them?) Or Limewire (too many viruses) but I got them from the pawnshop.

Now I was pretty computer literate. When I was at Amherst College my first campus job was computer center supervisor and then I got to be promoted to the Fishbowl supervisor. (The Fishbowl was the high-end graphics lab—I did a lot of Photoshop and Illustrator. I also knew how to code HTML and make simple web pages. This was before Dreamweaver and C++ and XML and everything else.) I ended up getting fired for getting drunk on the job (shocker) and then I went to work in the cafeteria doing dishes. Big step down. Not until I got promoted to maintenance did I feel as if I were doing something acceptable again.

But anyway, we got a lot of computers at the pawnshop. Laptops and desktops. But we didn't want to sell them with people's data still on them. So it was my job to clean them off. So everyone's music files, I copied to my hard drive. I had gigabytes and gigabytes of music, an extensive collection of all genres. I really loved listening to music, and if you came to my apartment, I had music playing all day long.

So sometimes computers would come in real hot. Laptops (with or without chargers) that the people could not open because they were password-protected. "I forgot my password," they would say. And they were lying, and Brian knew it. But he had me. So he would give them $50 instead of $100 or $200 if it were working normally and they had enough to buy a bundle or some crack, and because of how the criminal underworld gossips (I mean, inmate.com) soon everyone knew to bring boosted computers to Super Pawn.

My technique was simple. I would open the machine and pull out the hard drive. Then I had the cable connectors and a power source and I would run the internal drive as an external drive off my desktop. I would format the drive and then reinstall Windows XP and Microsoft Office 2003. (I had discs from college. Everyone who went to Trinity got a copy of Windows Home and Office Student Edition.) Then there was this website called serials.ws. This was an international site that gave away product keys for software. So once you found one that worked, you just installed it over and over again in an endless number of machines. People just shared their codes.

So Brian would give me a laptop he couldn't open, and he'd get a laptop back preloaded with Windows and Office that he could sell at a ridiculous profit. Sometimes he would throw me some cash, but the money flowed freely between us.

But then a couple things happened. Amanda quit. She learned the business from me and had a connection at Northwestern Connecticut Community College for product from a family member and she went off to run her own eBay business. And a drug dealer moved in next door at Park and Tulip. So there I would be, carrying thousands of dollars of merch up my stairs, and he would be out on his lawn chair watching me. It no longer felt safe.

I found an apartment in Terryville, the next town over, only a half mile from where I grew up. But it was $550 a month and I got a two-bedroom on the second floor with half of the attic and half the basement and room to park four vehicles. It was further out in the country, but it was an upgrade. I moved all my media there. I was still going to all the pawnshops—three in Waterbury, the other in Bristol, two in Meriden, one in Seymour, and one in Ansonia, but my main business was Super Pawn.

Brian brought me into the business. "Why are you wasting your time lugging all the merch around? Just come here, take your laptop here, take pictures and list the stuff in the back room, store your boxes here, and just ship out of here. Most of your time and effort is transporting merch. And you don't have Amanda anymore. What do you say, Susan?" It sounded good. And I took him up on it.

The other thing that was happening wass Brian was growing. He had gotten a commercial business loan from Webster Bank and he bought the plaza his store was in. He was talking about expanding into commercial real estate, which he said had more money and less work than the pawn shop. He told me I should buy the pawn shop from him with Ava. I could have my own brick-and-mortar store and still do what I do but do his job. It was intriguing.

"I'm in grad school right now. I have to finish that," I said.

I took a year off from school after graduating with my degree in Women, Gender, and Sexuality and decided to study Public Policy Analysis for grad school. I had taken the LSAT because I thought maybe I would get a J.D. Then when I saw the other kids taking the test and the kids in my high school class that became lawyers I was really turned off. Not my people. So I was getting a philosophy of law and jurisprudence or a civics or government degree instead. Plus, I figured as artificial intelligence got smarter and could ace the LSAT, we wouldn't need as many lawyers because that type of work would be outsourced to AI. Not a good long term idea, but we would always need politicians, policy analysts, and policy wonks in government. It seemed a safer bet.

Brian understood. I told him I would start paying him with the proper lien documentation and begin buying the store. I would pay him 10k at a time in cash from the bank in a manila envelope and we would adjust the paperwork.

I started a new scam too. I started going to the post office in Terryville instead of Bristol. The girl who ran the place was named Fiona and she was as crooked as they come. It was a small post office. I'd pull up and she'd be smoking a cigarette in front of the post office or complaining she hadn't gotten enough sex. She was a disaster. Then I discovered she smoked weed. She always thought I was cute, but she always stressed she was not gay. Anyway, she would break the rules for me. I asked her if she could make a package disappear.

"No problem," she said.

"How about this. I'll give you an eighth of weed if you make a box disappear for me."

"Done," she said. "Just bring me the label. I don't even need a box."

I returned with the label.

"Acceptance," she said. "You're good to go. It's in the mailstream. I'll scan the label one more time when Julio picks up the mail to bring it for sorting. It'll look like it got lost."

Nice. I had insured that package for $600. Since I was clean now, I didn't want to actually touch weed, but there was this girl at the pawn shop who smoked. I asked her if she would put an eighth in a Priority Mail envelope and just hand it to Fiona in Terryville.

"No problem," she said. I handed her fifty. After the check came from USPS, I earned $550. I did that many times, always giving Fiona weed so she couldn't get me in trouble. And always using Heather from the pawn shop so that nothing had me appearing on camera for the post office. It worked really well. Fiona got high, and I got paid.

While this was going on I picked up a new hobby—poker. Texas Hold 'Em. They were constantly gambling at the pawn shop, whether it was setback for money or poker. So I sat in and I learned. As if by magic, it turned out that there was this couple in the rooms, Timmy and Wilma, who held weekly poker tournaments at their house on Friday night after the Friday night meeting. The tournament was $20 to buy in and $20 to rebuy. They would get between ten and fifteen people a week. It was more social than anything else but I learned the game.

Bet. Check. Raise. All in. Pockets. Trips. Set. Quads. Straight. Flush. Nut flush. Nuts. Stone nuts. A three-bet. Muck. Flop. Turn. River. Snowmen. Pocket rockets. Gay waiter. Big slick. Ladies. I learned how much to raise with A-Q or jacks. I learned how to trap, and how to hunt. There was a lot to learn. Playing A-10 or pocket 3's was different if you were on the button, the small blind, the big blind, or at the cutoff. Lots of terminology. Lots of strategy. Lots of fun. My brain took to it naturally. It was just a great combination of math (knowing odds or the likelihood of a card coming next or helping or hurting you) and psychology, getting in someone's head. Plus, you had the ability to bluff. And it was something that you were gambling, but there was skill involved, and you were playing against others, not the house.

After enough practice I took my show on the road. I started going to Mohegan Sun Wednesday nights. They had a $120 tournament with $10,000 guaranteed. So first place was around $3,000 and you could win that in one night plunking down $120 to start. Exciting. Plus you have to have stamina. The tournament started at 7pm and wouldn't end until 2 or 3am each week. So not only did you need math and psychology, but you needed extra sharp processing while extremely tired. I excelled at all of those things.

Then came my first big tournament. At these weeklies, we would get maybe a hundred or a hundred and thirty people. It was a small field. Then I read about the Foxwoods Poker Classic. They were having a ladies-only tournament in April. $300 buy-in. Two-day-long event. Sounded good to me. I went and registered (my license said "female") and they had never seen anything like me and the ladies were all ruffled that a transwoman was there—one cock in the henhouse is all it takes. People were not used to playing with or even looking at a transgender person. They were back on their heels. I used that to my advantage.

I made it to day two of the tournament. I remember at that point I was "in the money" meaning we had played it down from 300 entrants to under thirty. And I had a lot of chips. I called Brian and told him what was happening. He gave me some poker advice to take it down.

I went back for day two and crushed it. We were down to the four of us and they wanted to chop (split the pot). The clock stopped. If we stopped playing, I would walk away with $11,201 in cash. I said okay. We chopped the money. We spent another hour playing for the trophy, the jacket, and the bragging rights. And I won that. The trophy is still in my barrister's bookcase in my bedroom.

I didn't tell my parents. I drove to their house and just showed them a wad of c-notes. "I won this playing poker," I told my mom.

"How much is that?" she asked.

"Just over eleven thousand."

"Oh honey, please put that in the bank!"

Always in a fear-based world. I took half of it and opened a ROTH IRA for my retirement, took a thousand dollars to buy a collectible Burton snowboard, a jacket, and pants to go snowboarding, and I put the rest in the market and bought USO (United States Oil Fund, an ETF or exchange-traded fund) because oil had gone from $120 a barrel to $40 a barrel and I knew it would go back up. When I sold that position several years later it had doubled.

I had moved in with Ava a couple years prior. We had been spending every night with each other for two years and it was just the natural progression of things. The only thing was, she was in a condo in Farmington and we could not have all my merchandise coming there. So I worked out a deal with Brian. There was an empty back office in the plaza he owned that was unused. He would let me store all my stuff there, and he gave me a key. So I had business pinned down.

I was still working in the pawn shop, living in Farmington, and commuting to Bristol every day to list and ship, and I had earned a master's degree in public policy analysis. The next piece was completing my transition with surgery. So my sister was getting married in October, and my mother specifically asked me not to have my breast augmentation done until after the wedding. (I still wore a bridesmaid's dress, but she didn't want me to take anything away from my sister on her special day.) So I waited until right after.

My surgeon was this petite little man named Dr. George in Glastonbury. We had talked everything over. He had never operated on a transwoman before, but I had seen his work and it was awesome. So I handed over $5700 and went under the knife—my first and only surgery. I got 420cc saline under the muscle. Once they healed they looked fabulous. I was a 38D. And I felt complete. As part of my deal with the doc, when he was done he signed a simple letter for me that said on this particular date I performed surgery for the purposes of gender reassignment. (They now call this "gender affirming surgery.")

This was all planned out. At the time, under law, if you wanted to change your birth certificate or your passport then gender-affirming surgery was required. The implication of this was that this was bottom (genital) surgery, but it was not specified under statute. I consulted a civil rights lawyer. She told me to go ahead and have the top (breast) surgery and get the letter and send it in and they should change my gender marker. And that is how, even though I retained a penis, I was able to get a driver's license, a birth certificate, and a passport that all said I was born female. I was most definitely a gender pioneer.

I stepped up my poker game. Now that I had tits, I liked to flaunt them, and the poker table was an excellent outlet. I started buying slutty dresses and skanky heels, and I played a lot of poker. One of the things that happened on account of my chopping the ladies tournament at Foxwoods is that they took my picture and released it to the poker world. Immediately people questioned my gender, if I were a girl, and if I were allowed to play in the ladies tournament.

There's still a thread about it on a popular poker blog called Two Plus Two. An entire discussion about gender and poker. Turns out, I'm the first transwoman to play in (and win) an event. And people could not get enough of me at the tables. First I took my show on the road to Atlantic City. I took the Borgata by storm. The second event I played, a two-day deepstack event that had a $180 buy-in, had attracted 1100 participants. It was the biggest field I'd ever played in.

Well, after the first day of play (and it was a long day—I woke up at 6am, drove from Connecticut to Jersey, started playing at 11am, and played until 1:30am) I was the leader of the whole tournament. The Borgata poker blogger, "the Gorilla," as he was known, took my picture and called me the chipleader. Well of course I was wearing something slutty and my fake titties were hanging out. It didn't take long for another Two Plus Two thread emerged called "Chipleader with Tits." If you search that phrase on Google (and don't autocorrect to "cheerleader with tits") you will see the article even today, and when you do a Google image search and Google "Susan Sturbridge," that picture still shows up.

I ended up 11th in the tournament. Eleven out of 1100. It still paid $4400. Not bad for two days of work! I also played at Caesar's, at Harrah's, at the Trump Taj, at the Tropicana, and at Revel (back when Revel had just opened and it was spectacular.) I started making Atlantic City a monthly trip. Then bi-weekly. I would come down on a Tuesday morning, stay all day Tuesday and Wednesday (there were two guaranteed tournaments on Wednesday) and then leave Thursday night. I started to get all sorts of perks and coupons and comped rooms. I got to be friends with the woman who ran the gym at the Borgata so I could work out for free. I would work out in the morning, pick up a New York Post and read it and do a crossword puzzle while sitting in a bikini by the pool, then go in the hot tub for awhile, eat a comped lunch, then play poker all day and at night go out to the boardwalk or to the Pool (the club at Harrah's).

It was a fantasy life. Business was still going strong. Ava and I had never been closer. Money was rolling in, and I was investing to buy the pawn shop. Between Ava and I, we had put in over 100k towards buying it.

Then I started going out to Vegas. What a world! People just thought I lived there—they were always shocked when I said I was from Connecticut. I played at the Wynn, the Venetian, the Bellagio, the Aria, the Golden Nugget, and of course, the Rio. The first time I went out was for the World Series of Poker. They had a ladies tournament that was $1000 to enter. It was the most expensive tournament I'd ever played in. I wore a white dress from Frederick's of Hollywood with my tits hanging out, a pair of black sunglasses from White House Black Market, and 6" white platform heels. It was a show. I was 6'6" with those heels on. I lost the first day full house over full house. It broke my heart. But there was hope.

There was a "consolation tournament" the next day. It was sponsored by LIPS (Ladies International Poker Series) at their home base at the Golden Nugget (today it's at Planet Hollywood) and it was another ladies event that cost $250 and pulled in about 350 people. I came in the final table (top ten) and paid for my whole trip, as well as my failed bid at WSOP. I went next year. I cashed at the WSOP Ladies event. I came in 41st out of 967 women. It was my best showing at the World Series and I won about $4000 that more than paid for my Vegas vacation.

While I was focusing on my poker play, both at my home base (Mohegan Sun) and playing weekly tournaments there and at Foxwoods, playing monthly at Borgata in AC, and playing semi-annually in Vegas, Brian had hatched his own plan. He told me he was having a very special meeting and he wanted me to be a part of it. Monday night at 6pm when the store was closed. Six men arrived plus me. We had a meeting in the back room of the store. Here was the pitch.

Poker was so big right now. (Pokerstars had not been shut down yet and poker play at casinos and online had been growing every year.) And everyone who needed to play needed focus, concentration, and stamina. What was missing? A dietary supplement designed specifically with the poker player in mind. It's name? Poker Fokus. (Sounds like Hocus Pocus, right?) Brian was building a team. He wanted investors and team players to start a dietary supplement company with him. Two guys bowed out. Four were in, and there was me. "We don't want your money, Susan, we want your brain." I was, by far, the most educated of the bunch.

"What do you want me to do?" I asked.

"Everything," said Brian as he laughed and lit a Marlboro red.

"What do you mean, everything?" I asked.

"Well, we need a website. We need a manufacturer/distributor, we need artwork, marketing collateral, content, a formula, advertising, insurance plans, tax forms, and business incorporation. Think you can handle it?"

"If you pay me," I said. "You're going to need help with the artwork and the Photoshop and Illustrator stuff. I haven't done that in years and the programs have come a long way."

"I thought you might say that," said Brian. "Don't worry. I got a guy for that. I don't need art. My boy can do that, but we need content. And it all needs to look professional. And I'm sure there's all sorts of compliance and liability stuff, you know, what if someone takes it and gets sick or something? You know? Details. And I know you're good with details. So how do you like your new job?"

"I like it. Can I keep my other one in case we don't all become millionaires?"

"Of course," he said. "Listen, I didn't even tell you. I have four Dyson Animal vacuums and four Lincoln Electric welders that fell off the back of a truck. Ralph can load your truck to bring them to the office. You got your truck? We can move them to your unit."

I did have the truck. After the blue one finally died (the motor didn't die, God bless the 300 straight six, but the frame rotted and the bed collapsed on one side—it went to the boneyard) I got another F-150. An '89. Red and grey two-tone with a four speed stick and the same motor. I drove that thing into the ground. Then I was at my buddy John the mechanic's shooting the shit and his business partner comes out. "I have a truck for you. I know you're looking."

"How do you know it's for me?" I asked.

"Guess," he said.

"What is it, purple?"

"Oh my God yes, it *is* purple! Factory purple. It's a '94 with 120k on it. It's got a Back Rack and a diamond hatch box and it's four-wheel and it's factory purple. It's $3700. What do you say?"

"I'm in," I said. It was the perfect pickup truck for a 6' tall 38D transwoman. Big, bold, and purple. Ava bought it for me. What a nice gift!

Ralph loaded the merch into the bed and I drove the stuff over. A new company called Poker Fokus. I was excited. I was going to be in the supplement business. Now remember, Red Bull and Monster Energy existed at this point, but there was no Five Hour Energy or their competitors. It was a wide open market. Brian had already found a manufacturer, Venus Pharmaceuticals on Long Island. My first order of business was to check out their operation.

I drove to Long Island and went in. They had an enormous manufacturing floor. They made pills of all kinds, as well as powders, tablets, capsules, anything. They worked on the formula with you, filled and sealed the bottles, added your label, and shipped them wherever you wanted, wholesale. It was a very professional operation. I was allowed to tour the plant and I took pictures. They were perfect.

We agreed on the formula—an upper, two downers (hypnotics or sedatives) and some herbal stuff for our proprietary blend, Rhodiola rosea. So, caffeine (about as much as a cup of coffee), L-theanine and GABA, two chemicals that worked on focus and keep you calm, as well as the Rhodiola rosea as the wildcard. We all tried the first batch. Two somnific. We tweaked the blend. The second ones were perfect. The product really worked! It definitely gave you energy but not the jitters like Red Bull or Monster, and definitely calmed you down like taking valerian root or melatonin, or CBD (the other, legal chemical in marijuana, analogous to the theobromine in coffee).

Now I had to come up with all the text for the website and the marketing collateral. I worked with Carlos, the graphic designer who made pokerfokus.com. I set up the Paypal, shopping cart, back end of the site, as well as all content. He made the graphics. Our trademark was a slice of two playing cards, two pocket kings, for the K-K in Poker Fokus. The hand-crafted king playing cards appeared all over the site and all over our marketing collateral. Here is some of the text:

About   our   blend:

We are absolutely sure that you will be satisfied with our blend, because we know the care and study that went into designing this product. There are many supplements that increase energy with caffeine, or deliver B-vitamins, or energy drinks that fill your stomach with liquid. But only Poker Fokus can boast our Proprietary Blend, a special mix of GABA, caffeine, Rhodiola Rosea, L-Theanine, and 5-HTP, professionally blended from FDA-approved ingredients,   and   poised   to   revolutionize   the   poker   world.

Why do we feel our product is so ideal in comparison to all the others? The difference is in the details. Never before has such a collection of safe and effective ingredients been brought together. This incredible union of special amino acids, a plant-derived adaptogen, and natural caffeine—combined with B-vitamins—offers the serious poker player the chance at a better game.

Check for yourself—you won't find another supplement with the Poker Fokus Proprietary Blend. Compare our ingredients with others—this is so much for than a caffeine pill. Designed by poker players for poker players (with a little help from health professionals) our unique blend may just be your new secret weapon!

They rented a pipe and drape booth at WSOP, and went during the main event. (I had already gone to Vegas that year for the ladies tournament, but that was a month earlier.) They had all sorts of product samples, shirts, hats, hoodies, everything. By this time there was over 100k in this venture. They were big shots, all flying to Vegas while I shipped them everything and stayed back to handle order fulfillment and customer service. The thing was, only a few orders trickled in. To this day I don't know how they screwed things up. But the launch was a complete failure. They had bought a color ad in *Bluff* magazine (the main poker magazine) and they were selling and sampling the product and it just didn't get any traction. It was a product that worked so well. But this was a team of miscreants led by a scheister pawn shop owner. They were not your typical businessmen, and they failed.

I got paid a little. A few orders came in here or there. But Poker Fokus was a flop. In the end I was embarrassed to have taken part of it. I realize in the autopsy phase that it was just too narrow of a market we were going after. Truckers could use the stuff. Students could use this stuff. Anyone who needed to stay awake and stay focused could use it. But we went for too narrow of an audience. Then, the next year, Five Hour Energy came out and we were sunk.

"They stole our idea!" said Brian.

"No they didn't Brian," I said. "They did it better."

So there was 100k down the drain. Now at the time I didn't realize this was a Hail Mary pass for Brian. Brian had a serious gambling and drug problem and built up a ton of debt. Though I had over 100k invested in the store, he had borrowed money from a lot of other people too. His family members at the pawn shop were stealing from him blind. So he launched Poker Fokus hoping we'd be the next Five Hour Energy and all become millionaires, but he needed that million to get out of debt. Then it happened.

There was a sting at the store. Lucky for me I wasn't there. I showed up for work and Ralph was standing alone out in front of the store. The door was locked and the lights were off and it was 1pm. They were usually open 10 to 6.

"They raided 'um," said Ralph.

"What?" I asked.

"The feds and the State Police. They're all arrested right now."

"Seriously?"

"Hand to God."

"Wow," I said.

"Come back tomorrow," said Ralph. "I'm sure Brian's wife will bond him out. Al's not so lucky though. He's gonna' go to the federal pen."

"Holy cow!" I said.

"Yeah, it's bad."

It made the papers. This was not the only pawn shop they hit. It was coordinated. They had brought stolen Dewalt drills to every store the week before, with an undercover officer posing as a booster. They had already passed the serial number off as stolen. Then they tested to see which stores reported the sales, and if they reported the serial numbers correctly. The other stores got shut down too, because they changed the serial numbers on the forms when they contacted the police about what they had bought. So, thinking the item is hot, if the serial is ending in 6494, they would just report it as ending in 9646, and that way they got to keep the item. Brian didn't even report the sale. It was a minimum $10,000 fine and a loss of the pawnbroker's license.

Additionally, Al was busted. Al handled all the gun sales and purchases. There were a lot of federal firearms documents that needed to be properly recorded for a sale, and properly stored for retrieval. The feds set him up. They sent in a young, busty blonde woman selling a Glock. When it came to the paperwork she said she couldn't fill out one of the forms. Al let it slide. Well that hot, young blonde was an ATF agent. They nailed Al for illegal purchase of a firearm, with a mandatory minimum six months in federal jail. Super Pawn was broken. Brian's cousin Anthony had an outstanding warrant for assault two and failure to appear. He got caught up with all this too even though he didn't work there and only hung out there. He got sent to Osborn Correctional.

The next day the store opened and the remaining men looked beaten. I walked in slowly.

"I'm glad you weren't here, Susan. It was awful," Brian said. "I lost my license, pawn and precious metals, Anthony is locked in Osborn and Al is out on bond but he's going away for at least six months. And now I'm open but only for redemptions. We're not allowed to buy anything else from people. We're out of business."

My heart sunk. If he were out of business, then so was I.

"Can I still buy the place?" I asked. "Get a pawnbroker's license and take it over from you?"

"Yeah, but you'll need more than what you put in. The business is worth 1.2 to 1.4 million and you only gave me 100k."

"Well quite frankly Brian, I don't really agree with your valuation. I think it's more like 800 or 900k, tops."

He laughed. "Well, you're still a little light. What are you going to do?"

"Okay then. Cash me out. I'll take my 100k back."

"Okay, but I'm going to need a little time to get that together."

"I understand. But I don't want a check. I want cash in a paper bag like I paid you."

"Understood. I'll give you a down payment tomorrow."

I went back to the unit behind the sports bar and took a look at my merch. I needed to liquidate. If he were going to cash me out, he probably had to sell the building, which would mean I wouldn't have that rent-free storage space. Not to mention Ralph had been sleeping on my futon in one of my side rooms because he was homeless, boosting for money for alcohol. What a disaster.

The next day Brian gave me 12k in cash.

"Thanks," I said. "When is the rest coming?"

"I need to sell the building. It's gonna' take time."

Time indeed. He never sold the building. The trustee took it from him. He declared bankruptcy a short time later. I personally lost $88,000. It was my life's savings. I heard from Brian's brother, a life insurance salesman, who called me. Brian disappeared and was MIA. I never saw him again.

I had a nervous breakdown. Even the Depakote and the Geodon I was on were not enough to stop the flood of anxiety I had that made me manic and then psychotic. I didn't get high or use over it—I had nine years clean—but I ended up in the psych ward.

My parents and partner decided that the best place for me would be the psych ward at St. Francis Hospital, a Catholic hospital in Hartford. They had a very good reputation and they were Catholic like me. Absolutely terrible mistake. Turns out, on intake, they classified me as a "male with breast augmentation" rather than a female. They locked me on the male unit with all the other men. Though I didn't have a roommate, I was surrounded by men, recreated with the men, and was treated as a man. After a few days of taking Haldol and having my wits returned, I complained to the nurses and my psychiatrist. I explained that my driver's license, passport, and birth certificate all listed me as female. They would hear nothing of it.

For eleven days I was segregated, made fun of, and sexually harassed. The men knew I was transgender—I had D-cup breasts—and most of them mocked me. One of them continually hit on me and said he had been in prison and he understood women like me and he wanted a piece. I hid. I filed complaints. I filed grievances. Nothing went anywhere. They were a Catholic institution and Catholics (well, these Catholics) did not believe in sex changes and even if I had undergone bottom surgery, they probably would have referred to me as a man who'd had a penectomy. They believe that birth sex is immutable. There are a lot of people who think that way. I just tend not to socialize with them. After eleven days I was released back into the arms of my girlfriend. I told Ava I was going to sue them for negligence. I just needed to find the right lawyer. But along the way to doing that, something else happened.

A MISTRESS

In 2011 I had over nine years clean and I had three sponsees in the program, Alexis, Virginia, and Jennifer. Apparently these three cisgender females wanted the recovery that I had. It was very much a treat to have three sponsees. They called me everyday and it gave me an opportunity to look at how I was working my program.

And my own program was not perfect. I remember a couple of things in particular. The first was, the program was always about living in the present and not projecting into the future. So I became intrigued by the idea of planning versus projecting. I ran a business, so I argued I needed to plan for my future. But I was not supposed to project. Business was all about projecting about earnings, growth, sales, and inventory. No one in the program could give me a good answer.

I also thought a lot about buying merchandise from the pawn shops. People in the program knew what I did—it was a program of complete honesty. I shared with others about how I made a living. I rationalized. I justified. Merchandise from the pawn shop wasn't stolen. I had a receipt. Good title. I had a legitimate business. I could fool some of the newcomers, but the oldtimers saw through it.

"You're still stealing," they would say. "It's old attitudes and behaviors. You have to get clean and trust in God that you will be okay without dealing with criminals."

I couldn't handle such introspection and I guess I didn't have enough faith. I bucked them. And now that my main supplier vanished, my tertiary business was small and hit-or-miss. Though my business was still running, my main supplier was gone (along with my life's savings) and I was just buying random stuff from the other pawn shops. I went from doing about 500k a year in sales down to 60k.

I needed a new job, so I got a job with a company called Stanford Prep. They were a tutoring outfit out of Santa Monica, CA and were looking for SAT and ACT tutors to work online. I aced my SATs, and after they interviewed me, I immediately got the job. Being the progressive California liberals that they are, I'm sure they liked that I was trans, and also that I had a master's since most of the other candidates only had BA's or BS's. So I started working as an SAT tutor, turning a new leaf.

When I transitioned, I'd always had my own business because I was nervous that no one would hire me. But I got this job all on my own. They wanted a transwoman to indoctrinate high schoolers. How much the world changed from 2003 to 2011. It was good honest work. The hours were shitty—I usually worked six to midnight—but the pay was good. It was part-time, and I worked down my eBay inventory so I could focus more on tutoring.

I had a sponsor named Joan who I was working the twelve steps with all over again. Right at this point I was at step four, talking about character defects. Two of them were dishonesty and promiscuity. I had cheated on Ava more than once, with women and with men (more on this in an upcoming chapter). So I was being rigorously honest and I wrote about all my indiscretions in my step-writing document that I kind of hid on the desktop of my computer.

So it was a nice June day. I was with my sponsee Alexis and another woman Terry and her son Jeff, who was eight. Terry was also in the program and lived in Bristol. We had taken a ride out to People's Forest in New Hartford and Riverton to get some sun on the rocks and swim in the cold Farmington River. Jeff had also brought a fishing pole and some nightcrawlers, convinced he would catch a trout. Us girls were having a lovely day in our bikinis. It was around eighty-five degrees and sunny. And then I got the call I'd always been dreading. It was Ava.

"Susan," she said curtly. "I read your fourth step. Please don't come home tonight. Good bye." Click. Shit. My mouth was agape. The girls knew something was wrong. I explained the whole thing to them and they all felt for me.

"She shouldn't have been snooping around on your computer," said Alexis. "What was she even looking for?"

"I don't know," I replied, crying, distraught. But when Ava said something like that I dare not disobey.

Both the women told me I could stay with them for the night. I chose to stay with Alexis because she didn't have a child. We left soon thereafter—I brought everyone back to their cars, then Alexis took me out for a sushi and sashimi combo, my favorite dinner. We retired to her dumpy apartment in the west end of Bristol on Wolcott Road. I found out that she had the same landlord I'd had at Park and Tulip.

As it got later and later, she told me I could sleep in her bed with her. She told me to get comfortable. I didn't have any other clothes.

"Just take your shirt off," she said. I was standing there in my bra. She took it off and began rubbing my nipples. You can guess what happened next. We had sex twice that night and twice in the morning. The sex was infinitely better than any intercourse with Ava.

The next day I spent with Alexis. She was working at Nordstrom selling women's clothing and she called out. We went for a hike, talked some more, and then it was time for me to go. Ava had called me and told me to come home. She had processed everything and wanted to talk.

Alexis said to me, "Can we keep doing this?"

I said I didn't know. It was a *huge* no-no in the program to sleep with your sponsee. It's called "thirteenth stepping." It's not ordinal—it's a cardinal sin.

"But don't you think I'm sexy?" she asked.

"Yes, very," I responded. She was about 5'6" and a 36DD with short blonde hair and sparkling eyes.

"I knew you wanted to sleep with me when we met," she said.

"I did not!" I fired back. "You always wore those smocks. You never had a shape."

"Those aren't smocks, you loser. Those are Lilly Pulitzer blouses and they cost about $150 apiece. I bought them at the Lilly store at the Westchester [mall]."

"Well, isn't that nice. They weren't flattering. I didn't know you were a double-D until I saw you in a bathing suit."

"Preppy girls don't show off their boobs," she said. "We're ladies on the street and freaks in the bed."

"Amen to that!" I said. "I gotta' go. I'll see you soon."

She gave me a sensual French kiss.

"You will see me tomorrow, woman."

"Okay," I said. And with that, I realized I was not going to stop having sex with this woman any time soon.

So how did I meet Alexis? At a twelve-step meeting in Bristol. She was living with her parents in Bronxville in Westchester county. Her mother had a fashion forecasting job at a trend forecaster in the City. Her father was an executive at Key Bank. She had gotten an English degree from Loyola University in Maryland, got a desk job in publishing, and went off the deep end with opiates. She loved Perc 30's and Oxys and Dilaudid and straight up morphine. All of her cash went to drugs. Her parents gave her credit cards at Neiman's and Sak's and Barney's and she maxed all of them out. I'd never seen someone so irresponsible with money.

Then she hit bottom. She went to a rehab in New York State, and for aftercare they told her going home or back to the City was going to be a trigger, so she went to a halfway house. She ended up in Bristol, CT at a sober house run by a known criminal and tax evader. But she had a room and lived with women, and got a job in retail. (She worked at the Lilly Pulitzer store during high school and knew a ton about clothing and fashion.) She worked at Nordstrom and was stipulated by her sober house to go to twelve-steps meetings.

I met her Tuesday night in Plainville at the step study guide meeting. She walked in with some ridiculous lacy and obnoxious pink and green top with bold patterns and bright color, she never took off her sunglasses, and sipped an iced coffee. And when she shared, oh my God. The most nasal, affected, Valley Girl voice came out of her and nothing made sense. She heard me sharing one night about my eBay business, and she came up to me at the break.

"You sell on eBay?"

"Yes. Nice to meet you, Alexis." She was too stuck up to talk to anyone.

"Could you sell some clothes for me? I really need the money."

"Sure," I said. "As long as I get to earn a little."

"We can chop it 50/50. But the consignment store wants to give me $10 for this Tommy Bahama dress. It was $178. I'm sure I can get more than that on eBay."

I didn't even know what Tommy Bahama was.

And so it began, our business relationship. Ava was happy, because she saw me hustling for money. Alexis was happy, because she was making money. I was happy, because I was making money and helping out someone in the program. It was a win-win-win. Then I began to be friends with Alexis. I felt funny getting baskets of clothes in the parking lot of a meeting, or handing her an envelope of money in front of others. So I would invite her to meet me at Starbucks and we would share Frappuccinos or we would get sushi or Thai food.

And then one day she asked me to sponsor her. I asked if she were willing to call me everyday, go to meetings regularly, and write the steps. She said yes, so I agreed. She was a good sponsee. She wanted to work on herself, and she flourished with the one-on-one attention so integral to the sponsor-sponsee relationship.

Her biggest problem was money. She spent more than she took in. First of all, her mother doesn't cook. I learned this from multiple visits later to her home. So Alexis didn't cook. She went out for every meal. But that gets expensive. Her parents had bought her a car and paid for her insurance. She paid for her apartment and utilities and gas and phone and constantly eating out. Every single month she was a few hundred short and had to call Daddy for some more money. The first time she did it I didn't care—sometimes we have hard months. But then it just continued month after month after month and her parents kept obliging. This must have been a cheaper setup than to have her live at home.

She kept telling me that I didn't understand. She was preppy. (Whatever that meant.) She wore designer clothes, drove a Jeep, and spent lots of money. That was always her life. But her parents were trying to give her a taste of poverty so she would come to her senses. This was not Bronxville. Not Westchester county. This was a bad neighborhood in Bristol, CT. I tried to get her to face reality, but that is a challenge for someone who stops using but lives in his or her disease.

After we made love the first time I went back home to Ava. I showered so I didn't have Alexis's scent on my body. Ava was angry, and rightly so. First I tried to turn it on her and said she shouldn't be snooping around on my computer. I mean, what did she expect to find? And why keep reading it once you know what it is? But she would have none of it. She demanded I have an STD test. I obliged. She was not going to sleep with me until I did. Alexis's words ran through my mind—"you will see me tomorrow, woman"—and I told Ava fine.

The very next day I told Ava I was going to my regular meeting, which afterwards usually featured a pizza party and so I would get home late. She said fine. As soon as I was in the car I called Alexis. I couldn't remember the last time I was so excited. I could feel the energy all through my body like an amazing glowing warmth.

"Where are you taking me to dinner, woman?" she asked.

She kind of threw me off. "I thought we were going to the meeting," I said. "How about Bertucci's?"

"No. No Italian food. I don't like that dirty food."

"Okay," I responded. "How about China Pan?"

"Chinese food? You know that's too heavy for dinner."

"Okay. King and I Thai?"

"Perfect," she said. "Pick me up in fifteen. See you, Love," and she hung up.

Well I guess now I'm driving from Farmington to Bristol, then to Hartford, then back to Bristol, then back to Farmington. Kind of a lot of driving but whatever. I picked her up and she grabbed me and said, "Make love to me." So I did. Then we got dressed again and she said, "Take me to dinner." What could I do, say no? She had just given herself to me. I got Pad See Ew and she got Massaman Curry.

"Let's go to West Hartford and just walk around Blueback Square," she suggested. It was a nice night and I obliged. We walked around holding hands. It was interesting being with a woman my own age. When we were out together, a lot of people thought Ava was my mother, which did not happen with Alexis. It was very freeing. We finally sat on a bench and made out a little. She whispered in my ear, "Can you do it again?" I said sure.

We drove back to her apartment, had a repeat performance, and were laying in bed smoking Parliament lights with the recessed filters. She only smoked Parliaments. She didn't have cable and just had a small television with a DVD player. We watched Pretty Little Liars Season One. Finally it was around 9pm.

"I have to go," I said.

"Why?" To go back to that old lady? Just stay here."

"You know I can't. She thinks I'm at a meeting and out for pizza. I have to go home."

"Okay, bitch. Call me."

And with that I sped home to Ava.

"How was the meeting?" she asked me.

"Good."

"Who'd you see?"

"Heidi. Val. Maureen. Lou. Bruce with the neck tattoo. Biker Mike. It was a good meeting. Then we went out for pizza afterwards. To Max Pizza. I'm tired. I'm just going to bed."

"Okay, honey, I love you!"

"I love you too, Ava!" And night-night I went.

And that was the pattern literally for the next year. I would say I was going to a meeting, then instead I would see Alexis and we would have sex and go out to eat. Not only was this hurting my pocketbook and the miles on my car, it was seriously compromising my integrity. I was lying all the time. I was totally untrustworthy. I just no longer cared about telling the truth. Coming up on ten years clean, I stopped having rigorous honesty. I stopped being honest, open-minded, and willing. All I was thinking about was my own sexual gratification and my own selfish feelings. It was the opposite of a twelve-step recovery program.

When I was in rehab in 2017, I found out that the moment I decided to have sex with Alexis was the moment of my relapse. I identified my patterns—I was dishonest, I minimized consequences, and I was promiscuous. The manifestation of those traits led to my eventual relapse on drugs after over a decade clean. That was the relapse—the sex. The drugs were a natural consequence that came later. It was a little like eating a hot pepper. Choosing to eat the hot pepper was the reason your mouth burned, even if there was a short time when it wasn't hot. It was an inevitability.

All I did was rationalize and justify. Ava's job was really heating up. First there was an SEC audit. Then they were closing a mezzanine fund. Then they were fundraising for a fourth fund. She was constantly on the road, constantly travelling, never home, and when she was home, she was comatose. The money was too good for her to pass up. They were paying her many hundreds of thousands of dollars a year and she wanted to retire early. I didn't blame her.

But life was lonely for me. I didn't have the pawn shop, I had minimal eBay, and was working part-time online from my home. It was a boring life and I needed to spice it up. After a few months it was clear—Alexis was my mistress.

There were many opportunities for me to sleep over Alexis's apartment, but she preferred to sleep over mine. I had a queen bed instead of a full, and a big comfy white down comforter. I also had cable television and the internet. So, basically, Ava was gone a lot. They had another office in Chicago and so any time she had a meeting in Illinois she stayed over one night. Then they had companies all over the country and were constantly fundraising so they'd be flying all over to different states to talk to other bureaucrats about getting pension funds to invest, as well as other private investors. Ava thought I was spending many nights alone, but in fact I was never alone.

Then in November, Alexis and I took our first vacation together. I told Ava I was going down to Florida to play poker and sit on the beach. She was busy with work and couldn't come. My hairdresser had a second home down in Miami Beach and said he'd let me stay there for free. I had points for the flight from all my trips to Vegas, so Alexis left her car at long-term parking at UCONN Health Center down the street from my house, and we drove to the airport and left. Ava had no idea I was going away on vacation with another woman.

We had an awesome time. I had just run a half marathon. (I ran almost every day and was in excellent physical shape. Mentally, spiritually, and emotionally was a different issue.) We stayed on Alton Drive and I would run to Ocean in the morning and into the strip in Miami Beach and then run home. About nine miles, while Alexis laid in bed. I'd never seen anyone sleep as much as Alexis. If she could, she would sleep twelve hours. She regularly slept ten.

I never even went to a poker room. We spent all of our time on the beach, and if it were raining, stopping at all the boutiques. We went out for Mexican and Japanese and Spanish and seafood. We would drive into Miami at night. It was awesome. We had rented a black Mitsubishi Galant and drove everywhere. I even took her to Key West for a day. We saw a drag show and went to strip clubs and ate paella, crepes, and key lime pie. It was lovely.

Then our last day we were driving up A1A in Miami Beach. She had started kissing my neck (she was constantly horny) and I started laughing and the next thing you know, bam! We hit a taxi at about 25mph. No airbags, but it was a big impact. The cops came. The taxi driver said he was hurt. He was lying. He was setting up a lawsuit. The female cop (nicest police officer I'd ever met) stood up for us. She said if he were hurt she would call him an ambulance. He refused. He said he would drive himself to the hospital—he just wanted it in the report. She said no way. Ambulance or you go on your way. He finally acquiesced. Scam artist. I guess it takes one to know one.

Luckily there was no damage to the car. Since no one was in front of the cab all the energy just got transferred to his vehicle and there was no crunch. Like two pool balls colliding. The officer gave me a written warning for following too close, no ticket but at fault if the guy claimed anything on insurance. I was just petrified she'd send an accident report to my home in

Connecticut, Ava would get the mail and read it, and see I had a passenger. The jig would be up. But no such thing happened. We arrived back home and no one was the wiser.

In the meantime I had found a lawyer to bring a civil action against St. Francis. They were in Middletown, CT, the Fleeman Law Offices run by Judy and her husband Craig. Judy and Craig were bleeding heart liberals who had rescue dogs and sat on boards of a bunch of local non-profits. I got referred by a friend, went to their dumpy office, and brought my medical report from St. Francis.

They told me I had a good case. Connecticut had just passed a law called "An Act Concerning Discrimination," which added gender identity and expression to the list of protected classes. So, being transgender in Connecticut was now the same as being black or Asian, and it became illegal to separate, segregate, or discriminate against someone for being transgender. And Judy and Craig wanted to go bigger. They wanted to file the case in Federal Court in New Haven so we could appeal to the Federal District Court if we lost.

It was a very intersectional and interesting case, because we were pitting religious liberty against gender non-discrimination. (Many later cases addressed such issues, like a baker or a florist not serving a gay couple because it was against their religious beliefs.) We were saying it was a tort and illegal for the Catholic-run hospital to house me with men, to treat me like a man, and to note me in their charts as a man if I had already had surgical sex reassignment. My birth certificate clearly stated I was a female.

They were taking the case on contingency—meaning no upfront fees, but they take a third of the money if they win. If they lose, there are no costs. They believed in the case. I regularly went in for meetings with them for planning and for them to get additional information. They told me the media might get involved with this one and I needed to be ready. I laid in wait.

I was falling in love with Alexis. After a year, she told me to just leave Ava. "You don't want to have sex with that old lady," she said. "You want to sleep with me. We can make a life together. My parents will buy us a house. We can have a family. A nice little daughter named Erika and dress her in little preppy Vineyard Vines clothes. And a son, who hopefully would be gay and we could dress him up even cuter in little boy's clothes. Life will be really good, honey. Trust me."

But I held back. Every month she was short on cash. She slept too much, was unmotivated, worked a go-nowhere job, was lazy, couldn't cook, rarely cleaned, and clung to being preppy like it was a religion. I couldn't pull the trigger. I'd been with Ava for seven years. We lived together. She was smart, successful, skilled, motivated. Just infertile. So I did want to have a family and be a breeder and pass on my name (or Ava's) to children more than I liked the loving, caring, and compassionate older woman I was coupled with? It was pretty heavy. So I just paused.

"Honey," I said to Ava, "I'm taking a vacation."

"Susan, your whole life is vacation! What do you need to get away from?"

"I'm just stressed," I said. "I need some time and space to think, to plan my next move and next job and career path, and, well, I just need some time to myself." She understood. Alexis was not as understanding—I got the same spiel.

"Why won't you take me with you?" she asked.

"Honestly, Alexis, I just need some time alone. I'm not breaking up with you. I'm just taking five days in Vegas to play poker."

"Who goes to Vegas by themselves?"

"I have friends there if I get bored—some women I met on the poker circuit. And Brian's cousin Manny lives at Bellagio. He's a bookie and just plays 5-10 all day. He was involved in Poker Fokus. I can always talk to him."

"But why don't you want to be with me?" asked Alexis. "I'm your girlfriend."

"Honestly, Alexis, I just need some space. Give me the five days and we'll be back together as soon as I get back."

So I took my vacation. It was great. I got a room deal from the Rio, and plus I liked their rooms because they are all suites. I had also made friends with the woman who ran the spa so they let me work out and go in the hot tub for free. Being trans did have some perks—everyone remembered me everywhere I went for services, even if it were only once or twice a year. So I got to the Rio and rented a Hyundai Sonata and spent my time at the Wynn playing 1-3 and at Bellagio playing 2-5 with a $500 cap.

Then I went to the Venetian. It was during their Deepstacks Tournaments so the room was swollen. I played a 10am daily for $80. I was doing well in the tournament, but there was this one guy I couldn't read. Mostly I had trouble with reading Asians, but this guy was white, and bald, and wearing dark shades. I couldn't get a bead on this guy.

Anyway, I look down. Snowmen. Pocket eights. I raise 5x. Everyone folds but him. He had a big hand. The flop comes A-K-8. I hit my set. I was first to act, so I check my bottom set. He checks. Turn is another king. Now I don't know what to do. I have a full house, eights over kings. But if he has A-K (I put him on A-K or A-Q) then he has a full house kings over aces and he wins. I wanted to read him. I paused after the turn and just looked at him. Did he have a boat? He was stoic, the perfect poker face. I hadn't seen him make any indication at any hand, and now we were in a big one.

At the time I was wearing a beaded black tube top from White House Black Market and a white mini skirt. I had an idea. Without taking my eyes off of him, I reached into my shirt and covered my entire left breast with my right hand. Then I slid the left side of the top down for a second, and back up. He started laughing. So did the other guys at the table. They knew what I was up to. The only other female at the table looked disgusted. I said bet, and I bet the pot. He thought a second and folded. I pulled the chips toward me and started stacking them.

"You got me," he said. "I wasn't expecting that!"

"I know," I replied.

We kept playing for a while more, then took a break. Apparently at the break, the woman at the table told the floor person that I flashed someone at the table. They were in the process of reviewing the footage (there's a camera at each table). So we kept playing. All of a sudden one of the floor staff taps me on the shoulder.

"We need to talk to you," he said.

"I'm in a hand," I replied.

"No, you're not. Dealer, muck her cards. Get up."

I followed him over to the corner of the room. He told me I had flashed another person at the table and the casino had a zero tolerance policy for lewd behavior. I pled my case and explained the situation. He was in no mood to argue. Within a moment, there were two security guards next to him.

"I want to talk to your supervisor," I said.

"Fine." He made a call. This enormous man in a brown suit approached me. He had to be 6'6". Taller than me in four-inch wedges and he was barrel-chested. A very imposing man.

"I'm the floor manager. How can I help you?"

I proceeded to explain that I had not flashed anyone. I told him I had covered my entire breast with my hand. I asked him to review the tape. He said he had, and he insisted that what I had done was illegal. I pleaded with him.

"Look at your waitresses! They show more of their breasts than I did! And they work here!"

"I can either have you arrested or you can leave with these security officers. They will escort you to your vehicle. And you are trespassed from the Venetian and Palazzo forever. We have facial recognition on our security cameras. If you come back in here, we will arrest you for trespassing. Are we clear?"

I nodded and went back to my car. I was shocked. My poker buddy Dan later told me at least it was just the Venetian—that's a single property in Vegas. I could have been trespassed from all the Caesar's and Harrah's and the Rio or the Quad, or the Bellagio and Planet Hollywood and the Aria, the Cosmopolitan, and the Vdara. "Be grateful it's just the Venetian," he said. I told that story at every other tournament ever. Whenever anyone would bring up Vegas, I would tell them that I was banned for life from the Venetian. I would tell them the tale, and I entertained hundreds if not a thousand people with my escapades.

So I was feeling sort of dejected—that's not what I expected to happen—and I went back to my suite at the Rio to relax and process. After watching some Fox News in the room to decompress, I decided to go work out. So I got my gym clothes on and went to the spa, where they let me in gratis. I stole a couple granny smith apples from the massage area and had some flavored water and went to the gym to start working out on the elliptical machine.

The television in the gym was on Dr. Phil. Now, I never watch Dr. Phil. I think he's a big windbag, but on this particular show, he had a woman on whose son was in a coma for smoking something called "spice." They talked about it more. Apparently, it was called "K2" or "incense" and was inert plant matter sprayed with synthetic cannabinoids. It did not show up on drug tests, was easy to purchase, and was legal. I'd never even heard of such a thing. (Remember, I had ten and a half years of having had no mood or mind-altering substances.)

I Googled it on my phone. There was a store that sold it on the same road I was on, on the other side of the freeway, at a tobacco store. They sell it at a tobacco store, I thought. That kid in the coma was probably allergic or something. How strong could it be? They sold it at bodegas. So after my workout I drove to the tobacco store.

I went in and bought a little glass pipe I used to smoke weed out of and asked about incense. He showed me their selection—various baggies, vials, and small bottles of something that looked like marjoram with different numbers on the side that corresponded to strength. There was 5x, 10x, 20x, 25x, 50x, etc. I asked the proprietor which he sold the most of.

"The Godfather," he said, and pulled out a little film canister with a photocopied black-and-white picture of a don. "Twenty dollars."

"I'll take it," I said, and with that I went back to the car.

I put a tiny bit in the bowl and started driving east away from the highway and the Strip and toward the little strip malls. The light turned green. I took a hit. It took my breath away. Like pot, but much stronger, much faster acting, and a much faster comedown. It was like the crack of pot. I was delirious for about five minutes, driving on a three-lane road just with the flow of traffic so I didn't get any public attention. This was *not* like smoking tobacco. This was stronger and more addictive than weed.

The switch was flipped in my head. After ten-and-a-half years clean I remember thinking, I will do this drug every day until I'm at the old folks home in a rocking chair in my eighties. They say in the program that one is too many and a thousand is never enough. How true that is! I drove all over Vegas just smoking the incense—the good thing about Vegas is that you can't really get lost, because the streets are basically a grid and you can always orient yourself with the Strip.

After awhile I got hungry and stopped at a Thai restaurant for dinner. (Being an out and not passing transwoman in a strange city, I always choose Thai. In the Thai culture, the transwoman is known as a 'kathoey' and has a place in society. So I always assume that where there are Thai people, they're not going to spit in my food, and they will respect me.) I went back to the Rio and smoked myself to bed.

My sleep was interrupted and I got up around 5am. It was just getting light. It was my second-to-last day of vacation and I wanted to experience this drug the way I used to smoke weed—outside in nature. So, I took a drive up to Mount Charleston, which is a ski area, and there's a trailhead at Mary Jane Falls, which one of the locals had suggested to me.

I took the long hike up the switchbacks to the top of the hill and there was this beautiful little waterfall. I was the only one around. Because I was at an elevation it was probably seventy degrees instead of ninety. There were trees and green grass. It was temperate. I smoked the last of my Godfather. When I was done I hiked back down to my Sonata down from 7500 feet to the desert floor. Except the unexpected happened.

It was a 35-mph zone, but a steep and winding road down. I was going about fifty, I turned the corner and there were three big mule deer walking across the road. I swerved sharply, lost control, and rolled the car over so it slammed into an embankment broadside and on its roof. All the airbags deployed. I had never been in an accident like that.

I extricated myself out of the car's broken window, hyperventilating. I was literally hanging upside down by my seatbelt. I got out and just started screaming. I had never been so terrified and I had never been closer to death. It was definitely my Higher Power showing me what He could do now that I'd chosen the wrong path.

I walked down the road (my phone had no service) and luckily there was a campground about a quarter mile down the road. Some campers having coffee heard the wreck and had walked out of their camp to the road to see what happened. There was a landline emergency phone at the campsite, and someone called 911. It took a little while for the ambulance to come—this was an incredibly desolate area off Kyle Canyon Road.

I had a slight knee injury somehow and was bleeding and had just been traumatized. The ambulance scooped me and brought me to the hospital. I got checked out relatively quickly, and was discharged with a script for pain meds, which I was happy to take. I hailed a cab and took it straight to the car rental company at the airport terminal. I explained to the woman what had happened. Essentially, the car was totaled on account of animals on the roadway, I would not be returning it, I just got out of the hospital, and what did I have to do next.

She had me give a formal statement to Budget, and that was it. I took a cab back to the tobacco store, bought a couple Godfathers for me when I got home, and I left the next day on a regular flight with a big bandage on my knee.

I was not at all worried about the car. I had an American Express gold business card for my eBay business, and one of the perks of the card was that you got free collision coverage on your rental car from AMEX Assurance, a subsidiary of American Express. So, I called them and filed a claim. It wouldn't even count on my own car insurance as an accident because I was using AMEX's service. They took all my information and a report and they said I should be all set. The card was not in default, I'd always paid my bill, and I declined the rental company's coverage. As a cardmember, I was covered. And I skipped out of another problem.

I got home safely on a direct Southwest flight into Bradley Field in Windsor Locks. I drove my Saab 9-5 Aero back to Ava and my house and told her everything (except the part about the incense and the pain meds) and I pretended to still be clean. And I was clean, wasn't I? Didn't what happened in Vegas stay in Vegas? I mean, I had two little containers of incense but after that I'd be done. Just a little respite from the constant stress of two full-time relationships with two different females.

That was the net result of getting a mistress—it led me back to using. I didn't understand until I went to rehab in 2017 that the relapse happens before you pick up the drug. It happened when I got a mistress, and then the drug use was inevitable. In the same way, when the program folks say "one is too many and a thousand is never enough," such is also true. And if I thought I was going to stop after those two vials and the pain med script, I was crazy. In the program they also say that when addicts use drugs, our ends are always the same—jails, institutions, and death.

I already had ended up in an institution for the first time, and jail and death were just "yets" for me.

So I picked up with my relationship with Ava where I left off, except now I told her I was going to smoke cigars from time to time. (I needed something to cover up the disgusting smell of the incense.) She didn't really mind—most Arabic men in her family smoked and she was not averse to it. I went right back to Alexis as well. I was still her sponsor, after all, and I hid my incense use from her too. But awakening the Beast had other consequences I didn't see at first. They manifested themselves soon enough.

BOOSTING PROFESSIONALLY

Around the same time that Rugbykingpin went under, I found out that Alexis had been boosting. I sort of expected it deep down, but now I knew for a fact. She's lost her job in Dresses at Nordstrom not because of boosting (they never caught her stealing) but because twice she had accidentally walked in on women undressing in changing rooms, thinking that the rooms were empty. They were both accidental, and the first time all that happened was she got a talking to. Turns out that once she started dating me, she came out as gay at work. I never told her to do this nor did I encourage her to do it, but she had a hard time listening to me at all.

But she was tired of asking her dad for money each month. So she started stealing, well, dresses. The reason I didn't know at first was because she kept bringing me so many clothes. She told me she was purging her closet, and was driving back to Westchester to get more. I had a steady stream of high-end clothes on my eBay account. Ava didn't notice—she was thinking she was concerned that she was going to be arrested and incarcerated for some questionable financial filings she had signed.

"I can't go to jail," she'd say. "How would I get my chapstick?" I told her she was a woman and wasn't going to jail. It was just a deposition for the SEC. I told her not to worry, because she was an honest person and not a criminal. The system helps people like Ava.

Sometimes Alexis would give me something not in her size. She told me that she was going to Salvation Army or Savers and the consignment stores from time to time when she wasn't working and was finding bargains to arbitrage. She was scrappy, like me with the CDs or DVDs or books, and I encouraged that.

Turns out it was all boosted. She was stealing from Nordstrom. Then she came out as openly gay, so her boss knew and her coworkers knew. Then she walked in on those women changing and they thought deep down that she was trying to see other females undressed. She wasn't (she had me) but the second time it happened there was really no excuse. Seriously, she's just an airhead and a screw-up, not a pervert. But Nordstrom's didn't want to be sued. They canned her.

So she came clean with me. I was her lover and her best friend. She should have. She told me on breaks she would go in the backroom and just grab whatever was lying around (usually pieces bound to be in transit to another store) and just shoved them into her enormous purse. One item a day. Every day. Retail between maybe $75 and $400 every day. And I had been processing them for her. I looked at it as a bonding opportunity.

"Listen," I said. "I used to boost from Nordy's too."

"You did? How did you do it?"

"Well, I was working there when I was twenty-one and living at my parents' for a little while before I went out West again. I got a job in Men's Furnishings. At first I stole nothing, but then I saw how much returns were hitting my commission and sometimes I only made my draw. So there was this woman who left to have a baby and was on maternity leave. So who gave a damn about her returns? I got her employee number off a receipt, memorized it, and if I got a return, I just punched it in under her number and I didn't take the hit."

"That's smart," said Alexis. "Why didn't you use the code for no receipt or say it came from another store?"

"Well, I did that a few times. This woman came in from the Providence Place store with a bunch of men's shirts. When I processed the return I wrote down that clerk's number. I used that a bunch of times too but then I just felt like a scumbag. I mean, it's one thing dinging a girl on maternity leave when it doesn't affect her. It's another thing to just screw over some random clerk in Providence."

"Screw him," said Alexis. "He probably had a small dick anyway. Don't even worry about it Susan."

The other thing I did was I boosted cufflinks and money clips from the display island. I would act like I was stocking stuff, then every day bring one piece home stashing it in my pants in the backroom.

"Why didn't you just put it in your purse?" asked Alexis.

"I was a boy then, honey."

"Oh yeah. I forgot. It's so much easier to boost as a girl." Duly noted.

"Then," I said, "Sarah and I were driving across the country in the VW bus, I would visit a Nordstrom's, tell them I was on a road trip and had just graduated college. My uncle had given me these cufflinks as a graduation present but I didn't wear those kinds of shirts. And they would give me cash. Two hundred, three hundred, four hundred dollars."

"Wow, you crushed Nordstrom. What happened there, you left to go cross-country?"

"No, I got fired in April before we were leaving. My boss did an internal audit because the department wasn't making enough money but our sales were on target. He figured out what I was doing. I got confronted with the evidence, and you know the bro code—deny 'til you die— but they fired me anyway. Good thing I'd already grabbed two or three thousand in cufflinks! That made the summer much better!"

"You are one crazy bitch, Susan. I didn't know you did all that."

"Well, Alexis, I was using. When we use we lose our moral compass."

"I agree," she said. "Listen. Susan. I have to confess to you. I've not been clean. I've been buying klonopin and tramadol from my friend Vanessa and I've been getting high. I'm sorry. Do you want to break up with me? I know you're clean."

What was this? Guilt was all around me. Even though she was my mistress, I wanted some semblance of honesty between us.

"Alexis, I need to be honest with you too. I've been smoking incense."

"What do you mean, incense? Like sandalwood?"

"No. Like Spice. K2. Fake pot."

"Susan!" she looked shocked. Then her face changed. "Do you have any?"

I looked at her. I guess we were going there.

"It's in my car."

"Well, share it bitch!" she said.

"Okay."

I went down to the Mercedes and got out my hidden pouch. I brought out a glass pipe and some incense.

"Where do you get this stuff?" she asked.

"I get it at Lifestyles in Waterbury."

"What is 'Lifestyles'?"

"It's a head shop."

"Are they open now?" she asked.

"Yeah, 'til nine or ten, I think."

"Then let's go, bitch. We'll smoke in the car."

And so it started. Now I had a partner who didn't know I had a mistress and she also didn't know I was getting high, and now I was getting high with the mistress. Ack! I brought Alexis to Lifestyles. They had a paper list of different names of different incense (they had Bizarro and Mad Hatter and AK-47 and Crazy Monkey and Black Lion and Diablo and Lights Out) and prices and sizes of pouches. Nothing was on display. If you asked for incense, they'd hand you the price sheet, you would say what you wanted, they filled the order, and you could even use a credit card to buy your drugs.

That was another problem I was having—debt. I had just sold Alexis my Saab 9-5 Aero and I upgraded to an older Mercedes E-Class. I paid cash. But cash was getting more and more scarce. I was smoking a ton of incense. Also, I was buying klonopin and xanax and perc 30's. My addiction was full-blown. Not to mention the cough medicine which was also doing again. I went from one hit of K2 to full-blown addiction, and it happened amazingly quickly.

So I made a decision. I wasn't going to pay any of my credit cards. I mean what were they going to do? They couldn't eat me! (Brian had always said that about debt. I was cursing the day I met him and me squandering 100k.) So I maxed all of them out with cash advances and purchases. I opened store cards at Express and Victoria's Secret and J. Crew and Ann Taylor. I bought gift cards with all my credit and maxed them out, then sold the GCs on eBay. Then I just stopped sending in my payments. At first they were nice, calling and saying, "It appears you have overlooked a payment." Then they got nastier and nastier. But for now, with a Mercedes that was paid for and a pile of cash in my safe, I assed out on 25k in consumer debt. I wouldn't see the effects of that for many months.

Around this time I got a letter from AMEX Assurance Company. I'd forgotten about the Hyundai I totaled. They, apparently, had not. They denied my claim. I called the customer service number. She broke it down for me. They couldn't prove I was operating the vehicle or if someone else were, and if someone else were, this act would have voided my coverage.

"I was the driver. I had no passenger," I said. "Check the report of the ambulance company."

"We did, Miss Sturbridge, but you never spoke to the police."

"I never saw any police!" I said. "The ambulance took me away before the police got there."

"Yes, we know that. And the responding officer tried to locate you in the hospital but you had already been discharged."

"How, exactly, is that my fault?" I asked. "Why didn't the cop tell the hospital to hold me until he came?"

"Well, we're denying the claim."

"Can I get a copy of the police report?"

"Yes, we'll mail it to you."

They did. The report identified the driver as "Operator One" and not as Susan Sturbridge. I called the Nevada State Police and explained the situation. They told me I had to make incident report changes to my local State Police barracks. They could add a sworn statement and the report would then be changed. I went to the Troop in Hartford and made a statement that I swore to in front of the officer. I stated I was operating the motor vehicle and there was no passenger or second operator. I also said I hadn't violated any terms of the rental contract. I mailed it to the Nevada State Police and faxed it to AMEX Assurance. They would review the new information and get back to me in sixty days. Shocker.

So Alexis got a job at Joseph A. Bank, the men's clothing store that's always advertising "Buy one, get two suits free." It turned out her boss at Nordstrom before her and had gotten a promotion to district manager at Jos. A. Bank. She told Alexis that if she ever needed a job to let her know. Plus, Alexis was in touch with her buying klonopin, tramadol, and finally, suboxone. This is around the time I directly got involved with the boosting.

"I can't steal from there," said Alexis after passing a bowl of K2. "There are cameras everywhere and the clothes are too big to fit in my purse. But if you can come in, a second person, we could take so much."

"What would the second person do?" I asked.

"Well, I would put together like four or five suits from the basement stockroom and put them on the pole as if they were a prepaid phone pickup order. You would walk in, pretend you already paid for them, and walk out. Then, you leave, go to another store, return the merch, get a gift card, and split it with me. What do you think?"

"I say I'm afraid of going to jail. Alexis, if I get caught stealing, I go to men's jail. Not women's jail. And I have 38D tits. I would be raped and sodomized and probably killed. It's literally a death sentence for me. But I'll tell you what I will do."

"What's that?" asked Alexis.

"Are you willing to split three ways?" She thought about it.

"Could we do it more than once?" she asked.

"Yeah."

"Okay, what's the plan, Stan?"

"Well you know Heather from Super Pawn?"

"The one with the huge rack?"

"No, Alexis, that's the other one, but Heather has nice tits. Anyway, she's a pothead. If I tell her I'll pick her up and she'll make $100 for an hour's work, she'll do it. So, you get $1200 in merch. She'll pick it up and bring it back and get a $400 gift card, then I'll sell it on eBay and net $300. A hundred for me. A hundred for Heather. A hundred for you. Even Steven. What do you say?"

"Call the bitch."

We did that five or six times, actually. Heather was working at Dunkin Donuts at the time and was very happy to make an extra c-note. Addiction is definitely a progressive disease. At first I didn't want my hands dirty at all. I would orchestrate, set up the deal, process the fencing of the gift cards and handle the money, but no hands-on boosting. It was only a matter of time before that changed.

Every time I take suboxone, I vomit. I guess that's a good thing because it means I'm not an opiate addict. The first time I took suboxone I was driving my old 1999 F-150 to Bronxville to move some items for Lauren. It was green, and it had a rack and a box. I bought it for $2000 from a firefighter in Watertown. It had a little hiccup in the transmission when I bought it but it ran for another 12,000 miles before the tranny went. I sold it for salvage on eBay when it broke down and got $671 for a truck with a busted tranny that you couldn't move without a winch. I had put a big iron cross decal on the back window.

So I was driving the old Ford to Westchester and I ate a half a suboxone strip. I got to the Danbury mall (Alexis wanted to boost from L.L. Bean, which was easy because of a fairly liberal return policy and no security tags on items under $100.) That was one of the stores where the magnet worked. Oh yeah, I had bought Alexis an *implement*. It was a specially-designed magnet that took off security tags. But only at Nordstrom, L.L. Bean, Anthropologie, and Victoria's Secret. Vickies was the easiest to boost from with the magnet, but they had a cap on how many items you could return without a receipt. So you would get to this certain point and then you would get this weird receipt that would say you could return this time but future returns would be denied for ninety days. It meant that you were hitting it too hard.

The magnet was about the size of half a baseball and fit in your palm. It had a small notch cut in the top of it. You would put the nub of the security tag in the notch and the whole thing would release and come apart. I always told Alexis that there would be enhanced penalties for getting caught with the "device" (as we called it) and she never did.

Anyway, she had the magnet and wanted to stop at L.L. Bean (there was one in Danbury and one at Evergreen Walk in South Windsor). So she told me taking the suboxone would get me high. She got it from her boss who used to sell half of her suboxone strips to a prison guard who would sell them to the inmates. A tricky business if you ask me, since all the strips came in packaging with barcodes and someone could track the barcodes if your drugs were diverted. And who was going to buy a suboxone strip that came in a dime bag? Nobody except an inmate. So I never got involved, but I figured it would be a good way to make an extra few hundred a month by selling the suboxone, but I never had the balls to go to a doctor and run that kind of scam. I needed a dirty doctor and didn't have one.

Regardless, the first time I took it we went to Danbury from Bristol. I stopped the truck and just vomited all over the parking lot. And the problem was I just couldn't keep liquids down. So I drank a Gatorade so as not to become dehydrated (it was in the middle of summer and very hot) and then I would throw that up too. It happened a second time as well.

So, Alexis went to L.L. Bean and did her business, grabbing me a dress as a gift which was very nice. She got her gift card and was happy, and I drove her to Westchester, where we proceeded to hit Lilly Pulitzer and C. Wonder, which is a defunct brand run by Tory Burch's ex-husband. I loved their stuff and was very sad to see them go out of business. And of course, Nordstrom. Nordstrom was great because they would give you cash without a receipt. But you had to be careful there. They had cameras everywhere and obedient and attentive staff. But it was still the same m.o.—grab an armful of clothes, walk across the store to a different department's dressing room. That girl helps you because she wants the commission. And you have to have your boosting bag.

My favorite was Brooks Brothers. The store has a good reputation. Good reliable bag that could take a beating. So you go to Brooks Brothers and say you need a gift for your girlfriend or boyfriend. You buy the item (which you are going to return) and then you ask them to wrap up the item in a gift box. They have excellent gift boxes that have an elastic that goes around them and keeps them closed. Then you leave the store, take the item out of the box, and put it in the trunk. Then you have an empty gift box in a navy blue bag that looks like you went shopping at Brooks Brothers and bought a gift.

Once inside and the box is emptied, you have something that will hold two dresses or four blouses and be held closed with the elastic band. It's the perfect crime. And with the magnet it's even better, because these stores are used to people setting off the alarm if they try to steal. So if you can deactivate the alarm, you are ahead of the game. There are no cameras in the dressing rooms, so you just need to make sure that the clerk has not counted what you have. As long as that is okay, the merch is up for grabs.

Vineyard Vines definitely had the best return policy—God bless Shep and Ian. They didn't even ask for an ID with a return, so you could tell them any name you wanted and there was no way to track the returns. Nordstrom is the next best because they give cash, but they also try to search the transaction on the computer. You must do a very specific thing—you need to know the name and zip code of someone who shops a lot at Nordstrom. Then, when you are returning something, you just say it was a gift from that person. The clerk pulls up the history, and they will see many transactions but not the one you fabricated. This lends more credence to your story, instead of just saying Jane Doe bought it for me and they look and there's no such name in the system.

This is what experienced boosters do. You need the name of anyone in the system, and then you will be more successful. The same goes for Tory Burch and Tommy Bahama, but they pay you with a merchandise credit. But those credits go for good money on the secondary market. Our other favorite store was Lilly Pulitzer, which is owned by the Oxford Group, same owner as Tommy Bahama. They had a very lax policy.

Alexis used to always wear Lilly, and I had never even known what it was until I met her. I found out later that Lilly Pulitzer (the woman) was prone to spilling her food and drinks on herself when she ate and drank and so she wanted to design clothes that you could spill stuff on and not see. Ergo we have these very bright and busy prints that are Lilly's signature pieces. Toward the end we were boosting from Lilly. There was a store on Greenwich Avenue in Greenwich and one at the Westchester Mall and a couple in Jersey.

But we hit them all. Lilly Pulitzer, Tommy Bahama, Vineyard Vines, Nordstrom, Tory Burch, Anthropologie, Athleta, J. Crew, everyone. It was getting to be a full-time job. And other things in my life were beginning to unravel.

SEX ADDICTION

AMEX Assurance had denied my claim again. It's difficult to think about insurance companies intentionally trying to engage in tortious conduct and malfeasance and denying claims they should pay. Don't get me wrong—it was not a small claim. I had totalled a brand new Hyundai. With towing charges, rental charges, loss of use for the company, etc., the bill was a hefty 24k.

I started getting letters directly from the lawyer at Budget Rent-a-Car looking for money. His name was Edward Letourneau and I spoke with him on the phone. I explained how I was not working right now (the tutoring company had changed their business model and wanted only full-time tutors) and I had no money. I explained the situation with AMEX. I told him to go after them. They had already tried that but AMEX was stonewalling.

"We're going to sue you," he said.

"Well go ahead and get a judgment. There's nothing to attach," I said. "So go ahead." And I hung up.

Not a week later a marshal served me with a writ and summons to appear in Nevada. *Malco Enterprises dba Budget-Rent-a-Car vs. Sturbridge*. In Nevada, you didn't write a written answer—you had to appear at a certain time and place. And I'm sure I'd have to appear more than once. Even a Gotta-Get-Away cheap flight from Southwest was $226 one-way to Vegas. I couldn't just move there and I couldn't afford to go back and forth. So I did what any other good criminal would do. I basically ignored the lawsuit.

While this was happening, I called my attorney Craig. There had been no action on my St. Francis case yet. I told him I had a new tort that I needed him to represent me on, but it would not be a contingency situation. In lieu of a retainer, would he allow me to volunteer at the law firm one day a week ad infinitum to pay for his representation? He talked it over with his wife Judy and they agreed. Henceforth, I became a volunteer for the Fleeman Law Offices and began to learn the paralegal trade.

The firm did personal injury, medical malpractice, social security and disability, wrongful death, and criminal cases. They had two attorneys, three paralegals, and me. I started driving to Middletown once a week. I began by just going through all the scanned documents, figuring out what to name them, what case they belonged to, and moving them to the correct folder. This was bitch work—the most tedious job at the firm—but just being there and looking at documents I learned a lot.

With respect to my Nevada case, Craig tried to represent me and sent a letter of representation to Edward Letourneau. What they got was a big, fat, no thanks. He said Craig was not licensed to practice in Nevada, and to represent me in the case was illegal. He backed off fast.

"So what's the game plan?" I asked.

"Let them sue you and let them get a judgment. That 24k judgment will go on your credit report. Sorry. But it's only enforceable in Nevada."

"What does that mean? They can't get the money?"

"No, because you're out-of-state. So they can attach your assets in Nevada. But you don't have any. So they would have to do what's called 'domesticating the judgment' which will mean hiring a lawyer on contingency in Connecticut to come after you here. But the second they do that they'll only get two-thirds. 16k. I don't think they'll take that kind of hit. So it's a stalemate. They'll wait for you to start earning money and when you want to buy a house and can't because of the judgment, they'll get paid. They're playing the long game."

"So essentially," I said, "If I don't care that my credit is destroyed, this will just be on my record indefinitely but they can't collect it?" I was thinking if we needed a house, Ava would just buy it (or, I guess, Alexis's dad) and I could pay cash. So it was an empty threat.

"Exactly," said Craig. "In fact, let it play out. It could turn out that we could sue AMEX Assurance under CUIPA [Connecticut Unfair Insurance Practices Act] and get treble damages. If that happened, you would get a judgment for 24k against you, then you would sue AMEX and get twenty-four times three, uh, 72k. I keep 24k, 24k goes to Budget, and 24k goes to you."

"Let's do it!" I said. This guy knew how to boost and sue.

"Let it play out," he said. "Just keep working here for now. You're an asset to the office."

So now I had a couple more things going on. Maybe earning 24k for crashing a car, and waiting on about 60k for being housed with men for eleven days at the hospital. The future was looking good.

So I needed to open another eBay account and another Paypal account. The way the tax laws worked, Paypal would send what's called a 1099-K to you that showed your yearly sales figure so that the IRS could keep track of eBay sellers. So when I had Rugbykingpin, my 1099-K would say 100k in sales or 200k in sales or whatever. That goes on your Schedule C and allows you to calculate your income tax.

If you sold under 20k a year, you didn't get a 1099-K. The money was tax-free, as if you had had a tag sale. I was up to 17k for the year on my eBay account and Paypal account and I had a stack of gift cards and I did not want to pay tax. So, like any good criminal, I cheated.

I went to the town of Farmington and filed for a trade name certificate. The name of the business was called "Candace Claymore." Under description I wrote "online sales." I knew the town clerk (she had been in a book club with me when I was at Trinity) and she just rubber-stamped it no problem, no questions asked, and I paid the five dollars, got a couple mints, chit-chatted with the ladies at town hall, and left.

I called Berkshire Bank, a small local bank. I told them I needed to open a small business account and had some questions. They transferred me to a woman named Priscilla in Plainville. We went over everything and she told me to come in and open the account. I drove to Plainville, the next town over, and walked into the branch.

You know the feeling of being in a thunderstorm and it's going to lightning and all the air is just charged with electricity? That's what happened when I saw Priscilla. We both just checked each other out for a couple of seconds, and then a huge smile.

"Would you like a coffee?" she stammered.

"Yes," I said, not taking my eyes off of her and walking over to the Keurig.

"No, I'll make it for you," she said, locking eyes with me and walked over. We reached the machine at the same time and our bodies touched. Lightning.

She stood *right* next to me. "I like your dress," she said.

"Oh, it's Tory Burch," I replied. "I got it at Nordstrom." What I should have said was that I boosted it from Nordstrom.

"I have to be honest," Priscilla said, "When you said your name was Susan I was confused because you sounded like a man. I didn't know what you were going to look like. But you're beautiful."

I stared at her face. "I like your eyes." She blushed.

"Come in my office." She was the branch manager.

I couldn't remember having this kind of chemistry with someone since Svetlana in college. My whole body was tingling and my pulse was up. I felt like I had just done a line of coke. My stomach was full of butterflies, and it wasn't going away. She was making love to me with her eyes.

"So what kind of account do you need?" she asked.

"Just the basic small business checking. Honestly, I just need a debit card that says 'Candace Claymore."

"Why?" she asked.

"Oh, that's my stripper name," I said, arching my back and displaying my rack. "Just kidding, I'm not a pro. But I am a poker player."

"Oh, that's great! So why the account?"

"Honestly, Priscilla, people have gotten to know me under my old poker avatar Rugbyingpin and I just need a new online alias."

"Rugbykingpin. Did you play rugby?"

"Played and coached. I used to love teaching women how to hit other women."

"I wouldn't know how to hit another woman," she said.

"I could show you how to properly make contact," I said.

Her hands and arms were so feminine. She was about 5'7", brunette, B-cup, thin, Italian-looking, bright eyes, gorgeous legs, just a ten. She smiled and looked down.

"I'm sorry," I said. "I didn't mean to offend you."

"You're not. I've been offending you," she said. "I haven't stopped staring at your chest. When did you get those done?"

"Six years ago. 420cc under the muscle."

"I want to get mine done," she said.

"You don't need it," I responded.

"No, this is all padding," she said. "Fancy Vickie's bra. I have no chest. I really do want to get them done."

"But it would take away from your beautiful face. With a face like yours you don't need big tits." She smiled warmly.

"Okay. Let's get this account done. Some questions." With that, we did all the paperwork and made the account. Within a half an hour I had a new debit card that said "Candace Claymore" on it. We were ready to part ways. She grabbed me one of her business cards. "If you have any questions or if you need anything, just reach me on my cell. I hope you come in here again." With that we got up and hugged each other goodbye. I told her I'd be back soon.

It was right around Christmastime. As I did every Christmas, I made a batch of citrons (candied citrus peel) with a bag of grapefruit, a bag of oranges, and a bag of lemons. I was precise—I stripped away the pith and boiled down the skins and candied them and dried them all over the dining room and sprinkled them with sugar. It was always very meditative. I would always bring my little laptop downstairs and just watch Netflix while I completed the mind-numbing work. I can't remember if I were watching *Breaking Bad* or *Sons of Anarchy*. But I made the citrons for the old Italians in my family on my mother's side and I made a bag for Priscilla.

I went down again, two days after I'd been there and walked into her office. She was alone. She saw me and jumped up to hug me.

"Susan!" she said happily.

"Merry Christmas!" I said and handed her a bag of citrons with a bow.

"Citrons?" she said. The fact that she knew what they were made me very happy. Undoubtedly Italian. "You made these?" she asked.

"For you," I replied.

She smiled and touched my arm. "I have something for you," she said and handed me a gift. I opened it at home, but it was a nice travel mug from Dunkin Donuts filled with a bag of Dunkin coffee. Very sweet. I sat down and we talked. She was divorced, a gym rat, a runner. She loved to ski and snowboard. She lived in Torrington (kind of far). She had a dog, used to drive a Cadillac ATS and now drove a Chevy SUV.

"I would've creamed my panties if I saw you pull up in an ATS," I said. She blushed. I told her I had an E-class and a green Ford F-150 (the purple one had gotten in an accident some time ago). Then she asked me about my living situation. I lied.

"I live in a condo in Farmington that I rent from a lesbian woman that lives there. She's my roommate." I figured Priscilla could see that I had a joint bank account with Ava so I had to say something. I lied again. "We actually have a joint bank account so I can pay her electronically for all the bills."

"Smart," she said.

"So, I'd love to, like, go to the gym with you or something sometime. Like, we could work out together," I said.

"Yeah," she said. "Since I got divorced I run in the morning and I go to the gym after work. So sure, we can work out. Or, we could just get dinner."

"Yeah," I replied. "I think dinner sounds great."

"I am taking a long weekend to go skiing in Vermont with some girlfriends this weekend, but let's go next week. How about Thursday? I get out at six in a meeting with the West Hartford branch."

"Okay. Can I take you to the sushi buffet in West Hartford?"

"I've never been," she said. "Sure."

You can learn a lot about someone by watching them eat, especially when they can choose from many options. Also, it's good to see how she handles chopsticks and how she eats her sushi and sashimi.

"Text me over the weekend," she said. "I'll be waiting to hear from you." We hugged goodbye again, this time for a longer embrace, and with that, I had a date.

I dare not tell my partner or my mistress. And wasn't this crazy after all? I already had Ava. For almost a decade. Ava who loved me and was devoted to me. We had gone to Montreal and Miami Beach and NYC. We had flown to LA and Beverly Hills for Svetlana's wedding. (I was in the bridal party as a bridesmaid. I loved how Svetlana considered me an ex-girlfriend, and included me in her life even though I only saw her once or twice a year.) We lived together. Made a life together. Cooked and cleaned and slept in the big puffy white bed together. My Princess. My Pepper. My Auntie. My love.

Then there was Alexis. She was an idiot who slept too much and couldn't pay her bills, but we had chemistry. Our sex was astounding—she was the absolute perfect match for me in bed. Sex was never the strong point with Ava, but that was not important to me. Sex, in essence, is a very small part of the day, and we'd all heard of lesbian bed death when two women in a long-term relationship are bonded more emotionally and the act of intercourse becomes less important. So I had Alexis for sex. What was I doing with Priscilla?

I came to realize what it was. Now that I was a woman and could feel feelings, I got addicted to the rush of endorphins and phenyl ethyl amine that accompanies having a crush on someone. As a man I barely felt that, but with eight milligrams a day of estrogen and four hundred milligrams a day of progesterone, the feeling was overwhelming, like an earthquake or a pent-up sneeze. I wanted that "first date feeling" and all the joy that accompanied it.

Priscilla and I did text over that weekend. I asked her if she thought I was cute, She said, "OMG you are the cutest." Some of the texting got a little more explicit. I changed her name in my phone so Ava wouldn't find them. I cherished those first texts.

Also, I would have swapped out Priscilla for Alexis any day. I mean, a little older and divorced, but a successful, enterprising career woman like Ava who worked out and could support herself. Hell, I'd buy her a set of tits if she wanted them! But I didn't know about her sexuality. We'd have to have our dinner.

She was late getting out of her meeting and was apologetic. I told Alexis that Ava wanted me home and I told Ava I was seeing a girlfriend in the program for dinner. We each drove our own cars to the sushi buffet, and walking in with Priscilla I felt like a million bucks.

"Oh, hello!" said the hostess. "So nice to see you again!" People remembered me everywhere I went. I guess there were just not a lot of 6' tall 38D scantily dressed transwomen in our area.

Over the course of the three-hour date--they had to kick us out--I learned what I needed to know. Priscilla had never been with a woman, but she wanted to try it. (She was essentially "bi-curious.") She liked that I was a transwoman because it would be a "safe" first experience with a woman with some familiarity to the experience. She was instantly drawn to my warmth, my smile, my grace, and my body. This was going to be a great experience, I could tell.

We passionately kissed goodnight and went our separate ways. I couldn't stop thinking about her. I had a crush. Apparently she couldn't stop thinking about me--the next day she texted me to say that. I felt warm blood rush to my face and breasts. I had lied to Ava about going on a date with Priscilla, but not about meeting her. I mean, she wanted to know where I got the Christmas present from. I just told her that the Plainville branch manager at Berkshire Bank had given it to me, and we had a new contact if we had any banking issues.

We had our second date the next week. I had stopped down a couple of times to talk to her--the tellers and the other employees there knew that something was up--and she asked me to get lunch with her Friday since she was seeing her family all weekend. We went to an Italian bakery in town and had a lovely meal. She introduced me to her friends that ran the bakery. I totally knew what she was doing. I understood. I was a transwoman. Would this be acceptable to old friends, who were used to seeing her only with men?

I never got to find out. Over the weekend, Ava said to me, "I have to talk to your friend Priscilla. At the bank. I'm going to open this new money market account and I'm going to put all the Paypal money into it. They are offering a better rate to new customers, and I'm an old customer, but maybe your friend can override it for me. You want to come with me?" Now *that*, I did not want to do.

"Why don't you just go to the Farmington branch. It's closer." She looked surprised.

"Honey, you know business is all about relationships. Let's use yours and she can meet your partner. It'll be fun. I can't go Monday because I have meetings but I'll go Tuesday. Let me know if you can make it."

I had to tell on myself. I went down Monday and she was in a meeting. I waited for about a half an hour, drinking coffee after coffee. She was finally available.

"Hi, Susan!" She hugged me in the branch in front of her coworkers instead of in her office, and she squeezed me tight.

It pained me to tell her, but I explained how I lied to her when i first met her and my "roommate" was really my "lover" and we'd been together for over a decade. Then I fessed up and told her I had a mistress for three years and I was torn between the two women and didn't know what to do. Then I'd met her and my world got turned upside-down, and I thought that maybe I could just somehow maneuver out of both of those relationships because if it worked out, she had everything I wanted in a partner.

She wasn't pleased. She didn't pull away, but she was more cautious. Then that was depressing because I realized she wanted me just for the sexual experience and not as a partner. So, a splash of cold water and a dose of reality, and all because Ava was going to come into the bank. I also came clean with Alexis. It felt good to confess. She was furious.

"What the hell, Susan! I'm not enough for you?! I do whatever you want all the time!" she fumed.

"It's not like that," I said. "I just want that first date feeling."

"What does this bitch look like?" asked Alexis. I showed her Priscilla's Facebook picture. "Oh, she is hot! I'd sleep with her. From now on I forbid you to see her without me. Do you understand? Or we're through."

"Got it," I said. A bird in the hand.

So soon enough we were making another trip to the Wrentham Outlets. We were all decked out in our finest dresses and leggings and boots, and Alexis said we should stop in the bank on the way.

"Just go in and get some cash so you can pay me for the gift cards. And introduce me to Priscilla." So I did. After that last meeting, I had gone to other branches and was avoiding Priscilla. I just didn't know what to say anymore. She welcomed me with a big hug into her office.

"This is Alexis," I said, "My girlfriend I told you about."

They shook hands. Wow, my mistress meeting the woman I'd just dated. Crazy. Alexis told her we were going to the outlet malls to do a little shopping at Tory Burch and Kate Spade. They had a conversation about clothes and sales and then we went on our way.

"She's beautiful," said Alexis. "Let's get the three of us together."

"For sex?" I asked incredulously.

"Yeah," said Alexis. She was always talking about this sort of thing. We'd done it before with men, but not with a woman.

"How do you suppose I broach that subject with her?" I asked.

"Figure it out Susan. Just ask her. She likes you. Just see what she says."

I had to think about that one. We got our boosting done. We ended up shopping at Victoria's Secret and Alexis was cursing the security tags, but she had her magnet. We ended up clearing $1800 for the day and had a nice shrimp and sirloin dinner at Outback.

In hindsight, I see that when I got the magnet for Alexis that was the end of our boosting. We had already used up Nordstrom. We hit Athleta and Vineyard Vines and Tory Burch and Henri Bendel and Talbots and Brooks Brothers and Coach and Michael Kors. We were running out of road.

After Alexis started using the magnet, I realized that this wasn't boosting--it was larceny. And if they could have caught one of us with that tool, it was an enhanced penalty. I just didn't want to do the time. The magnet scared me. But Alexis loved it. The first day she brought me two Anthropologie gift cards, two $600 dresses from Nordstrom, and a pile of $50 push-up bras from Victoria's Secret.

"The magnet changes everything," Alexis said. "Now I can boost a thousand-dollar dress from Special Occasion and a twelve-hundred dollar blazer from St. John. And I don't even need to sell to you--I can go right to the consignment store or the bridal store and get cash."

I didn't realize she resented having a monopoly or monopsony situation. I went back to Priscilla and gave her a pitch. She was lukewarm.

"Honestly, Susan, I'm not gay. I just find you attractive. I can't sleep with your friend. But you can still call me if you want."

Not the answer I was hoping for. I broke the news to Alexis.

"Screw that bitch anyway, she's ethnic looking. C'mon. Let's smoke a bowl." And we did.

This was not the first time I'd stepped out on Ava (or I guess in this case, Ava and Alexis). Four years into our relationship I got introduced to this transwoman Deirdre. She worked at Barnes Group in Bristol and had transitioned on the job. She had everything done-- facial feminization surgery, breast augmentation, and vaginoplasty. We bonded over being trans and talked a lot.

About a year later I was at her house for a party Thanksgiving weekend on Friday. There were a bunch of gender-nonconforming people there. As the night wore on, people got a little tipsy (I didn't--I was clean at the time) and one by one they went home. It was just Deirdre and I on the couch. She kissed me first.

We were like animals until we got our clothes off. Honestly, I'd never seen a fake vagina before and I was interested. Deirdre was a lesbian and had gotten her surgery done two years ago--it was her first go-round. And then it happened. My organ didn't fit. No matter what we did. I came to the realization that this was not a typical vagina, that is, moist and stretchy. It was something wholly different. She got more and more upset. Finally, I just used the tradesman's entrance and we finished the deed.

She was crying afterward. She didn't understand. She did everything they said to do after her surgery. She used the inserts to help her new vagina open and make it as wide as it was supposed to. It just wasn't wide enough. She was distraught. I reminded her that she liked females and that most females didn't have penises and I was an anomaly. That did make her smile. We never had sex again, but we remained friends. And I learned from that point on I would never have bottom surgery. It was a good lesson to learn.

Then I got my tits done and the floodgates opened. What seems like such an innocuous change makes such an enormous difference. First of all, straight and bisexual men were now attracted to me and bisexual women were also attracted to me. I was anomalous, different, bold. Tony was the first one to reach out to me. I was at the auto parts store in West Hartford buying an air filter. After I rang out and walked to my car, a man followed me out and stopped me.

"I'm sorry, Miss. I never do this but I just saw you and I think you are the most beautiful woman I've ever seen. Please text me." And he gave me his number.

I liked his approach. Direct. Honest. He was attractive, too. Latino, well-built, short, dark hair, cute face, muscular. I did text him, and a short time later I was at his apartment giving my tits their first test-drive. I ended up sleeping with him, and besides his impressive manhood, I also liked that he ignored my genitals. He treated me as close to being a natal female as possible. And that's how I like to be treated. There was nothing gay about Tony--he was all man, and once I got a taste and I liked it.

I was getting hit on all the time by women too. My sponsor, Elizabeth, was an ex-bodybuilder who now worked third shift at a printing company running the big presses at night that made glossy ads. She had been my sponsor for a few years now, and I really liked our relationship. She was affable and very available. One night she threw a big women's party at her condo and had a bunch of women in recovery over.

That's when I met Ann. We had instant chemistry, and went to talk in the basement of Elizabeth's condo where she still had her own tanning bed from her competition days. The next thing we knew, both of our shirts were off and we were comparing our girls. Elizabeth came downstairs.

"What the hell is going on down here?" she asked. "Geez. I just wanted to let you know that there's cake. Put your clothes back on."

I did all this while Ava was upstairs socializing with some of our other friends. Ann made me promise I'd call her, and I took her number.

I called her the next day, and she invited me over. She lived in a ranch house in Wallingford, renting the basement from her landlady. She definitely had mental health issues--was bipolar, but was not treating her disease like I was. But I was drawn to her because she reminded me of me when I was not medicated. We ended up sleeping together, and the sex was just excellent. I guess I had come to fully realize that sex with the other man or other woman is always better than with the partner you see every day. It's clandestine. Naughty. Illicit.

I began visiting her more often. On our fourth visit, we had just consummated and then she pulled out a bowl and started packing it with some weed.

"What are you doing?" I asked. "I thought you were in recovery. You go to program for Christ's sake!"

"Yeah, I started smoking two years ago. But I like the meetings and I keep going. The weed is just to help with my mania--it calms me down." She passed the bowl to me. I sat staring at it. I had years clean at the time and the temptation was very strong. Then I thought about what my first sponsor had told me--no matter how good your network is, at some point you will be face to face with temptation and you won't be able to call anyone. And at that point, it's just your Higher Power keeping you from using. I passed it back to her.

"I have to go," I said, struggling to find my clothes that were strewn all over the floor. I ran out of there. It was 10:45pm. I needed to call someone, anyone, but unless I called California I'd be waking someone up. I called the only person I knew I could--Elizabeth, my sponsor--and told her what happened. I don't know if she were more mad at the fact that I'd cheated on Ava, that I had slept with her best friend, or that her best friend had been lying to her for years about being clean. She was pissed. A day later she fired me as a sponsee. I was heartbroken, but I didn't stop the behavior.

Even before I found Alexis I was hooking up with men. All these trips to Atlantic City, I put myself on a transgender dating site and apprised men of my travel plans. There were two guys I used to hook up with in AC that lived in the area, and then when I would come down (later with Alexis, who would join in as well) I would give them some company. Dressing slutty was empowering to me. I would be dressed super sexy late at night at the casino by myself. What did I think was going to happen? I'm sure I had a reputation at Mohegan but I didn't care. That was my home base.

There's something very empowering to me to sleep with a straight or bisexual man. It validates me as a woman when a man treats me as a woman. When I sleep with a female, there's something about me anatomically that still makes me feel like a man. So I prefer sex with men but I prefer to couple with women.

And that's how my life went--a complete sex addict, sleeping with a partner and a mistress and as many men as I could find. But being on this path made me feel empty. Like a sinner. Atrocious. I just wanted fidelity with Ava. Unfortunately, that wouldn't come until later.

By this time it was 2015. The Fleeman Law Firm had offered me a full-time gig as a paralegal and I took it. After volunteering for two years doing bitch work I had a full-time job and a title. I was working in Middletown, commuting from Farmington, and I was just about to give up boosting. In fact, two things happened that made me stop.

The first thing is that we went to Kate Spade at the Wrentham Outlets with our Brooks Brothers boosting bags. I had always told Alexis I didn't like using them there, because they had a Brooks Brothers outlet, and they used different bags. She said no one would notice that. Well, a sharp clerk did, or she'd been watching us for some time.

We walked into the Kate Spade Outlet with our empty bags and the clerk at the front politely said, "Oh, let me take those for you, ladies."

Alexis said no thank you, but the clerk persisted.

"I'll take those and put them behind the counter."

She took our empty bags, clearly feeling that they were empty, and stared at us. The jig was up. We pretended to shop for a little bit, then took our bags and quickly left. That's the thing about preppy high-end stores--even if they catch you they are nice about it.

The second thing that happened was that I got a letter from the loss prevention department at Tommy Bahama, saying that due to my pattern of non-receipted returns, I was not allowed to return anything without a receipt. Furthermore, it implied that I was a criminal, and was very insulting. At least they had some sort of loss prevention. Those two things happened within a week of each other.

So I stopped boosting. Though I was addicted to the rush and the easy money I decided to end it. I had never been caught (besides the Kate Spade incident and the Tommy Bahama letter) or charged with a crime. I got off *very* lucky. I should have been in prison for a long time. Though I credit myself with being highly skilled and hitting low-risk and low-security targets, I'd still managed to boost about 30k worth of merch. I could live with that. Retire at the top. Go out on a high note. So I devoted myself to being a paralegal. Then something crazy happened.

So money was tight with the mistress and all, so I looked to my life insurance policy. Once Ava started living with me (knowing I was an addict) she made me get a life insurance policy for 100k in case I went out and used and died. It's a ghastly thought, but reality. So, I paid thirty-two dollars a month and had this whole life policy where I invested the money like having a brokerage account.

So when I needed a little extra money, I called Lincoln Benefit Life. The customer service rep said as of that day, the maximum I could withdraw was $584.00. I had a paper withdrawal form that I had to fax in. One of the fields I could choose was just "withdraw maximum" as an option, and I checked that. Anyway, I went into the bank the next day, and it turned out I had $5584.00 deposited into my account.

I did not act surprised. Calmly, I withdrew the whole amount and was just counting c-notes. Clearly, it was a clerical error. Someone had typed a number in twice. They caught it the next day and attempted to withdraw the full amount that Friday and there was insufficient funds. They tried again on Monday. Same result. Now my account had two overdraft charges. I went to the branch manager (this was at the credit union, not Priscilla's bank) and asked her why I was getting those $35 charges. I told her I did not authorize those withdrawals. They rectified it, and I pocketed the money.

Not so fast. Lincoln started calling me. I didn't pick up. They wrote me letters. I wrote, "Return to Sender: Refused." Then they sued me (imagine, the nerve!) in small claims court for $5000. They claimed "unjust enrichment." I had told Ava what had happened. She told me to keep the money and make them come after me. (Remember, that's what her company does.) So I had the chance to make a response.

I told them that I had checked off "withdraw max" on the form (which I had a copy of and attached as an exhibit) therefore $5584 was the maximum I could withdraw, as determined by the company themselves. They were livid. As the court date approached, I got my strategy down. I would tell the judge I never read any statements, just threw them out, I had no idea what was in that account, so why was I being sued? Ignorance is bliss. Ava warned me that might not work.

"Offer to settle with them instead," she said.

"What, like offer them $1000 to drop the suit?"

"No. Offer them $500 and see if they take it. Remind them that small claims cases are not appealable [she learned that from me!] and $500 now is better than $0 if they lose." That was ballsy. Right up my alley. So I did it.

When you go to small claims it's always the same. They call the cases. When they call your case you say "plaintiff," or "defendant," and then they know which cases have both parties there. If both parties are present, you can see what the other side looks like and then you meet them outside the courtroom to talk about your case.

This lawyer was very smart--he had all his ducks in a row. He had every single statement and knew everything about my account. I said hello and gave him my pitch.

"Impossible," he said. "You never even put $5000 worth of deposits into the account. You know it's a mistake."

"What if I think that's my legitimate ROI [return on investment]?" I continued.

"How could you have an ROI that high? These are index funds!"

I played dumb, though I day-traded for years.

"I don't know what you mean. These are complicated investment vehicles that I don't understand. I'm not in finance. I don't have an MBA. I like civics. This is Greek to me."

"But there are your statements," he said, handing over a stack of papers. I pushed them away.

"I've never seen those," I said.

"Well, we mailed them to you."

"Well, I throw them in the trash."

"You must have looked at them."

"Prove it," I said. He was at a loss for words. "How about this," I countered. I reached into my purse and pulled out five crisp hundred dollar bills. "I'll give you $500 to settle this right now. You know small claims cases can't be appealed, and maybe this magistrate will side with me. Do you want to roll the dice or take $500 in your hand?" He paused.

"I need to make a call," he said. I nodded and he walked out of earshot. He came back. "We'll take the $500," he said. I handed it into his space. "No, no, not today. I'll withdraw the case after a continuance if you mail us a check. I'll have a release ready for you." He looked dejected, but he was doing his job. He didn't make the decision. I sent the check as promised and they withdrew the matter. I made $4500 not boosting and suing, but getting sued.

Then there was the matter of Tommy Bahama. Tommy Bahama was just like Lilly Pulitzer in terms of price points and customer service (they are owned by the same company, Oxford) and the only difference was that they had cameras in their stores. I guessed this was because they sold men's clothing as well, since Lilly was the same company and they had no cameras. But of course Tommy still didn't have cameras in the dressing rooms. So, again, we would take five or six pieces of clothing into the dressing room, and a bonus would be if I found a dressing room with clothing in it already left by a prior customer. Those were just free clothes.

Tommy Bahama was special out of all the stores, because I sued them for defamation of character and got a favorable settlement of $2405. Here's how it went down. Remember I said I got a letter from Tommy via FedEx that said I could no longer return anything to their stores? Well, I was appalled. After I got it, they ran a promotion. For every two hundred dollars you spent they gave you a fifty dollar gift card. So I bought eight hundred dollars worth of items and got four gift cards, then I sold them on eBay for $120 and then I returned the clothes after they were redeemed. Or tried to. The assistant manager knew who I was but didn't know Alexis. She confronted me. She told me that I was not allowed to return anything to the store. I explained that I could, provided I had a valid receipt.

She checked a special loss prevention book that had the letter they had sent me in it. She reviewed it and said I could return something with a receipt. So I brought back the items in order to get the free $120 in gift card profit, and I asked the assistant manager (who refused to give me her name) if just *she* thought I was a criminal, or if it was the entire store. She told me, "anyone authorized to take returns." I knew at that moment I could sue for defamation and win.

Additionally, Tommy's loss prevention department had made a misstep. They had sent the identical FedEx letter stating I couldn't return anything to their stores to Alexis at her apartment, but with my name on the letter. So, Alexis comes home to find an express envelope that was addressed to me at her address. She called me immediately.

"What the hell?" she said. "I just got a letter from Tommy Bahama addressed to you at my house. Where did they get my address?"

"I don't know."

"Can they do that? My landlady is pissed. She thinks I have someone who's not on the lease living with me. I had to talk to her for ten minutes and tell her it was an error. I don't know if she believed me. What are we going to do about this?"

"I'm going to sue them," I said.

I sent them a demand letter for $2500. I chose that number because I figured that's what the most bargain basement lawyer would charge for a retainer. So, because it would cost them $2500 to litigate (think about it--even a cheap lawyer is $300 per hour, plus at least $50 per hour for paralegal time--do the math). Therefore, I simply asked them for the legal fees it would cost them to fight me. They were *not* pleased. They said that they would vehemently oppose my position and vigorously defend themselves. So I filed suit. First came the demand letter. It read as follows:

Dear   Attorney   Georges,

The following is a demand letter. If the issues enumerated in this letter are not disposed of within thirty calendar days, legal action will follow in the Connecticut jurisprudence.

I want to first thank you for your grace in handling my previous litigation—as always I am seeking a fair, just, and equitable solution to my new issue in the same manner as the first.

My   new   issue   is   as   follows:

I received an important Fedex from Tommy Bahama dated 6/9/2015, which was a brief primer on return restriction. I now faced particular restrictions on my behavior at Tommy Bahama stores. That was fine. As I already stated in court on the record, I have male friends at Mohegan Sun because I am a poker player there and when any one of them asked me if I'd like a gift, I always suggested Tommy Bahama as it is one of my favorite stores. I then returned the gifts only to have Tommy Bahama void the gift cards and force me to go to court in order to collect what was   rightfully   mine.

You could imagine my surprise when I received a phone call on Tuesday 6/16/2015 from a young woman named Alexis Granger. She had met me in the past at a book signing event for my third book, as Ms. Granger follows transgender authors. She told me the following:

Alexis came home to find a note from her landlord. She had a Fedex package for her apartment and she needed to pick it up in the office. She went to the office and her landlady stated, "If you have someone else living at your apartment, you need to disclose it to the office." "Why do you ask," replied Ms. Granger. "Because you have a Fedex coming to your home that is not yours." It turned out that the Fedex was addressed, "Susan Sturbridge, 1175 Huntington Avenue, #310, Bristol,   CT   06010."

My prior address was in Terryville, CT.. I have not lived there in eight and a half years. My current address is at the top of this letter. Where is this coming from? Are you trying to harass me   for   suing   you   before?   I   do   not   appreciate   it.

So, your sending a random woman a Fedex with my name on it was incredibly odd, but perhaps you thought I was somehow attached to that address? Because I never have been.

Then Ms. Granger recounted how she had called the customer service number for Tommy Bahama after assuring her landlady that while the Fedex was not for her, it was for someone that she knew, a local author in the LGBT community. Customer service suggested that she call the closest store to her (Westfarms) to see why this letter was sent out.

When she called, she spoke with Julian (I do not have his last name—he is tall and light) who then informed her that this Susan Sturbridge individual had been caught engaging in criminal behavior. Julian further advised Ms. Granger that Susan Sturbridge was under surveillance by the   store   and   that   Susan   Sturbridge   was   dangerous.

Ms. Granger reported this entire episode to me, as she was simply on the other end of the line listening to this slander. She told me she'd looked me up to advise me what a store was saying about me to its customers. Slandering transgender individuals, queer individuals, or anyone else is   not   acceptable   in   our   current   public   policy   arena.

I have no idea how many letters like this have been sent out. One person happened to let me know. I do not understand (outside of vengeance for me suing your company before) why you continue to embarrass me and defame me to the public. I am not one to engage in criminal activity of any sort, and I have no reason to be under surveillance. If you believe I have done something illegal, I suggest that you contact local law enforcement and lodge a complaint, at which point it would need to go to a judge to get an arrest warrant and arrest me for something. Please   don't   tell   living   breathing   people   that   I   am   a   criminal!

That   is   slander,   defamation   of   character,   and   harassment.

I have an offer to close this matter. A single payment of $2,500.00 in liquidated damages and I will sign any agreement you like stating I will not sue Tommy Bahama in the future.

If you do not accept this generous offer to allow you to avoid a potential lawsuit on the record documenting systematic slander, defamation of character, and harassment of a member of a protected minority group under the Connecticut jurisprudence, I will be forced to ask for $5,000.00   in   court   when   I   file   the   lawsuit.

I   look   forward   to   hearing   back   from   you.

Best   regards,

Susan Sturbridge

Tommy Bahama wrote a scathing letter back and would not pay the demand. So filed a complaint with the Hartford Judicial District and had a marshal serve the papers on their process server in Hartford. Sometimes a demand letter works, and sometimes you need to file suit. The complaint read as follows:

COMPLAINT

Plaintiff is an individual and is now, and at all times mentioned in this complaint was, a resident   of   Hartford   County,   in   the   State   of   Connecticut.
Plaintiff has resided in Farmington, Connecticut for over eight years and has during all this time enjoyed a good reputation, both generally and in her occupations as a paralegal and as a   customer   service   associate.
Defendant, Tommy Bahama R&R Holdings, Inc., is now and at all times mentioned in this complaint was a corporation organized and existing under the laws of the State of Georgia, with   its   principal   place   of   business   in   Georgia   in   Fulton   County.
Plaintiff is informed and does believe that the Defendant is legally responsible for the events and happenings referred to in this complaint, and unlawfully caused the injuries and damages   to   Plaintiff   alleged   in   this   complaint.
On June 12th, 2015, the Plaintiff received a letter dated June 9th, 2015 from the Defendant via FedEx which stated that the Plaintiff was no longer allowed to return merchandise to the Defendant's retail establishments without a receipt, nor would the Defendant accept returns made on items purchased with gift cards issued by the Defendant.
This June 9th, 2015 letter was the direct result of a prior lawsuit filed in Connecticut Small Claims Court, Sturbridge v. Tommy Bahama R&R Holdings, Inc, wherein the Plaintiff was awarded $872.19 plus entry fee and service costs, totaling $967.94 after a trial in front of Magistrate   Susan   King.
In this small claims suit filed on February 2nd, 2015, Tommy Bahama had voided four gift cards in possession of the Plaintiff totaling $872.19 which came into Plaintiff's possession after returning gifts that several males purchased for the Plaintiff at the Tommy Bahama retail store located at the Mohegan Sun Casino in Uncasville, CT on the Mohegan reservation. Defendant held that merchandise was not legally obtained and answered the complaint as such. Magistrate King found at trial that the Plaintiff was in fact owed these monies and that Defendant   had   acted   improperly.
Plaintiff received a telephone call on June 16th, 2015 from a young woman named Alexis Granger. Granger had received a FedEx at her residence addressed to: 'Susan Sturbridge, 1175 Huntington Avenue, #310, Bristol, CT 06010.' Plaintiff has never resided at this address.

Plaintiff was unaware of who lived at this address. Plaintiff never gave Defendant any other address besides her own residence when conducting business in their stores. Plaintiff has only ever had a single customer number at Tommy Bahama.

Granger, curious as to why she was getting a FedEx from Loss Prevention addressed to a transgender author and poker player, called the Defendant's local store located in West Hartford, Connecticut at the WestFarms Mall. She spoke to 'Julian,' a store employee, who proceeded to explain to Granger that the Plaintiff was a criminal, had stolen merchandise from their stores, and was under surveillance by the Defendant.

Granger disseminated this information to the Plaintiff via telephone and stated she kept the letter in case it was needed at a further point in time. Granger asked the Plaintiff why the Defendant would characterize her in such a manner, with the only explanation being that Plaintiff had previously recovered monies from the Defendant at trial and the Defendant was seeking to slander her.

Plaintiff denies any and all characterization of criminal behavior. Plaintiff's only relationship with the Defendant is through a previous court case. Plaintiff does not know how many other letters like the one Granger received were sent out.

The letter and phone call to Granger clearly exposes the Plaintiff to hatred, contempt, ridicule, and obloquy as it frames the Plaintiff as an individual engaging in criminal acts. The letter is prima facie defamation, as it is addressed to the Plaintiff at a third-party's address and originated from the Loss Prevention Department of the Defendant.

Additionally, Plaintiff visited the Tommy Bahama retail store in the WestFarms Mall in Farmington, CT on December 6th, 2015 on or about 5:00pm with the intention of returning items purchased with cash on November 27th, 2015 totaling $647.67 from the same store. Upon reaching the register, the manager informed Plaintiff that she was unable to accept returns from the Plaintiff, and cited a certain letter sent via FedEx to the Plaintiff's residence. Plaintiff explained to the manager (she refused to give her name) that this letter merely stated that Plaintiff could not return any items purchased with gift cards or merchandise credits. The manager then stated that she would take the return. When asked who else at Tommy Bahama was under the impression that the Plaintiff was a criminal, the manager responded 'anyone authorized to take returns.'

As a proximate result of the above-referenced publication and dissemination, as well as misleading employees at Tommy Bahama stores, Plaintiff has suffered loss of her reputation, shame, mortification, and injury to her feelings, all to her compensatory damage in the amount of $5,000.

WHEREFORE, Plaintiff demands judgment against the Defendant, for: Compensatory damages;
Interest as allowed by law;
Costs of suit; and
Such other and further relief as this court may deem just and proper.

They answered the complaint in boilerplate fashion, and I waited until our status conference in court to meet opposing counsel. The two female judges met us and I told them I agreed with the scheduling order we had crafted. I then told the lawyer, Attorney Biscayne, that if he wanted to talk about settlement I was open to it. A few days later I received an email from him with an offer for $1000. Of course, I rejected it--it cost me $405 to file the suit, so I thought that the remaining $595 was just a pittance. At least they made an offer.

So we met in person, on the 34th floor of Cityplace at his office, where I got a Keurig cup of coffee in a mug with his firm's name on it. Very fancy. But I expected no less from Tommy Bahama. We had a good negotiation. I made it very clear that I believed all I had to do was prove that I was not a criminal. He flatly disagreed. I then told him that the $1000 was a pittance and that I needed $2000 plus costs ($350 for filing suit and $55 for the marshal) and the lawyer agreed. So I made $2000 by suing the corporation for defamation and then settling before trial.

Of course I had to sign a release saying I would not sue them again, and also, that I wouldn't set foot in any of their stores for twenty years. Not a problem. I was out of the boosting game, and why did I need a $60 ashtray in the shape of a fish or a $200 bathing suit? They paid me $2000 to never talk to them again and I took it. I had now started boosting and suing--suing the very people I was stealing from. I think it was ballsy and exciting, and I couldn't wait to tell others about it. It wasn't enough that I ripped them off for probably five grand, I wanted to add insult to injury. How dare you tell me I can't return to your store any more. Just for that, I'm going to sue. And that's how it went, my first legal case in "real" civil court, not small claims. And there were just more and more. Why boost for $100 here or $200 there when I could use my big girl words and sue for $2000 or more at a time? It was an epiphany, and it continued.

THIRD BOOST AND SUE: PORTFOLIO RECOVERY ASSOCIATES

It was around this time that I got my first arrest in my home state of Connecticut. I had been playing in a poker tournament at Mohegan in the afternoon and got knocked out really early, like in the first two hours. Just blew $300. I was supposed to spend my whole Saturday there, but that got cut short. So I went to play cash. I was in the big blind with K-6 of diamonds and it got checked around. The flop was 7,8,9 or diamonds. So I had the second nut flush with an open-ended straight flush draw. All the money went in, and the guy a few seats over from me turned over A-5 of diamonds and I lost $200 in about ten minutes. I decided to leave.

I was pissed. I had just blown $500 in a little over two hours and I had zero accountability with either woman, so I decided to go get high and go for a hike. I drove up Route 2 away from Mohegan and stopped at the drugstore in Colchester, the first real town on the way home and about a thirty-five minute drive to West Hartford where I was going to hike. So I ate the pills and got back on the road, knowing I'd be sober until I got where I was going.

Big mistake. A car had flipped on Route 2 and the highway was blocked until they moved the vehicle. I sweat and waited. And waited and waited. I could start to feel the high. And I was still in traffic. I drove down the breakdown lane and got off the first available exit and just headed west toward home. I never made it.

I got pulled over by the Rocky Hill police for crossing the yellow line and speeding. They immediately knew I was high and arrested me. When I passed the breathalyzer (I'd had no alcohol) they told me I had to submit to a urine screen. Well, when it came time to pee, I couldn't. One of the well-known consequences of taking large doses of DXM is the inability to urinate for several hours. So they told me I was refusing the test. I explained I wasn't refusing but that I couldn't go. They called it a refusal and once I was released I got a notice saying DMV was suspending my license for six months for a chemical test refusal.

I appealed it. My endocrinologist wrote me a very professional letter saying that I took large doses of the diuretic aldactone (on account of being transgender) and that I might not be able to pee on the spot without a large amount of water available, something I was not afforded in lockup. (Aldactone is given to transwomen for an off-label use. It turns out that this diuretic, when taken in a large dose, causes skin to become smoother and body hair growth to slow to almost nothing, including the added bonus of making existing hair finer. To this day I don't have to shave my legs because I don't have any hair.)

I won the hearing. The hearing officer took one look at me being transgender, was a bleeding heart liberal, and let me off without a punishment. For your first DUI in Connecticut, you just take ten to fifteen drug and alcohol classes, watch a couple movies, go to a MADD impact panel where you hear from people that have killed or seriously injured people in DUI accidents, then the case is nolled, and you have no record. So that's what happened to me. No record. No license suspension. No consequences. Easy breezy.

Around this time I'd also lost my job at the law firm. Turned out, the couple who were the lawyers got divorced and the firm fractured. I was mainly doing work for Craig's cases, and now that he was going to be on his own without his wife's caseload, he said he just didn't have enough work to justify having his own paralegal. So, last one hired, first one fired, and I started collecting a healthy unemployment check.

Now I was able to go to the World Series of Poker again and play the $1000 ladies tournament. (I got let go in May and the tournament was at the end of June.) My license wasn't suspended, so I decided to drive. I'd driven across the country many times in my life and was accustomed to it. I asked Alexis to come with me and she totally said yes. She had gotten a small job as a substitute teacher, but she wasn't working that late in June. So I told Ava I was driving by myself and took Alexis and took off.

Now my license was suspended in Ohio because of an earlier incident so we took I-40 there, through Tennessee, Arkansas, Oklahoma, and the panhandle of Texas. I had stopped boosting. I quit while I was ahead. But Alexis had not. She had me stop along the way at different tack and Western stores so she could steal riding apparel. (She had also started riding horses again for recreation like she used to as a child. The woman with no job and no money had boosted expensive equestrian apparel and was hanging out with the girls at the stables.)

So we ate a lot of steak dinners. Alexis had never been out West so there was a lot to see. We finally got to Vegas. While I played poker, she went swimming, went in the hot tub, went to the gym, took drugs, you know, had a vacation. I was out of WSOP on the first day. Karma's a bitch--I guess running away with my mistress to Vegas angered the poker gods.

When we were done in Vegas we went and visited Utah like I always do, at all the beautiful natural parks. Alexis couldn't have cared about natural beauty--she liked designer clothes and shopping, not the rock formations in Zion or Arches or Bryce. Then we got to Colorado and all she wanted to do was to buy some legal weed. So I advised her we would stop in Glenwood Springs (we were arriving via Grand Junction) because I explained to her that it was a more affluent town.

The weed store was great. It was a two-family house with the first floor just selling medical marijuana and the second floor just recreational pot. They had a glass full of joints for $10 apiece. A guy who had just walked in just bought a joint, paid and left. Just like a liquor store. Alexis consulted the girl behind the counter and picked her poison. There was just a whole table full of gallon glass jars full of bud. It was unreal. She dispensed it into a green pill container, and on the pill container it listed all the chemicals used to grow the pot. Like an ingredient list. Alexis gave her eighty dollars of my money (she had long run out of her own) and bought a quarter ounce of herb.

We went back to the car and we drove to Aspen. Alexis had never been there, but had heard so much about the wealth and the life there. But instead of doing anything touristy, she took to going and boosting from the Marmot store and the North Face and a high-end specialty dress shop. I waited patiently and didn't steal. She had gotten really ballsy. Then we got back in the car and I told her we were going to go over Independence Pass at 12,000 feet and it was such a beautiful road through the top of the Rockies. Well she had smoked so much of that excellent weed I'd bought her that when we got to the top and I wanted to take a little hike, she was dizzy from the elevation and we had to go. We were having two different vacations, but sharing one vehicle.

On our way back on I-70 and I-80, she demanded we stop in Cleveland. She told me there was a Lilly Pulitzer store there and she had some merch to return she had boosted on the way out to Vegas when we had made a quick stop in Pennsylvania. I explained to her that I couldn't drive in Ohio because my license was suspended. She had no interest in driving. In fact, throughout this 5,000-mile road trip she hadn't driven a single mile.

We went an hour out of our way to Cleveland so she could return some dresses and boost some more. I would've been mad, but she came back to the car with a $500 gift card and apologized for running out of money. At least that was something toward gas. Otherwise, she was pretty much a freeloader. We drove (more precisely, I drove) through the night and got us back home at 3am. I dropped her off and went home to Ava.

It was at that moment I didn't want a mistress anymore. I had driven 5,000 miles and she drove zero. I wanted to see National Parks, beautiful places, play poker, and relax. She wanted to get high, steal from stores, and have sex. Not only that, in spending eleven days with her alone, I found her to be a vapid, vacuous, empty vessel. She was a trust fund baby. Waiting for her parents to die so she could get her inheritance and destroy herself more quickly. At once I was profoundly repulsed by her, and just wanted to be faithful to Ava. It was a turning point for me. And it took driving across the country and back to see I had no future with Alexis. I needed to top being a sex addict and focus on my home life--that's what needed work.

Breaking up was easy. We had no mutual property and no joint bank accounts. I had a few things of hers she demanded back and she had a few things of mine I wanted, and we took care of that exchange through an intermediary. And that was the end of my mistress. Five years. Five long years of losing my ten-and-a-half years clean, bankrupting my business, and cleaning out my bank account. She had decimated me. Time to rebuild. But before that could happen, there was the issue of the unpaid credit cards.

Debt doesn't actually go away--it changes form. And this is what I learned. Basically, only one of two things happens to unpaid consumer debt: it is charged off, or it is sent to collections. The vast majority of consumer debt is charged off. What this means is that the company takes the $5,000 you owe them and "writes it off" as bad debt. So, come tax time, they compute your debt as a loss, and so the company makes $5,000 less for the year, which saves them $5,000 times 35% corporate tax rate in America. (So, they pay the federal government $1,750 less in taxes.) What does that mean? It means society pays. Or, more exactly, our children and grandchildren pay. That $1,750 in less income tax revenue just gets added onto the national debt, which we will eventually inflate our way out of or default on, just like I defaulted on my credit cards, and either way it's just not my problem. Again, a victimless crime.

The other debt gets sent to collections. What this means is that your $5,000 in debt (a 'debt instrument') gets purchased by a company called a collection agency for somewhere around $500 to $750 dollars, which the credit card company receives as payment, and it is off their books. The collection agency is then able to, by law, send pretty harassing pieces of mail and can call you up to eight times a day about the money you owe. Additionally, these companies report to the credit bureaus and put this debt on your credit report. So, for example, when I went to this hospital in Vegas after flipping the Hyundai, there was a $250 balance the insurance didn't cover. When they sent bills I ignored them. Eventually the bills stopped coming, but when I check Credit Karma, there's a $246 debt on my report. So if I were to ever apply for a car loan, home loan, or personal loan for the next seven years, I have to pay off that $246 first with the proceeds before receiving my money.

It's an interesting system. I say this because while consumer debt in a credit report will clear off in seven years, if you get a misdemeanor conviction in Connecticut, it can be expunged in as little as three years. A felony can be forgiven in five. So, in a way, Connecticut treats not paying civil debt harsher than committing a felony! In my case, I knew medical debt cannot attach (which means they couldn't garnish my wages, if I had any wages to begin with...) and my credit was totally shot anyway so I would not be applying for any new loans anyway.

The other thing that can happen with collection agencies is that the debt is big enough, and it's in their best interest to sue you. So, I owed Berkshire Bank $7,400 on a credit card. (Sorry, Priscilla.) I had gotten it with an intro APR of 0% and loaded it up, then when the time period ended, I defaulted. They were not happy. They sold the debt to a collection agency called Portfolio Recovery Associates, a foreign entity doing business in Virginia.

They harassed me for some time. They called six to eight times a day. They sent a letter telling me that I owed them $7,400 and I had thirty days to dispute it. Thirty days after that, they mailed me all of my statements as proof that I owed them the money. I ignored them. Then, I got served.

I was sued by the Law Offices of Howard Lee Schiff out of East Hartford, one of the largest debt collection firms in New England. They represented Portfolio Recovery Associates. After the marshal dropped off the complaint, I read it, and it was pretty straightforward. I decided to fight it. After all, I was a paralegal. I knew how to write pleadings. This was my first opportunity to do defense work (in a civil setting) rather than plaintiff's work. I figured, worst case, I lose, they get a judgment against me, I had no wages to attach, and they would be out the money. The whole process took around nine months.

Most people, when they get sued by a debt collection attorney, simply ignore the writ and summons. Thirty days elapses from the return date, the firm makes a motion for something called a 'default judgment,' the other side does not appear or object, default judgment is granted, and then wages and bank accounts are attached and the money is forcibly removed.

I filed my appearance pro se. Then I filed an answer. In my answer, I told them I was not responsible for the majority of the debt because my card was being used by another party (my mistress, which was true) and therefore I was not liable for the purchases made on the card. It was short, it was sweet, and it was a legitimate defense. I also did my research on Google Scholar and found something interesting--it always paid to dispute the chain of title of the debt instrument. You see, I was being sued by Portfolio Recovery Associates, but who were they? I had a credit card from Berkshire Bank. How did this other company have the right to sue me?

Turns out, my Berkshire Bank (small, local bank) card was actually serviced by a national bank Elan Financial. It further turns out that Elan Financial merged with another national bank named BankNorth. Then BankNorth sold the debt to Portfolio Recovery Associates. There were several steps in the chain of title of the debt instrument, so in addition to saying I wasn't responsible for the charges, I said that Portfolio Recovery Associates lacked standing to bring a civil action against me.

It was an excellent strategy. In response to my answer, the plaintiff continued the suit. Next, I was sent a packet of documents known as "Requests for Admission," and "Interrogatories and Requests for Production." The former is legalese for a list of questions which you admit or deny. There were about fifty questions. The latter is legalese for a set of questions (interrogatories is just a fancy word for questions) and then requests for copies of documents, such as any exhibits you may use at trial, or pieces of information the plaintiff might not have that you will be using to prove your case.

It is a requirement in a lawsuit to answer appropriate questions from the other side. The process is known as "discovery" and is a fundamental piece of a civil action. You can object to questions outside of the scope of the action, but Howard Lee Schiff is a mill--they cranked out probably 3,000 cases in a year just in Connecticut. So this is all boilerplate.

If one does not answer the questions, or answers them evasively, the other side can win by default. So I answered the questions. Truthfully. I gave them my mistress's name and address and said she was using the card. I told them that sometimes Ava threw out my mail without showing me so that I did not necessarily receive every document in question. I stated I was not responsible for all the charges and had just not disputed them up until this point. I questioned the signatures on the documents they sent me to prove they had valid title to the debt instrument. I picked out one of the signatures of a bank V.P. and claimed he didn't actually sign the document (I mean, they have thousands of these cards in collections) but it was "robo-signed," which makes it an illegitimate transfer of a debt instrument. I hit them with everything I could.

They paused, then fired their biggest salvo yet, something called a "motion for summary judgment." This is basically a trial using papers. They attached a memorandum of law and exhibits, including all my answers to their questions, all my statements, and all their debt title transfer documents. The packet was over a hundred pages. It was my biggest challenge yet.

I was not intimidated. I stood my ground. I wrote an objection, and then researched my own memorandum of law. I'd never written one before (paralegals generally don't write them--that is saved for attorneys) and I had to use Google Scholar instead of LexisNexis. It took me days. I looked through hundreds of cases, and I finally hit on something I thought I could win with. I argued several things. First, that a motion for summary judgment is only suitable when there are no issues of material fact, and that it is the burden of the party looking to end the case to prove there are no issues of fact. I proved that there were. Second, I argued that common law dictated the timeframe on disputing charges on a credit card. They argued that I had to dispute the charges that were not mine within sixty days, and I argued that common law stated you could dispute charges after you were taken to court for the debt. Lastly, I argued that the Uniform

Commercial Code (UCC) dictated the rules for transferring debt instruments, and that this code states that the signatures on documents have to be original and not robo-signed.

They sprung into action. They even filed a reply brief that thwarted my position. I was unfazed. Then we waited for the judge to make a decision. I got it in the mail just like any other decision from the court--six pages in a plain envelope. The judge found my argument compelling and granted my objection--I had won the case! I couldn't believe it! I thought they would steamroll over me because I'm not an attorney--I'm a paralegal. They're professional debt collection lawyers. But I believed in myself, and I did the hard work. And I won!!

Portfolio Recovery Associates, vanquished, withdrew the case. I got a letter from them saying I owed them nothing. $7400 debt disappeared. I framed that and hung it in my office. I got out of the debt legally, using the judiciary. I felt on top of the world. But I wasn't done yet. Time to sue the law firm.

You see, one of the things the judge said in his six-page decision was that one of the documents that the plaintiff had used to prove their case was hearsay and violated the rules of evidence. It was a signed document that should have been notarized. (Otherwise, someone could literally create a document in Photoshop and it could have been completely falsified.) I realized that this act--introducing hearsay evidence in a judicial proceeding like a motion for summary judgment--was tortuous and I could sue. So I made a new complaint--*Sturbridge vs. Law Offices of Howard Lee Schiff* and had a marshal serve the debt collection lawyers. I was only a paralegal, but I felt emboldened by my victory. The complaint looked like this:

COMPLAINT

First Count: Negligent Infliction of Emotional Distress

The Plaintiff was a Defendant in an underlying civil matter titled Portfolio Recovery Associates   v.   Susan   Sturbridge.
From her Motion to Strike (108.00) back in April of 2016, the Plaintiff argued that the collection agency which the Defendant represented in the underlying matter did not hold title to the instrument in question. The Plaintiff continued to argue this particular logic throughout the entire underlying matter, culminating with an Objection to Motion for Summary Judgment and attached Memorandum of Law (131.00) that was sustained by the tribunal with a Memorandum of Decision (133.00) on 10/11/2016. The documents at 131.00 and 133.00 are attached herein as Exhibits   1   and   2,   respectively.
While preparing her complete defense of this erroneous action, the Plaintiff suffered harm in the form of monetary losses for processing costs, lost work hours due to time spent preparing case material in aforementioned underlying action, and severe emotional distress. The Plaintiff was emotionally distressed and her mood negatively altered as a result of the prospect of being wrongfully sued for a debt that she did not owe by a scavenger debt collecting outfit. The emotional distress suffered by the Plaintiff was severe enough that it might result in illness

or bodily harm. Specifically, with respect to harm, the Plaintiff was forced to see her endocrinologist and double her daily ingestion of micronized progesterone (also known as Prometrium®) in order to stabilize mood and assist in healthy sleep to make up for the emotional distress and insomnia she was feeling as a direct result of this distress. The Defendant's conduct in the underlying matter was the proximate cause of the Plaintiff's severe emotional distress.

Additionally, the Plaintiff contends that the stress caused to her in the underlying action was foreseeable: the Plaintiff cares a great deal for her reputation to the point that she sued clothier Tommy Bahama for defamation in the jurisprudence, and only withdrew the action because it settled out of court. That the Plaintiff cares to this extent about her reputation is evidenced by this other lawsuit. It is foreseeable that the Defendant's failed attempt to wrongly sue the Plaintiff would cause severe emotional distress.

The Defendant's conduct created an unreasonable risk of causing the Plaintiff emotional distress. The Defendant is in the business of delivering terrible news to all the individuals that they come in contact with as they are a scavenger debt collecting outfit. Attempting to sue individuals like the Plaintiff who did not owe any monies as alleged is behavior that causes an unreasonable risk of distress to anyone, especially when the court ruled that there was no cause of action and the matter was dismissed.

The Defendant's conduct caused an unreasonable emotional distress to the Plaintiff because of the nature of their business. They are a scavenger debt collection outfit who profits off the misery of defendants. The Plaintiff alleges the following facts to prove to the tribunal that the negligent infliction of emotional distress count is not defective because the Defendant's conduct caused an unreasonable risk of causing the Plaintiff emotional distress. The Defendant brought a fraudulent action against the Plaintiff in the underlying matter, Portfolio Recovery Associates v. Susan Sturbridge. The basic facts surrounding this underlying action are that the plaintiff Portfolio Recovery Associates purportedly held title to a debt purportedly owed by the Defendant Susan Sturbridge, an assertion roundly rejected by the tribunal after a failed Motion for Summary judgment at which point the case was rightfully withdrawn. The Plaintiff in this action, while the Defendant in the underlying action, proved through motions and a Memorandum of Law that defeated the Plaintiff in the underlying action was using illicit practices to collect a debt that they could not prove belonged to the Plaintiff in this action. The judge in the underlying matter stated on the record (attached herein) in his decision that the firm of Howard Lee Schiff, P.C. had entered illicit documents into a legal proceeding, because they believed that once they filed suit that this Plaintiff would simply be scared and attempt to settle the debt. (They made an offer for approximately 85% of the debt to settle early in the process.) Of course they could not collect the debt because they were offending public policy, something the judge saw through. Regardless, the Defendant's actions in the underlying matter were an attempt to scare, to frighten, to coerce, and to cause emotional distress to the Plaintiff by the very nature of their attempts to collect an uncollectable debt. Whether or not this Plaintiff ended up winning the case, the Defendant's actions were meant to scare, frighten, coerce, and cause emotional distress, and through these despicable tactics their actions caused an unreasonable risk of causing the Plaintiff emotional distress.

The Plaintiff alleges the following facts to demonstrate that the Plaintiff's distress was foreseeable. In the underlying action, the Plaintiff was being sued for between seven and eight thousand dollars that she did not owe. While having to fight valiantly against such a despicable scavenger debt collecting outfit, the Plaintiff literally had to create all of her pleadings from scratch as she was a pro se Defendant in the underlying action. It is absolutely foreseeable that when a law firm engaging in illicit behavior to attempt to collect uncollectable debts comes after an individual, and that individual not only has to research contract law and financial instruments, but also the Connecticut Practice Book and the jurisprudence more generally without a J.D., that individual's stress would be foreseeable.

With respect to the third of four necessary components of facts that must be alleged to prove negligent infliction of emotional distress, the Plaintiff repeats the contention stated in paragraph 3: The emotional distress suffered by the Plaintiff was severe enough that it might result in illness or bodily harm. Specifically, with respect to harm, the Plaintiff was forced to see her endocrinologist and double her daily ingestion of micronized progesterone (also known as Prometrium®) in order to stabilize mood and assist in healthy sleep to make up for the emotional distress and insomnia she was feeling as a direct result of this distress. The doctor, at the Plaintiff's request to quell the emotional distress inflicted on her by the Defendant, decided to up the Plaintiff's hormone dosage to the highest safe dosage on the hormone progesterone in order to counter the deleterious effects of the underlying offensive lawsuit that was the proximate cause of this emotional distress. Furthermore, on occasion the doctor also prescribed a dosage of clonazepam (Klonopin), a potent benzodiazepine whose direct result is a lowering of stress, a stress that was caused by the Defendant's tortious conduct.

Lastly, to the fourth allegation which must be made with respect to a complete claim of negligent infliction of emotional distress, that the Defendant's conduct was the cause of the Plaintiff's distress, the Plaintiff submits paragraphs 1 through 10 as a complete allegation that the Defendant's harmful, tortious, and illicit actions caused the Plaintiff's emotional distress. These actions are extreme and outrageous given all of the circumstances, and these extreme and outrageous actions caused severe emotional distress to the Plaintiff. As a direct and proximate result of the Defendant's negligence, the Plaintiff has suffered the following damages:

a.   Pain;
b.   Suffering;
c.   Anguish;
d.   Loss   of   Enjoyment   of   Life's   Activities.

Second Count: Violation of the Connecticut Unfair Trade Practices Act (Connecticut General Statutes § 42-110a et seq.)

Paragraphs 1--12 of Count One are hereby incorporated into this Count as if fully set forth herein.

At all times material, Defendant was a 'person' within the meaning of C.G.S. sec. 42-110a(3).

At all times material, Defendant engaged in trade or commerce within the State of Connecticut.

In the underlying action Portfolio Recovery Associates v. Susan Sturbridge, the Defendant in this action wrongfully sought to collect an uncollectable debt from the Plaintiff. The Plaintiff challenged the title of the debt in her motions, and in their Memorandum of Law accompanying their Motion for Summary Judgment and even in their Reply brief, the Defendant had absolutely no argument against this fact.

Whereas many individuals, when sued by scavenger debt collection firms, fail to fight allegations in the jurisprudence, the Plaintiff asserted her rights and argued against the Defendant without violating Practice Book. When it came time for their failed Motion for Summary Judgment (attached here as Exhibit 3) the Defendant wrongfully used hearsay evidence in a judicial proceeding by providing an unverified piece of information as seminal to their assertion of a clear title to the instrument. The judge in the case of course would not let such an egregious act go unheeded, and he issued the decision in Exhibit 2 specifically stating that the Defendant had violated the Rules of Evidence.

The Plaintiff contends that the Defendant regularly enters unauthenticated documents into legal proceedings in Connecticut courts. Through a discovery process which will include the parsing of public documents from well over 2,000 cases filed under their juris number, the Plaintiff will prove that the Defendant's behavior in the earlier action was not an isolated incident but rather a pattern of behavior by the agents of the Defendant.

The Plaintiff is awaiting data from the State of Connecticut Department of Banking who stated that within the statutes of limitation, there are a significant number of complaints against the Defendant lodged with the State of Connecticut for purported illicit practices.

Primarily, the Plaintiff contends that the tribunal is aware that there is no appellate authority as to whether a Plaintiff must plead other specific instances of unfair practices on the part of an corporation in order to satisfy the allegation of a general business practice, and that superior court decisions are split on this issue. Given the remedial nature of the Connecticut Unfair Trade Practices Act, and given that it is to be liberally construed to give effect to the legislature's intent, the Plaintiff contends that the allegation of a general business practice in the complaint is sufficient to demonstrate a violation of C.G.S. § 42-110a et seq.

The Plaintiff contends that the practice of submitting documents which are not authenticated in a legal proceeding that can result in a summary judgment against a defendant in a collections action is an act that is neither fair, nor just, nor equitable. When the title to the debt instrument in question was challenged, instead of arguing against the Plaintiff's position, the Defendant sought merely to circumvent justice by creating a document without an affiant that could very easily have been created on any computer, submitting this document as if it were fact. This action, while it may not be illegal under common law because of plausible deniability, most certainly offends public policy, as it is immoral, oppressive, unethical, and unscrupulous.

The Plaintiff contends that this behavior harms consumers. If only 1% of their cases were defective due to the admission of unauthenticated documents into legal proceedings, that would amount to between twenty and twenty-five illicit judgments of an average of around five thousand dollars per instance. Creditors who are being wrongfully sued by the Defendant are at risk for their credit scores to worsen, which increases borrowing costs, their wages or receivables being attached, and their assets in bank accounts being seized, all of which significantly harm a group of consumers.

Defendant's conduct as alleged herein violated the Connecticut Unfair Trade Practices Act (CUTPA) in that the conduct was unfair, immoral, unethical, oppressive, unscrupulous and/or deceptive and has caused substantive harm to the Plaintiff, as demonstrated in the first count, and has the ability to harm other consumers, a fact that will be evidenced through a discovery process.

Pursuant to C.G.S. sec. 41-110g(c), a copy of this complaint has been mailed to the Attorney General and the Commissioner of Consumer Protection.

As a direct and proximate result of the Defendant's violations of CUTPA, the Plaintiff has suffered monetary damages. This monetary damage (in the aggregate of copying, printing, and mailing costs as well as lost work hours and lost productivity) is enhanced by the negligent infliction of emotional distress claim, which is included within this second count as per paragraph 13, and is hence the total of the losses experienced by the Plaintiff as a result of the Defendant's CUTPA violation.

As a result of the Defendant's violations of CUTPA, the Plaintiff further asks for treble damages.

With respect to whether or not an attorney or law firm can be sued under CUTPA, the Plaintiff is utilizing the logic of the larger purview put forth in Heslin v. Connecticut Law Clinic of Trantolo & Trantolo, *190 Conn. 510 - Conn: Supreme Court 1983, wherein the Commissioner of the Department of Consumer Protection, Mary M. Heslin, sued an attorney's offices utilizing the CUTPA statute. This is prima facie evidence that CUTPA can be liberally construed to be applicable to attorney's offices, specifically when the conduct offends public policy. Specifically, the ruling reads at 520, "Federal law thus provides us with strong precedents for concluding that CUTPA applies to attorneys. Such a conclusion is buttressed by the fact that it comports with the decisions of other jurisdictions construing substantially similar legislation. Reed v. Allison & Perrone, 376 So. 2d 1067, 1068-69 (La. Ct. App. 1979); DeBakey v. Staggs, 605 S.W.2d 631, 633 (Tex. Civ. App. 1980); see also Matthews v. Berryman, 637 P.2d 822, 826 (Mont. 1981). It comports as well, obviously, with the enforcing agency's view of the statute, a recognized aid to statutory construction. Board of Trustees v. Freedom of Information Commission, 181 Conn. 544, 551-52, 436 A.2d 266 (1980); Connecticut Light & Power Co. v. Public Utilities Control Authority, 176 Conn. 191, 198, 405 A.2d 638 (1978). It comports, finally, with the liberal construction to which a remedial statute such as CUTPA is entitled.* Hinchliffe v. American Motors Corporation, *184 Conn. 607, 615 n.4, 440 A.2d 810 (1981); see General Statutes § 42-110b (d). As Professor Davis has pointed out, complex new business arrangements inevitably "bring forth equally intricate governmental mechanisms requiring effective exercise of the administrative power of investigation."* Davis, Administrative Law Text (3d Ed.) § *3.08, p. 67; see also* Bates v. State Bar of Arizona, *supra.*

The Plaintiff thus argues that the broadly reaching and remedial CUTPA statute does apply to attorneys and their offices, and the Defendant cannot merely assert that CUTPA does not apply to them by citing attorney-client privilege. This Plaintiff doubts whether the Plaintiff in the underlying matter, Portfolio Recovery Associates of Virginia, would desire that the Connecticut law firm they contracted out a disputed debt with a bad chain of title should use illicit practices to collect a debt. When a firm hires an attorney to enforce a contract, their posture should reasonably be assumed to expect the best legal representation possible, but not one wherein their hire seeks to circumvent the jurisprudence by entering illicit documents into proceedings. Portfolio Recovery Associates would not want the Law Offices of Howard Lee Schiff to violate the Rules of Evidence, since they would then stand to lose their underlying action and be responsible for fees and costs and not collect the debt. Therefore, the statement that The Law Offices of Howard Lee Schiff cannot be sued under CUTPA because of their desire to give the best representation possible to their client and the privileges therein is faulty in its logic: the contractor would not want their hiree to violate the Rules of Evidence and hence lose the case. Their behavior is offensive to public policy and should be considered a violation of CUTPA.

WHEREFORE, Plaintiff demands judgment against Defendant for:
Compensatory *Damages;*
Punitive *Damages;*
Interest *as* *allowed* *by* *law;*
Costs *of* *suit;*
Such other and further relief as this court may deem just and proper.

THE *PLAINTIFF*
Susan *Sturbridge*

They were livid. They filed all sorts of motions and did not prevail and the clock was ticking. I had to learn how to object to all sorts of pleadings. They were wasting valuable hours on this legal proceeding that was just wasting company time. I got a call from one of their representatives to come in and talk about a settlement.

I knew from my time at the Fleeman firm that taking something to trial costs money. There's paralegal time and attorney time and document preparation and exhibits. It would have cost Howard Lee Schiff thousands of dollars to fight little old me. So we talked it out. I told them

I spent $350 to file the lawsuit, and $55 to pay the marshal to serve them. With printing costs and postage costs I was looking around $450 in fixed costs I'd already put in. I told them that if they were debt collectors instead of attorneys I could sue them for up to $1000 under the Fair Debt Collections Practices Act. So I asked for that. $1000.

They talked about it and settled. I got a check for $1000 a week later, and I withdrew the case. And I earned $550 from the debt collection lawyer. And that's the story of how I screwed a credit card company out of $7400, got sued, won, then sued the law firm that sued me, and not only did I not pay the $7400, I was $550 richer from the process. Not too shabby.

More was coming. I just didn't know it at the time.

FOURTH BOOST AND SUE: ANTHEM AND RUSHFORD

While Tommy Bahama was in suit I ended up totalling my Mercedes. I was with Alexis on a boosting trip to Greenwich Avenue in Greenwich. They had a Tory Burch, a Vineyard Vines, Zara, and a Lilly Pulitzer among other stores, and a lovely Starbucks to have a double espresso to start the boosting day. A winter storm was imminent, but we were trying to get done before it came. It had just started snowing when we got to the Merritt Parkway to head home.

I was near Fairfield driving in the left lane behind another car, going about thirty miles per hour in the snow. A little Nissan Sentra in the right lane started to lose control and ended up stopped sideways across both lanes. There was nowhere to go. I had to make an instantaneous choice--strike the car in front of me and most likely total my Mercedes, or strike the Sentra broadside into the driver door and perhaps severely injure or kill the passenger but most likely save my car. I totalled the car.

The cleanup from this was really, really bad. Not only had I totalled a beautiful luxury car, I had done so with my mistress in the car and a trunk full of boosted merchandise. I drove my car one exit until it overheated (the radiator was in pieces) and got into a commuter lot. I called my parents. (How could I call Ava, to come pick me up with my mistress?) They trudged out in the snow and brought Alexis to her apartment and were incredibly angry with me.

When I went to my mechanic and told him I needed another car, he told me I was shit out of luck. He had some Mercedes that cost 25k and up that were out of my price range, or he had his sister-in-law's blue Chrysler Town and Country minivan. One owner. Mint condition. 150k. $2500. I took the minivan. Later, when I stopped boosting, this vehicle came in very handy.

So when I stopped boosting, I still had a drug habit that needed to be paid for somehow. As an addict, I'm scrappy and industrious, so I invented a new business--oven parts. It all started accidentally. My father (who is always on Craigslist looking for deals) called me to say someone in Farmington had just posted a free oven for pickup. He said to call them, then bring it to the scrapyard. (This is when they were paying around ten cents a pound for light iron.) I could drive to Bristol and make ten dollars for nothing.

Smart, I thought. I got the oven and asked the owner what was wrong with it. He said two of the burners had stopped working and it didn't broil. But otherwise it was fine. So I brought it home. I looked at the digital timer--it must be worth something, I thought. So I popped the panel off the back, undid the wires, and there were four screws holding it in. I popped out the control unit. It said, "Spitfire control" on it with a number and letter combo that was most certainly a part number.

I checked it on eBay. New that part was $125, used it was $75. I listed mine for $65 and it was gone in a week. In addition to that, I pulled off the knobs ($15 for the set), the switches (between $5 and $15 apiece), and the two burners that worked ($20 for one, $40 for the other) and I sold everything within a month. And a business was born.

By the time I'd gotten it down pat, it was easy. I'd pay anyone $50 for a working glass top stove, or $20 for a working coil top stove. I parted them out in my garage, listed the parts on eBay, and scrapped the body of the oven in Bristol at the scrapyard. Everything had value. A four-prong cord. A front piece of glass. The inner glass pack from the door. The bake and broil elements. The thermostat.

Pretty soon, I had a very healthy and legitimate business. Within two years, I was carrying over 300 items in inventory worth over 20k. The business worked. And it was easy. I now always had an excuse to not be home--"Ava, I'm picking up an oven in Springfield, then I'm going to part it out and bring it to the scrapyard." Sometimes I'd get two ovens a day, some days I would scrap three. Always working. Always high or drunk. I was smoking a lot of weed (one of the paralegals at Fleeman gave me her dealer contact in New Britain who always had great weed cheap) and taking a lot of Coricidin.

In late 2015, I picked up a contract job that went from September to January at Connecticare in Farmington. Once I had interviewed for the job and knew I was going to have a drug test, I gave up the pot. But I never stopped everything else. I told myself I could do this. Corporate job with a badge ID. Business casual attire, so I got to use my paralegal clothes, most of which were boosted from Nordstrom or L.L. Bean, or White House Black Market or Ann Taylor, and eighteen dollars an hour to start. I thought I'd love it.

The first day at orientation I was reminded about working at a corporation. (The last time I did this was at the former Fleet Bank when i was eighteen years old.) I immediately knew I wouldn't get through this job clean, and I called my dealer after work the first day and got high on weed that night in lieu of going to a meeting. My illness progressed quickly. Pretty soon I was using every day on my breaks, after work, drinking, taking pills, opiates, benzos, anything my dealer had. My life was spiralling out of control. My addiction was rapidly taking over my life. Ava gave me an ultimatum--go to rehab or get out of the house.

I obliged. I had Anthem Blue Cross Blue Shield health insurance and everyone we talked to said I would do great in the program at Rushford, a subsidiary of Hartford Healthcare Corporation, running a rehab in Middletown. My psychiatrist wrote me a referral, as did my PCP and my endocrinologist. Then one day at work in December, they called me and told me they had a bed open.

"When do I come?" I asked.

"Now," they said.

I told my boss I had a medical issue and had to leave and I drove home. I packed a bag and went down to Rushford.

What happened next was unbelievable. They discriminated against me for being transgender. Once they saw that I was trans, they withdrew their offer of the program and sent me home, claiming I needed a "private room" based on my gender identity. I was mortified. They blatantly violated my rights. I was absolutely livid. I went back the next day to claim my "private room." (I put getting clean in front of my ego and wanting to be treated the same under the law.) Then they told me that my insurance denied me, after waiting there all day. I knew Rushford accepted my insurance, so I was confused. I went back home dejected and went back to work.

Ava and my mother both knew I'd done my absolute best to get into rehab, and they knew that Rushford had treated me badly. So Ava didn't kick me out, but told me I still needed to go. I asked her if I could stay until my gig at Connecticare was done (another month) and then go to rehab if I didn't use. She agreed. I didn't use for a couple days, but then I went right back.

The next thing I tried to do was go to CVH (Connecticut Valley Hospital) and go to rehab there. It took a month of calling but I finally got in. When I came in I had to strip naked.

I said to the woman there, "You know I have a queer body."

She said, "We've had transwomen here before. Take your clothes off."

I did and it was a non-issue. Everyone treated me really well. I had a quad and shared a room with three other cisgender females. I showered with the other females. I went to groups with the other females. Except for having to get up at 5am every day to use my electric razor, and the fact that none of the women would let me watch Fox News, Fox Business, or CNBC, it started off as a good experience.

Then the fifth day, one of my roommates stopped taking her schizophrenia meds. She would be up all night pacing around the room, telling everyone she was going to stab them in their sleep. We all complained. There was nowhere to move her. We just had to deal with it. I didn't feel safe. Then we started having DBT groups, which is Dialectical Behavioral Therapy. This might work well for sufferers of borderline personality disorder, but not for me. I complained to the social worker.

She told me this was a 45-day DBT program. I told her I understand that the State wouldn't run a twelve-step rehab and make you believe in a higher power, but I told her DBT didn't work for me. I'd had it in an IOP before. It's nonsense psychobabble and I wanted NA or AA. She said tough. I checked myself out on the eighth day and had my mother come and get me. If I had only stayed for the 45 days and gotten clean, how much my life would have improved! But I wasn't ready for recovery yet. I guess I hadn't lost enough. I hadn't hit bottom.

No one was happy when I left, but they knew I had wanted to get well. When I got out, I got a copy of the denial letter from Rushford that came from Anthem. The letter said the reason I wasn't accepted into that rehab was because my "drug of choice was synthetic marijuana," and not DXM or opiates. Those bastards! This was malfeasance! I did the intake with the nurse. I said I'd done the incense, but not that I needed rehab because of it! I specifically said I was there for DXM and opiates, and my referrals from three different physicians said the same. Then it dawned on me. They didn't want me there. They lied to Anthem so that I would get denied so that they didn't turn me away for being transgender. I was livid! Now the wheels were turning. I was going to sue.

When I told my father I was going to sue Anthem, he said, "For what?"

"For denying me rehab," I said.

"They won't pay you a penny," he said.

"Watch me," I replied.

I crafted a demand letter and sent it to their service of process address, but I did not ask for a dollar amount. This is what the demand letter said:

Dear   Anthem   Representative,

My name is Susan Sturbridge and I suffered unfair treatment by your company while attempting to enter the Rushford Center, Inc. in Middletown, CT on December 3, 2015.

The purpose of this letter is to inform you that I have prepared but have not yet filed a civil complaint in the Hartford Judicial District. Please note that if I am forced to file this complaint, you will be properly served as per Connecticut Practice Book 8-1, and on account of the allegations under CUTPA, the Attorney General and Commissioner of Consumer Protection will also be served with this complaint. Additionally, I will petition the State of Connecticut Insurance Commissioner as per C.G.S. sec. 38a-817 for a hearing on your conduct in an attempt to obtain a cease-and-desist order that will objectively turn our pending trial into a hearing in damages.

You have fourteen days from the date of this letter to initiate a meaningful settlement conference with me. Simply reach out to me via telephone or via email. I look forward to speaking with you in   person   about   this   unlawful   act.

Please allow me to be incredibly clear. I am a capable and competent individual who is not afraid to publicly attack your company on account of your clear CUIPA and CUTPA violations in our Connecticut General Statutes. If you have any question about my commitment to publicly helping stop your unfair insurance and trade practice, feel free to peruse my Connecticut CHRO complaint, which is slated for a public hearing in the coming months. At that hearing, I must publicly admit to being an addict, therefore there is no deterrent effect vis-à-vis intimidation around   a   public   admission   of   this   fact   as   articulated   within   this   complaint.

Additionally, as a member of both Mensa and Intertel I assure you that the level of discourse I will bring to the table surrounding the issue of unlawfully denying claims based on the precise chemical attributes around a particular drug of abuse has only been augmented by my years working as a paralegal and my holding an M.A. from Trinity College in Public Policy Analysis. Do not underestimate my will nor my ability to present this case to the tribunal and handle motions, discovery, and pretrial--I have been a pro se plaintiff in the Hartford J.D. on more than one   occasion.

I am giving you this fourteen-day window to initiate a meaningful settlement conference with me as a courtesy--consider this a demand letter. If you believe that you will prevail on a Motion to Strike, feel free to ignore this request. I warn you, however, that pro se plaintiffs are given more leeway than attorneys in the Connecticut jurisprudence, and I hopefully have laid the groundwork for a well-reasoned and meaningful Objection to Motion to Strike that is built into my complaint in paragraph 14. Let's settle this case before it becomes a bigger issue than it needs   to   be.

Warmest   regards,

Susan   Sturbridge

I attached my draft complaint to the demand letter, which read as follows:

COMPLAINT

First Count:
Violation of The Connecticut Unfair Insurance Practices Act (Connecticut General Statutes Sec. 38a-815 et seq.)

1. At all times relevant to this Complaint, the Plaintiff Susan Sturbridge is and was an individual residing in the State of Connecticut who had purchased a health insurance plan through the Connecticut Health Insurance Exchange from the Defendant, Anthem Health Plans, Inc. (hereinafter, "Anthem") and was lawfully insured under the Affordable Care Act at the time of this   complaint.
2. Defendant, Anthem, is now and at all times mentioned in this complaint a domestic stock corporation organized and existing under the laws of the State of Connecticut, with its principal business   address   at   108   Leigus   Road,   Wallingford,   CT.
3. The Plaintiff is informed and does believe that the Defendant is legally responsible for the events and happenings referred to in this complaint, and unlawfully caused the injuries and damages   to   the   Plaintiff   alleged   in   this   complaint.
4. On or about December 2, 2015, Plaintiff received a phone call on her cell phone around 11:30 am from the Admissions Department at The Rushford Center (hereinafter, "Rushford") located at 1250 Silver Street in Middletown, CT. The nature of this phone call was to inform the Plaintiff that a bed had opened at the inpatient drug treatment facility and that she should promptly pack an overnight bag and drive to the facility to initiate an inpatient stay in the residential   treatment   program   at   Rushford.
5. Due to an unforeseen circumstance at the hospital wherein due to an unanticipated contingency the Plaintiff was required to stay in a private room per direct order of an agent and/or employee of Rushford, the Plaintiff could not be admitted on 12/2/2015. She was informed of this exigency at approximately 6pm on 12/2/2015 and was instructed to return on 12/3/2015 for   an   admission   to   the   unit.
6. The Plaintiff complied with the facility's request, arriving on 12/3/2015 to seek admission to the inpatient drug treatment unit at Rushford. She was informed around 3pm that day that she would be denied admission to the inpatient unit specifically because her "drug of choice" (the

most-abused drug whose use necessitated a hospitalization) was synthetic marijuana.
7. Explicitly, the agent and/or employee of Rushford charged with navigating insurance protocols disseminated that the Defendant did not consider this particular chemical a drug of abuse necessitating an inpatient hospital stay due its pharmacology and neurochemistry. On account of this reasoning, her pre-authorization for an inpatient stay was denied and she was turned   away   from   chemical   dependency   treatment.
8. Synthetic marijuana is a man-made preparation of inert dried plant material treated with a plethora of synthetic indole alkaloids. Specifically, the chemicals that were abused by the Plaintiff (and the reason she was petitioning admission to Rushford) are chemically similar to and bioidentical to five Schedule I drugs. Those five chemicals are 1-pentyl-3-(1-naphthoyl) indole   (JWH-018),   1-butyl-3-(1-naphthoyl)   indole   (JWH-073),   1-[2-(4-morpholinyl) ethyl]-3-(1-naphthoyl)indole   (JWH-200),   5-(1,1-dimethylheptyl)-2-[(1R,3S)-3-hydroxycyclohexyl]-phenol   (CP-47,497),   and 5-(1,1-dimethyloctyl)-2-[(1R,3S)-3-hydroxycyclohexyl]-phenol   (cannabicyclohexanol;   CP-47,497 C8 homologue). As analogues to these indole alkaloids of abuse, their Schedule I status prohibits their use in medicine and government agencies have identified these chemicals as having a high abuse potential, established effects of withdrawal after dependence, and demonstrated   lethality.
9. The Plaintiff contends that the Defendant denied her admission to the inpatient unit because the Defendant did not consider addiction to analogues of Schedule I drugs enough of a problem to necessitate an inpatient hospitalization simply because the drug itself is legal to purchase in the State of Connecticut by individuals over the age of eighteen from online sources. However, the Plaintiff contends that since the Federal Analogue Act (21 USC § 813) treats criminal prosecution of sales and manufacture of these compounds to be illegal, the medical community should   treat   their   use   as   the   same   as   a   Schedule   I   drug.
10. In so doing, the Defendant has unreasonably ignored a significant portion of the widely-available medical corpus built upon both public and private case studies and research that explicitly states the abuse potential of indole alkaloids found in synthetic marijuana to be significant, its addiction physiologically and psychologically harmful, and its lethality demonstrated.
11. The Plaintiff contends that denying an individual attempting to enter an inpatient treatment center on a voluntary basis upon the written advice of a significant number of different medical doctors is a violation of C.G.S. sec. 38a-816(6)(F), specifically because the Defendant's "liability   has   become   reasonably   clear."
12. The Plaintiff further contends that the Defendant's denial of coverage is likewise a violation of C.G.S. sec. 38a-816(6)(N), specifically because while the Defendant did issue a written denial, such a document was "not a reasonable explanation of the basis in the insurance policy in relation to the facts or applicable law for denial of a claim," as it stands in direct opposition to the   guidance   of   the   Federal   Analogue   Act.
13. Due to the behemoth size of the Defendant's insurance business spanning many different

states, and the number of claims that must be processed in order to total an annual revenue of over eighty billion dollars, the Plaintiff contends that denying individuals inpatient treatment for the abuse of synthetic marijuana is a secular and systemic practice of the Defendant and is not an isolated incident pertaining to the Plaintiff. On account that this behavior is not simply an atypical incident due to the number of Connecticut hospitalizations for synthetic marijuana use (including but not limited to episodes of convulsions, seizures, psychosis, and cardiopulmonary irregularities), the Plaintiff contends that such denials are a general business practice of the Defendant.

14. Furthermore, the Plaintiff contends that the tribunal is aware that there is no appellate authority as to whether a Plaintiff must plead other specific instances of unfair settlement practices on the part of an insurer in order to satisfy the allegation of a general business practice, and that superior court decisions are split on this issue. Given the remedial nature of the Connecticut Unfair Insurance Practices Act, and given that it is to be liberally construed to give effect to the legislature's intent, the Plaintiff contends that the allegation of a general business practice in the complaint is sufficient to demonstrate a violation of C.G.S. sec. 38a-816.

15. On account that the Plaintiff was not granted admission to the inpatient unit at Rushford by the Defendant, her abuse of synthetic marijuana continued and effectuated several more hospitalizations for overuse as well as continued dependence on and abuse of these dangerous chemicals. The Plaintiff continued to engage in self-destructive behavior until she was hospitalized at a different inpatient facility after her insurance contract with the Defendant was terminated in 2016 and her new insurance carrier approved the very claim the Defendant denied.

16. As a direct and proximate result of the Defendant's violations of CUIPA, the Plaintiff has suffered the following damages:

        a.   Pain;

        b.   Suffering;

        c.   Anguish;

        d.   Loss   of   Enjoyment   of   Life's   Activities

Second Count
Violation of the Connecticut Unfair Trade Practices Act (Connecticut General Statutes sec. 42-110a et seq.)

1-16. Paragraphs 1-16 of Count One are hereby incorporated into this Count as if fully set forth herein.

17. At all times material, Defendant was a 'person' within the meaning of C.G.S. sec. 42-110a(3).

18. At all times material, Defendant engaged in trade or commerce within the State of Connecticut.

19. Defendant's conduct as alleged herein violated and continues to violate the Connecticut

Unfair Trade Practices Act (CUTPA) in that the conduct was unfair, immoral, unethical, oppressive, unscrupulous and/or deceptive and has caused substantial harm to the Plaintiff.
20. Pursuant to C.G.S. sec. 41-110g(c), a copy of this complaint has been mailed to the Attorney General and the Commissioner of Consumer Protection.
21. As a direct and proximate result of the Defendant's violations of CUTPA, the Plaintiff has suffered the following damages:
a.   Pain;

b.   Suffering;
c.   Anguish;
d.   Loss   of   Enjoyment   of   Life's   Activities
22. As a result of the Defendant's violations of CUTPA, the Plaintiff further asks for treble damages.

Third   Count
Negligent Infliction of Emotional Distress

1-22. Paragraphs 1-22 of Count One are hereby incorporated into this Count as if fully set forth herein.
23. These actions are extreme and outrageous given all of the circumstances, and these extreme and outrageous actions caused severe emotional distress to the Plaintiff.
24. As a direct and proximate result of the Defendant's negligence, the Plaintiff has suffered the following   damages:
a.   Pain;
b.   Suffering;
c.   Anguish;
d.   Loss   of   Enjoyment   of   Life's   Activities

WHEREFORE,   the   Plaintiff,   Susan   Sturbridge,   prays   for   the   following:
A.   For   monetary   damages   in   excess   of   fifteen   thousand   dollars;
B. For additional punitive damages for Defendant's clear violation of CUIPA and CUTPA;
C.   For   prejudgment   interest;
D. For permanent or temporary injunction, restraining order, or other order prohibiting the Defendant from engaging in practices in violation of applicable law including, but not limited to, C.G.S.   sections   38a-816   and   42-110b(a);
E. For an Order awarding the Plaintiff such other and further relief as the Court deems just and proper.

THE PLAINTIFF,
Susan   Sturbridge

I thought it was a valid point. If under the Federal Analogue Act that K2 would be considered a Schedule I drug for criminal purposes, civilly it should be treated the same way. The good part was not asking for a dollar amount. By giving them a deadline but no dollar amount, they had to respond. And they did. The lawyer emailed me. What did I want? I threw out a ridiculous number--500k. He said, we'll give you $5000 to settle and not sue us. I was reasonable. I told him I was a paralegal and knew how much it cost to take a matter to trial-- around 20k for this type of action. He said he couldn't do over $7500 without approval from the higher-ups. I said deal. He sent me a release, I got a check for $7500, which I proudly showed to my father.

Then there was the conduct of Rushford. I could not prove that they lied to Anthem to make it impossible for me to get into rehab, but I could prove something else. Through their conduct--telling me I needed to be housed in a substantially different way than cisgender females, they had offended public policy by being in violation of Connecticut's 2011 "An Act Concerning Discrimination," which made it illegal to "separate, segregate, or discriminate" based on an individual's gender identity.

I met with Craig and bought him lunch, asking him if it were better to flat out sue them civilly (I could do it pro se and keep 100% of the recovered funds) or take it to the CHRO. There's something in Connecticut called the CHRO, which is the Commission on Human Rights and Opportunities. They handle all cases of discrimination--age, race, ethnicity, creed, religion, sex, sexual orientation, etc.--and they adjudicate these matters. It was my first complaint to the CHRO. I formatted it as a civil complaint, even printing it on pleading paper, so it was patently clear to them that if they did not settle the matter in the confines of the CHRO, they would be subjected to a public suit. The text of the complaint was as follows:

COMPLAINT

First Count
Violation of An Act Concerning Discrimination (Connecticut General Statutes Sec. 46a-64)

1. At all times relevant to this Complaint, the Plaintiff Susan Sturbridge is and was a transgender individual living her life legally as a female as defined by applicable Connecticut General Statutes, having completed the biological transition process from male to female, including hormonal treatment and surgical sex reassignment.
2. Defendant, Rushford Center, Inc., (hereinafter, "Rushford") is now and at all times mentioned in this complaint was a nonstock corporation organized and existing under the laws of the State of Connecticut, with its principal place of business in Connecticut in Middlesex County.
3. Plaintiff is informed and does believe that the Defendant is legally responsible for the events and happenings referred to in this complaint, and unlawfully caused the injuries and damages to Plaintiff alleged in this complaint.

4. On or about December 1, 2015, Plaintiff received a phone call on her cell phone around 11:30 am from the Admissions Department at Rushford located at 1250 Silver Street in Middletown, CT. The nature of this phone call was to inform the Plaintiff that a bed had opened at the inpatient drug treatment facility and that she should promptly pack an overnight bag and drive to the facility to initiate an inpatient stay in the residential treatment program at Rushford.
5. To the best of the Plaintiff's knowledge, at the time of this telephone call, the Admissions Department at Rushford had not been made aware of the fact that the Plaintiff was a transgender individual.
6. The Plaintiff complied with the facility's request, arriving around 1:00 pm after driving to Rushford. The Plaintiff stayed in the waiting room until around 5:00 pm, at which point she was introduced to two employees and/or agents of Rushford, and the two of them initiated a meeting with the Plaintiff.
7. The nature of this meeting was to discuss the details of the inpatient housing for the Plaintiff. Both individuals informed the Plaintiff that they needed to know more about her before they could assign the Plaintiff a bed, specifically inquiring about the external morphology of the Plaintiff's genital region.
8. The Plaintiff refused to answer the question, and stated she would gladly provide identity documents in the form of an unexpired Connecticut driver's license that lists her sex as female, an unexpired U.S. passport that lists her sex as female, and a Connecticut certificate of live birth that lists her sex at birth as female.
9. The employees and/or agents of Rushford stated that such documents were insufficient and irrelevant, and were instead focused solely on the external morphology of the Plaintiff's genital area, stating that they needed to know the answer to the question for 'medical reasons.'
10. The employees and/or agents of Rushford were not disputing that the Plaintiff is and was a female (as during the meeting the Plaintiff divulged that she had undergone surgical sex reassignment) and were not attempting to house the Plaintiff in anywhere but the 'female side' of the residential treatment facility, but were rather making certain inquiries as to the exact nature of the Plaintiff's surgical sex reassignment.
11. The Plaintiff contends that addiction is defined as a disease by most medical associations, including the American Medical Association and the American Society of Addiction Medicine, and that this disease (apart from issues like erectile dysfunction) has absolutely no connection to the external morphology of the genital region.
12. The Plaintiff continued to refuse to answer the questions of the Rushford employees and/or agents until they explained to her that if she did not answer this invasive personal question she would be denied admission to the inpatient unit, after she had already been called earlier in the day and told a bed was available to her the evening of December 1, 2015 and had been waiting all day for said bed.
13. The Plaintiff truthfully answered the question posed to her, as she believed that seeking treatment for her addiction was more important at that moment than her dignity and integrity, deciding to surrender her will to Rushford and place treating her disease of addiction above her

hormonal issues and non-traditional internal morphology of genitals, chromosomes, and gonads.
14. Immediately after this response, the Plaintiff was told that she would not be given a room in the inpatient treatment center on the night of December 1, 2015. When the Plaintiff protested, the Rushford employees and/or agents explained that they would be willing to allow her to sleep in a hospital bed in an affiliated facility, but that the Plaintiff would be financially responsible for her transportation there as well as the cost of the room for the evening.
15. Additionally, the two employees and/or agents stated that the reason for this decision was because the Plaintiff required a 'private room,' something that would only happen the next day after another female patient was discharged. The employees and/or agents stated that the Plaintiff's gender identity required her to be housed separately and in a different manner than if she had been a cisgender female.
16. The Defendant's website, under the header of 'Mission and Values,' states the following: '...We treat those we serve and each other with kindness and compassion and strive to better understand and respond to the needs of a diverse community.' It further states, '...We work as a team to bring experience, advanced technology and best practices to bear in providing the highest-quality care for our patients and families. We devote ourselves to continuous improvement, excellence, professionalism and innovation in our work.' Lastly, it states that, 'We act ethically and responsibly in everything we do and hold ourselves accountable for our behavior. We bring respect, openness and honesty to our encounters with patients, families and coworkers and support the well-being of the communities we serve.'
17. The Plaintiff contends that Rushford did not act in keeping with and upholding its mission and values as Rushford was not willing to admit her to their residential treatment program on a non-discriminatory basis.
18. The actions of the Rushford employees and/or agents amounts to de facto discrimination, as specifically prohibited by C.G.S. sec. 46a-64(a)(1) and C.G.S. sec. 46a-64(a)(2).
19. The Plaintiff contends that offering someone a room with a bed, discovering the individual is transgender and then withdrawing the offer amounts to de facto discrimination under aforementioned applicable Connecticut General Statutes.
20. The Plaintiff contends that telling a transgender individual that because of her gender identity she will need to be housed in a separate facility from others, a facility that does not specialize in the disease of addiction, even for a single evening, is de facto discrimination under aforementioned applicable Connecticut General Statutes.
21. The Plaintiff contends that giving a transgender individual a 'private room' rather than a double room with a roommate like every other cisgender individual who visits this residential treatment facility is given, is de facto discrimination under aforementioned applicable Connecticut General Statutes.
22. In order to be absolutely certain that the behavior of Rushford's employees and/or agents was not an isolated incident of discrimination against the Plaintiff singly but is instead ongoing discrimination against a protected class of individuals as a whole, the Plaintiff returned to Rushford on the afternoons of May 13, 2016 and May 17, 2016 for clarification. At those visits

the Plaintiff held brief meetings with a different employee and/or agent of Rushford during each respective meeting. Each time the answer was the same, from four separate and distinct employees and/or agents of Rushford that all stated it was the practice of Rushford to house transgender individuals seeking residential treatment in a separated and segregated manner, in direct violation of the Connecticut General Statutes.

Second Count
Negligent Infliction of Emotional Distress

1-22. Paragraphs 1-22 of Count One are hereby incorporated into this Count as if fully set forth herein.

23. These actions are extreme and outrageous given all of the circumstances, and these extreme and outrageous actions caused severe emotional distress to the Plaintiff.

24. As a direct and proximate result of the Defendant's negligence, the Plaintiff has suffered the following damages:

    a.   Embarrassment;

    b.   Humiliation;

    c.   Pain;

    d.   Suffering;

    e.   Anguish;

    f.   Loss of Identity;

    g.   Loss of Enjoyment of Life's Activities

Third Count
Violation of the Connecticut Unfair Trade Practices Act (Connecticut General Statutes sec. 42-110a et seq.)

1-24. Paragraphs 1-24 of Count Two are hereby incorporated into this Count as if fully set forth herein.

25. At all times material, Defendant was a 'person' within the meaning of C.G.S. sec. 42-110a(3).

26. At all times material, Defendant engaged in trade or commerce within the State of Connecticut.

27. Defendant's conduct as alleged herein violated and continues to violate the Connecticut Unfair Trade Practices Act (CUTPA) in that the conduct was unfair, immoral, unethical, oppressive, unscrupulous and/or deceptive and has caused substantial harm to the Plaintiff.

28. Pursuant to C.G.S. sec. 41-110g(c), a copy of this complaint has been mailed to the Attorney General and the Commissioner of Consumer Protection.

29. As a direct and proximate result of the Defendant's violations of CUTPA, the Plaintiff has

suffered   the   following   damages:
    a.   Embarrassment;
    b.   Humiliation;
    c.   Pain;
    d.   Suffering;
    e.   Anguish;
    f.   Loss   of   Identity;
    g.   Loss   of   Enjoyment   of   Life's   Activities

30. As a result of the Defendant's violations of CUTPA, the Plaintiff further asks for treble damages.

WHEREFORE,   the   Plaintiff,   Susan   Sturbridge,   prays   for   the   following:
A.   For   monetary   damages   in   excess   of   fifteen   thousand   dollars;
B.   For   additional   punitive   damages   for   Defendant's   clear   violation   of   CUTPA;
C.   For   prejudgment   interest;
D.   For permanent or temporary injunction, restraining order, or other order prohibiting the Defendant from engaging in discriminatory practices in violation of applicable law including, but   not   limited   to,   C.G.S.   sec   46a-64(a);
E.   For an Order awarding the Plaintiff such other and further relief as the Court deems just and   proper.

THE PLAINTIFF,
Susan   Sturbridge

The way the process goes is this: you make a complaint. The respondent responds in thirty days, and then you can rebut their response. Then you have a mediation where both parties appear with a lawyer from the State of Connecticut and try to hammer out a deal. If that doesn't work, they would hold a public hearing on the matter at hand, after which there would be a "trial" in front of a magistrate, who would enter a judgment and award damages as he or she saw fit.

So after I filed the complaint, they retained a very pricey Hartford law firm. Their first move was to have what was known as a pre-answer mediation. They did this to test my temperature. I would have nothing of it. They were going to have to answer my allegations, and I was not going to dismiss the complaint without a response.

I agreed to the mediation. We met in Waterbury with a state employee, not an attorney. She asks me what I wanted.

"1.21 million," I said.

I did the calculation based on the size of the yearly revenue at Hartford Healthcare and computed the punitive damages they would receive by looking at other cases. She told me we weren't going to settle today.

"Fine," I said. "Then they can answer."

Their answer was straight up offensive. They played it off as if I needed a private room because I was bipolar and had a mental illness and not because I was transgender. It was a decent strategy, but that was just not what occurred. They lied. It was a little sad. Then I realized I was putting Hartford Healthcare right up to the wall, and they were lying to save their own asses. Wouldn't I do the same thing? I sent a rebuttal. It went like this:

I was a victim seeking to make my life better by going into an inpatient program, and now I am being victimized again as Attorney Fritz has created a false and parallel narrative that is a simple misrepresentation of fact. First of all, Attorney Fritz attests that a Rushford employee "became aware of the fact that the Complainant had male genitalia when she provided the observed urine sample during her vitals assessment." This is simply an untrue statement. While I did have to give a urine sample as part of my vitals assessment, I was not observed. I was alone in a bathroom, returning the cup to the associate and was not viewed. Clearly, Attorney Fritz is making this false statement as she then does not have to address the behavior of the employees who had to ask me at the 5:20 pm meeting if I had a penis.

In fact, what specifically happened was that the two women that did my intake did not know that I possessed male genitalia and had to ask the question. After I answered truthfully that I had, I was specifically told the following: "We need to give you a private room then." I responded, "Why wouldn't I get a roommate?" They replied, "Many of the women here have been raped or through sexual trauma as a result of their using, and we couldn't have you be placed with a roommate because what if she saw your penis?" I then asked, "Exposing one's genitals is a crime. What makes you think I'm more likely to commit a crime because I'm transgender?" To which they responded, "Sorry, we cannot give you a roommate. You may only enter this facility in a private room." This narrative, while standing in direct opposition to the one provided by the Respondent, is nonetheless what actually occurred.

Furthermore, it must be noted that the only time I exposed myself to anyone at Rushford was during a "skin check" (stripping down to the underwear) as part of the intake process on 12/3/2016, which was a clinical medical process where my breasts were viewed. In relation to the nurse's statement that I exposed my breasts to her, this is a complete fabrication by the Respondent. I will admit, I was nervous, I felt like a victim, the employee asked me if I would be "more comfortable on the men's side of the unit." I got so scared that I would be placed with men that I do admit to pressing my breasts together to show cleavage and then saying, "would you put me in the men's unit with these?" However, she never saw my nipples or the entirety of my breasts. And while had I done that in public it might have been considered in poor taste, I certainly did not "flash" the employee or "expose myself to the employee" any more than anyone would see while I'm working out in a sports bra at the gym.

Another issue which seems to be misunderstood by the Respondent is the notion of a transgender individual being "post-op," which I am, and in the memorandum it states that I told this to a Rushford employee. (In order to alleviate any confusion, I am attaching a copy of the letter from my surgeon stating he changed my sex with a surgical solution.) Top surgery is the only pertinent surgery to transgender individuals. Bottom surgery, and the morphology of the genitals, has absolutely nothing to do with being transgender. Therefore, whether or not I have a penis is irrelevant. What is relevant is that I have breasts. If I remove my top in public I would be arrested for indecent exposure. This is because I am a female. This is the exact reason I pressed my breasts together to create cleavage to show the employee of Rushford that I was being victimized by being asked if I wanted to be housed with men. Top surgery is everything. And I explained to the woman on the phone that I was a post-op transgender woman on hormones so that I would not have any of these problems, and that they would instead understand I should be housed like any other typical female.

However, Rushford found a creative way to discriminate against me. Once I got there and they knew I would not accept being housed alone like a second-class citizen and in clear violation of Connecticut statute, they purposefully told the insurance company the incorrect drug of choice (synthetic marijuana as opposed to dextromethorphan hydrobromide) on the paperwork so that I would not be admitted because insurance wouldn't pay for me to go and this would all go away. While they claim in their answer that I was sent there on a referral by my psychiatrist stated to me firsthand that he had written down on the form that I needed rehabilitation for an addiction to dextromethorphan hydrobromide and not synthetic marijuana. This was echoed by referral forms from the other doctors all in possession of the Respondent. This act stands in direct opposition to the position taken in the Respondent's memorandum, which states that they were not in violation of the law because they did not intentionally discriminate against me. This is false.

In summary, what my genitalia look like has absolutely no bearing on my sex. My driver's license, my passport, and my birth certificate all state that I am a female. This is because I sought a surgical solution to my transgender status and am now a post-op female on hormones (please see attachment). The Respondent has fabricated an untrue story whereby they have stated that an employee and/or agent of Rushford saw my genitalia (this is a lie) and they also stated that I needed a private room because of my 'boundary issues' and not because I was transgender. Another lie. I never exposed myself to any nurse, though I do admit to pressing my breasts together to show cleavage in order to stress that it would be criminal to place me in a male unit. In direct opposition to the Respondent's answer, I would submit that my mental state and 'boundary issues' were not an issue at my time of admission, as I had just been working at Connecticare as a telephone customer service representative and had never been written up or had any problems at all in that job. Lastly, the Respondent further discriminated against me by intentionally writing the wrong drug of choice on the intake form so that my insurance would not *pay and I would be turned away. They did so on 12/3/16 because they knew I would make a fuss if placed in a private room away from my peers, an action that was going to be taken to protect the other females from my penis and not because I had a 'boundary issue.'*

I hope that the hearing officer sees through the Respondent's poorly executed ruse and finds in my favor that discrimination in violation of appropriate Connecticut General Statute did exist.

Susan Sturbridge

I was worried we weren't going to settle. I readied myself for a public hearing. I got together a list on Facebook and on my phone all of the LGBT people I knew, all the activists I knew, and I made a list. I sounded the alarm. I wrote them all a letter to ready for our public hearing. Here's how it read:

> *Dear   Fellow   LGBT   Activist,*

You are receiving this correspondence because I am in need of assistance--for over a decade I have tirelessly fought for the transgender community, taking every possible opportunity to speak publicly about the rights of gender nonconforming individuals. I changed sex publicly and wrote about the process in my second book, and since then have continued my activism from the poker table   to   the   classroom   to   the   boardroom.

I now find myself in the situation wherein I was discriminated against back in December of 2015 by the Hartford Healthcare Corporation, a leading Connecticut healthcare provider that treats many transgender and cisgender individuals. I have attached a copy of a letter I authored back in May to Hartford Healthcare's chief legal counsel and Senior Vice President, as well as a draft copy of the civil complaint I am going to file in the Hartford Judicial District in the coming months.

Presently, this issue is being handled by the State of Connecticut Commission on Human Rights and Opportunities. I got a chance to speak yesterday with one of their representatives in the Waterbury office, who informed me that due to the nature of my complaint (Susan Sturbridge v. Rushford Center) it will be slated for a public hearing in the coming months. I need your help at this   public   hearing.

Many transgender individuals were so very pleased by the landmark 2011 "An Act Concerning Discrimination" adding gender identity to Connecticut protected classes that we failed to consider what would happen if an entity dared violate our newfound rights. For all of the transgender individuals, for all of the gay and lesbian and bisexual individuals, for all of the allies   in   our   movement,   this   law   is   only   as   good   as   its   enforcement.

We now have a fresh new opportunity that has been dropped into our laps to bring our struggle for equal treatment under the law into the forefront once again. According to the CHRO representative (as well as my own large amount of research) this appears to be the first action brought to both the CHRO and into the Connecticut jurisprudence more generally that cites a violation of the protections contained within An Act Concerning Discrimination for gender nonconforming individuals. Specifically, my CHRO and civil complaints allege a violation under Connecticut General Statutes. sec. 46a-64(a)(2), which states it is illegal '...to separate, segregate, or discriminate on account of...gender identity."

In terms of my specific issue, in the coming months the CHRO is going to hold a public hearing on this violation, and this will give us a precious opportunity to show our support for Connecticut's generous LGBT civil rights in the public arena. I need bodies at this hearing. I cannot stress this enough. I am in the process of planning a "Statewide Transgender Rights Action Day" for the date of the public hearing. I do not yet know if the public hearing will be held in Hartford or Waterbury, and I do not yet know the date or time.

Though that is in the future, we need to start planning now for this substantial event in the path for equality for transgender individuals in our state. That is the reason you are being approached at the early stages of this process.

I look forward to meeting with you at your convenience to discuss a plan for how we can best civically engage those who seek to violate the law and bring a public discussion about how to best penalize an organization that has been systematically and systemically discriminating against the transgender population in our state since the law was passed in 2011. To the best of my knowledge, the respondent has changed their protocols and policies since the interaction I had with them back in December 2015 and no longer is in violation of statute, but this does nothing to address the five years of discrimination felt by our community.

Since the six-year statute of limitations has not yet run on the new Act Concerning Discrimination, it may very well be possible to create a class-action lawsuit against Hartford Healthcare by all transgender individuals that sought treatment or had treatment at Middletown's Rushford Center since 2011. This is above and beyond my capability as I am not admitted to the bar, however my civil complaint to be filed under the Connecticut Unfair Trade Practices Act will seek to recover substantial punitive damages from Hartford Healthcare in order to deter other businesses engaging in similar conduct.

I have a great deal more information and research on all of these topics, and I also have a well-reasoned plan of action for my own civil case and the arguments therein. Though I have not yet retained counsel, I will not require legal assistance until after a certificate of closed pleadings and claim for trial list has been filed and the pretrial date has passed, something that will not occur for at least a year. Right now I just need help organizing. I am going to need every single transgender individual, every single transgender ally, and every single gay, lesbian, and bisexual individual to support our fight for equality at this public hearing on our upcoming Statewide Transgender Rights Action Day.

I will need help from you personally as well as your organization to bring this to fruition, and am looking to hear any input I can receive from your groups in terms of strategy for creating the most potent Action Day that we can.

Feel free to reach out to me by mail at the aforementioned address, via email, or via phone or text on my cell. If you are not already friends with me on Facebook or if you have not connected with me yet on LinkedIn, feel free to utilize whichever platform you prefer.

Let's combine our many little lights together into one enormous beam to illuminate the continued need for vigilance around the fair, just, and equitable treatment of transgender individuals in our state. Let's make an Action Day and let's make it great!

Warmest regards,
Susan Sturbridge

Well, we had our second mediation. This time it happened in downtown Hartford. After we couldn't reach a resolution in the pre-answer mediation, Hartford Healthcare changed counsel to a more affordable, lesser-known Hartford firm (most likely they were billing them at a lower hourly rate to save some money) and they now appeared. I showed up to the mediation fifteen minutes early and was greeted in the lobby by the mediator. He wanted me to lay out my case to him.

I laid out all of my documents. I had the complaint, response, rebuttal, etc., and I also had with me a bound collection of eleven cases I had studied. Each one was a CUTPA claim, a great statute for bringing a claim under because you can be awarded treble (triple) damages, and can receive punitive damages in addition to compensatory ones.

Compensatory damages are meant to be payment for pain and suffering or whatever is the ascertainable loss. Punitive damages are different. The way they work is, when a company is found guilty of engaging in an illicit business practice, they basically get "fined," or "punished" for their offense to public policy. And as tortfeasors, they pay the victim, not the state. So, I had studied the eleven cases I came in with and had figured out the average percentage of annual gross revenue and the percentage of annual profit that amounted to the punitive damage award.

Hartford Healthcare had a very high gross revenue but a slim profit margin--they were operating like a Target or Walmart. I also brought with me their consolidated financial statement with the key numbers highlighted. I calculated the punitive award to be between 200k and 1.2

million. And then there were compensatory damages for the negligent infliction of emotional distress.

The lawyer for CHRO told me that by far, I was the most prepared complainant he'd ever met, and I accepted the compliment. I told him to start with the 1.2 million figure. He came back and said they were not going to talk to me unless I was going to be more reasonable. I told him to go back with the 200k number. He disappeared and returned.

"They're starting at 5,000," he said. It's fair. The cost of a retainer for a lawyer. It made sense.

The mediator said that the numbers are really far apart. He said, what are you really willing to settle for? I explained my logic. Per my public policy analysis degree, I learned that nothing can be certain in government and civics. So, to get around this theoretical hurdle, policymakers have decided that in public policy, 95% certainty means something is certain to happen, leaving a 5% wiggle room. So take punitive damages of 1.2 million. Let's say Hartford Healthcare is sure they will win. That still leaves an axiomatic uncertainty of 5%. Thus, 5% times 1.2 million equals 60k. That's my offer. 60k. He disappeared and came back.

"They'll do 15k," he said. "That's their final offer."

"I need to make a call," I said.

I excused myself and called Ava. She always was my go-to and had been to other corporate mediations before.

"So they're offering you 15k to drop the suit?" she asked.

"Yes."

"What do you think you would get if you took it to trial and won?" she asked.

"Somewhere between 200k and 1.2 million, but it's not a given since this is the first test of the transgender nondiscrimination law. If the judge likes me or likes LGBT people, he might come in high. If he's an old wrinkled prick who's slightly homophobic, the result could be really low. It's a crap shoot. It depends on the judge."

"Do you have any say over what judge you get?" she asked.

"No. Caseflow does that." I responded.

"Take the 15k, honey," she said.

"Why? I could earn so much more," I replied. "And I'd be setting a legal precedent that could help the next generation of transgender people in Connecticut and everywhere else in the country. I could be a pioneer. A leader. Why not do it?"

"If you knew you'd get a million dollars, I'd say do it," she said. "But the reality is, if you don't, then you go on the public record saying you're an addict, and that's forever. You might never get a real job. It's not worth it. Take the 15k."

I went back to the mediator and told him I'd take the deal. He was slightly disappointed. He wanted this to be the first test case of the new law--he was so excited to meet me because he thought this was going to be the first test. But I played it safe and he understood.

The check came a week later. You'd be amazed at how fast you can spend 15k when you need to. But for at least a short time, I was on top of the world. *Not* going to rehab had netted me

$22,500 in settlements. I thought that was even better than getting clean, taking the money. Boy, was I wrong.

HOW TO RACK UP THREE DUIS

My first DUI (technically, my second, since I had one two years earlier and it was expunged after I completed the pretrial diversionary program) was an accident. But the reason I drank was definitely Ava. Saturday night we'd gotten in a fight. I didn't remember what it was about. Since I'd been using, I'd been fighting with her a lot more, even though we'd been together for eleven years.

So I woke up on Sunday, went to 8:30 mass like I normally did, and was about to go to the gym--my normal Sunday routine. But I checked Craigslist and found a free oven in Newport, RI. (I almost never checked Rhode Island Craigslist, but it was a gorgeous Sunday in July and I thought I might want to go to the beach.) The listing had only been up for twelve minutes. I called and said I wanted it, the man gave me the address, and I was going to leave that minute. I asked Ava to come with me.

"I have to go to the gym," she said. She was a bit of a gym rat.

"But honey, we can have a great day in Newport and stop at the beach and I'll take you to lunch."

"Yeah, I'm gonna' pass," she said. "I want to go to the gym."

"What is wrong with you?" I asked. "I'm your girlfriend. I just organized a trip to Rhode Island for us on a beautiful sunny day where the money I'll make parting out the oven will pay for the day. And you don't even have a class to go to Sunday morning--you're just going on the bike and the elliptical. Come on!" She was still mad from the night before.

"You go," she said. "I insist."

I grumbled and got into the minivan. I just felt like my relationship wasn't working anymore. I called my dealer--he was on his way to New Jersey to pick up his woman. I didn't want to use cough medicine because I'd be high and have to move a 140-pound oven on a hand truck. The last time I did that I dropped one on my foot and cut myself pretty badly. So I stopped at the liquor store and grabbed a Four Loko.

I wasn't aiming to get drunk--just get a little buzz and feel better. I finished that Four Loko in about forty-five minutes and stopped at another liquor store and got another. I finished that as I was rolling into the Asian man's driveway with the free stove. We loaded it in. I was now in Newport by myself. I really didn't feel like going to the beach alone. I wanted my girlfriend. So I stopped at one last liquor store and grabbed one more Four Loko and drank it really slowly.

I came home on Route 2. I was in East Hartford and I got pulled over by a state trooper. He said he'd gotten a couple calls about my vehicle, swerving and changing lanes illegally. I didn't trust him as far as I could throw him. He asked if I'd been drinking and I said I had but I was under the legal limit.

He gave me the walk the line test, and I saw there was no line on the ground. I remember a couple drunks in my DUI classes saying if they ask you to walk the line and there is no line, the test is invalid. I failed the test and was arrested. I refused the breathalyzer and said I would take the urine. He brought me to the barracks in Hartford, the same place where I'd given my statement about the rental car.

I was locked in a cell for about thirty minutes and then a woman appeared with a cup.

"Time to pee," she said.

"Actually," I said, "I think I want to talk to my lawyer."

"It's a little late for that," she said.

"But I haven't called him yet," I explained. "I want to call him now."

"No. Pee in the cup."

"Are you refusing to let me call a lawyer before I submit to a chemical test?" I was incredibly lucid.

"If you don't pee, it's an automatic suspension. I'm not going to ask again."

I peed. I figured I was not over the limit by this point. I was wrong.

Several weeks later the urine test came back--.12. The limit is .08. I had a mandatory 45-day license suspension. It sucked. My parents and Ava drove me around everywhere. It was so embarrassing. Then I had to get an IID in the car (this is an ignition interlock device) in order to drive for a year once the suspension was up. It cost $175 to install and $75 a month, and you had to go back to the garage once a month to have it "calibrated." If you missed an appointment, the car was in violation mode and you would have to keep the unit for another month. Same went if you blew and you were over the limit--you had to bring it back and have it reset within seventy-two hours, and you were penalized another month.

It was as awful as it was embarrassing. I had to blow into my car to start it. My friends laughed at me. Ava and my parents refused to drive my car. It was just a disaster. I just focused on my ovens. Business was going well, I was selling a couple thousand dollars in parts a month, and I was scrapping out three or four ovens a week.

I hadn't forgotten about the DUI, but I was playing the delaying game. At my first appearance, they asked me if I wanted a public defender or if I would use my own lawyer. I told them neither.

"I'm a paralegal. I can handle all the pretrial motions."

The prosecutor told me that this was not wise. I had to remember that he was my adversary.

Next meeting I asked for a continuance. The police report wasn't ready yet and they had nothing for me. I filed my paperwork for discovery. It looks like this:

REQUEST FOR DISCOVERY

As filed in accordance with Practice Book § 41-5, pursuant to P.B. § 40-11, the Defendant asks that the Plaintiff disclose in writing the existence of, provide photocopies of, and allow the defendant in accordance with P.B. § 40-7, to inspect, copy, photograph and have reasonable tests made on any of the following items:
(1) Any books, tangible objects, papers, photographs, or documents within the possession,

custody or control of any governmental agency, which the prosecuting authority intends to offer in evidence in chief at trial or which are material to the preparation of the defense or which were obtained from or purportedly belong to the defendant; (2) Copies of the defendant's prior criminal record, if any, which are within the possession, custody, or control of the prosecuting authority, the existence of which is known, or by the exercise of due diligence may become known, to the prosecuting authority; (3) Any reports or statements of experts made in connection with the offense charged including results of physical and mental examinations and of scientific tests, experiments or comparisons which are material to the preparation of the defense or are intended for use by the prosecuting authority as evidence in chief at the trial; (4) Any warrant executed for the arrest of the defendant for the offense charged, and any search and seizure warrants issued in connection with the investigation of the offense charged; (5) (A) Any written, recorded or oral statements made by the defendant before or after arrest to any law enforcement officer or to a person acting under the direction of or in cooperation with a law enforcement officer concerning the offense charged. In addition to the foregoing, the Defendant requests the prosecuting authority shall disclose in accordance with any applicable constitutional and statutory provisions, any exculpatory information or materials that the prosecuting authority may have. Additionally, as filed in accordance with P.B. § 41-5, pursuant to P.B. § 40-13, the Defendant hereby requests the names and (subject to the provisions § 40-13[f] and § 40-13[g]) the addresses of all witnesses that the prosecuting authority intends to call in his or her case-in-chief. In keeping with § 40-13(a), the Defendant hereby requests the Plaintiff make a reasonable affirmative effort to obtain.

THE DEFENDANT
Susan   *Sturbridge*

I formatted it the way a lawyer would, and I wrote it exactly the way I would for our criminal cases at Fleeman. I went to my next court date.

"I'm here to pick up discovery," I said.

"It's not ready," said the prosecutor.

"Then I need another continuance," I said.

Granted. About thirty days had elapsed since my request for discovery had been made. The prosecution had, by state law, forty-five days to issue the documents, or else the case can be dismissed. I waited until the 46th day, then mailed in via certified mail a motion to dismiss. It looked like this.

Motion to Dismiss

In accordance with Practice Book § 41-8(1), the Defendant hereby files a Motion to Dismiss due to defects in the institution of prosecution, specifically because of a flawed discovery process. In accordance with Practice Book § 40-5(6), the tribunal may dismiss the charges for a failure to comply with discovery.

On November 18, 2016 the Defendant filed a Request for Discovery (attached as Exhibit A) in accordance with Practice Book § 41-5. In a failed attempt to fulfill this request, the State's Attorney provided an in-person delivery of documents at the Defendant's last court appearance, specifically, the Defendant was handed a copy of the police report associated with this docket number. At present, the statutory forty-five days has elapsed since the discovery request was made (as dictated by Practice Book § 40-11) and no further materials have been made available.

In addition to this report, however, the Defendant requested "copies of the defendant's prior criminal record" as well as "pursuant to P.B. § 40-13...the names and (subject to the provisions § 40-13[f] and § 40-13[g]) the addresses of all witnesses that the prosecuting authority intends to call in his or her case-in-chief."

These discovery requests were blatantly ignored by the State's Attorney's office, placing them in violation of Practice Book, and the Defendant asserts that these requests were ignored because the Defendant is a pro se woman acting as her own attorney rather than an attorney admitted to practice in the State of Connecticut.

Such a clear procedural violation exposes the weakness of the State's case against the Defendant, and the Defendant hereby prays to the tribunal for relief, specifically that the case be dismissed for these egregious missteps by the State's Attorney's Office.

THE DEFENDANT
Susan *Sturbridge*

I showed up at court again to argue my motion to dismiss. When my case was called, I got to go in front of everyone in court and make my case to the judge. He had a copy of my motion, and when he listened, he actually listened to me. I felt like he treated me like a lawyer and not a criminal. No one at court was pro se. He heard my argument. He asked the state's attorney if he had the discovery. The prosecutor held it up.

"They have provided their discovery," the judge said. "I'm denying your motion to dismiss."

"Thank you, Your Honor," I said. "Please give me a date about six weeks out and I will be ready with another motion to dismiss." He gave me another date. Then I did something stupid.

It was late December of 2016 at this point. We had made it through the holidays, and I got in another fight with Ava. It was bad--we were yelling at each other and she told me to leave. I got in my minivan and drove to Somers to pick up another oven, but not before stopping at CVS and buying some cold medicine.

I felt high when I got the oven. Then I put Mohegan Sun (my home base) into the GPS. It routed me through eastern Connecticut on roads I'd never been on. I was getting higher and higher. The next thing I knew, I was in Willimantic and my minivan crashed into a cemetery fence. It all seemed like a dream. I guess I was tripping. Plus, I had taken some klonopin with the DXM so I was really intoxicated. They arrested me for DUI, my second.

After they impounded the car, I called Ava after they'd released me on a non-surety bond around 2am. She sent an Uber for me because my phone was in the minivan. She continued to enable me. We picked up the minivan and assessed the damage. No front bumper. Dented hood. Dented fender. I couldn't drive to people's houses and pick up ovens with that! So I went and got a new hood and new bumper cover for $500. I kept scrapping ovens.

"Aren't you worried about those DUIs, honey?" asked Ava.

"I got it under control," I said. I was already filing a motion to suppress and a motion to dismiss on the first one. They never let me call my lawyer before they gave me the urine test. That's illegal under statute. "I'm going to get the urinalysis thrown out and then they'll either give me a deal and plea it down to reckless driving or they're going to dismiss it. If we need to go to trial, I'll hire Craig at the last minute. In terms of the second, I told the officer I had a seizure. I passed out driving at 20mph. I wasn't intoxicated. Then if the urine shows DXM, I'll just say it was a therapeutic dose and I had a cold. No problem." She had her fears allayed slightly.

I made my first appearance in court in Danielson for the Willimantic DUI. The judge was not like the judge in Manchester. He sent everyone to jail! It was crazy! An 18-year-old kid was on probation. He gave a dirty urine for marijuana.

"You failed a drug test," he said. "You had a six-month suspended sentence. You will now serve that sentence." And the marshals took him away in handcuffs. Holy cow! I just got scared for the first time. I plead not guilty and got out of there fast.

I appeared again ready to dismiss my first DUI in Manchester. I had already filed the pleading that looked like this:

MOTION TO SUPPRESS

In accordance with the filing requirements of Practice Book § 41-5, this pending matter has not been assigned a pretrial conference at this time, therefore this motion to suppress evidence is timely.

The Defendant is moving to suppress the urinalysis evidence within this case because there are several defects in the State's Attorney's actions that negatively impact its admissibility as evidence at trial. Specifically, Connecticut law at § 14-227a(b)(1) clearly states that the Defendant must be given the right to contact her attorney before providing a urine sample. The Defendant has held from her first interaction with the State's Attorney that this was the case and that evidence was inadmissible per statute. In addition to this grievous error that is a clear defect in the State's case, the State is also in violation of § 14-227a(b)(2) because the urinalysis results were not delivered to the Defendant within the timeframe dictated by statute. Because of these errors in following Connecticut law which occurred while collecting and processing purported evidence, the Defendant hereby moves that the evidence of a urinalysis test be suppressed in this action.

THE   *DEFENDANT*
Susan   *Sturbridge*

I started arguing my case to the judge.

"I don't know if he discriminated against me for being transgender or what, Your Honor," I began. "But he violated the Connecticut General Statutes."

I was courteous, professional, and I addressed the entire court. The judge let me speak for a little while and then he interrupted me.

"You can't argue a motion to suppress right now," he said. Remember, I'm not a lawyer.

"Why not?" I asked. "It's a pretrial motion and we're in pretrial."

"That would be heard before trial at an evidentiary hearing. We used to hold those in pretrial, but now they've been combined with the trial so we only have to call the witnesses once. So, we can set up another date, you can make your argument, and the officer can testify. If at that point the tribunal grants your motion, the evidence would be suppressed and you could make your motion to dismiss."

"Okay," I said. "Set it on the docket for pretrial."

"No problem," said the judge. "Mark it down for judicial pretrial in five weeks."

And I left again. Now, my strategy hadn't backfired, but it was becoming riskier. If I took the deal and didn't go to trial, they'd probably give me community service and no jail time. But what if I weren't as smart as I thought I was? What if my motion to suppress didn't work and I was facing a trial with a urinalysis test of .12? I would lose. They could sentence me to six months. Life was getting riskier. Then, tragedy struck.

My minivan died. I had just gone to Winsted with my friend Bob to pick up a Jenn-Air range for parts, and I had dropped him off, and my motor made a horrible noise and made a loud "pop" and I felt like I was missing a cylinder. I brought the car home slowly and checked it out. One of the spark plugs had ejected right out of the socket. It could be repaired, said the mechanic, but at 220k it was time to send it to the boneyard. It was a great car--I bought it for $2500 and put 70k on it without any mechanical problems. I had my mechanic remove the IID and the car went to the junkyard. Now I needed another car.

I wanted another minivan, as I could pull the seats out and fit two ovens inside a covered space, which was even better than a pickup truck. In the interim I went to Budget (ironically) and rented the cheapest car they had, a Nissan Versa. I surfed looking for cars and didn't find one.

"I'm going to Mohegan," I told Ava.

"No you are not! You are cleaning the office. There are oven parts everywhere!"

"No, I'm not," I said. "I'm going to play poker."

"Don't you leave!" she yelled.

"I'm leaving," I said, and slammed the door. Self will run riot.

I drove the fifty minutes to Mohegan, planning to play all night. Instead, I lost set over set and then ran into quads. I lost $600 at the 1-2 table in thirty minutes. I was disgusted. I hatched a smart plan. I would buy some cold medicine, not enough to get too high, and take a drive. No chance of getting caught. Not a problem.

I drove all over the state. Then, I was in Rocky Hill on the Silas Deane Highway and got stopped for speeding in a speed trap. Apparently, even though I could walk the line, I failed the gaze nystagmus test. Arrested again. DUI number three. There was no getting out of this one. No way. There were empty packages of cold medicine in the passenger seat. And I was driving a rental car that (of course) had no IID in it. A separate charge.

I surrendered. At least I thought I did. I said I would go to rehab. I took the money I'd made from Rushford and checked myself into Highwatch Farm in Kent, CT, the same place I'd met my Silver Hill counselor Mike in 2002, had a spiritual awakening, and stayed clean for over a decade. I was not disappointed. First of all they treated me amazingly--I was not discriminated against for my gender identity, shared a room, a bathroom, and a shower with other females. This place got it right.

One day we all got special coins with a picture of a bird on one side and some writing on the other. The CEO spoke to us. He told us that there's a bird called the godwit that lives in Australia. Because of its density, unlike many birds, it could not float in water, and couldn't swim. Every year the godwit flies 6,000 miles to summer in Alaska. If it stops flying, it will die. Yet, this bird has the faith to traverse that huge distance. And he said our recovery had to be like that--we needed to flap our wings constantly, working our program of spiritual fitness continually, or we will die.

Highwatch is a very special place, a place filled with spirit, warmth, and great food. The people who ran the place wanted me to spend longer than the three weeks I'd signed up for. But I was ready to go. I gained ten pounds there in twenty-one days. I mean, would you like the strip steak or the swordfish? The food was ridiculous. And like a lot of the men and women there, without drugs, I ate.

Well, I got out and my parents took my back to Terryville where my minivan was. I told them I was going to go see Ava, got in my van and left, blasting my music. But the first stop I made was at the head shop to buy some kratom. Kratom is this Southeast Asian plant called Mitragyna speciosa, used by many in place of opiates, as it has a mild euphoric effect. But I wanted it for appetite suppression. I bought two bags of the Bali capsules and ate twelve on my way to Ava's.

Within twenty minutes I felt the effects, a mild euphoria and an increased heart rate. Going into Highwatch I knew I had to stop the cold medicine and the weed and the benzodiazepines and the opiates, but kratom? It was harmless. Mild. Plus I had to lose the weight I'd gained at Highwatch. I used only kratom for about a month, and then I lost the weight. After that it wasn't going to be enough. After all, addicts say "one is too many, and a thousand is never enough." I wanted something stronger.

Before that happened, I had another court date in Danielson. I had brought a discovery request with me to court. I checked in with the prosecutor who looked at my request (same as my last one for Manchester court) and smiled.

"You wrote this?" he asked.

"Yes."

"It looks like a lawyer wrote it."

"Thanks for the compliment," I said. "I'm a paralegal."

"Well," he said, "Paralegal or not, I'm locking you up."

I was stunned. "Excuse me?" I said. "Why?"

"Because you were out on bond from this jurisdiction and you picked up a third DUI in Rocky Hill. You are a danger to yourself and society."

"You mean I purportedly got a third DUI," I reminded him. "I'm not guilty until the state proves my guilt beyond a reasonable doubt."

"So, you're telling me that you're not guilty?" he asked. "Of three different arrests by three different officers? I don't believe it. I'm raising your bond. You're going to sit in jail until this case is adjudicated. What if you pick up your fourth one? And kill someone? I'm not going to have that on my hands." He was totally serious.

"Then I want a lawyer," I said.

"No problem. I'll give you a continuance for one week to get one."

"One week!" I exclaimed. "That's crazy! I need four weeks."

"No way I'm giving you four weeks," he said. "We'll leave it up to the judge."

Oh my God. The judge that sends everyone to jail? I was about to soil myself. How was this happening? The judge gave me two weeks. I immediately left and called Craig.

"Craig," I said, "You have to help me! I got three DUIs and now the prosecutor in Danielson wants to lock me up! I seriously need you!"

"Wait, what?" he said. "Three DUIs? Susan…"

"I know, I know, Craig. I screwed up. Are you available two weeks from today?"

"Yes."

"I need you to come to Danielson for me and appear. Please help me!"

"Calm down," he said. "I'll appear for you, Susan. Let's meet Friday to discuss these cases. At Emporium. 1pm."

"I'll buy you lunch, Craig."

"Okay. See you then."

And with that, the man who trained me to be a paralegal became my counsel. Things just got progressively harder.

MY BEST ADVOCACY AND WORST OUTCOME

Craig ordered the falafel sandwich and a black coffee. "Susan, you have some serious exposure here," he said.

"I know," I said.

"No, I don't think you understand. If they give you minimum sentences consecutively, you're facing one year, four months, and two days in prison." I was devouring a reuben. I hadn't had breakfast.

"Craig, I'm not going to jail for a year and four months. That's ridiculous!"

"Susan, I don't think you understand. That's the minimum. You could be locked up for five years." I had never actually doubted my own innocence.

"What do you mean, five years?" I asked.

"The maximum for a third DUI is five years in prison. That's serious!"

All of a sudden my reuben didn't taste as good as before.

"Well, Craig, that's not going to happen. I'm sure you can get me out of one DUI of the three. Then I'll be facing four months. And there's home confinement. I'll be on the ankle bracelet in my own bed, watching my own television, and having sex with my own girlfriend. It'll suck, but you're allowed out of your house to work, so I won't lose my tutoring job. And I can run eBay without leaving the property. Just get me out of one."

"Well, I only have the discovery from the one you gave me from Manchester, the first one. I'll review everything and get back to you on that. When I go to Danielson shortly I'll take a peek at their discovery. And what about Rocky Hill?"

"Guilty," I said. "Certainly. I'm definitely guilty. You have to get me out of one of the other two. That's it. Work on it. I trust you."

We parted ways. The next time I saw Craig was the week after in Danielson court. My parents brought me rather than me drive, in case they raised my bond and locked me up. What would the judge make it? I had no idea. I gave my mother $5000 in cash. I told her if they raised my bond, listen to Craig, and you can bond me out up to $50,000. I couldn't imagine getting a higher bond than that, though I'd seen the judge give a couple 10k cash only bonds for drug dealing.

I didn't really think I was going to get locked up. I'm a rich white girl from Farmington on DUI charges that were from stops where no one was injured. The $5000 was just a precaution. Craig went in to see the prosecutor and was there for a long time.

He came out and said, "They are okay with you doing something called 'intensive pretrial supervision.' You'll have to check in with a probation officer once a week and give urines. If you give a dirty urine, then they lock you up. But, you can still drive, and no ankle bracelet. Can you live with that?"

"Absolutely!" I said, giving Craig a big hug. My mom hugged him too. After I appeared in front of the judge, the prosecutor made his intentions clear, and I started IPS. After seeing the bail commissioner and paying Craig $1100 in cash, I was a free woman once again. The bail commissioner said I had to report to Hartford probation this afternoon, and told me my P.O.'s name was Mike.

"Be there at 3pm."

"I will," I replied, and my parents drove me back to Ava's.

I met with Mike. He was a petite man, but cute, and had been a military policeman in Iraq, a police officer in Chicago, and had been doing probation for the last fifteen years when he was in Connecticut. We had a long conversation, about politics, religion, public policy, and the law. I liked him. He was smart and direct. My first appointment was ninety minutes. He told me that after that he would only see me for thirty minutes at a time. I peed in a cup for him, and went home.

Then I went back to Manchester court for my pretrial. I showed up and told the prosecutor I needed a continuance to hire counsel--I didn't feel comfortable proceeding ahead naked. They gave me a month. Then I appeared in New Britain for Rocky Hill and entered a plea of not guilty and went home.

The walls were closing in. I could feel it. My time was running out. I was running out of continuances, running out of goodwill, running out of road. It was exactly the same thing that happened when the boosting was coming to an end--I could just see it from above. Things were changing. The noose was tightening.

Then I went back to Danielson court. The woman prosecutor greeted me.

"Hello, Susan."

"Hello. I'm here to argue a motion to dismiss," I said, referring to the motion I'd made since I'd never received a copy of the police report.

"I don't have that motion," she said, shuffling papers.

"Well I sent it certified mail," I said. "I have the tracking number. Just a second." I started rummaging through my purse.

"I'm not interested in that," she said. "Go wait for the judge." She pointed to the door.

Frazzled, I left and sat in court. They called my case and I went in front of the mean judge. The prosecutor spoke first.

"Your Honor, the State is ready to make an offer to the Defendant," she said. "The State is offering a thirty-day sentence and eighteen months probation."

"What?!" I exclaimed. "You never offered me anything!" The judge was quick to react.

"Did you share this offer with the Defendant?" he asked.

"No," she said.

"Didn't you have a lawyer here last time?" the judge asked.

"Yes. He was here for bond only," I replied.

"Well," said the judge, "I'll give you four weeks to accept or reject the offer. Come back then."

I was stunned. My shenanigans weren't going to work any more, but I had gotten a gift. Whether it was intentional or an oversight, the prosecutor had treated this as a first DUI rather than a second. So instead of four months I got one month. I know I had to accept the error and take the deal. Now I knew I was going to prison.

I panicked. So far as I knew from all the men in program, transwomen went to men's prisons. I verified this with my friend Bob who was on disability and sold suboxone for money. He had been in Osborn.

"They send the he-shes there," he said. "There were a whole bunch of them in there."

Then I validated this further with a transgender activist I know. She had spoken at a different men's facility a month ago. She confirmed that there were transwomen in that facility as well.

Hell no! I'd been a woman for fourteen years! I had 38D breasts. I would be sexually assaulted, raped, or killed by a bunch of men. This was a death sentence. The first thing I did was get really, really high. I woke up in the emergency room, overdosed, and you know what? I was still going to jail.

So the next day when I was better, I authored a position statement for the Department of Corrections on how they should deal with me. I mailed it to everyone I could in the prison system--doctors, lawyers, wardens, the commissioner--everyone. Then I prayed. This is what it said:

May *4,* *2017*

To *whom* *it* *may* *concern:*

Executive summary: I am a MtF transsexual who identifies as a female, has a female's birth certificate, who has both 38D surgically augmented breasts as well as male genitalia and needs to be remanded to the Department of Corrections for an extended time due to multiple DUIs. I believe the best possible outcome for someone in my unique situation would be home confinement, a program I qualify for based on my charges, but I would also be completely accepting of being remanded to York Correctional Facility were I to be placed in general population and not segregated. I believe that being placed in a men's facility or being placed in York but being segregated will result in irreparable harm and I would greatly fear for my safety, and I am attempting to lobby the Department of Corrections to be sure that my basic human rights *will* *not* *be* *violated.*

My name is Susan Sturbridge and I am a transgender woman who has spent the last ten years living in Farmington, working, and living a normal life. Due to a couple of bad decisions (specifically, I am currently being charged with multiple DUIs) I find myself in a situation where I will need to be incarcerated for a time yet to be determined. I have a very unique situation when it comes to where I would need to be housed for the time period of incarceration due to the fact that I have a queer body. I do not believe that the Department of Corrections has a specific policy in place in terms of how they are to deal with the transgender incarnation vis-à-vis incarceration. To the best of my knowledge (I spoke with a psychiatric APRN named Alicia at DOC) the DOC is in the process of delimiting a policy at present.

Let me offer some background. I am presently thirty-seven years old. Though I knew when I was a small child, when I was twenty-three, I decided to begin transitioning from male to female, as I had always felt like a female. By age twenty-four, I had saved my sperm (in order to preserve my genetic material in case I ever wanted to have a biological child) and had started on a hormone regimen. I have been seeing the same endocrinologist since I began this transition some thirteen years ago. My doctor is a staunch advocate for the transgender community and is a visionary for transgender rights: he has helped a great many transmen and transwomen like myself utilize modern endocrinological medicine to manage our condition. It should be noted that I do not believe in a diagnosis like 'gender identity disorder' or 'gender dysphoria.' I believe that the transgender incarnation is a strictly physical malady that manifests itself in an endocrinological disorder whereby the infant child is born with the incorrect gonads, which in turn morphs the transgender infant into something that he or she did not want to be, and that this birth defect can be corrected with a proper hormone regimen. Thus, I corrected my birth defect with a pharmaceutical regimen of estrogen (Estradiol), micronized progesterone (Prometrium), and aldactone (Spironolactone).

Then came 2009. I had just received a Master's Degree in Public Policy Analysis from Trinity College in Hartford, CT. At that time in our jurisprudence, the State of Connecticut had not yet changed its laws about transgender individuals changing our birth certificates without surgery. That law was subsequently modified several years ago. So, in 2009, a transgender individual was required to have 'surgical sex-reassignment' in order to obtain a new birth certificate. (The federal government also required this type of surgery to obtain a corrected passport, but that law was changed several years ago as well). I made the argument in one of my books that if the State of Connecticut wanted transgender individuals to have surgery in order to obtain an identity document, the state should pay for that surgery.

In October of 2009 I paid for my own surgical sex reassignment. However, I did not go the standard route. There are norms within the transgender community when it comes to transsexuals, who are transgender individuals who elect to have surgery to alter their bodies. I identify as a transsexual, because I am a transgender woman who is what is called 'post-op,' meaning I have undergone surgical sex reassignment. With respect to transsexuals, there are pre-op (meaning these individuals intend to surgically alter their sex, but for whatever reason, they are in the process of changing sex and have not physically had surgery yet) transsexuals. There are post-op transsexuals, like me, who have undergone surgical sex reassignment and are completely "the other sex." Lastly there are 'non-op' transsexuals (who would more accurately hold the moniker 'transgender') who take hormones so that they experience life as the opposite sex and attain secondary sex characteristics (like facial hair or body hair or breasts depending on the chromosomal sex) but have no interest in having surgery. Any of these individuals can legally change their sex on their Connecticut birth certificates, regardless of any surgeries. When I speak about the 'standard route,' there is a standard set of surgeries for transmen and *transwomen. For transmen, there are three basic surgeries: double mastectomy (surgical removal of breasts or 'top surgery') and then metoidioplasty (surgical creation of a phallus from an enlarged clitoris) or phalloplasty (surgical creation of a phallus using skin grafts). The metoidioplasty and phalloplasty are considered 'bottom surgery,' however most transmen only undergo top surgery, because bottom surgery is so expensive and the results are not always optimal. Transmen are often not satisfied with their bottom surgeries, thus most transmen undergo only top surgery. The result is that transmen end up as men with vaginas, still possessing queer bodies. For transwomen, there are two basic surgeries: breast augmentation (surgical enlargement of the breasts or 'top surgery') and vaginoplasty (surgical creation of a vagina and clitoris by inverting the penis and using existing nerves and skin to create the artificial genitals) or 'bottom surgery.' In the same way that the bottom surgery is usually optional for transmen, the top surgery is likewise optional for transwomen.*

Therefore, when I speak of not going 'the standard route,' I opted to transition from male to female by undergoing top surgery for the purposes of surgical sex reassignment as opposed to bottom   surgery.

I had 'top surgery' in the form of breast augmentation in Glastonbury, CT in a surgery performed in October of 2009. The doctor authored a notarized letter that was sent to the State of Connecticut Office of Vital Records which was required to change my sex on my birth certificate to female. I felt (and continue to feel) complete after my top surgery. I opted not to have bottom surgery, as I felt physically complete as a woman with a pair of breasts. My logic is simple--it's the secondary sex characteristics (breasts or lack thereof, facial hair, etc.) that are the visual cues that enable individuals to parse other individuals and assign them a sex of male or female during an interaction. Having a real pair of breasts makes me a woman, because what is between my legs is between myself and my partner, not the general public.

Enter our situation now. What is between my legs is now an issue to the public, because as part of my punishment for multiple DUIs, I will be required to be remanded to the Department of Corrections for a certain timeframe that will become clearer after subsequent court dates, and hence be subjected to a public sex-segregated space. I have a dilemma. I have a driver's license, a passport, and a birth certificate that all state that I am a female. I have 38D breasts like many other females. I wear female's clothes, have a female's name, have a female network, and have been a tireless advocate for other transgender females like myself. Though I retain male genitals, I am not a male. Those are the only thing that is remotely male about me, but that's because I have a queer body, with breasts and a penis. I am a woman with a penis, not a man with breasts. This is an important distinction to make, and one that is recognized by the laws of the State of Connecticut.

Therefore I see three situations that can unfold in front of me. I could be sent to a men's facility. I could be sent to York Prison in Niantic. Or I could be offered home confinement. Allow me   to   elaborate   on   all   three   of   these   situations.

First, I could be sent to a men's facility. The Department of Corrections could make the decision that penis equals male. Susan Sturbridge is male because of her genitalia. We will discount her gender identity. We do not care that she has breasts. She is a man with breasts, as determined by her immutable sex at birth, and though she has had surgical sex reassignment, it was top surgery and not bottom surgery and the DOC is going to judge the sex of an individual based solely on the morphology of the genitals and not on the gender identity, or even the presence of a sex reassignment surgery if it is only 'the top.' If this were to happen to me, I can tell you at this moment that I would need to be placed in protective custody. If I were in a locked room full of males who have no respect for the law, I would be raped or killed. No question. I have 38D breasts. These are men who are locked up without any women in their purview. This would destroy my bodily integrity, and I would likely be forced into protective custody to serve out the entirety of my sentence alone, which is not fair, just, or equitable. I am not violent. I am not malicious. I am not malevolent. I did not hurt anyone. There would be no reason why I should have to serve my sentence in protective custody. That is just not fair.

Second, I could be sent to York. The Department of Corrections could be more progressive with how they treat transgender women. After all, not only do I have breasts but I have a female's driver's license, a female's passport, and a female's birth certificate. I am a female. So I could go to York. I would be amenable to this solution, with certain caveats. First of all, I would need to continue my hormone regimen, as this is not just for mood but also for bone health. I would be amenable to go to York if I were given my hormones, because the DOC would have to consider them medically necessary pharmaceuticals. Second of all, I want to be part of the general population. There would be no reason why I couldn't be a member of the general population. As I have already said I am not violent, not confrontational, not malevolent. I am educated. Erudite. I would spend my time reading and writing. I would have no problems with any other inmates. However, the DOC may not be amenable to having me in the general population. In addition to my queer body, I am also six feet tall and 250 pounds. According to several DOC sources that I have already spoken with, it appears that if I were sent to York, on account of my non-conforming genitals I would be separated from the rest of the population. (I know this makes no sense, but I suppose the thinking is I would rape someone because I have a penis? Even though I am not a sexual deviant and have had the same partner for twelve years, somehow the thought process is that I am somehow the threat at York and I would need to be separated from the other women for their safety? Kind of like the antipodal conclusion as in a men's   facility.)

If I had to serve out my sentence at York and had to be separated from the rest of the population on account of my non-conforming genitals, I would contend that this behavior was illegal based on the verbiage in An Act Concerning Discrimination (Connecticut General Statutes §46a-64). This law states that it is illegal to 'separate, segregate, or discriminate' against an individual due to his or her gender identity. I believe I could make a cogent argument to the tribunal that if the DOC were to send me to York and then separate me from the rest of the women because of my nontraditional genitals, that this would be illegal under current statute, specifically violating §46a-64(a)(2). I would be 100% fine going to York if I could be in the general population. However, if I would be separated in York to serve out my sentence this would   be   illegal   under   statute   and   not   the   best   solution.

Third, I could be given home confinement. I qualify for the program based on the victimless crimes I have been charged with and my specific type of offense of public policy. If I am given home confinement I can continue to work on my fourth book, adding to the knowledge base of our state, as I have authored three books already. My bodily integrity would be intact--I would not be exposed to harassment, verbal abuse, sexual assault, rape or worse. I would have full access to my doctors and my medications. Also, I am gainfully employed as a contract employee working as an SAT and ACT tutor. I am a gifted tutor who has helped hundreds of high school students get into the colleges of their choice, and this is work (along with other types of similar work) I could continue to do for this company from my home computer without leaving my   home.

When one looks at the three choices that the Department of Corrections faces with respect to me--men's prison, women's prison, and home confinement--there are two of these options that would likely result in my basic human rights being violated, and a third that allows me to continue being a positive and productive member of society. Placing me with men is a violation of my rights as a legal female in the State of Connecticut. Placing me with females and then segregating me is a violation of my rights as a legal female in the State of Connecticut. Granting me home confinement allows me to keep my basic human rights, my dignity, and it preserves my ability to continue substance abuse treatment. The Department of Corrections has had enough time to parse this--An Act Concerning Discrimination changed the law with respect to transgender individuals on October 1, 2011. There is no reason why right now the DOC cannot have a cogent policy in place when someone like me with a queer body gets arrested and is forced into incarceration. I am accepting my fate--I accept that I need to be incarcerated, I accept responsibility for my actions, but I will not accept my basic human rights and basic rights as   a   female   under   Connecticut   law   be   abrogated.

The way I look at it is simple. I am a woman. I have all sorts of documents that prove this. I have jumped through every hoop and done everything that the State has required to legally become the woman I have always felt myself to be. And still, I fear that if the DOC even is forward-thinking enough to place me with my fellow females for incarceration, I fear that there will be too much push back about integrating a woman with a penis into a population of women without penises. Like I have said again and again--if I can go to York and not be segregated, provided that I can maintain my medically-necessary hormone regimen, I will gladly accept this fate. However, I'm just not that sure if it's that simple. If I cannot get home confinement then what we need is a test of the new An Act Concerning Discrimination. I am more than happy to work with the Department of Corrections on helping implement a cogent policy around transgender inmates, and I have no problems being remanded to their care, provided I am placed   at   York   in   the   general   population.

Respectfully   submitted,
Susan Sturbridge

Then I found out that DOC is overseen by the executive branch, not the judicial. I'd met the governor before, at a fundraiser, so I wrote to the man at the top. I hadn't gotten any responses for four or five days. I was starting to get worried. That accept or reject date was rapidly approaching. Then something happened--my Higher Power intervened.

I had sent a group text to the fifteen most important friends I had in my life explaining the situation. I was soon going to jail, for at least thirty days, up to a year, or it could be home confinement. I just didn't know. My friend Jackie wrote back to me. She was very good friends with the highest-ranking Republican in the state legislature, Irena Semanski. She told me to forward her my letter, and she would have Irena read it. I did just that. This was a Tuesday.

Thursday, Jackie called me. Irena had called DOC, and they were having a meeting about me on Monday. On Sunday, Jackie called again. Irena says, off the record, you're going to York (the women's prison) in Niantic. But don't tell anyone. I was overjoyed. They had that meeting Monday. Tuesday my lawyer called me.

"They're sending you to York with the women," he said. "The state is going to respect your gender identity."

Again I was thrilled. Besides one other high profile case in the media, I'd never heard of another transwoman going to York. I was a gender pioneer once again. Jackie called me again.

"Irena wants to meet you," she said. We set up a date and Jackie picked me up in Farmington and drove me to the State Capitol. We met with Irena in her office, along with her sister (another state rep), two staffers, Jackie, and me. We had a lovely conversation. She really just wanted to know how as an educated erudite young woman I'd gotten myself into this predicament.

"It all started when I got a mistress," I said. They all laughed coyly.

"Oh, we all understand that," they said. We talked for an hour.

Irena said to me, "When I got your letter I was incensed. I called the Commissioner and told him, this woman is going to York to be housed with females!"

What a country! I'd sent out twelve letters, and it turns out, I just needed to call one of my best friends who knows a high-ranking Republican lawmaker, who just calls the head of the whole DOC and simply demands that my rights are not abrogated. Unbelievable!

I told Irena I was worried about being segregated. I was afraid that even if they were to house me with women, because I was transgender they would treat me differently and house me in solitary confinement. She assured me they would not.

"They had that Monday meeting to talk about how to handle this whole thing. They don't want a lawsuit. They want you in and out as quickly as possible. Don't worry, Susan. If they mistreat you, just reach out to my office." Irena was confident.

How nice it was to have my own state representative lobbying for me! We all took a group picture and put it on Facebook (she insisted on being my friend) and Jackie brought me out for sushi and then home.

Now I wasn't scared. I was empowered. I called Craig and explained I was worried about solitary confinement. I explained that my psychiatrist had written a letter saying that because I was bipolar, segregating me was likely to cause me stress enough to produce a manic episode from which I might never recover. I asked if I should point out to their lawyers what had happened the last time someone tried to segregate me in a sex-segregated facility at Rushford.

"Agitate, agitate, agitate," he said. "Make it so they don't want you there."

So I sent in a letter to their chief legal counsel and cc'ed the commissioner of the Department of Corrections. The letter read as follows:

May   18,   2017

Dear   Attorney   Specter,

At the suggestion of counsel, I would like to try to head off a potentially dangerous situation for me during my upcoming stay at the York Correctional Institution in Niantic. As a direct and proximate result of alleged criminal conduct, I will be facing remand to York on either May 24, 2017   or   June   9,   2017,   respectively.

I was advised to submit to you a copy of the documents that came to fruition over my last stay at a sex-segregated residential institution. What's incredible about this CHRO case is though the terms of the settlement are strictly confidential, I feel confident in disseminating to you that I received a five-figure settlement and I was never actually housed improperly in an inpatient/residential capacity. Simply the appearance of impropriety led the Defendant to quickly settle for a five-figure monetary award. I am can attest with certainty that were a situation to arise wherein my rights under Connecticut General Statutes § 46a-64(a)(2) were violated by any other corporation or state agency that was charged with housing me in a sex-segregated space and I were actually housed for a period of time, the settlement would be orders of magnitude greater.

For the sake of both posturing and optics I intend to clearly state that this is not a threat in any way, as I'm absolutely certain in this era of transgender rights visibility that the Department of Correction would never segregate me on account of my gender identity, obviously housing me in the general population at York. I am simply presenting these data in the hope that on the smallest chance that anyone at DOC would unintentionally or negligently disregard Connecticut civil rights law (that has been active since October 1, 2011) everyone is keenly aware of exactly what transpired   after   the   last   unfortunate   abrogation.

Basically, I want you to know that while I admit fully that I have offended public policy through the violation of criminal statutes, and will be a convicted criminal after either May 24th or June 9th, this does not mean that my civil rights under C.G.S. can be abridged. I am an activist. I advocate for transgender rights. I majored in Women, Gender, and Sexuality at Trinity College in Hartford during a B.A., and then received a Master's Degree in Public Policy Analysis. I have furthermore worked as a paralegal, have authored two nonfiction books and a fiction book, and am a member of two high I.Q. societies, American MENSA and Intertel.

While all that does not eliminate that I am an addict, and bipolar, and transgender, it means that not only am I well versed in the law, but also in its enforcement, its creation, and our jurisprudence more generally. While I admit I will be convicted of violation of criminal statutes and am more than willing to serve my sentence, I want to make it patently clear that I have worked tirelessly for the rights of others, including myself.

I do not want to sue you. I do not want to have to make a CHRO complaint about you. I don't want litigation, legislation, nor abrogation. I expect to be treated like every other female at York. I will not accept segregation or confinement on account of gender identity. I want to be completely transparent, as I could be in your stead for an extended length of time. I just want us all to be on the same page before I come in and join the general population.

Please review the attached documents. If you have any questions about the Rushford/Hartford Healthcare matter, please direct them to the attorney who oversaw our mediation.

If you have any other questions about my position, feel free to reach out to me directly on my cell phone or via email.

Best   regards,
Susan   Sturbridge

I attached all the documents that were seminal to the Rushford CHRO case so that they could review exactly how I treated those that mistreated me, and let them chew on that. My lawyer explained to me the same thing the women I knew in program had said. There were two sides to York--the east side and the west side. Before you get placed, everyone has to spend a week in medical, which everyone said was the worst. Then they split you according to the crime you have committed. People with DUIs were on the east side, the good side. You were in a dormitory setting. There were no locks on your doors. If you wanted to go walk around outside, you waited for count to clear, then go outside for two or three hours. You took alcohol and drug education classes. Plus, you could still get home confinement, which would mean go to medical, get an ankle bracelet, and come home. The other people on the east side were the people that had been convicted of drug crimes. They had less freedom than the DUI folks, but it was still good.

"You don't want to go to the west side," my friend Barbara told me. "I was there for months awaiting sentencing. You're locked in a room all day, and then when you get out of the room, all the people there were bad criminals, many of them were violent. Don't worry. You'll be on the east side. I was there for the last two months of my sentence for selling oxycontin. It's much better. You'll be alright."

Things were looking up a little bit. I finally went to court on the first DUI in Manchester for judicial pretrial. I brought Craig. He came out of the prosecutor's office.

"One-hundred-fifty hours of community service. No jail time. No fines. A year probation." Ava ran up and hugged him. I could handle this. I could do this. There was only New Britain left for the third DUI. That was the wildcard, and what I was afraid of.

We all went to that court date, Ava, me, my parents, and Craig. He went in to speak with the prosecutor. I was facing a year minimum. He came out smiling with his thumbs up. He called us together.

"Forty-five days," he said. Ava started to cry, and hugged him.

"How did you do that?" I asked.

"I played dumb," he said. "I went in and said, 'I don't really do criminal cases,' and they laughed at me. I told them the truth. You were on disability for being bipolar, you were an addict, and you were transgender. I told them that the DOC didn't want you there. You got a year sentence with forty-five days to serve followed by two years of probation, all to run concurrent with the thirty days from Danielson.

"So I'll be out in forty-five days?" I asked.

"That's what it looks like. I'll get to make an argument for less with the judge. But for now, plan on forty-five days."

Unbelievable! We went from a year, four months, and two days down to forty-five days. I thought about my failed stint at CVH. This could be like going to rehab. I could handle it. We all hugged Craig and went home. I had a court date in New Britain on July 6th, and a court date in Danielson on July 7th. I just had to wait one more month to get sentenced.

I started getting as high as I could. Ava had taken away my wallet because I kept buying drugs, and she had taken away my car. I was under house arrest with Ava until I was sentenced. I bucked her every chance I could. She went to the gym, and left me home with no purse, no wallet, and no cellphone. That was, I couldn't take an Uber to my dealer's house, or to the drugstore and buy cold medicine, and had no money to buy drugs. As soon as she left, I left her a note.

"I'm taking a walk. 9:30am." And with that, I put on a cute little running skirt and a skanky top. I walked to Berkshire Bank in downtown Farmington. I'd been to that branch plenty of times. They welcomed me when I went in.

"I'm really sorry," I said. "I don't have my ID. I just need to take some money out of my checking account." The teller looked puzzled.

A different woman at a different window said, "We know who you are, Susan." She looked at the other teller. "Go ahead," she said to her. I took out a hundred dollars and got a coffee to go.

I walked down Route 10. Ava thinks she's going to control me. I'll show her. I can get high even when she takes away everything I have. I walked all the way to CVS and bought three boxes of Coricidin and an Arizona iced tea, went to the parking lot, and took the drugs. Then I walked another mile to the gym. I said hello to the little girl at the front desk, and asked to use the phone. I called Ava.

"Where are you?" she said. "Did you use?"

"No. I walked to the gym," I said. "Can you come and get me?"

"Yes, honey," she replied. "I'm sorry I left you to go to the gym."

As soon as I got in the car I could feel the effects of the DXM. She knew I was high right away.

"I'm bringing you to your parents," she said, and drove me to Terryville. She dropped me off with a purse and phone and no clothes. She said she would drop off clothes. "I can't watch her twenty-four hours a day," she said to my mother. "Tell her she's kicked out of my house until after she's done with jail."

And she meant it. She dropped off the clothes later. I would come to find out that this last two weeks I spent with my parents would be the bottom that got me clean. Even though my parents were on me like white on rice, I still managed to get high. I would go out on the porch and say I was going to smoke a cigar, then walk down to the Rite Aid down the street and steal some Coricidin or Mucinex.

Sometimes I walked down to the CVS about a half mile away and did the same thing. They couldn't stop me from using. Then one day they were sick of me doing this every time I went out, so I sat on the porch and my mother watched me. This went on for two days, then I couldn't take it anymore.

"Mom," I said. "Give me back my purse, and my wallet."

"No," she said flatly.

"Okay, then I'm calling the cops. I'm thirty-seven years old. You can't take my things. I'm not a child."

"If I give you your purse and wallet, you are taking your clothes and everything out of this house and you are not coming back. Ava already kicked you out, and you won't be able to come back here. You can spend all the rest of your money on hotel rooms and Ubers," she said.

I told her fine. I brought out all my luggage, called an Uber, and waited. My driver arrived.

"I'm sorry. I just need a short ride, but if you don't mind waiting a minute while I check into a hotel, you can give me a ride to Bristol so I can pick up a script."

"Sounds good," he said.

He brought me to Jay's Motel and I paid my sixty dollars and got a room. He was a gentleman and brought my bags inside. We got back in the Toyota and he drove me to CVS in Bristol. He put the destination into the GPS. Almost immediately, Ava called my cell phone.

"Why are you going to CVS?" she asked.

"I'm not," I said calmly.

"You are," she said. "You just went to Jay's Motel and now you're going to CVS."

"What, did you hack my Uber?" I asked.

"You use the same password for everything, so I just requested a notification every time you take an Uber."

"You bitch," I said, and hung up the phone. The Uber driver was just laughing at me. He knew it was my girlfriend. She called me back.

"I'm calling your parents," she said. "Please honey, please, please, *please*, just go home." She started crying. We were almost to CVS.

"I gotta go," I said, and hung up. She called again. I put the ringer on mute. "Thanks for the ride," I said, and gave him a five dollar tip.

I went into CVS. They had five boxes of Coricidin behind the pharmacy counter. More than three was an overdose, but I needed six to get high twice. Five would not do. But I didn't want to take another Uber to Stop and Shop to find more, because I feared Ava or my parents were on their way to intercept me at CVS. I bought three boxes and a watermelon juice, went outside, and took the drugs. I called another Uber, and got taken back to the tiny motel.

Almost immediately, there was a pounding at the door that I knew was the police. I ignored them, all the flashlights and noise, until finally the little Indian woman from the front desk appeared at the door. Two Terryville cops came into the room. I explained I was naked. They were doing a wellness check. Ava had called them and told them I was a danger to myself. I wasn't high yet, so I engaged them, explained I wasn't high, that I was just watching TV, and they left.

This was my bottom. The high lasted three or four hours. Then I wanted more. It was 2am. There were no Ubers in the area. I was going to have to walk. I put on my shoes and started walking in the dark to Bristol. It was reminiscent of when I rode my bike to get the women's clothes--I had lost control of myself, of my actions. I was crazy. I made it to the first store that was open twenty-four hours. Apparently, my mother had anticipated this and contacted Bristol police. My patterns were that easy to discern by others. They stopped me and asked me if I were Susan.

"Yes," I said.

"Your mother called us," he said. "She's on her way here to get you and take you home."

"I was just going to get some cigars at Fast Freddie's," I said. "There's nothing illegal about that."

"You walked from Terryville just to get cigars?" the cop asked. I shrugged my shoulders.

"I really like to smoke."

My mother showed up. I told the cops I refused to leave with her. I would walk back to the motel. The cops insisted I go with my mother. It was 3am.

"If she promises to bring me to the motel and not to her house," I said. They conferred and she agreed. We drove back in silence. When I got into my room I waited ten minutes, fuming. I wasn't high at all now, but couldn't sleep. So I put my shoes on and did it again. I walked the four miles at 4am into Bristol. I walked to Price Chopper, the first twenty-four hour store.

All they had was Mucinex. I boosted a 28-count box, which was more than enough to get high, and bought a drink. But when I got outside and started to take them, I felt as if I were going to quickly vomit. I walked to Stop and Shop, the next twenty-four hour store, the one that had the Coricidin. I never made it there. Ava's white Lexus pulled over.

"Get in," she said.

"How did you find me?"

"Susan, there's only one road to Bristol. And you were on it."

She brought me back to the motel. People were driving to work, starting their days. I had no job. No car. I was staying with my parents, and was going to prison in a week.

"Let this be your bottom," Ava said. She understood that twice in one night I walked between towns to fulfill a bad drug habit. She brought me back to my parents in silence.

That day I had my weekly meeting with Mike. He was angry with me.

"Every urine has come back dirty," he said.

"Your test is corrupt," I said. "It says right on the urinalysis that the test is 77% accurate. So, 23% of the time you'll get a false positive. I'm not getting high. I should be passing those tests."

"You're questioning the scientific validity of my tests?" he asked.

"Absolutely," I replied. "It's too high of a margin of error to take them seriously. That's the definition of reasonable doubt."

"Susan," he said calmly. "I need to know something. What would have happened if you had killed someone in one of your DUIs?" I responded almost immediately.

"Well, I'd probably be given a five to seven year sentence for vehicular manslaughter, and I'd probably serve eighteen months or two years and then be out again."

"No, Susan, not the punishment. How would you feel about taking a human life? An innocent human life?"

"How do you know they would be innocent?" I asked. "What if they were a wretched person that deserved to die and God was just using me as an instrument to take their life?" Mike said nothing. Finally, he spoke.

"When I first met you," he said, "I felt really bad for you. But now? I just think you're a sociopath. You belong in jail."

"Well," I said, "I'm going no matter how many urines I fail. You have no power over me."

"I just hope that when you get out, you stay clean," he said. "You have a lot to offer, but you have to stop using."

I'd been hearing the same thing for a long time. I knew I would have to get clean in jail. July 6th came around. I wore a plain dress, no purse or phone, and waited for Craig. The prosecutor said they recommended forty-five days to serve of a year sentence. The judge asked Craig if he had anything to say. He stressed that I was a transwoman, I was bipolar, I basically had a psychotic break, and I had a thirty-day sentence from another court. Would she entertain a thirty-day sentence to serve concurrently?

She agreed. With that, she imposed a thirty-day sentence on me. She asked me if I wanted to say anything.

"I want to thank the prosecutor for her compassion, and I want to apologize to the court for my offense to public policy." She thanked me, and the marshals took me away. I had just been remanded to the Department of Corrections.

A SKID BID

They call it a skid bid because you skid into jail, leave your mark, and go home quickly. The first thing after I was led out of court was a pat-down. There was a male marshal and a female marshal, and the woman asked me who I'd prefer to pat me down. Well, the man was cute but I didn't want to be sent in the wrong van! They put me in a holding cell all day, gave me a bologna and cheese sandwich ("court lunch," as it's called) then a short van ride to Hartford in shackles. Then a longer ride in a white bus with no windows to Niantic, and to a holding cell with about twenty women.

First you are given a prison ID with your picture and your inmate number on it that you have to wear at all times you are out of your cell. Then I was stripped naked by three women and given three pairs of elastic waist blue jeans, four pairs of white socks, four pairs of white underwear, three horrible bras, and three maroon tee-shirts. That is the uniform at York. You are also given a grey sweatshirt and a grey nightgown, which is really an oversized shirtdress.

They cataloged all my belongings and sent me to medical. I was in room 24, a single occupancy cell in 4 South. The next day I had court again, so they woke me up at 6am, gave me my meds and my breakfast (every meal is called "chow," and the cafeteria is called the "chow hall") and then stripped me naked again and checked me out and gave me my clothes back. I got to see Craig one last time in court.

I told him they were giving me my meds and allowing me to shave and to tell Ava and my parents that I was okay. I took another plea for twenty-nine days to serve concurrently, then waited on the steel bench with no cushion all day with another court lunch. Then I went back, was stripped naked again, and taken back to my cell again. The whole process is completely humiliating and dehumanizing.

Saturday and Sunday I was locked in a room by myself for between twenty-three and twenty-four hours a day with no human contact except to pass me meals and meds. I was given no books, no paper, no writing implements, nothing. Just stare at the walls for days.

Monday was better. I got to see the doctor, who told me I was going home on home confinement and would be leaving in ten days. And she also gave me a Bible to read. Tuesday, I met with the counselor and watched a video on the Prison Rape Elimination Act. He then told me that the doctor was mistaken, that I had a thirty-day minimum sentence, and I would leave on August 4th. In two days they were moving me to 2 South, Tier A. I would be an inmate just like everyone else.

Wednesday I met with this woman Lisa who worked for addiction services in Wethersfield, at the central office for the Department of Corrections. Her boss (a doctor) and her were in charge of drafting a set of protocols for housing transgender inmates in the Connecticut system. I asked her why I came in with twenty other women, and they were all housed in quads together, and I was all alone for twenty-three to twenty-four hours a day.

"Because of your anatomy," she said. "You have a working penis. You cannot be housed with cellmates."

"But you're segregating me. You're making me live by myself! I have no human contact all day. All the other women have bunkies to talk to and socialize with. I want a roommate."

"That's not going to happen," she responded.

"Well, what you're doing is illegal," I replied. "It is illegal to separate, segregate, or discriminate against someone for his or her gender identity."

"It's not illegal. We're respecting your gender identity. We respect that you're a woman. You're at York. It's your anatomy."

"Nice try," I said. "My anatomy, by definition, is what makes me trans. It is de facto discrimination and you're admitting to it."

"I am admitting it," she said. "What are we supposed to do? Give you a roommate and then you get her pregnant?"

"I can't get anyone pregnant. I've been on hormones too long. My testes have atrophied."

"I understand your position," Lisa said, "But talking with my boss before you came in, he said your penis would not work because of the years of estrogen. Then we found out when you got here that this wasn't true."

"That's only because I told you the truth," I replied. "If I lied to you, you would not have known that."

"Maybe if you were 5'2" and your penis didn't work, we'd be able to find you an appropriate roommate."

"So now you're discriminating against me for being 6' tall?" I responded. "I know I don't look like a cisgender female. But that's even more wrong to treat different transpeople differently. The law doesn't make that distinction. I will be sure to take care of this when I get out. But I'm not being combative or confrontational. I'm just happy not to be at a men's facility."

"I understand," Lisa said. "I'll check on you once a week. You'll be moving tomorrow. Everything will be much better." She left and drove back to Wethersfield.

Things improved dramatically the next day. I was allowed to go to Tier 2 groups (group therapy for drug addicts) and I got moved to my new room in 2 South. They made me stay in the handicapped room alone, with no cellmate. I had my own sink, my own toilet, and my own shower. The other sixteen girls in my program lived upstairs and shared two individual showers. My door was directly opposite the C.O. station--they watched me like a hawk.

So I was still segregated. (The prison would say "separated." "Segregated" means a different thing at York, meaning you wear a red jumpsuit and are in "Seg" for a punishment. Basically, it's twenty-three hours a day in your cell, but even in Seg, the women are given roommates.) I didn't have a cellmate. But I was only locked in my cell nineteen hours a day rather than twenty-three. You would be amazed at how much a difference that extra time socializing makes for someone! (I suppose, it's a 400% increase in recreational time.)

I met all the women. Because of everything I was told by the people I talked to in the program, I expected it to be much worse than it really was. The first one I met was Laura, an Italian biker chick who was crocheting a gift for her granddaughter. They did not allow knitting needles, but they did allow women to hook. Apparently, this was not allowed at the men's facilities because the men would shave down the crochet needles and make shivs to stab people. Boy was I in the right place. Laura managed a strip club during the day and sold Oxycontin at night. She sold it to an undercover cop, and here she was for ten months.

I met a woman Mary who was a social worker with the State of Connecticut and in recovery. She had about ten years sober, and then decided one Sunday night to have a couple of drinks. She went to a local bar, got hammered, blacked out, and stabbed a man in a blackout who later died. She was serving twenty-five years. There was another murderer on my tier, a woman who paid someone to kill a guard at Niantic. She was serving life.

Then there was Nadia. She reminded me of Svetlana and so I immediately liked her--a tall Ukranian girl with a thick accent who was just so adorable and fun to talk with. She was a baby. Twenty-two years old. Her boyfriend had posted pictures of her topless on Facebook, and she responded by burning down his blow-up Christmas decorations on his front lawn while his parents were home. Arson one. Three years. She had served half the sentence.

We got close over time, but only platonically. I was not here to have sex--extraneous sex was what started this whole damn process in the first place! I ate all my meals with Nadia. She braided my hair and threaded my eyebrows and made me "dinner" of ramen noodles with Adobo, garlic powder, and Sazon. It was nice to have a little friend in there. She told me I must have been a cute boy. She was a sweet, innocent, arsonist. She showed me how the women made make-up out of pastels. They used pastels for eye shadow, then mixed pastels with floor wax to make a crude nail polish. They trimmed each other's hair with toenail clippers.

She wanted to know if I would marry her so she could become a citizen rather than being deported back to Ukraine. I asked her a simple question.

"What's in it for me?"

"I'll give you fifteen thousand dollars to marry me," she said.

"I need more than that," I replied.

"Take it or leave it," she said. "But don't think we're having sex. I'm not paying for sex. If you want to have sex with me, I'm not paying you. You'd have to marry me for free."

"So wait," I said, "I can marry you and have sex with you for free, or you'll pay me fifteen thousand dollars to *not* have sex with you?"

"Yes."

Honestly, something happens to these women's brains when they get to York. A year and a half away from men and they are certifiably nutty.

Two of the women on the tier wore yellow jumpsuits. I asked one of them why they wear those. It turns out that if they are awaiting sentencing and have a high bond (a million dollars or more) or if they'd ever tried to escape, they were forced to wear yellow. This was a nutty place.

There were two women there who were in for robbery one. One robbed a liquor store with a rifle, then carjacked a couple at a gas station. She had served four of her five years. Then another got in an elderly woman's car, told her she had a gun (which she didn't) forced her to drive to the bank, took her purse and ATM card and checks, and robbed her without a weapon. The woman was seventy-nine years old, and this criminal was planning on stuffing her in the trunk of the car to leave her, but then she found out the old woman soiled herself and she felt too bad and just left her in the driver's seat. The woman had served four and a half years of a seven year sentence for robbery one, kidnapping, and identity theft.

Her name was Molly and she was one of the nicest ones toward me. So, everyone could buy stuff from commissary. Ava had sent me a hundred dollars via Paypal to buy food and toiletries and stuff. But because of the order scheduling, I would only have eleven days left on my sentence when my order would come in. I was starving there--I just couldn't eat the food. I had lost ten pounds in eight days in medical. All the food was in "slop" form. Some sort of gravy or sauce with a bunch of protein pellets and then a couple of pieces of chicken or beef. Breakfast was farina, oatmeal, cream of wheat, or grits, none of which I could stomach. I told the girls on my tier about how much weight I'd lost. Molly gave me a grocery bag full of food, along with coffee and creamer and sugar. Laura gave me a good toothbrush, and good soap. Someone else gave me shampoo and conditioner, and even a black eyeliner. They hooked me up! And they didn't even know me! Here I was, all worried about coming here and being ostracized, and it was just the opposite. It was a community.

I didn't find out what Molly wanted until a week later.

"Listen," she said, "I'm not gay. I only like men. But I will definitely rub your tits and you can rub mine to get you aroused and then I'll give you a handjob. I'm not gay though. But I respect your body. I haven't been with a man in over four years."

Any sexual act could be consummated either in the shower (I was not allowed in there because I had my own) or in the "lesbian lounge," the area by the washer and dryer that the cameras couldn't see.

After I let Molly do what she wanted with me, this other girl who was in for murder but not yet sentenced, spoke with me.

"I need something from you," she said. Her name was Sam.

"What do you want me to do?" I asked.

"Just have sex with me, please. I haven't been with a man in almost two years. I'm a sex addict. I touch myself every day. I just need a cock. I promise to satisfy you."

"How are we supposed to do that?" I asked. "Getting a handjob or a blowjob is one thing in that little space. But actual sex?"

"We can do it," she said, rubbing my arm. She aroused me. It was amazing how much pent-up energy there is in a women's jail.

So I ended up doing what both of them wanted. It felt good and made the time go by, gave me something to look forward to. And the women were so desperate for a human touch. The only thing that bothered me was that there was always an audience. You couldn't avoid it. If the guard saw me going into their shower for some privacy, I would immediately be given a ticket, and possibly sent to Seg. The only thing to do was to use the lesbian lounge.

The next day all hell broke loose. I was questioned by a captain and a lieutenant. Even though I am a woman, I remember the bro code--deny 'til you die. I knew they didn't have any video of the incident in question. They were basing their investigation on a third-party complaint--hearsay evidence--that would never pass muster in the judiciary. However, in prison, because of PREA, any inmate can make an anonymous complaint about any other inmate or any guard, saying they did something wrong sexually.

I told the captain that this was exactly what Lisa told me the girls would do to me. If there were a woman who was transphobic or didn't like me, she could just make up an allegation against me to threaten me and they would throw me in Seg while they investigated. Thankfully, my reputation with the captain preceded me, and they believed me over an anonymous tip. Not to mention that Molly and Sam denied it as well. (Any sexual contact in jail, even if it's consensual, is illegal and is a ticket, just a different type of infraction.)

When I told my drug class about what happened, they all said, "Welcome to York," and "everyone goes through this." Turns out, all the women make these sorts of allegations all the time, just to be catty. So, though I felt like I was being discriminated against, they were actually treating me like everyone else.

Then I got sent to Seg. It really was an accident, and it wasn't for sexual impropriety. A bunch of us were hanging out on the tier during recreation time, and one of the women asked me about my breasts. I gave them the stock answer--420cc under the muscle, saline--but this meant nothing to her. She wanted to know my bra size.

"Thirty-eight D," I said.

"No way. Show me," she said.

So I lifted up my shirt *with my bra on* and showed her. Apparently, come to find out, this is a big no-no in prison. You are not allowed to expose even your undergarments to any other inmate. They had me on camera doing it from the back, so they couldn't tell if I had a bra on or not, but it was enough to get me sent to Seg for the remaining eight days of my sentence. Realistically, they were looking for something to punish me for after I weaseled my way out of a ticket for sexual promiscuity. I don't think the captain was buying either one of our stories that nothing happened.

So I got the red jumpsuit. They put up a blown up picture of me and took away my ID badge. I was not allowed to leave the room except for an hour a day to go outside into a cage all by myself. I showered the same as the other women in showers that we were allowed to use Mondays, Wednesdays, and Fridays. We got one pair of underwear and one pair of socks. We were fed and given our meds through a hole in the door. No paper or writing implements. All I did was read and sing to myself. I read two books a day, every day, that were brought in with the food. Seg was the prison of prison. It was absolutely the worst possible situation to be in, and I hated every minute of it. Eight days without human contact for lifting up my shirt. No one said prison was fair.

Finally, it was August 4th, my time to leave. I got woken up at 4am, and was brought out of 3 North. I thought I'd be trading my red jumpsuit for my nice leopard print dress and wedges, but it turns out that you are not allowed to leave York in a dress. So they gave me a sweatshirt and a nice pair of grey Talbots slacks and put me and my bags on the white bus with no windows once again. Ava picked me up outside the courthouse in Hartford, and with that, my skid bid was over.

FINAL BOOST AND SUE: CHRO VS. DOC

Well the grand experiment of what would happen if we put an adult transwoman into a women's prison for thirty days was over. What had happened? The first eight days I was there, I was segregated and held in isolation twenty-three to twenty-four hours a day while my peers were living together in quads. Then I lived and recreated with the other women a few hours a day, I lived alone, separated from everyone else in the group. Then I was sent to Seg and had to share a shower with other women, after they told me I had to have my own room with its own shower under PREA. So, all of what they did was illegal under Connecticut General Statutes, and the time I spent in Seg was illegal under PREA. So what was I to do? Go back to CHRO of course! I wasn't going to let my rights be violated, even if I had offended public policy multiple times. Here's what the complaint looked like:

State   of   Connecticut,
County   of   Hartford

BEFORE ME, the undersigned Notary, on this seventh day of August, 2017, personally appeared Susan Sturbridge, known to me to be a credible person and of lawful age, who being by me first duly   sworn,   on   her   oath,   deposes   and   says:

I, Susan Sturbridge, experienced separation, segregation, and discrimination at the hands of the York Correctional Institution in Niantic, CT after being remanded to custody on July 6, 2017 for a   period   of   thirty   days.   Specifically,   I   was:

*--for four days withheld medically-necessary hormones that I ingest daily as part of a physician-directed hormonal regimen to treat me endocrinologically for a transgender condition, a condition   that   DOC   knew   that   I   suffered   from   beforehand;
--separated from my fellow inmates for the first eight days of my incarceration in 4 South where I   was   kept   in   a   locked   room   alone   for   twenty-three   hours   a   day;
--separated from my fellow inmates and kept in a handicapped room in 2 South away from the rest of my A-tier inmates (though I possess no handicap and specifically requested to change rooms), where I was kept in a locked room alone for nineteen hours a day with a private shower;
--segregated from my fellow inmates for the final seven days of my incarceration in 3 North in a room where my photo next to my door stated "house alone," where I was kept in a locked room alone   for   twenty-four   hours   a   day   with   a   community   shower.*

I believe that this is a blatant violation of CT Gen. Stat. § 46a-64(a)(2), which states that it is illegal "to separate, segregate, or discriminate" against an individual for gender identity.

I specifically asked decision-makers why I was being housed separately from other inmates, and a psychiatric APRN from the Wethersfield offices of DOC stated in so many words that I was being segregated because of my anatomy, specifically because I am a woman who retains men's genitalia. She knew that I was coming into York ahead of time because I had written a position statement to lobby for my going to York (attached here as Exhibit 1) in which I specifically spoke to the issue of being segregated.

The Department of Corrections violated my rights by housing me alone (rather than with a "bunkie," or, roommate) which is a punishment saved for only the worst-behaved and highest risk criminals.

Without a complaint like this, I have no doubt that such illicit behavior on the part of the DOC will continue, and they are aware that hormone therapy was withheld, and that I was housed in violation of statute, a major tort.

Susan Sturbridge

I attached a copy of the original position statement that got me a stint in York, and a copy of the letter my doctor had written that said holding me in seclusion would be detrimental to my mental health and cause me to decompensate. I sent copies to the Captain, the Warden, Lisa, the DOC lawyer, and Irena's assistant, with specific instructions for her to explain the situation to Irena. They were not pleased.

They hit me back with everything they had. I got a tome in return. Records of all kinds. They said I was a sex addict, that I had a functioning penis, and that they separated me for the good of the group at York. Their main defense was that under PREA, an individual is supposed to be housed with someone of a similar size, and that there was no woman my size at York. (This is a lie--I am tall and large, but I am not that much of an outlying data point that there were not a few women there who were my size.)

I had to write a rebuttal to their position. It was my right to rebut their assertions. I hit them back. Here's what I said:

The Department of Corrections has misrepresented fact to this commission in their response to my allegations of discrimination.

First, it is clear that I should have been placed at York CI for the duration of my sentence, as my birth certificate clearly states that I was born a female. The warden at York made it clear that once he discovered that my birth certificate stated that I was a female (regardless of external or internal morphology of genitals) then I should be housed with females. However, this does not mean that I was not discriminated against simply because I was allowed to be housed at a female-only facility. I was not treated like other inmates and was separated for being transgender, as their response states that their decision was made in part because of my non-traditional gender expression vis-à-vis the retention of male genitalia.

     I disagree with the Department of Correction's assertion that I was a "sex addict." I never have admitted to being a sex addict, I am not a sex addict, and this is patently false. The Department of Correction is misrepresenting fact purposely to make it appear that I needed to be treated differently than other inmates. I further disagree with the Department's contention that I have a "working penis capable of ejaculating." Allow me to be patently clear. I have been on hormones for over a decade. As a side effect of this regimen, my testes have atrophied, and I no longer produce viable sperm. I cannot impregnate a woman. If the DOC would have liked to have tested the ejaculate material that my body produces (clear seminal fluid that does not contain any sperm) then they would have been able to determine that I am unable to naturally impregnate any female. This being said, they could have housed me with a woman who'd had a hysterectomy or one that was post-menopausal if they were so concerned that I would be impregnating their inmates.

     I agree that in the privacy of a cell it would be easier for sexual contact to take place, however, this does not mean that I am more likely to participate in any sexual activity on account of being transgender. As a transgender woman, I am no more likely to break any rules at York CI than a cisgender woman, and to imply as such is discriminatory. What York CI is saying is that I cannot have a roommate (read: be treated like everyone else) because there could be allegations of rape and there would be no video footage showing that this had not transpired. I am no more likely to rape an inmate because I have a working penis than a woman who does not have a penis. This is prima facie discrimination.

     Further, the DOC denies withholding medically-necessary hormones because they are punting the football and claiming it is, in fact, a different state agency that handles medications. When one is incarcerated, one can only complain up the chain of command from captain to warden, and is not allowed to even contact a different state agency, either by telephone or via the internet. I made it flatly clear to Lisa (whom I met with once a week) that my hormones were being withheld, and she apologized to me, stating that the DOC had "dropped the ball" and that it was in my medical record that I was not given medically-necessary hormones for four days. Again, while a separate state entity might oversee the medications being brought into York CI, this does not mean that I could have had any way to contact this organization and right the tort committed by the DOC.

     I flatly disagree with the DOC's contention that while I was on 4 South (the medical unit) that I was treated like the cisgender individuals. Every cisgender individual (there were around twenty during the week I arrived) was housed in a quad with three other inmates as a preparation for a longer stay wherein these individuals would be housed with other people. I was not afforded this same happenstance. Instead, I was housed alone for the first eight days with no human contact for twenty-three hours a day, only allowed to leave the cell for the hour per day as specified in the Respondent's response. However, no one else was segregated. Everyone else was surrounded by three other inmates for that twenty-four hour period.

     In Hutto v. Finney*, 437 U.S. 678 (1978), the Supreme Court of the United States found that solitary confinement represents a type of punishment and therefore was subject to Eighth*

Amendment standards. To house a prisoner in solitary confinement is antithetical to our jurisprudence and is considered cruel and unusual punishment. There was absolutely no viable reason why I had to be in solitary confinement strictly because I possess a working phallus. Having one set of genitals or another, or being cisgender or transgender, does not take away one's rights via the Constitution of the United States. The case law surrounding cruel and unusual punishment under the Eighth Amendment to the Constitution must trump the guidance of the   *Prison*   *Rape*   *Elimination*   *Act.*

       With respect to the Prison Rape Elimination Act and its citation by the DOC as its reasoning for placing me in a solitary cell, this too is an unjust reading of the law. Also, since Connecticut state law bans discrimination based on transgender status, the DOC is not at liberty to cite a federal law that removes the protections of the state law under which they operate. I did not ask to shower or use a toilet in private. No one else was afforded such housing. On the Tier where I was housed in 2 South, there were approximately sixteen women that shared two showers. These showers were not communal--there were two showers with ante rooms to change away from any other inmates, and these were placed across from each other and were individual. There would be absolutely no reason why as an inmate I would be required to have my own shower. And if the CFR states that I must be given my own shower, then it is in direct contradistinction to Connecticut state statutes. Furthermore, once I was moved to RHU, I did not have my own shower and had to use the individual showers just like all of the other inmates. So apparently, DOC follows federal guidance when I am housed in the general population, but then when I am transferred to the Restricted Housing Unit and being punished, that guidance is no longer valid and I do not get my own shower. The DOC cannot have it both ways. I had my own shower for the first twenty-two days of my incarceration, and then used a group shower for my final eight days of my incarceration. These are two different methods of housing. One of them needs   *to*   *be*   *illegal.*

       I also disagree with the notion that "an in-cell shower and toilet helps preserve privacy for the Complainant as well as for any other inmate who would be upset by seeing male genitalia." How would another inmate see my genitalia? This is a factual impossibility. On the tier on 2 South, no one showers in their rooms but walks fully clothed to a shower area, at which point behind a closed door the inmate strips naked and then showers, then gets dressed again and emerges back on the tier. These are individual, not group showers in 2 South, therefore it is patently false that any other inmate would even glimpse my genitalia, as no one sees anyone else naked   *at*   *all.*

       With respect to being placed in the Restrictive Housing Unit, I am not sure why the DOC has included the first portion of their response, wherein they claim I had sexual relations with another inmate. As part of PREA, any inmate may make an anonymous complaint to the decision-makers about any other inmate or any guard or other prison worker. Therefore, a young woman who did not get along with me and was transphobic made a false allegation that I had engaged in a sex act. As the DOC clearly states, "both the Complainant and the inmate with whom she was allegedly intimate denied the allegation." This is because nothing ever happened.

I was not ever sexually intimate with another inmate. This was a false report made by a childish and immature inmate who could not deal with the fact that she was being housed near a transgender woman. I was told when I arrived by Lisa that I could be the target of untrue allegations by other inmates based on my gender identity. I understood this, and when it happened, I simply truthfully recounted the events and was not punished, since I had done nothing wrong.

With respect to the reason I was sent to RHU, supposedly "flashing" another inmate, allow me to be patently clear. First of all, I am a transwoman who looks like a transwoman. I do not "pass" as female and anyone who meets me knows that I was born what we currently understand to be "male" at birth. Thus, all the inmates on my tier wanted to know about my surgeries (if I had had any) and my body.

(This is not to mention that a young woman was in one of my groups that had been housed properly with me during a short stay at Connecticut Valley Hospital where I was housed with women, and she already knew the morphology of my genitals and told the rest of the women that I had a penis. I cannot stop the women from talking about me in prison, and thus any of the exhibits which attempt to prove that I was "talking about my genitals" all the time were patently false. There were actually two women in York CI that I knew from CVH and they spread all the information about my body and the shape of my genitals. Not me. This is impossible to stop.)

Thus, the inmates all wanted to know about my body. One day during recreational time, I was sitting around five or six inmates and the women were all asking me about my breasts. I explained to them that I had gotten breast implants eight years ago, saline implants under the muscle, and that I was now a 38D. One of the inmates told me that she didn't believe that I was a D-cup. "Show us," she said. So I lifted my shirt with a bra on and showed the women my breasts fully covered inside a brassiere. I had no idea that this was illegal conduct, but it turns out that it is against York CI policy to show your undergarments to anyone at any time. This is all that happened. No one saw my naked body. No one saw my breasts. They saw a brassiere. If this had happened outside of York it would not have been tortious conduct, however within the prison system it was, so I went to RHU and accepted my punishment.

Clearly, my time in RHU violated both federal law and Connecticut state law. Connecticut state law states that I cannot be segregated on account of my gender identity. Federal guidance suggests I need my own shower. In RHU I did not have my own shower and I was separated from the rest of the inmates. With respect to the signage that told the guards to house me alone, the DOC is misrepresenting fact and is trying to sweep this issue under the rug. There were other large (6' or 250 pound) inmates in the compound who I could have been housed with. There are 1500 women at York. It is laughable to state that there was no one else of my stature there to house me with--I am not that much of an outlying data point. There were other women who were my height or taller, and other women who were my weight or more.

With respect to Conn. Gen. Stat. 46a-64, this rule about transgender people does not just include public accommodation. I chose to cite 46a-64 because I believe that the DOC's role is to provide public accommodation. If the commission does not agree that this is public accommodation, under Conn. Gen. Stat. 46a-71. This rule states in Sec. 46a-71, (a) All services of every state agency shall be performed without discrimination based upon race, color, religious creed, sex, gender identity or expression, marital status, age, national origin, ancestry, intellectual disability, mental disability, learning disability or physical disability, including, but not limited to, blindness, (b) No state facility may be used in the furtherance of any discrimination, nor may any state agency become a party to any agreement, arrangement or plan which has the effect of sanctioning discrimination, and (c) Each state agency shall analyze all of its operations to ascertain possible instances of noncompliance with the policy of sections 46a-70 to 46a-78, inclusive, and shall initiate comprehensive programs to remedy any defect found to exist. It applies to every area of Connecticut, be it a place of business or the Department of Correction. DOC is a state agency and must follow state rules and cannot simply claim exemption because they are punishing individuals. It is still treating someone differently than cisgender females by housing them alone.

With respect to my comments to Lisa, I never made any comments about monetary compensation. This complaint is not pecuniary--I do not want the next transgender inmate to be housed the way I was in direct violation of Connecticut state law and the Eighth Amendment to the U.S. Constitution. This is a misrepresentation of fact. I never mentioned money to anyone while I was in York. This is a fabrication making me look bad. Furthermore, while I admit that I am attracted to both women and men, I do not admit to being a sex addict. This is a fabrication. The DOC's contention that I was housed the same way that any other cisgender 6' female would be is patently false. People in different cells are not the same exact size. They are of similar stature. There were plenty of other women at York that could have been my cellmate. However, the DOC did not give me a roommate and instead put me in solitary confinement because of my gender identity, not on account of my size. Housing an inmate alone is not a sound correctional practice, as the DOC claims, but rather has been shown by the courts to be cruel and unusual punishment. While the DOC may house other inmates alone for any number of reasons, they have already admitted that they housed me separately because they feared that I would rape another inmate, which is prima facie discrimination.

DOC engaged in tortuous conduct and will continue to engage in tortuous conduct until the CHRO or a judicial magistrate or judge issues a ruling about how DOC must handle transgender inmates. Transgender individuals make up approximately .6% of the population, and I have no doubt that there will be other transwomen that will be going to York in the future. To that point, I also claim that in addition to the discrimination that I felt, there are multiple transwomen being housed in men's facilities in the state and these transgender individuals should be immediately transferred to York. Their rights as transgender individuals have been abrogated and they have been mistreated by the DOC.

Lastly, the DOC needs a comprehensive policy regarding transgender inmates. They are citing the Prison Rape Elimination Act, but clearly when I was housed in RHU I was not afforded the purported rights of PREA, which stand in direct opposition to Connecticut Statute. I look forward to continuing my complaint in order to afford other transgender individuals fair

Respectfully   submitted,
Susan Sturbridge

I got my "day in court." We had a mediation which was similar to the first. They made it patently clear that there was nothing I was going to say or do which was going to make them send all the incarcerated transwomen to York to live with females. I explained to them that this was my only demand--I wanted other transwomen to be treated justly under the law. I told them that I shouldn't have had to contact a Congresswoman to be placed in the proper prison. And that there were dozens of other transwomen that were being illegally housed in men's prisons.

I told them that I was going to blow the whistle. I had contacts at National Public Radio, the Hartford Courant, and at local television stations. I was going to expose the DOC for all their rottenness and they were going to be held accountable for housing transgender inmates improperly. I told them that the iron was hot right now--transgender was a hot topic. The liberal media would eat it up, and they'd have egg on their face.

We ended up agreeing on $25,000 in hush money, and I took it, and dropped the case. Does that make me a bad person? Maybe. But I had to look out for myself first and foremost. Those other transwomen just weren't as resourceful as me, or they would have advocated for themselves. And yes, maybe my white male privilege I was raised with came out and I grabbed capital rather than helping others. But do you blame me? I got paid $25,000 to go to prison for a month--most transwomen don't make that in a year.

So I boosted and sued again, because that's who I am. Did I learn my lesson? That's up for you to decide. But I can tell you I put this all behind me and went legit. I bought myself a nice van for my oven business and expanded and hired a recovering addict in the program to help me with my business and drive me around. I got back together with Ava for good, without distraction.

And that's how you boost and sue. Ava wanted me to put that down too, go legit in all aspects of my life. But as we speak, a friend of mine told me that a dentist screwed up her tooth extraction and she had to redo it because of medical negligence. I told her I would write her a demand letter and a draft complaint to mail to the dentist's process server and we could probably grab a quick five thousand dollars. But I would only do it if she would give me a fifteen percent. She said yes, and so that's the next thing on my horizon, helping others to boost and sue, and taking my piece. I mean, if you can't do, you teach, right? And I'm all about for-profit education.

And with that I changed, not just from man to woman, but from low-life booster and scam artist to legal eagle and legitimate businesswoman, all with a little help from some settlements from private companies and the Department of Corrections. I didn't know anyone else who got paid to go to jail (unless he or she were innocent) but I never minded being a trailblazer.

See you in the courtroom!

AFTERWORD

In case you were wondering, this is what a memorandum of law looks like. Most of the time, these are written by lawyers as part of legal cases, and are never seen by members of the public. I had to write one to sleaze my way out of that $7400 of my debt. No one ever taught me how to do this--I had to teach myself. So, I picked up a new skill, and got paid for doing it. A memorandum of law looks something like this:

Introduction

The Defendant Susan Sturbridge is involved in a civil matter that the Plaintiff wrongfully characterizes as a simple debt collection issue. The Defendant has stated from the beginning of the civil action that she does not owe the debt in its entirety because a significant portion of the debts incurred were through unauthorized use of the card. Furthermore, the Defendant has asserted from the start of the proceedings that even if she owed part of the debt, that the Plaintiff did not hold title to the debt and therefore was not the correct party to collect it. Now with the latest Motion for Summary Judgment and accompanying Memorandum of Law, the Plaintiff is once again misrepresenting fact to the tribunal, a violation of which they are now guilty of a second time, in addition to the Defendant's first Motion for Sanctions which has not yet been ruled   *upon.*

With respect to the Defendant's first assertion, that she does not owe the entirety of the debt because of unauthorized use, the Plaintiff argues in the argument section within their Memorandum of Law that the Defendant must provide an evidentiary foundation to demonstrate that there is an issue of fact. Rather, the Plaintiff in filing their improper motion is seeking to usurp the right of the Defendant to seek discovery, a process that the Defendant has not yet begun as the tribunal has not yet set a status conference date to discuss the required dates for discovery, depositions, pretrial, et al. When the Defendant's discovery is completed, adequate evidence   *of*   *unauthorized*   *use*   *of*   *the*   *card*   *will*   *be*   *revealed.*
With respect to the second issue of fact--the chain of title of the debt--as part of the discovery process the Plaintiff turned over a fraudulent robo-signed document to the Defendant as proof of ownership. Common law dictates that if the validity of a signature is denied in the pleadings, the burden of establishing validity is on the person claiming validity, in this case, the Plaintiff. Therefore at this juncture in direct opposition to the Plaintiff's Motion for Summary Judgment, the Defendant is specifically denying the validity of the signatures on the document proffered by the Plaintiff as proof of ownership. Because of this denial, the burden of proof now shifts to the Plaintiff, which creates a specific issue of material fact that should be taken through the discovery process and through a jury trial rather than wrongfully through a summary judgment. This   *fact*   *stands*   *in*   *direct*   *contravention*   *to*   *the*   *Plaintiff's*   *assertion. Furthermore, specific case law exists at the appellate level that stands in direct contradiction to the case law cited by the Plaintiff in their Motion with respect to the burden of proof of the*

existence of material fact falling squarely on the movant and not the opposing party. Lastly, the Defendant filed a valid Motion for Sanctions against the Plaintiff dated September 10, 2016 (this particular pleading was not filed electronically and is not yet visible with a number on the State's judicial website, though it was certainly received by the Plaintiff as they filed an Objection to Motion for Sanctions [124.00]) which has not yet been ruled upon. If the Defendant's motion is not denied, this action would deny Plaintiff's counsel the right to represent the Plaintiff and significantly impact the case, and seriously calls into question through their abuse of the Practice Book the Plaintiff's ability to truthfully represent fact to the tribunal.

In light of these three issues, the Defendant requests that the court categorically deny the Plaintiff's Motion for Summary Judgment so that this issue can be decided at a jury trial.

Argument

Case law at the Appellate level stands in direct contradistinction to the claims made by the Plaintiff with respect to the suitability of a Motion for Summary Judgment

In her Answer and Special Defense (107.00) dated April 25, 2016 as well as in her Response to Requests for Admissions (119.00) dated August 25, 2016, the Defendant has always asserted that there were unauthorized charges made to her credit card account. In their Memorandum of Law accompanying their illicit Motion for Summary Judgment, the Plaintiff argues in "III" that when the Defendant received monthly statements and does not object to the charges, the Defendant is liable   for   the   balance   due   on   the   account   stated. The Plaintiff arrives at this conclusion, however, through a misinterpretation of case law that begins with Dunnett v. Thornton, 73 Conn. 1, 15-16 (1900). The Plaintiff is arguing this position based on the "account stated" theory of recovery and wrongfully concludes that Plaintiff is entitled to summary judgment on the basis of evidence that the Defendant received monthly statements and failed to dispute their content. Thus, the Plaintiff argues that because the Defendant did not dispute the amounts due that, therefore, the Defendant essentially acquiesced to all past monthly statements being true records of the amount of debt owed. The Defendant asserts there is evidence that the Appellate Court has ruled in a contrary manner, and a more appropriate case to base such a decision on in this situation is the one found in American Express Centurion Bank v. Head, 971 A.2d 90 (2009) 115 Conn.App. 10. In this case, which bears striking resemblance to the civil action at hand, the Plaintiff filed a Motion for Summary Judgment in what appeared to be a simple collections case. The Defendant objected to the motion, but the trial court decided in favor of the Motion for Summary Judgment, and "In a memorandum of decision filed on July 23, 2008, the court stated that the plaintiff filed documentation sufficient to support its motion for summary judgment and that the defendant failed to file any opposing affidavit or evidence sufficient to demonstrate that an issue of material fact existed. The defendant filed the present appeal on May 16, 2008." ibid 94.

The Appellate court issued their decision overturning the trial court's ruling on allowing the Motion for Summary Judgment by relying on Allstate Ins. Co. v. Barron, *269 Conn. 394, 405, 848 A.2d 1165 (2004). The Appellate court found the following: In seeking summary judgment, it is the movant who has the burden of showing the nonexistence of any issue of fact. The courts are in complete agreement that the moving party for summary judgment has the burden of showing the absence of any genuine issue as to all the material facts, which, under applicable principles of substantive law, entitle him to a judgment as a matter of law. The courts hold the movant to a strict standard. To satisfy his burden the movant must make a showing that it is quite clear what the truth is, and that excludes any real doubt as to the existence of any genuine issue of material fact.... As the burden of proof is on the movant, the evidence must be viewed in the light most favorable to the opponent.... When documents submitted in support of a motion for summary judgment fail to establish that there is no genuine issue of material fact, the nonmoving party has no obligation to submit documents establishing the existence of such an issue." (Citations omitted; emphasis added; internal quotation marks omitted.)* ibid, *94.*

Furthermore, the Appellate court states that, "In the present case, the defendant disputed the amount of debt alleged in the plaintiff's complaint, namely, $3824.97, when he denied all of the plaintiff's allegations in his answer to the complaint. The amount of debt allegedly incurred by the defendant was therefore a disputed material issue." ibid, *95. At the end of their decision wherein the Appellate court reverses the trial court's misapplication of a Motion for Summary Judgment, the judge writes, We conclude that in this case, submitting a monthly account statement that indicates the alleged amount of debt, and an affidavit stating that the defendant never disputed his monthly billing statements and that the submitted documents, some of which are essentially blank, are accurate copies of the plaintiff's records, does not satisfy that burden....Accordingly, we reverse the judgment of the trial court.* ibid, *95.*

This decision by the higher court should be used as guidance in this case as to the issue of the Motion for Summary Judgment, especially because the two situations are so very similar and this case originates from 2009 rather than a hundred years earlier.

II. Common law dictates the specific rules surrounding unauthorized transactions

The Defendant rejects the notion proffered by the Plaintiff that simply not disputing transactions as they arise on a month-to-month basis makes a debt valid. The Plaintiff holds that Title 15 of the United States Code, § 1643(b), sets forth the burden of proof as follows: "In any action by a card issuer to enforce liability for the use of a credit card, the burden of proof is upon the card issuer to show that the use was authorized or, if the use was unauthorized, then the burden of proof is upon the card issuer to show that the conditions of liability for the unauthorized use of a credit card, as set forth in subsection (a) of this section, have been met." Therefore the common law is clear--the burden is on the company the Plaintiff purchased this debt from, not the Defendant, to show that the charge is authorized. The Defendant has always held in this case that not all charges that make up the account were authorized, and cannot prove which ones were authorized until she received copies of the signature receipts that accompany the charges as part of the discovery process which the Plaintiff is seeking to preclude. The Defendant asserts the following, in keeping with Title 15 of the United States Code, § 1602(o), which provides: "The term 'unauthorized use,' as used in section 1643 of this title, means a use of a credit card by a person other than the cardholder who does not have actual, implied, or apparent authority for such use and from which the cardholder receives no benefit." As she has been a victim of unauthorized charges on her card, the Defendant furthermore asserts the following as defined in Title 15 of the United States Code, § 1643 (a): Limits on Liability. (1) A cardholder shall be liable for the unauthorized use of a credit card only if—(A) the card is an accepted credit card; (B) the liability is not in excess of $50; (C) the card issuer gives adequate notice to the cardholder of the potential liability; (D) the card issuer has provided the cardholder with a description of a means by which the card issuer may be notified of loss or theft of the card, which description may be provided on the face or reverse side of the statement required by section 1637 (b) of this title or on a separate notice accompanying such statement; (E) the unauthorized use occurs before the card issuer has been notified that an unauthorized use of the credit card has occurred or may occur as the result of loss, theft, or otherwise; and; (F) the card issuer has provided a method whereby the user of such card can be identified as the person authorized to use it.

The Defendant therefore offers that there are unauthorized charges on the card that under United States Code she should not be liable for, and simply not disputing the charges at the time they were made is not an indication that the Defendant has lost the right to claim unauthorized use, and that this statement is a factual issue that precludes a summary judgment.

III. Connecticut's Uniform Commercial Code dictates rules regarding transfer of instruments for consideration

The Defendant has claimed since the beginning of these proceedings (specifically within a Motion to Strike dated April 25, 2016 [108.00]) that the Plaintiff does not hold valid title to this debt they purchased from U.S. Bank, NA. In response the Plaintiff responded by producing "Exhibit B: Bill of Sale and Assignment of Assets," which is attached to this pleading. The Defendant asserts that the second signature on this document, specifically the signature by Joel G. Rebmann, Sr. Vice President, is an unauthorized signature on this document and that this individual did not have the authority to sell the instrument and that this robo-signed document was in fact never signed by this party. First, the Defendant asserts that under C.G.S. § 42a-3-416, Transfer warranties:

(a) A person who transfers an instrument for consideration warrants to the transferee and, if the transfer is by endorsement, to any subsequent transferee that: (1) The warrantor is a person entitled to enforce the instrument; (2) all signatures on the instrument are authentic and authorized; (3) the instrument has not been altered; (4) the instrument is not subject to a defense or claim in recoupment of any party which can be asserted against the warrantor; and (5) the warrantor has no knowledge of any insolvency proceeding commenced with respect to the maker or acceptor or, in the case of an unaccepted draft, the drawer.

The Defendant claims that under § 42a-3-416(2) all signatures are not authorized and therefore the transfer of warranties in this instrument are nullified. Second, with respect to § 42a-3-308. Proof of signatures and status as holder in due course: (a) In an action with respect to an instrument, the authenticity of, and authority to make, each signature on the instrument is admitted unless specifically denied in the pleadings. If the validity of a signature is denied in the pleadings, the burden of establishing validity is on the person claiming validity, but the signature is presumed to be authentic and authorized unless the action is to enforce the liability of the purported signer and the signer is dead or incompetent at the time of trial of the issue of validity of the signature. If an action to enforce the instrument is brought against a person as the undisclosed principal of a person who signed the instrument as a party to the instrument, the plaintiff has the burden of establishing that the defendant is liable on the instrument as a represented person under section 42a-3-402(a).

The Defendant has asserted in a pleading that she is questioning the validity of a signature on an instrument, specifically on Exhibit B by Sr. Vice President Joel G. Hoffman. Under Connecticut General Statutes § 42a-3-308(a) ("If the validity of a signature is denied in the pleadings, the burden of establishing validity is on the person claiming validity") the Plaintiff now has the burden of proof upon them to show that this supposedly authorized signature is valid. Therefore, the act of the Defendant creating this pleading necessarily creates an issue of fact that now should be argued in front of the tribunal in a trial setting, rather than in a Motion for Summary Judgment.

Conclusion

There are material facts that are disputed in this case, which would render a finding of summary judgment a miscarriage of justice. There are unauthorized charges on the card that the Defendant claimed in both her Answer and Special Defense as well as in her Response to Requests for Admissions, the existence of which being asserted in a pleading constitute grounds for denying the Motion for Summary Judgment. Second, the Defendant has made a claim of an unauthorized signature on a relevant instrument in a pleading, which is prima facie material fact that precludes a summary judgment. Lastly, pertinent case law at the appellate level holds the movant to a strict standard of scrutiny, thus when the Plaintiff simply asserts there is no material

fact to dispute, this does not satisfy the burden of proof required to render a summary judgment
against   the   opposing   non-moving   party.

For all of these reasons the Defendant holds that this Motion for Summary Judgment should be denied.

THE   *DEFENDANT,*
Susan   *Sturbridge*